THE TRUTH OF CARCOSA

THE TRUTH OF CARCOSA

JACOB ROLLINSON

NEW YORK

UNION
SQUARE
&CO.
NEW YORK

This is a work of fiction. Names, characters, business, events, and incidents are the products of the author's imagination. Any resemblance to actual persons, living or dead, or actual events is purely coincidental.

Copyright © 2026 by Jacob Rollinson

Jacket art and design © 2026 Rodrigo Corral Studio

Jacket copyright © 2026 by Hachette Book Group, Inc.

Hachette Book Group supports the right to free expression and the value of copyright. The purpose of copyright is to encourage writers and artists to produce the creative works that enrich our culture.

The scanning, uploading, and distribution of this book without permission is a theft of the author's intellectual property. If you would like permission to use material from the book (other than for review purposes), please contact permissions@hbgusa.com. Thank you for your support of the author's rights.

Union Square & Co.
Hachette Book Group
1290 Avenue of the Americas, New York, NY 10104
unionsquareandco.com
@unionsqandco

First US Edition: January 2026

Union Square & Co. is an imprint of Grand Central Publishing, a division of Hachette Book Group, Inc. The Union Square & Co. name and logo are registered trademarks of Hachette Book Group, Inc.

The publisher is not responsible for websites (or their content) that are not owned by the publisher.

The Hachette Speakers Bureau provides a wide range of authors for speaking events. To find out more, go to hachettespeakersbureau.com or email HachetteSpeakers@hbgusa.com.

Union Square & Co. books may be purchased in bulk for business, educational, or promotional use. For information, please contact your local bookseller or the Hachette Book Group Special Markets Department at special.markets@hbgusa.com.

Interior image by Shutterstock.com/Dmitr1ch (paper texture)

Print book interior design by Rich Hazelton

Library of Congress Cataloging-in-Publication Data has been applied for.

ISBNs: 978-1-4549-6262-5 (hardcover), 978-1-4549-6264-9 (paperback), 978-1-4549-6263-2 (ebook), 978-1-6686-5491-0 (audiobook)

Printed in Canada

MRQ-T

1 2025

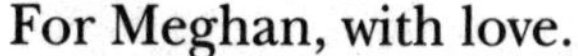

For Meghan, with love.

1

Two weeks after the first announcement of the Hasturian Guard's "special operation" in the city, their shortwave radio broadcasts fall silent. The next morning the mobile network comes back online, and rumors spread that the barricades have been dismantled. The militia have stood down, or holed up, or fled. There are other rumors, too. Houses destroyed, families disappeared, fires in the night.

Scottie can barely credit the stories. It's like they've come from some other place, another country, where people do barbarous things. Not England. But if they're true, he can't deny that the Guard have only done what they've always threatened to do. This is the *Will of the People*, about which the government-in-exile blustered and promised for years, right up to the point they were escorted to Dover.

If the rumors are true.

"Can you really believe it, Mr. Sol, what they're saying?" he asks, as Sol climbs into the cabin of the van.

Sol is in his forties with the soft, worn look of a middle manager. But his hair is unkempt, clothes disheveled, skin waxy. He's wearing a dirty delivery driver's jacket and jeans. He nods irritably.

Scottie is soft and unkempt in a different way, like somebody who's only just woken up. He's younger, with a soft beard and clothes that suggest time spent outdoors. He shrugs.

"I can't believe it."

Indeed, as they navigate the quiet roads toward the city, it's possible to pretend that all is well, that they're driving for pleasure in the England that was. New green leaves glisten with fallen rain. Stupefied pigeons rise late from the asphalt.

But smoke rises from the town, and on the slip road into the city a dozen cars are lined up with their doors hanging open. The verge is stained with dark patches, and somewhere over the rise a fire still smolders.

Sol slows to a crawl, wary, but the scene is deserted and the makeshift turnpike at the head of the line has been hauled to the side of the road. The route ahead is clear.

In the city, posters on the walls mark the stages of the occupation: Old advertisements are overlaid with flyers calling for allegiance to the Hasturian Guard, for racial unity, for the King, for the defense of England and the death of cannibals; emergency dispersal orders cover these; then handwritten curfew notices, signed "HG." Across the railway bridge, all bills have been ripped down and graffiti, neatly lettered in housepaint, begs for martial law.

"It's like a bad dream," Scottie murmurs. Sol says nothing. They pass barricades and burned-out houses: familiar roads made strange. Empty medical tents and stained brickwork.

"That was the Berryman." Scottie points at the charred remains of a pub. "I can't believe it . . . I can't *believe* it . . ."

Sol bristles. He seems to carry a burden of discomfort, some pain that sensitizes him to the irritants of the world: the uncomfortable seat, the sticky gears, Scottie's moaning.

"I can't believe it . . ."

"You'd better start believing it," Sol finally says.

"But it's so . . . *terrible*."

"You've been listening to the radio. They said what they wanted to do."

Again, true. But—

"But I . . ."

Scottie's eyes are wide. His voice falters. Sol realizes he's made a mistake. Up until this morning, Scottie was confident and practical about the situation they faced. It's clear now that he simply hadn't processed it. "I'm sorry," Sol says, but it's too late. Some barrier has broken in Scottie: The world has become very real to him.

"This is serious," he whispers, as if to himself. "This is *dangerous*! Maybe we should go back!"

"Scottie, I'm sorry. Take a breath. Remember the plan. We're here to find your friend. What's his name again?"

"Louis."

"Louis is going to help us, right?"

"Yeah."

"We're going to find him. Just like we meant to do before all this happened."

"But everything's changed!"

"Our plan hasn't changed."

"He could be dead."

"We don't know that."

"How are we meant to find him? This place is a war zone."

Just then they round the corner to the city center and reach a bus shelter plastered with paper: handwritten notes, photographs, printed posters. Sol pulls up beside it and scans the posters. The word "Missing," repeated over and over. Missing people, messages, instructions. *Have you seen? I lost you in . . . Sweetheart, meet me at . . .*

Waiting for you.

"What's Louis's full name?" he asks.

"Louis Barrow."

"What does he look like?"

"He's a white guy. He looks a bit like me."

"Like you, how? Scottie?"

But Scottie is looking across the square at the facade of City Hall.

A ladder. A pot of paint. A list of names painted in large white letters across the brickwork. At the top of the list is the word "COLLABORATORS"; an elderly man in a wrist brace is finishing the name "LOUIS BARROW."

* * *

The square is a surreal tableau. A single white Jeep with a UN insignia is pulled up beside the municipal fountain. Two soldiers in blue helmets stand guard beside a makeshift office: a generator, strip-lights, photocopier and filing cabinet, a litter of papers, tousled by the wind.

Two senior citizens are working under the supervision of a woman in a Kevlar jacket. Sol waits in the van while Scottie walks, hands-up, past the blue helmets. He points at the writing on the wall and pronounces the name in a trembling voice. One of the bureaucrats, an elderly librarian with a bandaged face, nods. She roots around in the filing cabinet and hands him a photocopied note. The note contains the address of a house in the city. Below is something else:

To the Relevant Authority,

Cannibal House
They know more than they tell.
These vermin change their skin with "E"-injections.
("E" for embryo)
They cannot stop the KING!

Louis Barrow, Trusted Citizen

"What does it mean?" Scottie asks. The librarian only shakes her head. She has a broken jaw.

"*Denuncia*," says the woman in the Kevlar jacket. She might be from Spain or Latin America. "The Hasturian Guard go one house, another house, another house . . . They follow these little *nota* from *trusted citizens* like this. Collaborators."

"And the people in the house?"

The librarian draws a line across her throat.

"Why?"

"Read the *nota*."

"It doesn't make any sense."

"No. None of this does."

Radios crackle. A blue helmet taps Scottie on the shoulder and tells him to *vamos* before the curfew.

"What curfew? Who's in charge here? Who are you?"

The woman points at her lanyard, which bears the UN insignia.

"Forensic fact finder," she says. "I'm not in charge. And I go soon, too."

"Then who's in charge?"

"In this city, now? Nobody knows." She sighs, turning back to the volunteers sifting through the papers. "They take a big risk to do this," she says, pointing at the list on the wall. "They want to tell the truth, what happened here and who did it. I can't tell them not to do it. And it helps my work. But after I go, they stay. What then?"

Paintbrush in hand, an elderly man starts climbing the ladder again.

"If you can leave, go," the fact finder says. "Find refuge."

* * *

Back in the van, Scottie hands the note to Sol.

Sol reads, wincing.

"Why would Louis do this?" Scottie asks.

Sol shakes his head. "I don't know. He was your friend."

"He wouldn't do this."

"Do you know the people in the note?"

"There are no names. Just the address."

"Do you know the address?"

Scottie reads it again. His eyes widen. Slowly, he nods.

"From long ago," he murmurs.

"Then we should go there."

Night has fallen by the time they reach the house. It's in a terraced suburb, the front gardens heaped with garbage bags, streets strewn with broken glass. There are remains of barricades, constructed from trash cans and shopping carts. Some cars have been torched, some broken into. Electric light is sporadic.

The house has been burned out. Scorch marks rise from vacant windows. Scottie stares at it. He seems to have collected himself.

"I knew this place a long time ago. Louis knew it, too. I never knew the people who moved in since. I don't see why Louis should have known them."

"Was your friend ever . . . *into* the Hasturian Guard?"

"No way. He wasn't like that. He didn't believe that *England for the English* shit."

"But he was close to *The Truth of Carcosa*."

"What do you mean?"

"People get compromised. It's a tangled web, believe me."

"Not Louis. He was on our side. He was my friend. He agreed to help us."

"Would you prefer me to go inside?"

"No. I need to do this."

Sol pulls a pair of bright yellow rubber gloves out of his jacket pocket and hands them to Scottie.

"If you find anything—if you find the files we wanted . . ."

Scottie nods.

"*Wear gloves*," he recites. It's a much-repeated warning. "*Don't read anything*."

⁂ ⁂ ⁂

Scottie follows the old route into the back of the property: over the fence onto the grounds of Hourglass Lodge hospice, across the hospice's wide green space and through the hedgerow. He jumps the final, low fence, pushes through thick yew growth, and emerges in a back garden. The moonlight is strong, and the garden looks well tended. Scottie steps up the garden path and pauses. He's in a familiar place that's changed in ways he doesn't yet understand; he should be cautious.

Some conservatory windows are smashed. Some are blackened and warped. Some have melted, running like sugar syrup to the ground. Scottie steps into the conservatory and pulls a flashlight out of his jacket pocket. Turns it on. Narrow beam. He starts to search. He has no specific hope of finding signs of Louis, nor the files Louis agreed to bring them weeks before. But he feels a responsibility, having known Louis, to bear witness to what he's done.

He shines the light over charred carpet, still soggy from the fire hoses. He finds furniture: the shell of a chair, springs and skeletal armrests; the charred remains of a table; a puddle that was a television set. Drifts of ash. Leaves, blown in from outside. Here, beside a door, intact but ajar, his beam illuminates a discarded spray can.

The room beyond is a downstairs bathroom. It has escaped the fire, but the bathtub is full of clothes and graffiti on the wall reads ACCESSION UNSTOPPABLE.

Scottie retreats from the bathroom. He shines the flashlight up the stairwell. The walls are black with soot, but a trail of discarded objects marks a path to the bedrooms. Things thrown from upstairs: a coat hanger, photo frame, picture book. Scottie climbs. The stairs complain with every upward step. The flashlight beam dances ahead of him, illuminating scorch marks and voids. On the landing he finds three doorways. Two doors were open at the time of the fire, and the interiors beyond are black. The third door was closed. Scottie heaves it open. The wallpaper inside is a bright, warm yellow, with a pattern of fairies or sprites—little smiling people with nutshell hats and dragonfly wings. Big smiles and wide eyes.

Scottie follows his flashlight beam into the room.

Inside, beside an empty cot, is a pile of empty food cans and ballpoint pens. Some squatter has been here. Before the fire, perhaps; but after the original inhabitants were removed.

These vermin change their skin with "E"-injections.

It can only have been Louis. After removing the family, Louis occupied their house. Here, he ate canned potatoes and fruit salad, and wrote until his pens ran dry. In *this* house, and no other: for old time's sake, perhaps.

Cannibal house. That's not what they used to call it. Scottie can't remember what they used to call it.

There's no sign of whatever Louis was writing. Scottie shines his flashlight under the cot. The plastic eyes of a stuffed rabbit stare back in alarm.

* * *

A few minutes later he trudges back downstairs. His hands are empty except for the flashlight, which is flickering now. His hands are shaking.

He stands in the center of the living room, still unable to fathom the enormity of what his friend has done. He can see it, but he can't comprehend it. He can't square it with the fact that just a few weeks ago, Louis was communicating normally. He'd agreed to help out, to deliver the files Judy and Mr. Sol were so adamant they needed. He was *on their side*.

Cannibal house.

Did Louis believe what he wrote about these people? And if not, what did he expect to happen to them, once the militia accepted the rumor? He, too, must have heard the broadcasts.

Scottie's flashlight beam returns to the ruin of the couch, and stops there. There's something about it he hadn't noticed before. Synthetic fabric has melted over the springs, creating a topography of ridges and rills where water from the fire hoses has pooled. Except in one spot, where the water has drained out of a low basin—lower, indeed, than other flooded parts of the miniature landscape. This spot should be completely underwater.

He pushes his flashlight into the lowest dip in the material. There's a small nick where water has drained out. He prods at the nick, and the ruined fabric falls away, revealing a yawning hole beneath. Unwilling to use his hands, Scottie kicks around the tear, exposing a deep hole in the living room floor. The flashlight beam meets water a few feet down—flooded crawl space—with flotsam jiggling in the ripples. A piece of charcoal. A dead rat, sleek and perfect. A plastic folder, sealed with parcel tape.

Scottie kneels down. He feels the cold soak through his trousers. With the flashlight between his teeth and one hand on the crumbling lip, he reaches out for the folder. He doesn't grasp it instantly. He must pat it, stroke it with his fingertips, before it spins on the water and drifts within reach.

There's a handwritten label on the folder. It lists two numbered items.

1. *The Truth of Carcosa—A Special Report by Louis Barrow.*

2. *Correspondence 1984 by Judith Bea and Cléophe Carrette.*

The Truth of Carcosa: A Special Report

By an Expert of Sound Mind

Concerned with Preventing Calamity

Louis Barrow,

~~of the~~ <u>formerly</u> of the Archive for Literary Investment

In fact, I am quite sane.

You will excuse the above abrupt preface. The thing is, I know how writings such as these are typically received. So let me be clear—no, this Special Report is not busywork for an unquiet mind. Nor some last-ditch effort to save my position. This work should be read as a serious and lucid message to those who are capable of waking to the danger, or the opportunity.

I Am Quite Sane.

Yet I might admit to feeling lonely. Not that my loneliness is pathological, nor even tremendously uncommon. In fact, until very recently I've cleaved to the belief that loneliness is a linguistic fact.

I refer of course to the theory that while signs—everyday words such as *pencil, razor, videotape*—are communicable, the realities to which they point are essentially unknowable unless they can be reached by our personal sensoria. And so that which is truly our own, our most powerful and vivid experiences, since they *cannot be touched*, also cannot be communicated.

I call these incommunicable signs *portents.* Portents are the lonely baggage of the self: our predawn fears, our intimate shames, the sad pearls of personal joy to which we cling when all else disintegrates around us. Fragments of memory and fantasy that linger after we wake up, put the book down, leave the movie theater. What our bodies know, and cannot say.

Let me illustrate.

When I open the door to the cold room at the Archive for Literary Investment, I know logically that I'm entering a climate-controlled depository of literary manuscripts and correspondence from 1971 to 2010. But I *feel* as though I'm entering something far stranger.

The door is heavy. It opens only after you swipe your access card on a reader, which produces an optimistic series of chimes: *diddly-DEE!* After which you hear the clunky magnetic lock disengage, and you pull the handle.

Heavy. You pull it open and it hisses as air currents exchange, and from inside you hear the air conditioning unit re-engage: *click, thunk, whir.*

You leave the warm office for the cold hum of the archive room. You smell the faintest acid odor of paper bleach and cardboard adhesive. Behind you, the door closes: the seals of frame and door near one another, rubber lips closing in, and the airflow sharpens, like a tiny inhalation: like a question, cut off.

The archive cold room contains sixteen rows, accessible by a single corridor. Therefore, as the door closes behind you, your view is of a single path, with a wall on the right and sixteen aisles on the left. At the far end is the fire exit, alarmed, never used, with a bold red stripe across its belly, declaring CAUTION.

The sixteen rows terminate in wall shelves. So if you walk into any row to locate your target text, and turn back to the main corridor, you need only turn *right*, and you'll find the office door, waiting to return you to the warmth and chatter of that communal space.

But what's this? Beside the handle you're gripping, your attention is arrested by a bold red stripe. CAUTION. This isn't the office door, but the fire exit. Instead of turning right at the corridor, you have—inconceivably—turned left.

This happens more than once. As you're leaving, some cockeyed instinct guides you left when you ought to turn right. Sometimes you catch yourself, mid-turn. Sometimes you stand before the fire exit, hand on the alarmed handle, CAUTION traced in negative on your eyelids, knowing—*convinced*—that on the other side of that barrier you'll find the office, with its fluorescent glow, keyboards tapping, the funk of old woolen clothes. You need only pull the handle and you will rediscover it.

This is what your body tells you. How does it get it so wrong?

Perhaps the sensory overload in the cold room baffles your instincts, overriding the internal compass and confusing short-term memory. But perhaps the repeated decision to turn left when you should turn right is *itself* significant. Perhaps your consciousness is responding to the presence of another form of geometry, something present within the cold room but alien to planet Earth—from some other system, perhaps, with a fundamentally different cartography and calendar.

This *feeling* of mine, this hint of other worlds—this I call a portent. As such, I cannot expect you, dear reader, to comprehend it. You may read all the words in this special report, and feel convinced that you've *sounded their ken*; but according to the theories that (until recently) delimited my perceptions, you cannot hope to grasp the true meaning of the *portents* within. We remain within our sense envelopes, scraping against our own internal surfaces, imagining what the outside world looks like.

This is what I mean, when I say loneliness is a linguistic fact.

The question of True Communication, as we might call the piercing of this envelope, is for poets and fanatics. They call it transcendence, or Accession, or nature, and they yearn for it with fruitless devotion. Grown-ups know True Communication to be impossible and leave it at that. Salvatore Archimboldi said it best when he called its pursuit the "last resort of heartbroken tyrants."

Which makes it particularly awkward to explain what I must.

In short, I have become convinced in recent months that we hold within this archive artifacts and fragments of wondrous, terrifying power. Simultaneously, I've felt the erosion of my envelope. I've become alive to certain portents hanging in the firmament of my own personal cosmos, like chinks in a previously airtight mechanism. I've come to apprehend that it isn't just my cosmos anymore.

Fearfully and full of doubt I type these words, and I leave to you the question of their veracity and moral valence, upon reading the rest of my report:

True Communication is possible.

We need not be lonely anymore.

The Yellow King is coming.

2

Sol sits in the darkness of the van's cabin. The engine is off, yet his hands grip the steering wheel. His left arm is rigid, but a careful observer might see him moving his right shoulder and elbow in tiny circular motions. He isn't stretching or exercising his arm. In fact, with each small movement, the fabric of his sleeve is scraping *oh-so-lightly* over his skin. And the permanent expression of discomfort on his face ripples with something like relief, something like pain. A careful observer might guess that Sol is teasing an itch he dare not scratch.

Scottie hammers his palm on the window and Sol jumps like a startled cat. Collecting himself, he gets halfway to unlocking the door before Scottie presses the folder against the pane. Sol catches sight of the label and freezes.

"It was in the house!" Scottie explains excitedly. "Louis left it there!"

Sol is paralyzed with fear and indignation. Scottie, his hands bare, is holding the files just inches from Sol's face. This, after all the warnings he's been given. Both Judy and Sol have spent hours trying to explain how dangerous the files might be. Sol's hands form fists. He can't speak. When it finally comes, his voice is a furious whisper.

"Why aren't you wearing gloves?"

Scottie, blinking: "Come on, unlock the door! We need to get out of here."

"Put it in the back, Scottie." Scottie looks confused. Sol gestures vehemently. *"In the back."*

Scottie, surprised and hurt, does as he's told. Sol lowers his fists onto the steering wheel. He opens his hands, with some effort, rubs his palms together, and wipes away the stress tears flowing down his cheeks. A near miss, perhaps. Or maybe nothing. He's still here, his nerves still vibrating with sensation. The likelihood that it could all have been taken from him, just a moment ago—it's difficult to calculate. Archimboldi's *The Truth of Carcosa* has filled his world with invisible land mines, and it's exhausting, trying to calculate where they might be. He can't do this alone. He needs to trust the people he's with.

* * *

"Why did you lock me out of my own van?" Scottie asks, once they're on their way out of the neighborhood.

"Why didn't you listen? I told you to wear gloves. I told you to be careful."

"I was careful, Mr. Sol."

Sol clears his throat. Winces. His forehead is beaded with sweat.

"The folder. Is it what we asked for? The files from the ALI?"

"One of them is."

"The actual manuscript?"

"No. Something else, an archive thing, like a list of letters. And there's something Louis wrote, too. A diary, I think. He calls it a report."

Relief and disappointment flicker briefly over Sol's face.

"Okay," he says. "It's a start."

* * *

They drive out of the suburb on a circuitous route. Mostly they see nobody. Once, passing a cul-de-sac, a cluster of wavering flashlights turns their way and a single shot rings out before Sol accelerates away. They reach a stretch of unlit highway, then quickly turn onto a service road. They pass through a quarry and onto a gravel trail that climbs into woodland. The headlights pick out young leaves, startlingly green in the blackness. They leave the gravel road and follow a pair of rutted tire tracks deeper into the woods. The van lurches from side to side as Sol struggles with the steering wheel.

Sol, who's been thinking hard, breaks the silence.

"How much did you read?" he asks.

"What? What makes you think I read anything? You warned me, didn't you? *Keep your distance, don't read it, wear gloves . . .*"

"And you didn't wear the gloves." Scottie says nothing, but the look on his face confirms Sol's suspicion. "Look, I shouldn't have expected you to understand, because you haven't seen what I've seen. I know today's been a shock to you. But I thought you pulled yourself together pretty well."

"Ha. We'll see."

"What do you mean?"

"I don't feel anything, Mr. Sol."

"It's the shock," Sol says. This isn't an uninformed opinion. Until a year ago, Sol took a professional interest in psychological responses to trauma. He could list the symptoms, if he chose.

"I think I should feel sad, but I don't."

"You feel numb."

"Not even. All I can think is how lucky I am that it was them and not me. How clever I am to live where I do. And my lucky parents, in their gated community . . . I didn't even realize how relieved I felt to speak to them this morning. And Judy's safe . . ."

Sol nods. Scottie looks down at Sol's hand, then blushes and looks away. Sol tries to hide the hand behind the steering wheel. Difficult while driving.

"What is it?" he asks.

"I'm sorry, I didn't think. Talking about how my people are safe when I don't know about yours. Have you spoken to your wife yet?"

"Who, Dulcie? Why would I speak to her?" Scottie points, and Sol realizes he's wearing his wedding ring. "Oh. She's not my wife. We're divorced. I kept the ring in my go-bag because . . . well, it's gold, you know? I don't know why I put it on that finger."

"Have you heard from Dulcie?"

"No. We're divorced. I'm sure she's fine. I hope so."

Silence.

"Is there anyone else you need to talk to? To make sure they're okay?"

"I don't want to talk about it right now, Scottie."

They drive. They're moving slowly now between close walls of undergrowth. Wind whistles through the gaps at the top of the windows, carrying the damp scent of leaf mold.

"I did read some of Louis's diary," Scottie finally says.

Sol nods. Long recovered from his earlier indignation, he's already considered the eventualities, weighed up the consequences. If Scottie read this diary and nothing bad happened, then the diary should be safe to read.

"I think you should read the whole thing," he says.

"I'm sorry I lied to you. I'm sorry I didn't take this seriously."

"You couldn't know. Not without seeing it. Even two weeks ago this whole thing could have been a fantasy, before the Hasturian Guard started . . ."

"Doing what they promised to do."

". . . but the plan doesn't change. We came to find information and we found it. You should read the diary. Read the other thing.

Make up your own mind. Otherwise you'll just be taking our word for it."

"I never thought you were lying."

"It's okay."

"It's just that lots of people come to our community with things they're running from. Lots of people have, um, non-mainstream ideas. We don't say they're crazy. We don't believe in that. But we have to be careful."

"I understand."

"Take me to the bonfire spot. I'll read them there."

They drive to a fork in the track, and choose the right-hand path. The trees here are older. Limbs emerge in the bright headlights and fall behind into the darkness. Eventually they reach a clearing and Sol pulls up.

Scottie climbs out into the cool air. He retrieves the package from the back of the van. As he steps back through the fumes and headlights, he hears Sol call to him.

"Once you've read it, you'll come to us, first, right? Me or Judy. No one else."

Scottie nods, and watches the red lights diminish down the lane.

At one end of the clearing, in a sheltered spot between covered stacks of firewood, campfire embers glow. Scottie carries the package over to the campfire and lays it down carefully on the sandy ground. He pulls a camp chair and storm lantern from beneath a tarpaulin and feeds the embers until the fire returns to life. Then once again he unpeels the tape around the plastic folder and pulls out the document labeled THE TRUTH OF CARCOSA: A SPECIAL REPORT.

It comprises perhaps a hundred pages of laser-printed sheets, smudged and stained, as though examined and thought over for long hours under difficult circumstances.

Scottie clears a space on the ground before him and lays the manuscript down. He takes the pages he's already read and places them face down to the left of the unread pages. Now he has two piles. As he reads, the pile on the right will shrink, and the pile on the left will grow. And however much he feels like his world might explode, like unimaginable calamities might be unveiled with every page overturned, the steady growth of one pile and diminution of the other is all he can predict will happen.

We at the Archive for Literary Investment have been victims of our own success. We are a relatively well-endowed archive with a diverse list of authors in our catalog. We have four manuscripts by Cecilia Burton. We have the fascinating correspondence between Jag Caruthers and his constellation of lovers that would form the basis of his *Dog Running Dog* trilogy. But these minor treasures are chronically overlooked. When people think of the ALI, they think of the Archimboldi Deposit.

The Archimboldi Deposit is the ALI's Big Deal. It's only become more of a big deal since that infamous will reading, following which the executors of the Archimboldi estate set about destroying any notebooks, manuscripts, or correspondence that fell into the scope of their attention. "Destroy with fire," the author's explicit, debatably lucid instructions. For years the legal drones of Giovanni, Metti & Metti, LLC have followed these instructions to a tee.

The ALI keeps the arsonists at bay, of course. Its own deposit was endowed in 1993—before Archimboldi's deathbed crisis—and agreed upon in bulletproof contractese. Our legal department is muscular, well trained, and frequently exercised. You should see them, bounding over the green in pursuit of their prey.

The ALI also benefits from its position within the Institute. If you don't recognize the name, you may remember the old Broadland University from whose (public, bankrupt) ashes the (private, thrusting) Institute arose. The Institute values the vast potential for returns inherent in the ALI's hard assets. One day, I expect, the Entrepreneurship & Partnerships department upstairs will announce the grand monetization plan they've been planning for years; but the fruit of their blue-sky thinking has yet to ripen, and for now, at least, our peaceful life at the ALI remains unmolested.

For context, the Institute is situated outside the city's circular highway. There are commons on two sides, where disreputable people still exercise their ancient right to graze. A famous river forms the final boundary. Across the river, private woods. Conifers. The Institute sits thus amid pastoral splendor while its brutalist design suggests an assemblage of concrete cogs and brackets. The buildings' facades glow pink when the sun strikes them, and the windows are square and generous. The ALI sits at the bottom of the Institute's heap of architectural gubbins, but still commands a decent view down the slope to the river. From my window I might see sails gliding past on a temperate day. I certainly see the pines rising into their own shadow and quiet, as the afternoon draws on. See their blackness building. Think, *you should get back to work.*

As for the nature of that work: I am an administrator. I administrate. My line manager Jan makes clear what's required in terms of productivity and professional deportment. There's a generally cozy atmosphere in the office. We share cakes and doughnuts, tea and coffee.

The only barrier to our otherwise warm communications arises from the issue of confidentiality—that is, when a colleague must work on a deposit under embargo or otherwise restricted. That category covers everything in the Archimboldi Deposit, naturally: Every item is a deadly secret never to be told, legally speaking, and is—*was*—meant to remain so until Monsieur Carrette completed his biography.

But I'm getting ahead of myself.

First: how confidentiality affects the office environment. Let's say a member of staff must work with an embargoed deposit. A visiting researcher needs to see certain materials, and our colleague Judith—let's call her Judith—is asked to locate them and assist by producing notes or transcriptions.

Judith is a happy-go-lucky intern, excited to gain experience in research. Having made no calculations about the trajectory of her career, she's indiscriminate in her affections, happily engaging all colleagues, from the managers down to the support staff (e.g., myself).

Then one day the cadaverous Mr. Holmes LLM descends from his legal aerie with an NDA clasped between his knuckles. The elders nod knowingly as he ushers Judith into an unoccupied reading room. When she re-emerges—dazed, trepidation and doubt on her face—she beelines for the cold room; thence, laden with folders, directly into a reading room. Upon her reappearance hours later, her transition from my world is complete. She's no longer the friendly innocent, willing to give of herself for free. Self-sufficient, grave, and aloof, she now holds knowledge in her breast she can never share.

When she looks at me, I try not to perceive pity in her eyes. For I have never been asked to sign an NDA, nor will I ever be. My researches, such as they are, are limited to the fraction of the ALI's deposits that are free from embargo.

I know the reason why. I recognize the impact of my past behavior. These current limits are resonances of the past; they are *consequences*, regardless of whether they feel fair.

* * *

Don't misunderstand me! I don't mean to be dramatic about the NDA issue. It's not as if friends get replaced by pod people the moment they gain access to sensitive documents. But the gap that appears when some know things that others may not chills relationships.

Then there's the thing about Judith.

Of course, I didn't pick the name "Judith" out of nowhere. I was sidling up toward discussing Judith Bea. So let's move from supposition to reality. Let's pose the question: Whatever happened to Judith Bea? Everything changed after she was given that assignment for M. Carrette. Arguably, indeed, Judith Bea's life fell apart. Try to call her or find any trace of her online. You'll get nowhere. Ever since she so dramatically left the ALI, she effectively no longer exists.

This is a great loss. I always liked Judith Bea. I still fondly recall the first real conversation we had. A fresh afternoon, out on one of the Institute's high concrete walkways. Coffee break. She gave me space on her bench.

"What are you doing here?" I asked her.

"Staring at live trees," she said.

"Live trees?" I was intrigued by her choice of words.

"I spend enough time staring at dead trees and hallucinating. I thought I'd give my brain a break."

"Staring at dead trees and hallucinating?" I said. "*Oh!* You're talking about reading!"

I laughed. I *liked* that she'd said this clever thing. Spurred to respond, I pointed out that the trees themselves—like all other physical matter on the planet—were made ultimately from dead stars; and all stars, live or dead, were formed from the cataclysmic destruction of innocent nebulae, themselves deriving from the still-more-cataclysmic explosion at the start of all matter, space, and time, the disastrous horizon at which we are staring back, always, in our sensitive and cognitive processes, although the magnitude of the catastrophe is ordinarily hidden by the immediate challenges of our day.

Judith was beyond impressed; she was stupefied. Speechless. Encouraged, I told her more about the morbid nature of the work we did at the ALI.

"We are wardens," I remember saying, after a few exchanges in this vein, "in a site of secular pilgrimage."

"Pilgrimage!" she repeated, as if savoring the word. Then, warming to the theme: "Yes, I see, and the academics are the pilgrims."

"Yes."

"Pilgrim's Progress."

I brushed past this non-sequitur.

"I sometimes think of the cold room as a reliquary."

"A reliquary!"

"It's something you hold relics in. I suppose it's not quite the right word. Perhaps 'crypt' is the right word."

(I meant *ossuary*.)

Yes, the conversation progressed amiably enough, I found her imaginative and kooky, and afterward I felt like I might be making a friend of my new colleague.

But it wasn't to be. You'll learn why.

The day things first started to shift for Judith—and myself, ultimately—was not long into the New Year. On this cold, wet day, I was manning the ALI's help-desk console. It wasn't my scheduled shift, but an email had circulated into every inbox in the office but my own, demanding immediate attendance at an Institute-wide presentation. My exclusion was probably a mistake, my colleagues told me. They'd update me once they came back.

So the office emptied, and I sat at the help desk. Nobody visited. I was alone, except for a single contractor working on an electrical fault in the lobby. It was peaceful. The help desk sits close to a bank of windows with a view down the slope to the river and high woods beyond. With the rain coming down in wind-blown squalls, flattening the grass in spirals and eddies, I found I could forget the strange politics of the office; I felt cozy; I enjoyed my view of the gentle little storm for the modest gift it was.

Movement in the shadows across the river roused me from my reverie.

Most of the time I understood that tall bank of conifers to be nothing but shadow, but it was possible to detect some gathering of light or darkness within it. I perceived then a gathering darkness. *Somebody's moving in those woods. Coming this way. Some inky spot will soon emerge from the tree line.*

And yes, a figure did appear, atop the near riverbank. The same presence I'd perceived in the woods. I understood it to have left the trees and forded the river in a straight, unbroken line—a line directed at myself.

Larger and more distinct the figure grew, as it crossed the grass. It sprouted legs and swaying arms. It became a man with a recognizable gait. Recognizable, but strange. Like a piece of paper being blown back and forth, wavering, progressing, and regressing simultaneously; despite his inexorable forward progress, his backsliding pace made me wonder if he would ever reach me.

I tried to see his face. I thought it was a pale-skinned face above a baggy old black suit. But the details evaded me. It was like looking at a white handkerchief, snapping in the wind.

He's a dancer, I said to myself. *He is dancing to me, but his steps will never bring him here.*

At that moment there was a bassy thud, a click, and the hum of electrical circuits returning to life. The lights came back on.

I turned and saw the contractor standing beside an open panel in the wall, pulling gloves off her hands with an expression of professional satisfaction. She'd just restored power to the office, having momentarily shut it down.

This struck me as a breach of protocol: The cold room's climate control is carefully designed and extremely expensive to run. Surely power outages would be planned in advance? I studied the contractor for signs of chagrin (or duplicity), but there was none. She was placid as she returned her tools to her belt. I noted the logo on her uniform: Xanthic Spectrum. A power company.

I realized that I'd been sitting in semidarkness for some time, yet because of my fixation with the figure in the window, I hadn't even noticed.

Oh, the figure in the window!

I turned back to see him, but he was gone. The field was empty, and the storm had ended.

Soon enough the contractor left and the rest of the office staff returned, worried looks on their faces. Apparently the CEO had serious news to impart: An employee had been assaulted. This colleague had been attacked by activists while attending a pro-democracy protest. Exactly what they'd been doing at this protest was unclear (and naturally enough their contract had been terminated), but the CEO stressed the importance of not allowing our work—especially that of the ALI, where this academic had finagled limited access to the Archimboldi Deposit—to be drawn into what he called the "ongoing culture wars."

After making a few off-color jokes about belonging to the "globalist elite" (Jan, for one, wasn't amused), the CEO had attempted to reassure attendees that the Institute was steadfastly committed to retaining and drawing value from the Archimboldi Deposit.

"He should be more careful," Jan whispered to me. "A year ago he could have gotten away with being so dismissive. But the people have legitimate grievances, and our leaders are finally listening to them." This wasn't the first time Jan, a "shy" supporter of the current populist regime—shy, at least, in the liberal enclave of the Institute—had tested these opinions on me. I responded as I did when she tested me in other ways, such as jokingly referring to Judith as a diversity hire: with a perfect blankness that she interpreted as approval.

3

Sol drives back to the fork in the track and makes a sharp right. He reaches a mulch parking lot along a grassy bank, and a hand-painted sign adorned with smiley faces and stick figures that says GREENWOOD COMMUNITY—GENUINE TRAVELERS WELCOME. His headlights illuminate snatches of rustic-looking constructions between the trees. Sol parks and kills the engine and weak electric light illuminates the cabin. He doesn't get out of the van.

He rests his head against the steering wheel. He breathes—long, calming breaths—and eventually his hands unclench and stop trembling. His lips move, as if in prayer or conversation. Sometimes, when he exhales, sibilant whispers leave his mouth. Only two words are audible, spoken in a torrent.

"Shut up shut up shut up shut up . . ."

A timer runs out, and the yellow cabin light turns off.

As if prompted by the change, he takes off his courier jacket and pulls up the long sleeve of the T-shirt beneath, exposing his right forearm. He scratches the exposed spot, longer and harder than comfortable, occasionally gasping with relief and pain.

Eventually he pulls the sleeve back down—gently now, over the raw skin—and takes a cell phone out of his pocket. He switches it on and waits for messages to appear. None do. But there is a missed call.

He returns it. No connection. He risks leaving a message.

"Nadia, I'm where I said I'd be. I'll turn my phone on tomorrow. Sunset."

Then he sits, staring at the screen. Eventually he makes another call.

No connection. He leaves a message.

"Dulcie, I just wanted to . . ."

He sits, wordless, until an automated operator offers him the option to delete and rerecord his message. He takes it. Tries again.

"Dulcie, I'm sure you're safe. I'm safe, too. I don't want to reopen old wounds but I dreamed about you last night—"

Deletes the message. Hangs up. Turns the phone off and puts it away. He climbs down out of the cabin, crosses the parking lot onto a path between tall bean plants, and walks to the community buildings beyond.

In the shadows behind the parked vehicle, a match flares. It's brought to the wick of a naphtha lamp, which glows with a warm light as the bearer approaches the van and inspects it, slowly, outside and in.

The CEO was right to fear drawing Archimboldi Studies into the political line of fire. Certain legal factors have already made the field particularly tense. Outsiders don't always appreciate how careful Archimboldi scholars have to be, especially those operating without the ALI's legal protection. For, following numerous lawsuits and the passage of the latest intellectual property bill (overreaching, even by the extraordinary standards of our current government), the onus to destroy the remains of Archimboldi's estate has extended to a requirement to burn—yes, "destroy with fire"—works that merely *replicate* those prohibited texts, or even *reference* them without the utmost delicacy. Respected scholars have seen entire print runs of books pulled off shelves, all because some reference was made to a diary entry from 1979 that had been added to the burn list.

Examples of this are numerous and circulate regularly at the Institute. One example was Dr. Eloise Osvald, an expert in Latin American magical realist poetry who attained the status of public intellectual thanks to her exemplary reading of Octavio Paz. Osvald's understanding of Paz's work was already understood to surpass that of her contemporaries, yet one day she came across letters between Paz and a minor figure named Jaime Bolo that seemed to unlock still more. This unlocking was transformative: As if she'd donned some magical glasses, what had previously been obscure in Paz's work became clear to her.

However.

Bolo had sent carbon copies of his letters to another of his regular correspondents, Salvatore Archimboldi. These copies had been bequeathed to a niece, then bought by a collector, then—naturally enough in the new order of things—seized by the executors of the Archimboldi estate and destroyed.

Osvald catastrophically underestimated the risk of using these letters. She reckoned that since Bolo's letters were addressed to Paz first, the Archimboldi claim on the originals was void. She misunderstood the power of GMM (as Giovanni, Metti & Metti are known) and the malleability of the new laws. She never expected her book launch to be raided or her publisher's office ransacked until the offending material was located and removed for destruction. Which, of course, happened.

You may remember when the MP for Teeside made that extraordinary speech in Parliament, calling the new intellectual property bill that permitted these actions a "monstrous hydra and affront to individual freedom"; or most likely you don't remember it, since that very afternoon there was that assassination, following which came the Immigration Emergency Referendum, the consequent suspension of elections and replacement of Parliament with the unelected Emergency Cabinet, and the myriad subsequent idiocies that have held us captive all these years.

Anyway, such is the capacity for carelessness to destroy a career in Archimboldi Studies and the premium placed on access to the ALI's secure vault. Academics use the phrase "Archimboldi Chalice": a wondrous cup, much desired, that can be enjoyed only in the sanctuary of the ALI; otherwise, it's sure poison to the drinker.

And given that Archimboldi was himself a foreigner and a refugee from a fascistic (sorry, "stability-oriented") regime, it's easy to see why certain patriotic citizens cheer the destruction of his works. I was aware, on that squally afternoon, of websites and servers dedicated to the subject (Jan had referenced a few).

And now, apparently, beatings.

It was in a somewhat reflective mood, therefore, that I started to prepare our largest reading room for the afternoon's scheduled visitor, M. Carrette, the official biographer of Salvatore Archimboldi, who was to take a lengthy dive into the Archimboldi Deposit.

Let me put on the record that I always liked M. Carrette. I didn't envy him. It was his burden to be the authorized biographer of the most hotly debated author of modern times. Anybody who penetrated the sanctuary of the ALI earned the scorn of the excluded, and no actor in the field had earned more scorn than M. Carrette, whose mandate was apparently secured through a deal with his publisher and an obscure UN cultural department.

He was subject to the most jealous scrutiny, gossip, and ridicule. Researchers would wrinkle their noses and groan when they learned that M. Carrette would be taking up their favored reading room. If they managed a glimpse of his reading list, they'd roll their eyes and say "of course," as if utterly bored by the workmanlike approach this *sanctioned man* was taking to their delicate field of expertise.

But M. Carrette seemed unperturbed by the flurries of academic vogueing his visits provoked. Borne forward by the wind in his greatcoat, he sailed weekly into the Institute, over its gantryways and high walks, stern eyes steadily fixed on the prize allotted him by fate and favor: the Archimboldi Deposit in the ALI.

At the archive Carrette was courteous and punctual. He knew what he wanted and usually gave us ample time to prepare it. I write "us." I don't mean me. But he recognized me when he visited. I might say we were nodding acquaintances. I liked him well enough to be dismayed by what ultimately befell him.

4

In the clearing, Scottie lowers the page. He inhales deeply, stretches his shoulders, and wiggles his lower back. The camp chair is uncomfortable. It's early and he's not tired, but he's troubled. He scratches his beard thoughtfully.

"I expected you back in the Longhouse."

The voice comes from across the clearing. It's a white woman, dressed in woolens and sandals, with her hair in a red kerchief. She is carrying a naphtha lantern spilling light from a misted glass orb.

"Hi, Fran," says Scottie. "Sorry. I wanted to take time and process things. You know, it's heavy, what's going on down there."

"Yes," Fran says, advancing into the clearing. "I expect it's very heavy."

When Fran speaks, she leaves long pauses between words. Newcomers find these pauses disconcerting, but Scottie's known Fran for years. He's used to her rhythms. He has time to slide the manuscript into its folder before she reaches the campsite. She pays little attention, focusing on unfastening a tarpaulin cover.

"You don't need to help me, Scottie. I'm only after kindling. I was worried about you. Did you see any trouble?"

"We . . . were okay. It looks like the fighting's done for now. The UN are here, Fran, can you believe it? But they say they're not in charge, it's still not safe. Down in the city center they've made this list of victims, hundreds, there could be thousands—"

Fran closes her eyes and bows her head. She shrinks into herself, still and impermeable as a stone, until Scottie peters out. This behavior is one of Fran's accepted quirks. It means *stop*.

Scottie sits quietly until Fran thaws.

"We had a meeting today about all the violence," she says, as if the conversation never stopped. "There's a lot of trauma in the community right now. We had a couple of resolutions. The first one is that people need to get off their phones."

"What?"

"We don't need to hear every piece of bad news every day. It's a matter of morale. And we're going to do a watch, taking shifts. Stop people coming in who don't belong here."

Scottie nods. "But," he says, "what if people come from the city, asking for help?"

Fran shakes her head sadly.

"Think about it. How many people down in that city want to escape, right now? If just one in a hundred people decided to come here, we'd have thousands swamping our community. We don't have the resources."

"Fran, we're supposed to help people . . ."

Fran's eyes look so sad. It wounds her to say no. *And yet* . . .

"Things are changing. Out there, and in here. We have to look to ourselves. Scottie, I want you to think carefully about the kind of things you tell people here. Think about your influence. And your friends, do they understand our rules? They've been through a lot. I don't want them spreading toxicity around our home, even unintentionally. Judy—"

"Judy's fine."

Fran stares at Scottie patiently. Her disapproval of Judy, who seems to have entranced Scottie into monogamy, remains unspoken for now. *Saved up*, Scottie thinks, *for one of the meetings.*

"And your other friend, the geography teacher."

"Mr. Sol is a lawyer."

"Does he understand where he is?"

"He respects the rules."

"Good. He must be processing quite a lot."

Scottie blinks. "Yeah."

"He looks unwell. Heaven knows what he saw out there. I was thinking I might lend a hand."

"Therapy? Massage?"

"Yeah."

Scottie suddenly feels protective of Mr. Sol. He can't pretend they're close friends—they only met a couple of weeks ago. But Sol did one good thing for Judy—one kind, brave thing. For that, she trusts him, despite who he used to work for. And if Judy trusts him, so does Scottie. So, despite the fact that everybody benefits from the therapies deployed at Greenwood Community, Scottie has a disconcerting feeling that he's handing Mr. Sol over to Fran in some way when he says, "Yeah, why not?"

M. Carrette was late that afternoon. I was standing in the ground-floor loading bay where the Institute's smokers choose to congregate. I wasn't smoking. It was my habit, on rainy days, to visit the smoking bay to enjoy the steady stream of water running from the gutters of the high walk above. The dripping and the breath of the wind.

I saw M. Carrette emerging from behind a trash can. He'd evidently chosen a hidden route to the ALI today. I assumed the academics were particularly thick on the high walks. However, I soon realized something was wrong. M. Carrette's normal composure was gone. He was hurrying, almost tripping over his brogues. I realized he was being pursued—and then I saw his pursuer emerge from behind another bin some fifty feet away, and I caught my breath.

It was the dancing man. Or something very like him. I saw a figure in black clothes—at this distance I could see that the garment was a suit, worn and dirty—with corpse-white flesh. But the strangest sight was his face: The features were both bulbous and blank, and if I were asked to describe it afterward, I wouldn't have known where to start. It was an approximation of a face. A photocopy of a printout of a face.

The man was moving in a beeline toward M. Carrette, who hurried toward the smoking bay with grim determination, greeted me politely, and thanked me as I unlocked the door for us both. He didn't look back; his only concession to the existence of the horrible man behind him was a dismissive wave of his wrist as the door slid shut, as if flicking a bogey from his well-manicured hand. Then we were out of sight of the interloper.

While brief, the incident left me with questions. What kind of connection could that derelict have with M. Carrette? Was a fresh force pushing its way into his jealously guarded work? Was the man an agent of a rival estate? A book burner?

M. Carrette and I walked to the archive in companionable silence. I asked him no questions, and I expect he appreciated my discretion. But once in the office it soon became clear there was a problem. M. Carrette became apologetic, yet resolute, and various members of staff wheeled documents about the place in a confused manner. A change of plan was occurring. A new sample was needed from the cold room. Work hours were required.

This is where Judith Bea came in. Soon enough Mr. Holmes loomed over her desk with an NDA in his hands. They disappeared and re-emerged and Judith hurried into the cold room. M. Carette hovered in the foyer, pretending he hadn't caused a problem. Judith passed me with a cart piled high with boxes. The top box was labeled 1984. I mentally noted this fact.

I watched Judith enter the most secure reading room we have. When she came out, she looked sickened. Literally sickened, as if in the early stages of a viral infection, when the world suddenly tastes bitter and burnt, and electric shocks start to shoot through you, and your body braces, on high alert, for the evil to come.

It's time to address why my name never sits on any archive access list. It goes back—well, it goes back as far as I chase it, this seed of shame; my school years, my birth—my conception, most likely. But for brevity's sake, let's say it goes back to my graduation year.

My first year as a qualified recipient of a Bachelor of Arts degree, I worked at a bar. It was the same bar that employed me before graduation, only now I worked full-time hours. Working in a bar had been fun as a student. It was an arty bar, and I knew its customers. There was a sense of something coalescing and growing—a collective pulse of people and ideas, everybody excited about the world, everybody so beautiful, with such firm, unwrinkled skin. And in the excitement of that time, it seemed, we *all* drank. We *all* took drugs. It was a glorious adventure.

Then we graduated, and that magical crowd of beautiful people slowly filtered away, to be replaced by strangers. And I was left. Still working at the bar. Still drinking. Still taking drugs. The strangers now surrounding me were also beautiful, but they were strange; and they were interested exclusively in each other.

I wasn't quite alone among the strange. Some of my cohorts had been taking seriously what others regarded as experiments with drink and drugs. After graduation, we continued our own research in increasingly esoteric directions.

My closest companions in this were Spider and Scottie. Spider's personal legend was that he'd spent his adolescence ingesting hallucinogens, which meant he'd already experienced the content of two or three lifetimes, and was a bored and cynical observer of his soul's journeys; so, out of ennui, he'd started investing in the full-body thrills offered by crack cocaine and heroin. Of course, he wound up on the streets. Later, actually, he mugged me three times. The first two incidents I thought he was just asking for money "as a friend." The third time I realized he no longer knew who I was. Only then did I understand the threat he'd been employing all along.

Scottie's nervous system was nowhere near as degraded as Spider's, so he was still excited about LSD and LSD analogues: 2CB, 2CI, 5-MeO-DMT. He dealt with chemists and filled his refrigerator with droppers full of compounds, for sale and ingestion. One famous summer he became convinced that his refrigerator was dying, and that he needed to consume his entire collection "before it went moldy." By the time he'd worked his way through his vials and droppers, Scottie had come to exist on the edge of an ever-bleeding vortex. Space-time was mysterious in its relationship with him. He lost his jobs, one after another, since there was no guarantee he would turn up in the right place at the right time. He was a baffled voyager tracing self-deleting circuits through the planes.

But this was later. Whatever unhappy terminus our journeys led us to, for a few months Spider, Scottie, and I were pretty tight. I write "tight," not "close," to give you a sense of the idiom. And because the relationships that drug trips engender are as illusory as the experiences themselves. I know I sound like a fogey. But the fact is, drug people are primarily interested in their own nervous systems. Were we even fellow travelers? Perhaps so, but on separate trains, waving at one another while our railroad cars rolled down parallel tracks. At dusk, perhaps. Night falling.

Scottie had head trips, Spider had body trips, what was my poison? Well, the fact is, one year from graduation, Spider and Scottie were the only people left who could tolerate me when I was drinking. I was barred from half the pubs in the city. Nobody invited me to parties: too many blackouts, too much aggression and sadness. Indeed, the primary condition of keeping my bar job became that I never touch a drop of booze on the premises, not one drop, never again. And to my credit, I didn't. I'd line up my "wasted" drinks outside the back door and down them all after my shift ended.

Don't get me wrong, if Spider or Scottie provided exotics I'd sniff them or smoke them. But for me, the daily journey began and ended with booze. Economical booze. Strong cider out of a plastic bottle craftily designed to signify rocketry, with attendant dreams of flight and destruction on distant moons. I don't know why I became this way. It was a strange year. There was something in the air. A frazzled after-party desolation, hanging in the atmosphere at dusk: Goodbye, beautiful friends. In this twilight, it felt like getting high was the only thing to do.

But *where* to get high? Spider had an unstable housing situation, and Scottie defended his room as his last refuge from all the fun we were having. I was in a protracted dispute with my roommates, so my place was never a possibility.

So we roved. We sat under bridges. We crashed parties. We'd get high in places that were arguably crack houses, but which were also the chaotic homes of lonely, vulnerable people. These were difficult spaces to be in. All of which was why I got so excited when I found out about the House of the Dead Man.

5

Fran bears her lamp between the last of the trees bordering Greenwood Community. This late at night there's not much to see. The central longhouse is built on towering A-frames, but the surrounding buildings are low, wooden constructions. Lamplight flickers in the cracks between planks. Some of the buildings are half-submerged in banks and ridges, accessible via steps cut into the earth. Fran walks toward one of these hobbit houses.

She follows a creaking duck-walk, and before she gets to the stairwell a voice calls out from within.

"Scottie, are you back?" A woman pulls aside the doorway's heavy curtain and looks out.

"No, Judy, sweetheart," Fran says. "It's me."

"Which one are you?"

"It's Fran."

"Have you seen Scottie?"

"He's not in the longhouse," Fran says lightly. "When are you expecting him back?"

"Later. He's out doing something important. I'm a bit worried."

Fran advances until the lamp illuminates them both, then sets it down. Judith Bea has dark skin and wavy hair pulled into a tight bun and she looks tired. She might be twenty-five or thirty-five.

"Oh, yes," she says. "You. Fran."

The one who fancies Scottie and talks like a priest.

"I'm sure he's fine," Fran says, sitting down on the top step. "Things have calmed down out there."

Bea breathes deeply. When she exhales, her knees buckle beneath her and for a horrible moment she is falling. Fran catches her.

"Please. . ." Bea mumbles, struggling free.

"Okay." Fran holds her hands up.

Bea settles on her haunches. She covers her eyes.

"I've seen these stories about what's happening . . ."

"That's down the hill. We're safe here."

"I wish I knew they were safe. Both of them. It's hard, not knowing. Being stuck here."

Fran gazes at her for a long time before speaking. When she does so, it's as though she's made a consequential decision, and momentarily, at least, Bea respects the seriousness with which Fran approaches matters.

"I'm sure you'll see them soon."

They rest awhile, listening to the wind shake the trees.

"I could do with a smoke," Bea says miserably.

Fran nods. "I can help you. Have you tried my tea? I've just finished drying a batch. I think there's some water on the boil—how about I bring you a cup?"

Bea looks dubious.

"What do you mean, *tea*?"

"Tea. Better than smoke. Not too heavy. More of a body high than a head high."

"Huh."

"If you're tired, and you're waiting, sometimes it's better to go to sleep."

Bea looks at her fingernails: bitten and cracked.

"Yeah, maybe I'll come over and get some in a bit."

"Maybe best not. We're going to have a meeting in the longhouse tonight."

"Oh."

She looks up at Fran, then looks away.

"Of course, you're welcome to join in. You know, you always are."

"I, um."

"No pressure, though. Scottie has explained about you. Where you are."

"*Has* he?"

Bea and Fran lock eyes. Bea looks for some kind of bond or recognition. She sees nothing that she understands in Fran's eyes—just that weird calm. Is it seriousness or zealotry?

"Alright, Fran, bring your tea round. I'll skip the meeting for now."

Fran smiles. Her eyes stay fixed.

"I'll just leave it outside your door."

Scottie had a girlfriend at the time. He always had a girlfriend. His fecklessness brought out a protective instinct in women. This particular girlfriend, Hattie, believed in auras and the healing power of natural living. She was always trying to persuade Scottie to drop out properly and join her in the agricultural commune that was perpetually being set up on the outskirts of town.

While this commune was nearly happening, Hattie saw no reason to commit to any rental arrangement. For nearly a year, therefore, she moved between friends' couches and Scottie's bed and other informal arrangements with interested parties. One day, Hattie learned about an abandoned house not far from my own, a property backing onto Hourglass Lodge hospice. Abandoned but not cleared out, and not squatted, because of the strange conditions of its abandonment.

The house belonged to a widow. It previously belonged to a married couple; then, as they'd initiated divorce proceedings, it went into escrow; then the husband, a publisher, who'd never moved out of the house that was no longer his, apparently killed himself. The widow entered the house to verify the mechanical facts of her husband's death, and never set foot in it again. She couldn't sell the property for complicated legal reasons, but being a woman of means, with property elsewhere, she had the privilege of simply leaving the property be. This she did. It moldered and dampened and grew into its own thing: the House of the Dead Man.

I knew none of these details at the time. I would be obliged to learn them later, in court. All I knew at first was that Hattie was squatting in an abandoned house that gave her nightmares and a sticky cough. She lasted a week there before rolling up her bindle and returning to Scottie's, shivering and coughing, telling spooky stories. She described a house where a tree grew in the living room and black mold pulsed across the walls. A house that clicked and groaned at night, where shadows melted behind moldy furniture and crumbling installations.

Naturally, Scottie wanted to see it. Spooked as she was, Hattie had enough of a teenage horror movie instinct to go back with Scottie, bringing snacks, a dropper full of LSD, and sleeping bags to lay over the mildewed marital bed. I, too, was curious about the place. I asked to see it. Scottie was comfortable with the idea, but Hattie resisted. Hattie, you see, hated me. She was like one of those dogs that knows you, and consequently hates you, and there's nothing you can do to compensate for the fundamental flaw it detects from your scent. Hattie knew that a place like the House of the Dead Man was a delicate thing, like a folktale or a saltwater meadow. She intuited that it wouldn't survive my clumsy attentions. And she was right.

Scottie led me to the House of the Dead Man on a Saturday morning in spring. To get in, we trespassed on the grounds of the hospice, then pushed through an unkempt hedge into the yard.

It was a wilderness. Knee-high grasses and wildflowers, an algae-choked pond, and sickly looking bushes straining against one another. The unmanaged growth continued into the house. A flooded conservatory led to a lounge where carpet grew moss. The tree in the living room was real: a muscular green mamba-shaped thing pressing into the center of the ceiling. The room smelled of mildew and old rot. It was teeming with spores from all sorts of fungi; welts crept across the weeping wallpaper.

I loved it there. You could settle into a crumbling armchair, soft like the carcass of some great animal, and feel the fungus adjust itself around you. Folding in around your body, holding you close, reassuring you that it would be your final comforter.

The bedroom was a haven for moths; every surface was littered with a dry crumbly paste. I enjoyed going into the en-suite bathroom and identifying the soaps and shampoos the prior residents rubbed into their scalps. I enjoyed cracking open the closets to find the tattered remains of their clothes. It was thrilling to know that somebody had lived a life there. Instinct told me they were dead; the house had consumed them; their mortal remains had been stretched tight, like a greenish, mildewy membrane. They *were* the house, and the house was a carcass.

I got drunk in it. I settled into the reeking squeaking comfy chair and I didn't get up again until I'd finished my three-liter bottle of cider. I remember that some hours into the debauch, Hattie arrived, and I was abandoned to explore alone like some shit-faced ghosthunter. I broke things. I swore. I reached out with my inner being to connect with the House of the Dead Man, its shadows and sounds.

Scottie and Hattie decamped in the morning. They seemed a little disgusted as they stepped over my spot on the living room floor. I stayed on. My head was reeling. The utilities had been disconnected long ago, so the only fresh water I had was a plastic bottle Scottie left behind. I portioned it out carefully over the course of the morning. Then I started working through the bookshelf.

6

Sol cleans his bowl and fork in an open lean-to attached to the back of the main hall. The sink is a scavenged industrial unit fed with filtered rainwater. His enamel bowl clatters against the sides as he scrubs it with a coconut-husk brush. Once finished, he balances the bowl on the heap of crockery drying on the drip tray. In the cool air, the burning sensation across his arm has calmed to an ache. He worries that the skin is broken and needs a dressing, but the itch has subsided for now.

The main hall is constructed along the lines of a Saxon longhouse, painted all over with Sylvan scenes. It contains a central fireplace around which social activities are encouraged to take place. Sometimes Sol is invited to join in. Sometimes the activities take a more intimate bent, and Sol is invited to retire elsewhere.

He prevaricates beneath the bare bulb of the lean-to: He needs rest, but he feels the instinct toward company, and the warmth of the central fire.

"Mr. Sol! So glad you enjoyed our food."

It's Fran. He hears her sandals on the duck-walk before her kerchief catches the light of the bulb and blazes red. Her eyes fix him in place.

"You look like you could use a rest."

Sol clears his throat and smiles. He likes Fran, but he never knows what to say to her. She has a habit of staring.

"I've been to the city and back."

"Was it horrible?" He nods. She stares. "Let's go inside and have a cup of tea. I'd love to talk to you some more."

Sol accepts. Fran, an authority of sorts in the community, probably wants to vet him. It's about time, he reckons: He's been living there a couple of weeks.

They enter the hall, which is empty of people and full of uncomfortable chairs and stale bedding. Fran decants what she calls raspberry leaf tea from a samovar in the embers of the fire and passes him a mug. It tastes bitter to Sol, as if it's been steeping for too long. He sits on a beanbag by the fire.

He expects Fran to say whatever it is she's been meaning to say, but she sits down on a collapsed easy chair directly behind him and without preamble starts massaging his scalp. Sol, disconcerted but not completely surprised, allows it.

For some time the only sounds are their breaths, the crackle of the hearth, and creaking of timbers above. Sol relaxes into the massage. It feels good. His scalp tickles and tingles. Then some threshold of pleasure is breached, and he starts to feel the swirls of electricity swim over his skull and down his spine until they seem to hold his body in suspension.

"How does it feel?" he hears somebody ask, far off. Some observer, who walked in unseen. Sol starts to answer, but it's Fran who replies.

"Sludgy," she says.

Sludgy?

The rest of the conversation he doesn't catch, and the observer leaves. Fran continues to work on him.

What's sludgy?

The heat and the tea are hitting Sol in waves.

Am I sludgy?

Sol wants to say something, but he can't. His mouth can form no words. In a numb way, he understands that he has lost control.

* * *

"What do you do in the big bad world, Joe Sol?" Fran's voice asks.

From some deep place, Sol hears his own voice answer immediately.

"I used to be a lawyer once."

"Yuk," says Fran.

"I used to work criminal defense."

"Double yuk. Nasty men doing nasty things . . ."

"I did that for a long time. Then I got a different job . . ."

Sol moves between the surface of things and the dark space beneath. In the moments when he returns to the surface, he can feel Fran's attention on him. Her face is inches above him. She might be sniffing him, or feeling with whiskers the space around . . .

"Your aura's all black with holes in it," she whispers.

Sol dives down, into the blackness of the past.

* * *

For a while, they called Joseph Sol the "footage man." He had a knack for digging up footage from the childhoods of the most dangerous and violent criminals. He could find videoclips of children—almost always little boys—at weddings and birthdays, looking excited, or lost, or thoughtful. He would pair the clip with accounts of the trauma they'd suffered during their childhood. There was pathos in the image of the little boy who'd shortly witness his own mother's murder by a home invader. This same sense of pathos would lead the judge, the jury—whoever needed leading—to rethink the life and crimes of the man who'd been that child. To cast them in a tragic and sympathetic light. Sol used these clips for sentencing. That was his specialty: a sentence-reduction expert.

He seems to be communicating this to Fran. Perhaps he is simply saying it out loud, but here in the darkness it feels like Fran is with him. Probing, asking: Didn't he feel guilty, doing these favors for such *nasty men*? He has to answer. He feels a compulsion to tell the truth like a tide rippling over his body.

He knew the footage work was morally complicated, but at base he regarded himself as a good man doing a good thing. He thought redemption needed the kind of serious reckoning with the past his work attempted. He didn't think it was a cheap trick. He knew he was manipulating the jury, but also that the convicted person would see that footage, too; they'd look closely, identifying that lost version of themselves. Perhaps their conscience, too, might be reawakened.

In grand moments, after a glass or two of wine, he told his wife that he believed in the power of his footage to change people for the better. And in vulnerable moments, after a glass or two more, she'd encourage him to admit it was about his father, whose war-inflicted traumas had caused explosions of rage and cruelty against his mother, his sisters, his son; but whose fundamental decency—underneath it all—was never doubted in the Sol family, not by battered wife or pathetic kiddies, until he lost his job, took his own daughter hostage, and was killed by the police.

And when all bottles were drunk and dawn was on the horizon, Sol would admit it was all about himself, really, because he was capable of everything his father had done, and found it hard to imagine any crime through anybody's eyes but the perpetrator's. Sol would get angry with his wife, at this point, as if she had pulled the rug from under the important work he did, the *being good* and *doing good* that constituted his professional contribution to society.

Wasn't it enough? he would demand of his wife. Wasn't it enough to know the roots of his motivations, and to push to do good in his work? Was some other declaration required of him, some catharsis or ritual cleansing? Was he supposed to cry now? Was he supposed to join a survivors' group?

It carried on like this for seven good years.

Then his wife fell pregnant and miscarried in the third trimester, and in the emotional melee that followed, Sol couldn't find a way of expressing the relief he felt in knowing that the child—a girl—would be spared the rages he carried in him; couldn't find a way of expressing this relief that would be non-harmful, wouldn't insert him into the center of the affair, the tragedy that wasn't his, really, since it was all his wife's body, her hopes, her hopeful decorations and toys, the ultimately fruitless flow of her ambitions to which he feared he could add nothing but the endlessly looping footage of his own angry self; and as the marriage dissolved, these fears manifested amply. His ex-wife's name was Dulcie. Dulcie meant "sweet."

Fran's voice, penetrating the depths: "You dream of her."

Sol hears his own voice now: "Sometimes. Less, now."

Things changed, he reflects, when he went to work for Giovanni, Metti & Metti. What Dulcie surely identified as final proof of his midlife crisis. Tilting at the largest windmill he could find.

"What do you dream about now?"

Although he feels compelled to be truthful, Sol is aware that GMM is taboo. His work there must remain secret. Luckily, he is cunning in his compulsion: He can answer honestly and keep his secret.

"I dream of Jennifer Donaghy."

Lying on the office floor.

"Is she your girlfriend?"

"No," he pronounces. "She's dead."

Fran's fingers pause. Then she leans into Sol's space again.

"Did she die recently?" she asks.

"Yes."

"How did she die?"

"Somebody hurt her."

"Who?"

". . ."

"Was it you? Did you hurt her?"

"No. I wish I'd saved her. She was my partner. She says I was supposed to follow her."

"Why are you here, Joe?"

"I'm hiding."

"What are you hiding from?"

Tell the truth and lie.

"The end of the world."

"Are you going to hurt us?"

"I hope not."

I liked the books in the House of the Dead Man. I'd completed a degree in Comparative Literature in Broadlands University (before its metamorphosis into the Institute), specializing in *fin-de-siècle* French poetry, so I knew my way around a bookshelf. These shelves held paperbacks, mostly, unusual editions from a different era, with cover designs featuring bad-taste cartoons and sleazy, airbrushed photographs.

It was a weird collection. There were smutty books and sad books. There was, in fact, some *fin-de-siècle* French poetry. As I read the books I found dedications and notes, and I learned that the dead man who once lived in the house was called Jonathan Crew. He was also the publisher of many of the books. As I read them, they fell apart. As such, I was obliged to skip forward regularly: A smug preface by some 1960s chauvinist became a baffling chase scene across Tuscany became a letter to an estranged son. I didn't mind the plot holes. The ruined pages joined the litter on the floor.

It wasn't just the books that had gaps. My memories of the House of the Dead Man overall have their own inconsistencies. I recall spending time in a basement room that couldn't possibly have fitted with the geometry of the house. I recall listening to music, although there was no sound system. Perhaps these fragments derived from the books I read. Perhaps I merely dreamed them.

I know I kept going back to that house. For more than a month, I couldn't stay away. Spider and Scottie and Hattie and all the others dropped out of my orbit. They didn't like partying with me in that sunken place. They could see I was spoiling the place, making it profane.

When the police came, they tried really hard not to arrest me. They seemed to have this notion about *kids being kids*, doing stupid but harmless things and being reprimanded, *no harm, no foul.* They wanted *me* to be a kid. Ignoring the bags under my eyes, my swollen face, they rousted me out of there like local sheriffs in a teen movie. *Stay outta the Crew Place, d'ya hear?*

But I didn't stay out. I wasn't some kid playing at breaking the rules: I was essentially in a *relationship* with the property. The details of this relationship remain unclear—I was mostly very drunk—but the word "portent" is apposite here. One might say that the House of the Dead Man was an all-encompassing private portent into which I hoped to be *subsumed.*

The neighbors noticed the noises. The second time the police came, they paid attention to the damage I was causing. Plastic bottles of piss lined up in the toilet. The clothes I'd pulled out of the closet to feed the moths. Ruined books, heaped in a pile at the bottom of the tree. The place had become a den for something feral.

And it was all business once they found my cocaine. They handcuffed me and drove me to a building full of sad and angry men. Because of certain things I said, an officer was stationed outside my cell, obliged to check through my peephole every five minutes to make sure I hadn't swallowed my tongue or caved in my head against the toilet.

There was plenty of aftermath, although no prison. Instead, written statements of apology to the family of the long-dead Jonathan Crew. Residential addiction treatment, which I'll discuss later. Community service. My name got in the paper. Only the local paper, luckily, so my family didn't get it in print. Mom and Dad had to do an online search to find out exactly what I did.

I won't get into all the details. Suffice to say, I ultimately sobered up. No, it wasn't the *short, sharp shock* of arrest and therapy. It took years after that particular crisis before I took real action. But it did happen. I stopped spending my time with Spider and Scottie and the other faces on the scene. I've already described Spider's trajectory. Scottie drifted into his own narrowing track of space-time, attended by the women who thought they could pull him out of it. Hattie's commune was finally established, and she lived there for a year before heading out for better things. She's a wellness influencer now.

I have a criminal record. I got my job at the ALI, and I'm grateful for it; but because of my record, I cannot access the Archimboldi Deposit. Not that I cared, for a very long time. Not that afternoon, when the dancing man swam up the lawn toward me, or accosted M. Carrette on his way to the archive. Not when Judith Bea passed me with the box labeled 1984, or when she re-emerged from the reading room, looking shaken and sad. That day I cared only about my own unease. I was sad, I suppose, to see Judith Bea graduate out of my little realm. I couldn't know at the time that she was a few steps from graduating out of everybody's realm—saying good-bye to society entirely.

7

"Okay," Fran says, and pulls her fingers away from Sol's head. This seems to take more effort than it should, like pulling her fingers out of a bowl of dough.

She sits back and observes the man she's been massaging. He's motionless, aside from soft, shallow breaths. Apparently still under.

He hasn't lied to her. But he's hiding something.

She shouldn't care. It isn't her practice to pursue strangers' secrets. But everything has changed in the last few weeks; Greenwood Community—Fran's community—has moved to the center of her priorities. Every morning she wakes up to crisp spring air and birdcall, and the knowledge that down the hill people are being killed; protecting this beautiful place in the world has become more important than anything else.

So what is it she mistrusts about Joseph Sol?

Footsteps nearby. A community member tiptoes between the furniture to whisper in her ear: "Fran, there's a car coming. Just a normal car. Can't see who's in it."

Fran nods.

"Go see," she instructs. The messenger tiptoes away.

Fran returns her attention to Sol. Her internal alarm bells are ringing; a decision has been made. A more radical procedure is needed.

"I'm sorry," she says, to the back of Sol's head. She knows he can hear her. "I don't like taking people deep without their consent, but I needed to know. But we always pay back, Joe. You gave us something, and we'll give you something in return."

Fran wipes her hands together, palm to palm, as if ridding herself of some unpleasant slime. Then, gingerly, she replaces them on Sol's skull.

⁎ ⁎ ⁎

From his space below, Sol feels the new motion Fran is using on his scalp. It produces a subtly different effect on his consciousness. As if once he was being stirred, and now he's being whipped.

Her voice: "Thank you for being honest with me before, Joe."

You're welcome.

"This is a place of healing, Joe. I'm going to teach you something that will help you heal. This is a lucid dreaming technique. When you have your bad dreams, there's something you can do to control it."

Hmm.

"I want you to remember an object that you often hold in your hand or keep in your pocket. What is that object?"

It's my toothbrush.

"Okay. Think about your toothbrush. It's your *focus*. Whenever you have a bad dream, and you are out of control, if you want to regain control, I want you to remember your toothbrush. I want you to visualize it so it appears in your hand. Can you see it?"

On the surface, Fran watches Sol's arm float up in front of him. With his eyes closed, he pantomimes inspecting something in his palm.

"Yeah . . ." he slurs through a half-open mouth.

There's something desolating about the drumming of rain on bus windows. Especially in winter, when the city lights up and the smeared and swimming shopfronts project an aura of hope, forlorn, just out of reach. Warm-lit pub interiors project exclusive community. People, together, luminous and inaccessible.

Such were my thoughts that evening as my homebound bus hauled me up the hill to Calendral Road and the windows of the Berryman trickled into view. I imagined how romantic it would be to cry, *Driver, stop!* Then to step from the bus door, umbrella upheld against the streaming rain—the sizzling bacon rain—oh and the hiss and lurch as the juggernaut made its friendly way onward—then to cross the narrow pavement, swing open that pub door. Warm air, soft light, and laughter spilling onto the street.

I no longer drink. But I'm only human. I pressed the bell and darted out of the bus to the waiting threshold of the Berryman.

I was barred from the Berryman long ago. It had previously been my favorite place: It was quiet and friendly, with two open fires. And it was a liberal place. In the era before such things were outlawed, it displayed posters in support of human rights. After I sobered up, it was the one pub I wanted to return to; after paying the landlord £500 to cover some damages I'd apparently caused, I was allowed to do so.

I stepped out of the rain and into the pub. The closing door shut off the rumble of the departing bus. My glasses steamed up. Some locals nodded and twitched at me. I waited by the bar, pretending to be interested in the display case and wiping condensation from my glasses, and after a long wait the landlord deigned to sell me an alcohol-free lager.

Carrying my drink to the back bar, I was astonished to encounter Scottie, bundled up in a gigantic damp shooting jacket at a table by the fire. On the opposite side of the hearth was another chair, on which somebody had placed a hyper-realistic cat figure, curled up in a hoop.

I hadn't seen Scottie in perhaps three years. I was impressed by the tableau he was making, dressed as an old-fashioned hobo by the fire, apparently staring down a stuffed cat. It was an extraordinary scene, yet somehow predictable: an image from an anti-narcotics campaign illustrating the pitiful state of long-term abusers.

Scottie, I remembered in that moment, woke up one morning to find his vision was upside-down. He was lying on a bed on the ceiling, and the light fixtures protruded from the floor, and through the misplaced windows light was streaming upward from some white-hot furnace far below. A doctor explained that his overworked cerebral cortex had given up flipping the image of his vision. Scottie claimed the condition lasted a day and never struck again, but I wasn't sure. I'd watch him trying to hold something—a glass of water—and getting squirrelly and suspicious, like he didn't understand how the water was staying in the glass, how to maneuver without provoking disaster. In these moments, I suspected his mirror world had fallen back upon him.

And now, in the Berryman, I felt an analogous blend of pity and contempt.

"Hi, Scottie," I said.

He raised a finger at me. He didn't take his eyes off the cat. This angered me. It seemed a high-handed gesture for a tramp in a damp coat to make to myself, a man in gainful employment, four years sober and tired after a long, righteous day.

Decisively I picked up the cat figure that was stealing his attention, but was surprised to feel it translate into a live cat in my hands, which rippled and twisted, flumping onto the floor with a yowl.

"Fuck's sake!" barked the landlord.

I raised my hands. Innocent. Confused. Not drunk. The moment passed. Pint glasses returned to lips. I sat.

"Shit!" I hissed. "I thought it was a stuffed toy."

Scottie nodded. He said: "I know, mate. It was."

He winked. And I realized that it wasn't just his dismissiveness that angered me: It was the absurd opacity of the man, the moronic hippie code of half-truths and secrets he carried. Infuriating. Just the kind of thing he *would* say!

Nonetheless, irritation aside, I won't deny I was intrigued to see my old companion.

"How are you?" I asked. "It's been a long time."

"I'm back in town for a few days. We're getting supplies."

"Oh yeah?" I said, as if he'd answered my question. "Where are you living?"

"Where are *you* living, Louis?"

"At the same place I've been for a while. Quite central. In the new section."

He smirked.

"Are you living the straight and narrow life?" he asked.

"Very much so," I said, more vehemently than intended.

"I heard you are a keeper of secrets now."

"Not quite. I work in the archive."

"Up at uni?"

"They call it the Institute now. It's fully private. Half the students are execs getting sponsored by their companies—"

"And you work there?"

"Yes. Nine to five, straight and narrow."

"Hah."

"What do you mean, *hah*?"

"Hah. Nine to five—just like you pledged you'd never do."

"No, Scottie," I insisted, imagining the kind of half-baked radical conversation he might have been referring to. "I never made that pledge. That was you and Spider."

Scottie narrowed his eyes.

"I don't think James likes being called that anymore."

"I don't think *James* cares what you call him as long as you give him money for crack. Have you seen him lately?"

Scottie didn't answer. Instead he continued his previous line of attack.

"You swore all sorts of oaths and made all sorts of promises when you were drinking."

"And none of them meant anything."

"Yeah! You were talking shit."

"I was sick, Scottie. We were sick, back then."

"Sick?" Scottie flinched again. He looked around the pub as if the lights had flickered. As if shadows had lengthened and whipped around like twitching tails and the undersides of things had made their presences known. "Sick?"

Now came the next surprise of the evening: I spotted Judith Bea. She was sitting alone, fiddling with her phone. She looked anxious and out of place. I'd always assumed she'd do her drinking in the urban-styled chain bars in the city center. My prejudice, no doubt.

She noticed me and waved, and I waved back, and so did Scottie, all familiar.

And my heart sank.

Judith Bea drank in the Berryman. Judith Bea knew Scottie Devine, the unlikeliest Casanova in town. She knew him better, it seemed, than she knew me.

But I didn't have much time to dwell on this discovery, since the biggest surprise was on its way.

Through the side entrance slid a gangly, matted-haired individual dressed as a poacher. A cousin of Spider's, I surmised—if not in reality, then in temperament. I assumed that his khaki jacket was full of weed; that intuition was immediately confirmed by the stank spreading through the bar as the poacher worked his way between the punters, scanning for a signal.

Judith provided one. She sat with her index finger extended, almost as if twiddling her bountiful hair, but also as if saying shyly, "Yes, me."

The poacher saw the gesture and stopped by her table to complete a furtive transaction. It struck me as a bit obvious, but being the only sober person in the pub means you tend to suffer what others ignore.

Next, the poacher scanned the room again and found Scottie, who—lo and behold—had raised his hand in the air like a keen pupil at the front of the class, pleading *please sir, ME sir.* I cringed. Over slinked the poacher, with his smell of damp and hair grease and skunk, and Scottie purchased a pillowcase-sized bag of weed in the most obvious manner possible.

They should've just exchanged money for goods over the table, like a legitimate barter. But these clowns showed each other the product and the items—*above the table*—then slid them *underneath* the table. Then they locked eyes while their hidden hands rummaged and rustled, struggling to pass these simple objects between them. A farcical display.

While this was happening, I tried to be as physically distant as possible without falling off my chair. Then my eyes caught Judith Bea's. She looked as appalled as me. We stared at each other, suppressed smiles creeping across our faces. Understanding passed between us for a few precious seconds, and it was delicious.

8

In the parking lot, near the hand-painted Greenwood Community sign, a hybrid car creeps into a shadowy corner and halts. As the engine dies, the cabin light comes on automatically, and the driver is momentarily visible before she switches it off: a Black woman in her early thirties wearing a university-branded tracksuit set.

She waits a few seconds in the darkness, allowing her eyes to adjust. In her bag on the seat beside her are a collection of items, including phones, a camera, and a microphone. She selects a surgical face mask and an envelope.

She dons the mask and softly opens the car door. She steps carefully on the mulch, white soles visible in the dark. She walks almost past the sign, then a gust of wind blows and she pauses, listening for the sounds of motion she thought she heard under it.

"Nobody here called a taxi."

A voice carries from some undefined spot of darkness nearby.

The woman puts her hands out.

"Easy," she says. "I'm a friend."

"Are you lost?"

"Who am I talking to, please?" No response. "My name is Nadia. I'm not here to hurt anybody."

"Why are you here?"

"I'm on business."

"We have all we need and nothing left to spare. We don't want to trade and we don't have any room."

"Okay."

"So you can go now."

"I'm not looking for trade or refuge. I wish I knew who I was speaking to. Would you mind if I got my flashlight out of my pocket? I have a flashlight. Just a flashlight."

"Leave it in your pocket. Stay there."

Footsteps move away through grass and fallen leaves. Nadia sees movement amid some silvery shapes in the middle distance, and the shapes resolve into crops: tall, spindly, swaying in her vision.

Then the footsteps return, and with them the warm light of a gently hissing naphtha lantern, and a view of the woman who surprised her. White woman, woolly jumper, suspicious expression.

"What's your business?" she asks.

"I'm looking for a friend. His name is Joseph Sol. I want to give him something I owe him."

"Give me a break."

"He's here, then?"

"What did he do? Why are you after him?"

"I assure you, I'm here to help. I'm no threat to your community."

"Mr. Sol isn't a member of our community. We could hand him over wrapped in a bow if we wanted."

"I'm not interested in that. I want to give him something."

Nadia waggles the envelope she's carrying.

"What is it?" the woman asks. Nadia holds it out for her. Suspiciously, she takes it. She squeezes and probes around the edges and the small, flat object in the center, like a slim notebook. "What is it, a book?"

Nadia nods, and starts to back away. Before she leaves the radius of the lamplight, she says, "It's a very valuable book. Please deliver it to him."

Jumper woman watches her retreat to the car, and hum quietly away between the trees. Then she's alone with the package.

She teases at the sealed lip until she's made a hole wide enough to peep through. She brings the envelope close and peers inside.

"Well, that was incredibly awkward, wasn't it?"

Judith had pulled her chair up to the fire as soon as the dealer left.

"What?" Scottie asked.

"You looked like you were wanking each other off under the table."

"Well, actually, Judith," Scottie lowered his voice, "I was buying *marijuana.*"

"I *know,*" Judith stage-whispered. "You've got it stuffed in your *trousers.*" She laughed. She seemed quite delighted with him. Women often are. It mystifies me. "I didn't expect to see you here, Louis," she said, turning to me. "I didn't think you . . ."

I showed her the label on my drink. She nodded. I made sense to her again.

"So, Scottie," I said, "I work with Judith at the ALI."

"The what?"

"The archive."

Scottie nodded. He locked eyes with Judith.

"So I've heard," he said.

"And you two . . ." I proffered.

"Oh, I've known Judy for ages," he said.

"Right."

Judith stopped looking at me directly. She seemed to be blushing.

"How long are you in town again?" I asked Scottie.

"Reckon I'll be heading back tonight."

"Back where?" I asked. "Back to your . . . compound?"

"You couldn't buy me a drink, could you, mate? I have this feeling that you might owe me a drink or two."

I didn't argue. I left Scottie and Judith to get their story straight and headed to the bar. The landlord took some persuading that the beer wasn't for me, and I had to buy myself a second soft drink. It gets tiresome, this pursuit of redemption. The thing is, readers, I'm not universally reviled. I've constructed a life for myself in sobriety, including relationships of mutual respect in spaces where my contribution is valued. At the ALI, for instance, although I'm formally invested with trust, I am informally liked by several people. I curse the instinct that drives me back to the places where I'm a pariah, to the people who'll never forgive me.

I was thinking about this as I returned drinks for Scottie and Judith. It must have shown. Scottie didn't have any more acid comments to share, and Judith kept giving me this apologetic smile.

"Are you really living in a commune or something?" I asked.

Scottie wobbled his head ambivalently.

"Kind of. We've got a piece of land that has access to the common. There are a few of us there."

"And you've come in for what, agricultural supplies?"

"Coffee. Toilet paper. Tampons. That kind of stuff."

"And a great big bag of weed."

"Yeah."

"I am astonished that you can still consume any kind of drug. There was a point, I remember, when a cup of tea would flip you into another dimension."

Judith laughed at this. I couldn't work out how much she knew. About Scottie's story, or my own.

"What doesn't kill you makes you stronger," he said.

"That's fucking bullshit, man."

"It's just weed," Judith said. "Makes you giggly, makes you sleepy. Makes you forget."

I smiled at this nonsense. Then I remembered the first real conversation we had, Judith and I, about pilgrims and reliquaries. My long monologue. She hadn't, I realized, been stupefied by my impressive display of knowledge and intelligence. She'd been stupefied by drugs. Baked. Out of her fucking tree.

"What are *you* trying to forget, Judy?" Scottie asked. He had that irresistible openness in his face: fellow traveler, fellow sufferer. Tell me your troubles.

"Huh," Judith said. "I actually can't tell you. Legally, that is. I'm contractually prevented from telling you about my work."

"Yeah, but—" Scottie blinked. He indicated the space around us. "This is the pub."

"Sorry. Louis understands."

"It's serious," I said. "There's a lot of money floating around these literary deposits, and lots of legal attention. And banging on about things in the pub is exactly what NDAs were invented to prevent."

Scottie made a farting sound.

"Go *on*," he insisted.

"I can't," Judith said. Scottie rolled his eyes. Ten years ago, we'd both have called her a *narc*. "I can't!" Judith persisted. But she could, if she chose, and she wanted to. That's why she said what she said next. Like a little teaser, for us, but also for herself. Testing the waters of indiscretion. Finding out what it felt like. "The truth of Carcosa begins in the cold room and ends in the reading room, and if Monsieur Carrette takes any notice of my notes—well, time will tell."

And my jaw dropped. Like a hungry patient, I let my mouth hang open. *The Truth of Carcosa* returned to me.

Back to the House of the Dead Man. We're in the living room. Mold and vegetation, the carcasses of furniture. I looked at a lot of books there, you see. More than you'd think, knowing how drunk I was. But the thing was—and this fact only returned to me when I heard Judith Bea say those words—I didn't really *read* most of them; many I simply pulled apart, but one book I read many times.

This book was by an author whose name, even then, provoked a little twinge of recognition. When I say it now, it conjures serious gravitas: Salvatore Archimboldi. The ALI's Archimboldi. The Big Deal. The book was from the 1980s and had a cover I can't recall, except to state that it was grotesque and confusing, as if the cover artist didn't understand what the book was about, or the author himself had been led astray. It was called *The Truth of Carcosa.*

I read it through, in one oppressively hungover afternoon. I recalled almost no details of the book. Details, in fact, seemed to repel me as I passed from page to page. I got impressions.

The Truth of Carcosa resembled a play at first. The play was strange. It seemed to be occurring at once in a fantastic kingdom called Carcosa, beside the lake of Hali, and at once in a nameless Latin American city, where a single traveler was attempting to secure a passport for onward travel to some unnamed sanctuary. Aside from the passport element, the plot seemed to involve a dynastic struggle and some philosophical meditation. I wasn't clear on that count. The overall effect, however, was like listening to a half-conscious man recount a recent argument, or overhearing a gentle lunatic on the bus. Lowering the book was like coming to, not knowing how long you'd been out for, where you went, or how you got that taste in your mouth.

The word "Carcosa" meant nothing to me when I first encountered it in the House of the Dead Man. Other than itself, that is. I mean, I didn't understand it to be part of a sequence. I hadn't yet heard of Robert W. Chambers, or his contribution, *The King in Yellow.* It would be almost a decade before I realized how significant a find *The Truth of Carcosa* had been; how utterly slipshod I'd been in losing it, in persuading myself that it didn't exist.

9

Sol feels Fran's attention on him like the brush of a feather. It penetrates his skin, his thoughts. She sees what he sees, as he sketches, through a slurred verbal shorthand, the locations common to his most frequent dreams. He guides her through iterations of childhood bedrooms and schoolyards. He takes her to the hospital. He takes her to a beach between tall rocks whose encroaching tide is an ever-present threat. At each location she walks him through the process of retrieving his focus—the toothbrush—and using it to gain some element of control: to close closet doors, open school gates, activate an engine in the seabed to flush the tsunami waves away . . .

Finally he finds himself standing before the gates of a hazy apartment complex: an out-of-focus mass of concrete with a sharp little balcony one floor up. Three police officers are standing on the balcony, looking in.

Fran's voice: "Whose house is that?"

I don't know. I never went there.

"Who's inside?"

My dad.

The officers don't move. They pose like little plastic army men.

"Do you know what happens next?"

Yes. But I keep it frozen. I didn't mean to show you this.

"Find your key, move on."

He inserts his toothbrush in the gas tank filler of a parked car and twists, and they move on to the campus of a modern commercial estate. The buildings are modern and uninspiring, medium-rise brick and glass. The street signs and logos are meaningless scribbles.

"This is new. Do you work here?"

I used to.

It's the campus of the regional GMM office.

"I feel like I recognize this place."

I told you I was a lawyer.

"It looks like the new estate across from the bridge . . ."

We need to get inside.

"Where did you work, exactly?"

Inside, inside!

The edges start to ripple and vibrate as Sol leads Fran to a doorway in a smoked-glass lobby. He presses his toothbrush against a card reader—*diddle-dee-DEE*—and ducks into the growing gap.

The room inside isn't the lobby. It's an expensively decorated drawing room, filled with artwork—paintings, ceramics, tribal fetishes. An armchair and sofa, both wrapped in a clear plastic film. Leaning against the back wall, beside a closed door, is a pair of shoulder-height gas canisters. Oxygen. Framing the door like a kind of portico is a structure of inflated clear plastic. An airlock. Sol can hear the hiss of the gas canisters and the whirr of a nearby pump. He becomes aware of his arm again. Itching.

"This is your office?"

No.

"Is it the home you shared with Dulcie?"

No! I've never been here before.

But he's seen it. He knows that it's a terrible place. A trap. He can't hear it yet, but something is going to start knocking on the door behind the airlock. The plastic structure is going to compress and crinkle like a stertorous intake of breath—*something* is going to make itself known here.

From his pocket he pulls his toothbrush, and he waves it in front of himself, expecting to wave everything away; but nothing changes, the hiss of the air and the whir of the pump continue, and then his sluggish brain pulls things together, and he thrusts the toothbrush through the sofa's plastic cover, and with an explosive venting of gases the scene dissolves.

You might assume that on hearing Judith Bea utter the words "the truth of Carcosa" in the Berryman I was plunged into a fugue of disbelief and horror, that my conception of the world was shattered, along with the fragile sense of peace I'd worked hard to attain in sobriety. You'd be right—and wrong. Sure, I was upset. I felt the upwelling of horror that threatened to subsume me in its gargantuan scale. But at the moment of my immersion, like the ringing of a bell, my therapy returned to me. It returned wholesale: its idiolect and cosmology; the names I associated with it—Dr. Bredsky especially—and the places they inhabited; the smell of the varnish on the cafeteria table in the refectory at Pentorgan House.

This return was surely prompted by some hypnotic trigger, testament to the skill of my therapist, Dr. Adriana Bredsky, in ensuring my sobriety in the most intense of crises. It's a shame that more addiction programs haven't adopted Bredsky's methods; I've never met a fellow addict who recognized the litany of terms—Accession bridge, *Kataluin*, Deferral—that became part of my vocabulary during my residential treatment.

I must have looked strange that afternoon in the pub, with Scottie and Judith looking on, as I sat with my hands covering my eyes in an attitude of prayer. I wasn't praying. I was repeating an old mantra that had only just returned to me:

This is my Bridge, my route to Accession.
Nobody can travel this Bridge but me . . .

I first encountered Dr. Bredsky when, during my state-mandated addiction treatment, I moved from the inner-city Laburnum Clinic to rural Pentorgan House for an intensive weekend course.

Pentorgan House, a private clinic on a government contract, occupied an old mansion with a beautiful garden and grounds. The interior resembled any other hospital, with bilious gloss paint and linoleum, except the windows were deep-set and the corridors narrow, with sometimes surprising angles.

I'd made little progress with my previous therapists. They seemed more like technicians than doctors; there was no artistry or intuition to the standard checklist they ran through to establish my psychic roadworthiness: *When did I feel sad? What did I think about when I felt sad? How did my body feel when I felt sad?*

Answering these questions, I felt a confected nostalgia for the old days of psychoanalysis. I'd always hoped my therapist would be some bearded degenerate, desperate to hear my dreams. I wanted to vent about my terrible childhood, my parents, my special collection of traumas; but these technicians of the soul offered no such opportunities.

Dr. Bredsky was different. She was a severe-looking woman with a default expression of superiority that I soon warmed to. I must have caught her eye while she was inspecting the common room. She found me ensconced in an armchair, reading an old book of Romantic poetry. She paused to ask a few questions, then left me to my reading.

The next day, however, I was given a series of in-depth medical tests. My entire body was precisely examined by new, strange nurses. The day after that, I found myself in Dr. Bredsky's private office. My case file was open on her desk.

She asked me to relate how I arrived in residential care. She didn't ask stupid questions about my mood, or shut me down when I "deviated" into the deeper reasons for decisions made by myself, others, and society at large.

I explained a lot to her and it felt good. I told her about the House of the Dead Man. I told her, too, about the books I'd been reading, and she was pleased that I read, and I felt clever in a way I hadn't since graduation.

After our first session, Dr. Bredsky issued a prescription. Since my mind was such a *fabulous maze*, she would give me a sponsored place on one of Pentorgan House's advanced courses. I needn't return to Laburnum Clinic, but could stay in the mansion undergoing a "special combination."

The special combination was two-pronged. I attended group seminars covering the philosophy of the program that Dr. Bredsky had developed. And I had special one-on-one sessions with Bredsky herself, centered on "practice"—which meant, since I was so literary, *reading*.

Each group seminar would focus on a handout covering a particular topic. Some of these pamphlets were practical, such as ways for managing high-pressure events; others were more esoteric; many showed a spiritual bent.

Well, as they say: Recovery strategies are a smorgasbord. You pick what works for you. I balked at the notion of submitting to a Greater Force, for instance, since I wasn't religious. However, the concept of Accession—"True Communication and the End of Loneliness"—appealed to me. The related process of "bridge-building" seemed a neat metaphor for creative work: solitary yet collaborative, your own "bridge" was a construction that was also a journey. Bridge-building was aimed at Accession; yet it couldn't be undertaken with the expectation of concrete reward. Accession—a "True Bridge Between Worlds"—seemed more of a motivating target than an achievable goal.

At least, that was my interpretation at the time. There were so many new words to interpret, some clearer than others. The word "Deferral," for example, which seemed to describe moments of fruitless crisis, I found hard to understand or remember. Conversely, I clearly recall the wistful, melancholy session we spent discussing *Kataluin*. *Kataluin*, our nurse moderator informed us, were agents of change. They appeared when momentous events were to occur. They precipitated those events, sped their immanence, intensified their effect. We were invited to share stories about our encounters with *Kataluin*.

Most people then described the arrival of interlopers who upended the balance of their lives: new friends and lovers who provoked a descent into destructive habits. According to this definition, Scottie and Spider were my *Kataluin*; I was about to say so when our moderator interrupted to clarify that *Kataluin* were not, in fact, human. They could take many forms. They followed a logic of their own, appearing suddenly and disappearing in a puff of destruction.

This was too mysterious for most attendees, and the seminar dissolved shortly thereafter, but I found myself keeping a satirical eye out for whatever pixies or gremlins were supposedly causing my misfortune.

Yes, we weren't forced to accept any one notion, but neither could we resist it all. As Dr. Bredsky herself explained in our inaugural seminar, we would need to believe in *something*, amid this litter of strange new phrases; otherwise, we'd be left to our own devices, which were proven (since we were here, our lives in smoking ruins) to be inadequate.

And so, the mantra entered my repertoire:

This is my Bridge, my route to Accession.
Nobody can travel this Bridge but me.

I hummed it like a nursery rhyme at Pentorgan House. It faded out of my life after I returned to the wider society, but that afternoon in the Berryman it returned with a vengeance. I shut my eyes and chanted. When I opened them again, Judith and Scottie had left me. The pub was full of strangers. My table was conspicuously isolated.

10

Sol sits in a greenish-grey hospital waiting room filled with old couches. The dirty windows are illuminated from below, casting light and shadows on the ceiling. Magazines cover the coffee tables.

"Back in the hospital," Fran says.

Sol perceives her voice like an itch on his spine, and he shrugs and wriggles, and eventually draws the toothbrush over his skin and flicks it at the adjacent couch.

Fran appears there, blinking.

"You threw me out," she says.

"It was getting uncomfortable," Sol says. He itches his arm.

"Why are we back here?"

Sol looks around. He realizes the tea must be wearing off. He's regained a lot of clarity.

"I'm not sure," he says.

"What's wrong with your arm?"

"Nothing."

"Let me see—" Fran leans in to touch him, but Sol waves his toothbrush and an instant later she's sitting on a couch opposite, out of reach. It takes Fran a second to recover her composure.

"You've picked this up quickly," she says, nodding. "I'm impressed." Sol itches his arm. In some distant corridor a door slams. "Have you spent a long time in hospitals?" Fran asks.

Sol shakes his head sadly.

"Not long," he murmurs. "A week. Not even."

"Was it the partner of yours? Donaghy?"

Sol shakes his head. It was Dulcie. The end of the pregnancy. The beginning of the end of the marriage. Somewhere off in the hospital, hammering starts.

"Am I safe in the community?" he asks.

"We're a healing community," Fran says. "We accommodate all kinds of people. Some people stay a long time, some shorter. We don't just throw people out."

"You're lying," Sol says.

Hammering.

"Remember the sign in the parking lot? We welcome genuine travelers. Just tell us the truth, and we'll help you. I know you're holding something back—not just from me, from everyone. From your friends Scottie and Judy."

The hammering doesn't let up. Doors open and close.

"I'd like to wake up now," says Sol.

The following weeks passed in a daze. At work, my professionalism remained intact, but the zest was gone. I'd get distracted, falling into the reverie of memory. I started to take extended breaks in the quietest staff room I could find. I was on the cusp of a new phase of my life, one which required a period of reflection before I could pass through the threshold.

I remembered, especially, how Dr. Bredsky led the "practice" part of my Pentorgan House treatment. It was an intimate, weekly one-to-one session. Since Bredsky knew my interest in *fin-de-siècle* French poetry, she selected older books to read: nineteenth-century poetry, Romantic prose. It thus felt natural when we started reading *The King in Yellow* by Robert W. Chambers.

The King in Yellow is a collection of interlinked short stories. The stories are connected by a fictional play also called *The King in Yellow.* This play is a work of art so pure, powerful, and corrupting that it's banned across the globe: a "beautiful, stupendous creation, terrible in its simplicity, irresistible in its truth."

The King in Yellow [play] is set in the dominion of the King in Yellow, a location called "Carcosa," by the lake of Hali. A person who reads the play on planet Earth empowers this normally distant Yellow King of Carcosa to action his dreadful urges and slake his thirst for power in the human realm.

You'll recognize the word "Carcosa." I did. Indeed, the moment Dr. Bredsky pronounced it, I felt a flood of apprehension, as if on the brink of remembering the contents of that book, *The Truth of Carcosa,* which had taken up so many hours of my life. But it was a false familiarity, a *déjà vu*: I recalled nothing extra.

Dr. Bredsky saw I'd gone pale, and confessed that she'd engineered the encounter. She'd placed *The King in Yellow* before me to provoke my memory and expose suppressed facets of my recent "unfortunate holiday." And if she couldn't shake my memories loose, perhaps I'd enjoy observing the recurrence of words, words that seemed to have a persistence of their own, acting like viruses, parasitical, undead, crawling through the void with infinite patience, waiting to find a reader to facilitate re-entry into the world.

And she was right—I did enjoy the recurrence of this word, "Carcosa." The notion of word as germ, stretching into past and future, added piquancy to our readings of *The King in Yellow.* Dr. Bredsky would also apply references to her esoteric philosophies to provoke reflection: *Was the narrator of "The Mask" a Cipher? Did "In the Court of the Dragon" feature a Deferral?* The answer almost always involved relating the story to my own life somehow, and I was endlessly grateful for the opportunity to tell Dr. Bredsky about myself.

By the time I left Pentorgan House, I'd concluded there was no book called *The Truth of Carcosa.* Its immanence within me had been a psychic blip—the result of my tremendous sensitivity (recognized by Bredsky even after my parents and teachers failed to appreciate it) to the signs and portents orbiting my envelope.

This fit the interpretive attitude I'd taken over the course of the treatment. I'd treated each concept in Bredsky's philosophy as an aid to personal psychic navigation: the mark on the map, not the thing itself. But years later, as I revisited those memories in the privacy of the staff room, a disturbing news event shook the foundation of this attitude. I learned that somebody had burned down my local library. Details were scarce, following the new policy of Harmonious Reporting, but it seemed a group of parents had become concerned that the books in their local library would hurt their children. Accordingly, they burned it to the ground. These parents faced no prosecution for their actions, since they were merely protecting their children from harmful words, and the library had been amply warned that its seditious pornographic translated literature was an offense to the new state of affairs in England.

Above all else in the steady cascade of disasters overtaking our nation—the arrests, assaults, detentions—the fact that these criminal parents went unpunished shook my old assumptions. If the state itself, the level-headed guarantor of rights and protections, could agree with such a literal, fundamentalist view of reading, then what was to stop me from abandoning my rationality, my interpretive posture? Why shouldn't I *believe* in words, the way lunatics and zealots do?

Why not declare that "Carcosa," the dominion of the King in Yellow, is a *real* place, the dominion of a *real* king?

The King in Yellow [king] expresses power through *The King in Yellow* [play], which recurs throughout *The King in Yellow* [novel]. Doubling is inevitable and labels are necessary. I might assume that you understand when I, referring to the fictional play, write: "*The King in Yellow* is corruption made manifest." But you may have slipped out of gear and started thinking of Chambers's book; or perhaps you've fallen through several trapdoors at once, and stand trembling before the King himself.

To indulge in this semantic slippage amused me. Why, I thought, should I bother to understand and accommodate a hostile world, when I could simply misinterpret it in my own favor instead?

I reconsidered the other concepts Dr. Bredsky had taught me: Deferral, Accession, Cipher, *Kataluin.* I did so in a new, willfully stupid way that matched our new, stupid England. The word "Cipher," for instance, I'd previously understood as a highfalutin idea about consciousness, a notion of the mind as a vessel for experience of the world. It now amused me to take the concept literally: The mind was a zero. Nothing. I visualized a nation overrun with empty minds, braying and hollering their emptiness, and despairingly, I laughed.

11

In the longhouse, Fran falls back onto the easy chair while Sol slumps forward. Fran seems tired, but satisfied: The session was long and intense, but evidently has its own rewards. It takes a minute for Sol to wend his way back to full lucidity.

"What was in that tea?" he asks eventually.

Fran shrugs. "Muscle relaxants, mostly. All natural."

"Huh."

"Do you feel any better?"

"I feel like I just woke up."

Sol stands up. His body does feel more energized. He chucks a couple of logs into the fire. He doesn't remember exactly what he's just been through. He feels good, in a disembodied way, but also as if he's been a little vulnerable.

"What have we been doing?" he asks.

"I've been teaching you about lucid dreaming," Fran says.

"Why do I feel . . . icky?"

"Do you always feel icky, after you've been free?"

There is a certain languid energy in the air. Sol wonders whether Fran is appraising him as a sexual possibility.

"I noticed you scratch your arm a lot," she says.

"Do I?"

Sol shifts the itchy arm behind his back.

"You've probably got allergies," Fran continues. "Most people do and don't realize it. I can take a look at it if you like . . ."

At that moment, a woman bursts in.

"You just had a visitor," she says to Sol.

All at once, the world returns to Sol: all the urgencies that the tea and the massage held at bay. The blood runs from his face.

"Who? Where?"

"She's gone. Name of Nadia. Said *you* knew her."

Sol nods, slowly. Adrenaline sweat creeps down his back.

"She gave me this."

The woman hands Fran a small, thin, leather-bound object. A passport.

Fran holds it up so Sol can see the illustration of a harp and the words ÉIRE/IRELAND.

"It's a good one," she says. "EU. And it's got your picture in it."

She opens the passport to the photo page. Sol can't see the illustration in the flickering shadows.

"But it doesn't have your name in it," she says. Fran looks Sol square in the eye. "This woman just delivered you a fake ID, Joe. What exactly are you mixed up in?"

* * *

It takes a while for Sol to start talking again, but it does happen. He must tell Fran enough, he realizes, that she doesn't consider him a threat. They return to the fireplace. He foregoes the tea.

"When I said I was a defense lawyer," Sol begins, "I wasn't lying. But that wasn't my most recent job. Until about three weeks ago, I was something called a research bailiff for a corporate law firm."

"What's a research bailiff?" Fran asks.

"It's private investigation work. I had to find people and deliver subpoenas to them."

"Right. Wait. I've heard about this. Who were you working for?"

"GMM."

She stands up. “Get the fuck out of here.”

“It’s true.”

“No, I mean get out. Leave. I can’t believe we had you here. This is a disaster.”

“It’s not what you think. I’m not like them.”

“Oh, you’re a nice guy who just happens to work for Evil Incorporated? GMM works with the Hasturian Guard. They tell the fucking *police* what to do. GMM makes people disappear—fuck, is that what you were doing, with your *subpoenas*?”

“I wanted to bring them down from the inside. I’m on the run from them.”

“Even worse! If they’re looking for you, then we’re all in the shit. They could come here.”

“Please,” Sol says, “I’m on your side.”

“Does Scottie know?”

“He knows everything.”

“I’ll kill him.”

“I can explain.”

“You’d better. You’d better have a bloody good reason to have pulled us into your shit. You’d better be trying to save the fucking world.”

12

Before she was exposed, fired, disbarred, doxxed, and sued to bankruptcy, a solicitor named Nadia Eze wrote a good blog about the nasty reality of work in the corporate legal world. The blog, *Lawyers and Liars*, had two aims: exposing the insidious creep of little-known laws that were eroding justice and freedom in the United Kingdom; and skewering the pompous hypocrisy of the major players in corporate law, the Magic Circle firms that positioned themselves on the profitable side of every turn in the national downward spiral toward what she termed *corporate autarchy and legalized kleptocracy*.

Eze specialized in in-depth profiles of legal tactics—SLAPP suits, strategic NDAs, arbitration clauses—and infamous precedents such as *In re: Albatross Hung*, which spawned a thousand injustices; she also produced sharp sketches of daily life in cutthroat firms, based on accounts of anonymous whistleblowers. Her series of articles on GMM amply covered both bases.

GMM, per Eze, was a kind of counter-WASP Catholic old-boys' club populated by adherents of Opus Dei and Militia Templi: nasty old men with signet rings and nasty young men with fashy mustaches. It did a huge amount of real estate management for the church, and work for trusts promoting pro-life, anti-communist tenets worldwide. Its overseas arms were muddy with African oil, cobalt, and uranium, while its domestic activities were entirely entwined with the promotion and further misuse of *In re: Albatross Hung*. They thought they were God's lawyers, Eze claimed, but it was a strange god that allowed them to suborn police officers into civil cases, ransack people's homes in pursuit of "infringing" material, equip bailiffs with stun guns—to operate, in short, a parallel legal empire without oversight from the overwhelmed UK criminal justice system.

So ran Eze's vituperation, for some pages, which Joseph Sol read when he was a happily married, underpaid defense solicitor. He'd imagined the GMM offices to be a granite building around London's Greys Inn, tall and narrow with baroque cornices and heavy oak doors. Inside, he fancied pale men in black clothes signed vellum contracts or counted guineas into a heavy wooden box.

By the time Sol started working for GMM, Eze was long gone, her blog periodically scrubbed from the archive sites that attempted to preserve it, and finally exiled by the new National Firewall. Sol had been divorced for some months. Everything was changing.

* * *

The GMM regional headquarters wasn't a castle full of ghouls. It was a modern construction in a commercial estate just inside the circular highway. The interiors were tasteful and modern, and Sol's new line manager, who was a woman named Jennifer Donaghy and didn't have a fashy mustache, was enthusiastic in listing the benefits that accompanied the job.

The onboarding started in a meeting room, then proceeded into a series of hot seats in the open-plan workspace. There were several hours of online training. *Modern Slavery Looks Like This.* Staff came and went around them. The atmosphere wasn't painfully formal, but there was a level of tension. The women were few, and tended to move in defensive formations, and none of them were older than Donaghy, who was Sol's age. Most were younger. There were young men, too, of course; and there were older men, in expensive suits, moving from room to room with tablets and flapping plastic folders.

Sol wondered whether he was reading too much into minor things. The reality of any operation was ordinary, he understood, whether the end result was food for the homeless or remorseless corporate pillage. But part of him suspected a false surface. He half-believed there was a hidden kernel somewhere, where GMM's true nature would be revealed—whatever that was.

"We won't be spending much time here," Donaghy told him, picking up on his alertness. "It's a hybrid role."

"I remember from the interview," Sol said.

"Your interview . . ." Donaghy began. Then she looked down at her nails. Pink shellac. She was wearing a dark, modest dress and smelled of perfume. He was sweating through his checked shirt.

"What about my interview?" Sol said.

"Funny question, but at the interview, were you wearing your old school tie?"

Sol blushed. Donaghy smirked.

"It worked, didn't it?" Sol said defensively. "I'm here, aren't I?"

"Well, Joseph, you are here, so something you did must have worked."

Sol got back to his training, but he felt discomfited and couldn't focus on his training video, a cartoon about subconscious bias featuring cats who'd been compelled to employ dogs, whom they detested. He turned to Donaghy, who was staring at him.

"I'm teasing you a bit, Joseph," she said. "Please don't take it personally. It's banter. It's the way we make friends around here. Listen, before we get into the field, I want to introduce you to a few people. One person especially. You haven't met Higgins yet, have you?"

"Higgins? No."

"He's very senior. But he's agreed to meet you today."

"What about?"

"He's my *mentor*."

She pronounced the word as if its true meaning sat somewhere between "boyfriend" and "father." The atmosphere suddenly felt unprofessional. Following Donaghy toward Higgins's office, Sol suspected he was about to glimpse GMM's true kernel after all.

One story that returned to me in my fallow period was "The Repairer of Reputations," a piece of speculative fiction set in 1920s New York—the heart of a vicious, proto-fascist American Republic—and narrated by a lunatic. Dr. Bredsky and I had read and discussed it over the course of an afternoon. The story was diverting (our lunatic, named Hildred Castaigne, believes he is the rightful heir to the American empire, but he has, in fact, been led astray by the King in Yellow; his royal diadem, stored in an elaborate, alarmed safe box, is revealed to be a trinket in a biscuit tin), but we focused on its political angle.

We talked about the difference between fascism in the modern world and fascism in Chambers's world. Dr. Bredsky made the valid point that we tended to regard fascism as a modern, stylistically brutal phenomenon, thanks to its contemporary visual code of shaven heads, camouflage, and firearms. But Chambers's New York was fascist without khaki. It was full of flags, gaily-colored uniforms, and handsome horsemen with polished sabers; Castaigne compared himself to Napoleon.

I drew Bredsky's attention to the opening of "The Repairer of Reputations": a happy list of the United States' colonial and genocidal adventures, military victory over Germany, infrastructure building, and reforms. It reflected the popular prejudices of its era: "the exclusion of foreign-born Jews as a measure of self-preservation, the settlement of the new independent negro state of Suanee, the checking of immigration, the new laws concerning naturalization, and the gradual centralization of power in the executive all contributed to national calm and prosperity."

It's hard to tell whether Chambers shared the opinions promoted here, since the story is narrated, as I have stated, by a lunatic.

I pushed Dr. Bredsky on the topic.

She suggested that sometimes an author might use a lunatic to express some essence of their era, the Zeitgeist whose form cannot be seen for what it truly is through sane eyes. Following the degradation of our nation's democratic functions in recent years, I wondered, on reflection, whether Bredsky had been warning me of events to come. To confirm this, one afternoon in my staff room, I scrolled a single day's news. To wit: A former MP heading a security firm declared that his employees were now going to be armed; he got an article published in a national newspaper about "globalist cannibal grooming gangs." The unelected Emergency Cabinet decreed that citizens of foreign heritage were to take a "voluntary" oath of allegiance to the crown. The national press railed in unison against our foreign allies' smug proscription against the death penalty, which could be administered hygienically, with provable scientific results.

Chambers's speculations had come to pass, I realized. Fascism was upon us. I had a fleeting vision of myself as the lunatic Castaigne, maneuvering to succeed in a world gone doubly mad. Although unnerving, this image was strangely empowering: As a lunatic, I needn't fight the tide or stand in judgment of it, only claim my own private victories when I could.

While my internal world took this sideways turn, Judith's progress continued apace. Winter became spring, and she was deep into her project with Carrette. He spent long hours in the Institute's reading room, requiring detailed preparation from Judith every day. They were both working hard, and we understood not to burden Judith with requests or distract her with small talk. We left tea and biscuits, like votive offerings, at her desk.

Judith seemed certain to get an acknowledgment in Carrette's book. There was talk of a conference paper, whispers of promotion. For those of us unhappy with the direction our nation was taking (an increasingly silent group), I suspect Judith represented a glimmer, if not of hope, then of normality. Suffice to say we failed to appreciate the strain she was under. I certainly didn't, caught up as I was with my personal research, subjecting the text of my own life to increasingly idiosyncratic readings.

Another story that returned to me in that period was "The Mask," a romantic tale about spoiled Parisian artists alchemizing living beings into marble. The many interesting facets of the story (and really, I must start blogging some of the insights that find no space here), are somewhat overshadowed by its consistent tone of nice-guy misogyny—something I raised when I first read it with Dr. Bredsky. She entreated me to look a little closer. I obliged, and was rewarded by moments of melancholy beauty scattered among the pages, as these bohemian children wandered through dark hallways in their *Parisien* mansion, smoking opium, dreaming, and encountering the ghosts of their own desires.

I suspect my reaction to the story was intensified by the romantic feelings I'd begun to hold toward Dr. Bredsky. These feelings between patients and therapists are natural and well known; age should be no barrier to love, so I feel no embarrassment in that regard. It shouldn't have been a problem. The problem arose when I broke into her office.

I'm not sure why I did that. Objectively, given that I was a mental patient with a history of criminal trespass, I shouldn't find it so surprising. Still, I can't help but see myself pursuing some trace of "The Mask" in my trespasses: the rays of moonlight, the polished sandalwood, the synesthetic effluvia of the "saddest music in the world" encountered by its young and beautiful characters. Perhaps I believed I was decadent, not criminal; perhaps she encouraged me.

I don't remember if it was day or night. I remember the Sad Ones (as I, in my fabulous diadem, now called my fellow patients) were eating a meal in the refectory, and Dr. Bredsky had exited the building, pursued by a noisome train of clerks and junior doctors.

The office was off a little windowless landing in the back of the house. Its door was one of three, one leading to a (locked, private) bathroom, the other to a little closet for computer equipment. The landing was carpeted and stale, and as I pressed open the unlocked office door, dust motes followed me into the room.

Here, in the center, were the two chairs we occupied in our one-on-one sessions. I resisted the urge to draw them closer together. Behind them was Dr. Bredsky's desk, an expansive oak item that conspired with the well-stocked bookshelves to give the room its impression of coziness.

I stood a while in a reverie. Then impulsively I moved behind her desk and pulled at her drawers. Locked. I sat on her chair and looked over the desktop. There were no personal items. I looked out the window and saw treetops swaying in the breeze. I looked around the office and realized it was larger than I'd thought: The bookshelves hid a narrow gap that extended the space into an "L" shape. The gap was given over to document storage: shelves of books, filing cabinets, and a neat stack of crates at the very end.

The books I didn't recognize, except one shelf dedicated to the complete published works of Salvatore Archimboldi, from

Bucolia to *Mulberry Sands.* The filing cabinets were old-fashioned steel constructions, dusted with grime. They were locked, their label slots containing blank sheets of yellowing paper.

On a hunch, I slid one of these labels out and flipped it around. My instinct was right: The back side of the paper displayed the original label: RESTEVO SEMIOTICS CONFERENCE 1978: A-K.

I moved on to the next two cabinets, to reveal labels for the same conference. The last two cabinets contained paper of a different grain, resolving into a different label:

NODE/CIPHER CULTIVATION PROJECT 1984: A-M.

I immediately identified that 1984 was the year of my birth. It stirred me to think of Dr. Bredsky working on her seminal theory that year.

At the end of the passageway, however, the stack of crates seemed to beckon me forward. Halfway to them, I perceived a label on the side. It read COURTESY OF ALBATROSS HUNG.

Since *In re: Albatross Hung* has become such a well-known legal phrase, it's clear now that Dr. Bredsky had acquired some element of the Archimboldi Legacy. At the time, I couldn't know this. I simply felt drawn to the crates by some force stronger than curiosity, a certainty that they contained something I would like.

Then I noticed the security camera.

It was a big, ugly, white thing, more like a probe than a camera, fixed to the wall above the crates. I'd been directly in its view, I realized, since I stepped behind Dr. Bredsky's desk. It had been recording me as I caressed her paperweights and sniffed her chair.

I was busted.

The sensible thing to do was to walk away, settle back into my normal routine, and wait for whatever consequences arose. Despite the aching of my heart, this I did.

The consequences came swiftly. The next day before group I learned that I needn't attend, since my recovery was complete. I'd made unprecedented progress through the curriculum, and I was cured! I was discharged within a day. The odd part of this brusque and impersonal off-boarding—mainly handled by junior doctors—was when Dr. Bredsky called me in for a final "debrief."

Her attitude toward me had changed, but not as I'd expected. I thought she'd be cold with me, but instead she seemed embarrassed, even deferential. She kept mumbling, and wouldn't look me in the eye. I signed some forms at the desk, and I could see that the adjoining passage was now empty: the shelves, filing cabinets, and crates removed. Only the security camera remained. A lawyer witnessed the entire procedure in silence.

And I was released, to relapse and restart alone, on my long, lonely journey to Accession. No one can travel this bridge but me.

Revisiting these regrettable memories in my fallow period afforded me no benefit. Then there came that wave of violence known as the "immigration riots." Famous and well-established people were promoting the idea that pedophilia was a foreign import. My more racist neighbors started patrolling our street. I became depressed.

I found myself sleeping an inordinate amount. I napped in the least-used staff room in the building, the one that smells of smoked fish and has a view of a shaft between high walls. The knack for napping is to drink a cup of instant coffee and hold a set of keys in your hands. As consciousness fades, your hand will relax. Eventually, you'll drop your keys. The commotion will wake you. I used this method to ensure that my naps were short, because there's nothing more desolating than napping in the afternoon and waking up after sunset, wondering what happened to the world you lost.

After one such "key" nap I awoke with a curious memory alive in me. I recalled the strange afternoon in Pentorgan House when I took a wrong turn outside the cafeteria. I thought I'd discovered a shortcut back to my dormitory, but after I slipped through a self-locking door (CAUTION), it clicked shut behind me, forcing me onward through a low, unpainted corridor, and shortly thereafter I found myself in a filthy cellar full of wine racks and lumber. In a daze, I wandered between rows of junk until I found a heavy, slanting trapdoor that opened up onto the estate grounds.

Treacherous slate steps led up to a lawn, and some artificial waterway (a moat?); then I emerged into a landscaped garden and, taking in the beauty around me, I understood why people called Pentorgan House a fabulous place to recover.

Wanderlust impelled me across the gorgeous lawn and down a path that led out of the formal gardens, then steeply down the side of a sheltered ravine. The ravine carried tall ferns and hogweed and a cold fast brook; everything dripped with water; and between the high trees before me I saw glimpses of the valley below, which to my shock and disbelief was completely full of long, low sheds, filthy yards, and chimneys. I was overwhelmed by a need to climb the hill again, to find a door back into that old castle, to find Dr. Bredsky in her cozy office and lay out my anxieties for her to salve.

Duly I set off up the hill. I thought I'd impress Dr. Bredsky with stories, like a child presenting his mother with something he found in the woods. But when I reached her office I found the door locked. I hovered for a second on the landing outside, and heard a sound—perhaps a click or thunk, or even a slurp—from one of the closed doors nearby.

It was the closet-like space where I believed Dr. Bredsky stored computer equipment.

Another sound. A gasp?

Was Dr. Bredsky in there with someone else? Was she injured? Had she *fallen*?

Was she lonely?

I slowly opened the door and peeked inside.

I understand now that Dr. Bredsky was merely operating a complex computer and surveillance system called the LIN (Live Information Node), the design of which I probably found confusing, since it was—as Bredsky explained—a blocky old PanOp Insights prototype with a primitive interface. I understand that the LIN was designed to capture data about clients, its thick white wires connected to the cameras that infested Pentorgan House. Logically, I know that these wires' resemblance to fat white roots or creeping tentacles was an accident of design. The acrid effluvia and rhythmic tick-ticking was an effect retroactively applied by my imagination to a scene I'd essentially misunderstood; still, that afternoon in the staff room, the vision as I first perceived it recurred: Dr. Bredsky, pinned to the chair by glistening, blubbery tubes, limbs akimbo as she submitted to the embrace of some hulking white *thing*, the room filled with the sound of *lapping*, like a fetid lake against the shore.

It felt uncomfortable to recall so vividly what I knew to be false. I chanted my mantra and meditated on the Cipher but couldn't be sure it was working. With conscious effort, I replaced the image in my mind with the true one: Dr. Bredsky lounging cross-legged before an outdated computer. Hearing the door open behind her, she turned; she raised her reading glasses, smiled, and said, "Louis, why are you looking so peaky?"

After recovering from this flashback I felt impelled to find out what became of Dr. Bredsky. Searching for her name, I was shocked to discover that she was in prison in Nevada. She'd allegedly presided over a sweat-lodge ritual that went wrong, resulting in a dozen deaths. My desolation was compounded when I returned to my desk to discover an official notification from Personnel that I was being placed on performance review. I had three months to remedy my working practices or I'd be terminated. This had nothing to do with the breaks I'd been taking; it was because I had "made inappropriate use of communications technology" on the premises.

I know what you're thinking, but in fact I *hadn't* been watching porn in the staff room. The only use I'd made of any "communications technology" was to search for Dr. Adriana Bredsky's name on my phone, foolishly forgetting to use a VPN, only twenty minutes before the Personnel email appeared in my inbox.

13

Donaghy led Sol to an office that appeared to be made from a material older and more sound than the rest of the GMM building—a core, around which the open-plan spaces and glass walls had accumulated like plaque. The worker bees outside had easy-clean carpets and motivational posters. Higgins had wood panels. A large oak desk. A humidor. Ashtrays. Passing through the threshold, Sol quickly understood that the present day and its silly rules were a rumor here.

"They're settling you in?" Higgins asked. He was grey and pink, slightly shriveled beneath an expensive suit and a friendly-uncle mask of skin.

"The onboarding's going fine," Sol replied.

Higgins smiled at the quaint language. "They're settling you in," he affirmed.

Donaghy nodded, vigorously, her ponytail bouncing around on her shoulders. The way she carried herself had changed in this room: She acted younger.

"You took an unusual path to reach us, I believe," said Higgins. "*Private investigation*."

"You make it sound romantic," Sol remarked.

"Wasn't it?"

"It was criminal defense work. I prepared character statements."

"For whom?"

"Defendants."

Higgins smiled indulgently.

"Who *paid*?"

"I was something of a free agent."

"No such thing."

"Ha." Higgins blinked. He waited. Sol relented. "Most of my jobs were financed by a trust. You'll understand if I don't name them. They supplied funds for the defense of people who qualified."

"People who *qualified*."

"All sorts of people."

"And you've been out there on the road, collecting stories about *all sorts of people* who've been getting in *all sorts of trouble*. And you say it wasn't romantic."

"It really wasn't."

"This was some *human rights* thing, wasn't it?"

Sol said nothing.

"An unusual route to our firm, wouldn't you agree?" Higgins asked Donaghy.

She made no reply.

"Well, that's fine, for one of our more orbital roles. I can see why Donaghy wanted you onboard."

Sol raised his eyebrows at her. This was his first indication she had anything to do with his recruitment. But she was gazing fixedly at Higgins.

"You made the right choice," Sol said. He didn't direct the statement at anybody. He allowed it to hang in the air, waiting for whoever wanted to claim him.

Higgins pulled a leather-bound book out from under his desk. No laptop or flapping plastic binder for him. He consulted some papers inside.

"Are you a *family man*, Mr. Sol?" he asked.

Sol had anticipated questions of this type. Nonetheless, he grimaced. A *family man*. The phrase reeked with connotations.

"That's a strange question," he said, eventually.

"How so? It seems pretty straightforward to me."

"What precisely does it mean? Do I have a family?"

"You could interpret it that way."

"Or does it mean, do I want a family? Are you asking me whether I'm fertile, whether I'm homosexual?"

"Homosexuals have families, I'm told."

"Or was I brought up in care, perhaps? I'm sorry, Mr. Higgins, it seems like an insensitive question."

"You don't have to answer it."

"I don't think I will."

Higgins smiled at Donaghy.

"You'll excuse me. I'm old-fashioned in my way. When I meet somebody, I like to get the measure of them as quickly as I can. Sometimes this can mean provoking a little."

"I didn't mean to get defensive."

"You have no reason to apologize."

"I'm not apologizing."

Higgins burst out laughing.

"Did you know, when I first met Ms. Donaghy, I asked the same question, and she answered straight away, 'Yes sir!' Didn't you, Jennifer?" Donaghy blushed. "Very keen, very *obliging*. What do you think of *that*, Mr. Sol?" Higgins prodded.

"Nothing," Sol said, appalled. "I don't think of it."

Higgins leafed through his folder in silence for a while. Finally he snapped it shut and looked squarely at Sol.

"I heard you wore your school tie to the interview," he said, with a chuckle.

Sol nodded, sighing.

"Perhaps not such a dyed-in-the-wool radical as your curriculum vitae—and this . . . *front* of yours—might suggest. Nonetheless, I suppose we must be a little careful around you, since you have *sensitivities*."

Sol shrugged.

"I'm a lawyer," he said. "I care about words. And I'm aware of employment law."

Higgins smirked.

"Laws change," he said. "You'll understand that if you last here. Laws change, but values—*certain* values—never go away."

Here he leaned back on his chair and indicated the wood paneling, oak desk, paintings on the walls: the old world persisting at the core of this apparently new building.

"Mr. Higgins told *me* the same thing when I started," Donaghy said, somewhat gushingly. There was something not kosher between Donaghy and Higgins. A wetness in Donaghy's eyes.

"And *she'll* be telling new starters the same thing," said Higgins, "from this same chair, with the same pictures on the wall." Donaghy looked coy. "It's true," Higgins persisted. "You underestimate yourself, my girl. You think *you* couldn't make partner one day, Miss Donaghy? Sit in this office? What do *you* think, Mr. Sol?"

Sol, feeling provoked, shrugged. "I don't know. Could be me."

"Could be you!" Higgins laughed a hacking laugh. "I like that! There, Jennifer, *that's* what I call confidence! Could be you, young man!" Donaghy forced a smile. Higgins cleared his throat. "Good. Pay attention. Look around. Take in your future office."

Sol did look around. He saw the old masters. The plush club chairs, on which they hadn't been invited to sit. The humidor—a huge thing, resembling a safe, but with light glowing from behind the frosted glass frontage (the logo a snazzy “XS”), humming quietly with oversized ventilation pipes occasionally hissing. A photograph on the expansive desk, positioned to face the whole room.

For a long while the photograph arrested Sol’s attention. It presented an expensively decorated drawing room interior, empty of people but filled with artworks—paintings, ceramics, tribal fetishes. There was an armchair and a sofa, both wrapped in clear plastic film. Leaning against the back wall, beside a closed door, was a pair of shoulder-height gas canisters. Oxygen? Framing the door, like a kind of portico, was a structure of inflated clear plastic. Sol recognized it—from films, perhaps, science fiction—as an airlock.

Higgins cleared his throat. He was tapping a cigarette out of a packet. The interview—or hazing, or miniature family drama—was over. It was time for Sol and Donaghy to return to the realm of hot desks and neon slogans.

* * *

“Clever of you to say you’ll take over Higgins’s job on your first day in the office,” Donaghy remarked.

They were in the corner of the Focus Zone. The room wasn’t empty, but every other worker was plugged into headphones and facing away: into screens, out of windows, at walls.

“I thought he was inviting it,” Sol said. “He acted that way after.”

Donaghy looked like there was something important and complicated she needed to communicate, but she couldn’t work out how. Finally she picked some words.

“He’s a *character*.”

“I can tell.”

"You've only met him once. He's my mentor. I don't expect you to be tugging your forelock at every middle manager, but Higgins is old school. And he's my—"

"Mentor. He's your mentor. I'm sorry, it wasn't my place. I misjudged the situation."

Donaghy raised a warning finger. "He doesn't forget, you know. Higgins is the man who keeps all the secrets."

"Good man to have as your mentor."

Donaghy looked hard at Sol. "Are you taking the piss?" she asked.

"No."

"It's not easy, here, you know. It hasn't been easy for me. Not always. Not like it is now, for the younger girls."

"I see."

Sol did see. Donaghy was the same age as him. It must have been hard for her, coming up in the old days, with the men and the banter. It showed in the way she carried herself, her body, around the office.

"So I appreciate what Higgins did for me," she said. Sol nodded. "Where are we at in the training package?"

"Data protection. Forty-minute video and test."

"It can wait. Let's go. I want to get out of here, back into the field."

Things were going badly at the ALI. Some colleagues disappeared at the peak of the latest "immigration riots." Our CEO instructed us to travel in pairs and stop wearing our Institute lanyards in public. Every morning we'd receive a bulletin about the latest development in the government's Emergency Cabinet, and what it meant for us. Apparently the current lot, an unsavory bunch by all accounts, were bending over backward and making all sorts of compromises to keep another set of ideologues out. These new barbarians were bent on tearing everything apart, including the Cabinet itself, and since sympathetic racists had started blockading the ports their demands were getting harder to resist. Jan privately advised me to start job seeking. Judith Bea fell ill.

Perhaps it was the stress. One day, after she'd been off work half a week, she sent me a message. We'd exchanged numbers long before, and I'd hoped that we might become more familiar (this hadn't happened). But she sent me a voice message that afternoon, asking whether I could do her a favor. She was very apologetic, and sounded ill, so of course I agreed. She asked if I could pick something up from her house and deliver it. Yes, I said.

The bus dropped me at the nearest stop, on the high stretch of Calendral Road, and I descended a strange, steep side road. It was flanked on both sides by high walls and tall trees. My memories of Pentorgan House were alive in me then, and as I progressed I recalled again the dripping pathways out of the grounds, the curious fear that impelled me into Bredsky's office, the grotesque vision I met of Bredsky in the embrace of her tentacular equipment. I had the dreadful sense I was heading toward some similar revelation.

But the scene at the bottom of the hill seemed quite ordinary. The lane terminated in a little Victorian cul-de-sac of tiny, terraced constructions. Drawing near, Judith's hand pressed against one of the windows. She called out: "Don't come too close. It might be dangerous."

When she opened her door, Judith looked grey and watchful in her toweled robe. I realized she'd been looking grey and watchful for weeks.

She placed a fat envelope on the step before her. There was an address stuck to the front.

"*Dangerous?*" I echoed.

"I might be infectious. I'm sick."

"Oh . . ."

"I'm sorry about this, Louis," she said. "This needs to get to Monsieur Carrette's place."

"You want me to post it?"

"He's got a place in the city now. The quickest way is if you follow the footpath under the bridge."

I looked at the package. "What's in it?" I asked.

"You know I can't tell you." That rueful smile. "Listen, Louis. It might not be so bad, you know, to leave the ALI."

"I'm not leaving."

"Of course not. But if you wanted to. Things are getting a bit . . . weird at the ALI, aren't they? There might be other places you could go."

"Things are getting weird everywhere."

She sighed. Nodded. Winced. I realized she was in pain.

"Will you deliver it?" she asked. "I'll make it up to you, once I'm better. Take you to the Berryman, buy you a shandy."

I knew I was going to accept, because I wanted to please her, and the favor she was asking was really a tremendous honor. Dozens of academics would have jumped at the opportunity to involve themselves in M. Carrette's work, and I, too, am an Archimboldian of sorts. I, too, have wondered what I would do if chance somehow made me the bearer of the Archimboldi Chalice.

"Okay," I said.

14

Donaghy finally took Sol out to the van. It was one of a fleet of GMM vehicles all made up in deep English-heritage blue. Once inside the van, Donaghy's demeanor shifted. She slouched and pouted, looked over the cabin controls like an old pro pilot.

"Now it's time for you to really learn about this job," she said.

This was the glamorous part of her role, Sol realized. She could make-believe as patrol cop or detective, going on a stakeout. She could act hardboiled, wisecrack and drive.

They drove.

Donaghy asked how much Sol knew about *In re: Albatross Hung*. Sol said he knew it was the basis of their work: seizing property, seizing books and letters, the legacy of Salvatore Archimboldi. Donaghy asked how much Sol knew about Archimboldi.

"I know what I've read in the papers."

Donaghy grimaced. She didn't trust the papers.

"There are tales told about that man," she said. "Careers made telling them, too. You should take what you've heard already with a grain of salt. The left-wing press are always building him up for being a poor exile or beating him down for being a pale stale male who died mad and left this big legal mess behind. Neither of these things are strictly true—you understand? He may have been poor once but he died rich. You saw the photo in Higgins's office."

"The one of a room? Furniture, knick-knacks?"

"That was Archimboldi's living room. It was taken the day he died. Evidence, obviously, for carrying out the instructions in his legacy. After they'd cleared out everything in the room, Higgins decided to keep that picture. Keep it there, right in his office, so he can see it every day. Think about what that means."

"He told you this?"

"Among other things."

"Why *does* he keep it in his office?"

"That's what I want you to think about."

"Yeah, but why?"

"Because it's *important*, Joseph. The Archimboldi Legacy is important."

"Why does he smoke in the office? It's illegal."

"Oh, don't get me started. He's such a *character*. And it won't be illegal for long. Things are going to change around here."

"Was Archimboldi mad?"

"No. His will was unusual, granted. But it *was* his will. He was *compos mentis* when he wrote it. Medically tested, twice. It was a watertight document, legally speaking, and it led to *In re: Albatross Hung* and everything that followed, like it or not. It's because of that document that we're in this business."

"So he wasn't mad."

"He wasn't fucking mad."

"Gotcha."

"Here's the setup. The part that doesn't go in your onboarding. Although if you've been paying attention you probably know some of this already. As per Archimboldi's will, one-quarter of the funds in Archimboldi's estate was released, on his decease, for his heirs. Three-quarters were deposited into a trust, under the stewardship of one Giovanni, Metti & Metti LLC. Us. GMM was given explicit dispensation to invest this sum in whatever stocks or shares they chose, provided that the total wasn't disposed as capital or exchanged under certain *yadda yadda* conditions, very important but not exactly memorable.

"What that means is, it had to stay ring-fenced. It could grow and grow, and they could move it around into different investments if they thought it would make it grow faster—but they could never spend it, or disperse it, or whatever, until certain conditions were met. They did invest it. They made the Archimboldi Trust grow. And it got big, Joe. Very big."

Donaghy made a gesture with her hands: an orb, growing. The van tracked briefly off-course.

"That's the situation GMM is in now. It has a gigantic asset under its control. Far bigger than they ever imagined. You'd think that the board would be pretty pleased with this situation. And on the surface, they are. But the fact is, it's now a burden to them. Higgins explained: The sum is so huge, so overinflated, it's unbearable. This *absolutely fantastic* fortune, just out of reach. It has a psychological impact on the firm: Every director, every CEO coming in has just one task, one yardstick to measure themselves against: What will they do to free the Archimboldi Trust?

"Of course you know the clause in the will: The entire fund can be released for disposition at the discretion of the trust manager once one condition is met. We'll get to that condition in a minute, but I want to focus on the first part of the sentence: *at the discretion of the trust manager.*

"You understand the implications of that clause? The 'trust manager' is a board of seven people. Imagine the machinations of that board! Imagine the politics of getting on that board and staying there. Higgins calls the Archimboldi Trust a curse. It's swallowed up whole lives, whole careers, all because of that one condition: *that the entirety of Archimboldi's correspondence, personal writings, journals, et cetera, be destroyed, in the presence of a notary public, to the satisfaction of a judge*."

This last bit she recited, like she'd seen the will herself. Like she'd heard it repeated, over and over, in oak-paneled back rooms. Like everything significant about it came back to her, Donaghy, the last sane inheritor to a world of mad men.

"There are exceptions, of course, in the will. Our friends at the ALI rely on those exceptions. It's complicated. They've got a strong legal department of their own. But outside of the ALI, we're still playing hide-and-seek. Hunting down the scraps of the Archimboldi estate.

"You might ask, how do we know what letters are out there? There's our research department, for one. And Enforcement. Enforcement is good at extracting information from the people they deal with—helping us move up the chain. In point of fact, certain people in the ALI talk to us. And there are so many busybodies on the Internet, monitoring things. Dedicated websites. It's a scrum. Some patriots cheer you on to find stuff; some traitors try to lead you astray. As soon as you find one cache, somebody posts another little tidbit, another rumor leading you to the next cache."

Sol jumped in: "I don't understand why they don't just appeal it up to a sympathetic judge. Surely somebody will see that the clause is unachievable. It's a basic premise of scientific thought that you can't positively prove any phenomena as true—"

"—only disprove it as false."

"Only disprove it. Yes."

"Therein lies the mystery."

"Yes, but why? Why don't they? If the whole setup depends on the *satisfaction of a judge*, then why don't they find the right judge?"

"They? You mean *we*, Joe. You're part of the team now."

"Yes."

"Maybe the judges like fucking with us."

"Oh, come on."

"Higgins says there's a kind of sibling relationship between lawyers and judges. Like brothers. You love them, you hate them, you can't do without them? And sometimes you do fucked-up things, just to fuck them up."

"And you believe that?"

"You find it unbelievable?" They were pulled up at a traffic light. They looked at each other. Sol searched Donaghy's expression for something like recognition. He didn't know what he found, before she broke eye contact. "Anyway, enough speculation. I'm going to let you know your role in all this."

* * *

They pulled into a parking lot behind a closed diner. Donaghy leaned close to Sol and pulled out a black briefcase from his footwell. It folded open like a doctor's wallet: Inside, like cigars or ammunition, were paper cylinders sealed with wax. Donaghy rested a finger above one of them.

"Silver bullets," she said. "Subpoenas. Your task is simple. Note that each subpoena features a gap for a label. That's because they're not *loaded* yet. When it's time to load one, I'll provide a label with the target's name. You will approach the target and confirm their identity. What's important here is *how*—it's vital that the target confirm their own name to you. You might mistake them for an old school friend, ask them, *are you such-and-such?* And if they say, *yeah that's me*, you then compel them to take the subpoena. Usually you can just give it to them. There's a social instinct, you see, to cooperate. Take advantage of that.

"Once they take the subpoena, delivery is complete. It doesn't matter what they do with it afterward, if they read it or chuck it in the trash. Legally, they're compelled to comply with the instructions within. Without getting into the nitty-gritty, the instructions are to render up evidence. That is, whatever scrap of Archimboldi's estate they've managed to squirrel away. Enforcement get involved at that point, and all the other robust elements of *In re: Albatross Hung* that get uh, mentioned sometimes—that's not something we need to worry about."

"Okay," Sol said. The "robust" elements of *In re: Albatross Hung* were familiar from Eze's blog. Targets were typically held, incommunicado, while their property was ransacked. There was no recourse: Neither the police nor the criminal courts had any role in the process; nominal courts were convened in boardrooms or golf courses or wherever corporate legal teams met.

Donaghy closed the briefcase. It was still morning and it was raining. The diner looked sad. If Donaghy wanted Sol to say anything more, she didn't show it. Instead, she reclined her seat and cracked the window. Behind the diner, pines were waving in the wind. The rain got harder, then stopped.

Quiet.

"What next?"

"I've got a tip," Donaghy said.

"We're going to deliver a subpoena?"

"Maybe. Maybe today's the day. Have you heard of Cléophe Carrette?"

"Biographer. He's doing the big Archimboldi book. Big deal."

"Big, big deal. Big backers. He has the run of the ALI."

"He's good, isn't he? He did the Jag Caruthers book?"

"He's thorough and careful. The Jag Caruthers book must have been a nightmare—three active lawsuits and an NDA."

"I didn't know about that."

"But he got it done."

"Are we waiting for him, then?"

"He takes this road in from London. I've been spending some of my downtime here, just in case we get the name through. I want to be the one who hands it over. You see, Cléophe Carrette protects his materials by never withdrawing them from the ALI—not even copying them. But what you need to understand is, if he ever did withdraw something, or even make a copy of something, and we located it *outside the archive*, it could legally be traced to its source. Which would make it the key to the ALI vaults. And once we got inside, it would be endgame for the ALI deposit—possibly, the whole Archimboldi Trust caper."

"How?"

"In re: Albatross Hung."

"But how, exactly?"

"I don't know. I have no idea how the laws work."

"What?"

Donaghy looked at him like he was a simpleton. "How many people in GMM actually know how *In re: Albatross Hung* works, do you think?"

"A lot, I'd hope."

"Fewer than you'd assume. It's . . . it's a huge body of law and precedent, and it keeps growing. Staying abreast of it is a full-time, skilled job. People specialize in different areas: Research knows their end; Enforcement certainly knows theirs. But in our firm, there's only one person who stays on top of *In re: Albatross Hung* in its entirety. One person."

"Higgins."

"Yes. I told you he was the keeper of secrets."

"Your mentor."

"Most people treat *In re: Albatross Hung* like a magic gun. You load it with bullets and fire it and watch the whole world come down."

"Huh."

Something unguarded in Sol's tone made Donaghy look hard at him. Just for a moment. Then it passed.

They waited. They listened to the radio. Wind blew in the trees above the diner's chrome facade. Donaghy's phone buzzed. There was no mistaking her excitement. Her fists clenched, her lips suppressed a triumphal grin; *perhaps this was it*. She read the message on the phone, and everything deflated. Not today.

"What's happening?" Sol asked.

"We're going back to town. Got a target."

"Not Cléophe Carrette?"

"Different name. Ms. Mona Trent-Mach."

"Did you really think it would be him?"

"We're targeting Mona Trent-Mach today."

Donaghy got busy inputting the name MONA TRENT-MACH into a label printer; soon the name whirred out of the top in a glossy ribbon. Donaghy checked the spelling, carefully, twice. This was important. Somebody's life was about to be changed.

"Pass the briefcase, pal."

Sol drew the case up from the footwell. It was heavy.

"You can open it. Do you want to put the name on?"

Like she was offering a treat to a child. Still, Sol nodded. He unzipped the case to reveal the subpoenas all lined up in a row, and found the space in the nearest rolled-up cylinder, and pulled the backing off the sticker and squared it carefully and pressed it down.

"Locked and loaded," said Donaghy.

After Judith shut the door, I retrieved the package. It was unexpectedly heavy, and upon straightening up I was overcome by dizziness. The clouds took longer than expected to clear from my vision, and a kind of nauseated unease settled in my stomach.

I set off down the footpath that Judith had recommended, between green-tinged wooden fences and overhanging wisteria glistening with drops. It was cold and the package was heavy. The route wound between residential areas, and after a few turns I started to feel lost. I knew the city was all around me, but saw only creosoted fences, cracking concrete, and animal droppings.

I began to perceive an unexpected change in the light. My surroundings had fallen into gloom, and as I looked up, the last blaze of sunlight departed the tip of the nearest tower block; dusk had come. Already?

With dusk, a noticeable change. Foxes started wailing from their backyard haunts, precipitating the baying of neighborhood dogs; and then, all at once, silence.

I felt the presence then, nearby. I knew exactly what it was: the *thing*, the shadow that had danced across the lawn to me that squally winter's day.

Gripping my package, I looked back.

Nothing. The alley behind was empty. Two rows of fence boards stretched toward a perfect horizon point. I felt intensely aware of the darkness around me. I had to force myself to turn back toward my destination (nothing there), and onward up that empty, foreboding lane.

It was *heavy*, this package. My arms ached. The passage ahead stretched impossibly far, and with every step it darkened. And the certainty grew within me that if I looked back now I would see him falling forward, dancing over the rain-slick concrete. I felt tingling on the nape of my neck: *a hand, reaching.* Instinctively, I ducked. I felt energies coursing through my spine. All forward motion had ceased, and with a sense of finality I allowed my head to turn back once more.

I was alone.

Then with a sickening pop of static he burst into my consciousness: a white mask resolving into writhing vermicular forms, a fusty funeral jacket forming and deforming in chaotic skeins, shifting voids where mouths and eyes should be. He reached out a crumbling hand for the package I carried, and I saw a gleam move across his finger, like the light caught in a drip of water, rolling to a point of departure, ripening, preparing for downward flight.

And in a mote of pure, sweet psychosis I received and understood the message, YOU NEED NOT BE ALONE ANYMORE, a message cherished by some craven, genius spark of myself that actually wanted to stop and welcome the certain death no doubt approaching.

But then, as if a spell were broken, I could move again, and the idiot in me was suppressed, and I ran. As I ran, the energetic static built up in my nervous system was expelled, my nausea subsided, and simple panic—oh, sweet adrenaline!—drew me from that nightmare alley and onto familiar paths, with streetlights and traffic, and it was like waking up and knowing it had all been a dream and—

"Oi!"

Pain in my head. I opened my eyes. I was on the ground.

Beside me was a pair of black boots. The boots led to legs shod in black canvas. As I raised my gaze I saw that the person standing above me was wearing a black uniform. I'd run into a security guard.

"Where'd you come from, then?" the security guard said. She was a woman with a shaved head and a facial tattoo. With the turn of her mouth, she seemed to be laughing, but she wasn't.

"I, uh . . ."

I realized that the package was no longer in my hands.

"Where'd you come from? *Parlez-vous* English?"

I was lying on the pavement of Sanderson Drive, a block from Carrette's flat. The sky was full black, and the streetlights yellow. I'd apparently blundered into a gathering of security guards—there was a cluster across the road, and a few more on this side. They all wore the same uniforms. Some carried litter-pickers and trash bags, others placards.

UNITY IS STENGTH, one placard said. Another: EVROPE HAS SEEN THE SIGNS.

Still another: HE WILL COME.

"Oi, cloth-ears, I'm talking to you," the woman said.

"I'm Louis," I croaked.

"All right, that's a start," the woman laughed, unpleasantly. "You local, then?"

"Yes."

Surreptitiously I felt the ground around me for the package.

"That's *good*." She nodded vigorously. "We're here to help local people."

The tip of my finger felt the texture of stiff paper. The package was safe beneath my leg.

"Who are you?"

"I'm Joanne. These are my friends. We're the Hasturian Guard."

The words held a niggling familiarity, but I couldn't place it. "Are you, um, a club?"

"We're activists. We stand up for ordinary people."

Joanne proffered her hand to help me up. I didn't want to take it and expose the package beneath me. Her expression hardened, however, so I took her callused hand and allowed her to lift me to my feet.

She saw me scoop the package up from the ground, and her smile disappeared.

"What's that, then?" she asked. "You a delivery driver?"

"No."

Joanne twitched. She looked like she was trying to keep something to herself; then she gave up, and let it all flow out:

"Four out of ten delivery drivers are illegals. What's wrong with Royal Mail? What's wrong with postmen? Why can't I say 'postmen' anymore? Why can't people just be proud of who we are?"

"I'm not a delivery driver."

"Where did you get that from then, someone's doorstep?"

"No."

"Oi, James," she called to one of the "activists" nearby. "We've got a doorstepper here."

The man who walked over was tall and rake-thin, and before he stepped into the streetlight I recognized Spider. His features were still gaunt, but he was clean now, and clean-shaven. His uniform was crisp and slick, his eyes harder than they used to be.

"This joker ran right into me," Joanne said. "And look what he's got in his hands. Running away, I reckon. They take stuff from our doorsteps, you see, James."

Spider looked through me, the uninterested stare of authority, and I feared he'd forgotten our connection. But he blinked, slowly, and said, "Nah, it's all right, Jo. He's one of ours."

"Oh. *Good.* Well. Hope to see you again soon, Louis. Maybe you'd like to join one of our litter picks."

I nodded. Spider pulled a card out of his pocket. He retrieved a pen and, pressing the card against Jo's back, wrote something on it. He handed it to me.

There was an insignia, and the words "Hasturian Guard: Trusted Citizen Pass." My name, along with Spider's name and signature, was on the back.

"In case you need it later on," he said. Joanne nodded, happily.

"Things are going to change," she assured me, as I walked away. "We won't be ashamed anymore. We won't be alone anymore!"

The Hasturian Guard were out in force, and I was watched almost all the way to Carrette's flat. To say I felt afraid doesn't cover it. I felt embarrassed for my country. I felt fearful less for myself than for my fellow citizens, those who'd come from far away and whose security was being stripped, layer by layer, with every passing month and act of Parliament. Approaching Carrette's property—a first-floor flat with a plain entrance between a chip shop (with a *Leave Means Leave* poster) and an estate agent—I felt keenly the significance of the color of his skin.

For the Hasturian Guard were pale-skinned like myself, and I could talk my way past them; but M. Carrette was Black, and if they cornered him he was never going to talk his way out of that.

15

The target's personal details arrived by email. Mona Trent-Mach lived on Sanderson Drive. She worked in a specialist digital compliance company in the city center. There were two options, according to Donaghy: spring her at the bus stop, or set up outside her house and doorstep her.

"Your choice," she told Sol.

"Do we know where she works, exactly?"

"Yes."

"Well, what if I go directly to where she works?"

"And say what?"

"Say I have a delivery for her."

Donaghy smirked.

"Do you fancy it?" she asked.

"Yeah."

"Attaboy."

⁎ ⁎ ⁎

Donaghy dropped Sol off and told him to call when it was done. He had an address and a picture on his phone. According to the picture, Mona Trent-Mach was white, well-groomed, and tired. She had glasses and red hair.

The digital compliance company was in an office building with an unmanned open lobby. The inside door to the elevator and stairwell was remotely locked, with an array of buttons on the intercom. Sol thought about calling up. He rehearsed what he might say. He was about to press the button when he noticed the fire escape door was ajar. He took the back stairs instead.

Trent-Mach's office was on the fourth floor. He climbed ten short flights of stairs and looked through the fire door's reinforced window. He saw the back of an office. Nobody in sight. The handle on the door said CAUTION THIS DOOR IS ALARMED. Sol thought about it. It was a gamble. Much of the time—about half the places he'd worked in—signs like these were used as a deterrent, and there was no alarm. He looked at the edges of the door, to see whether it was used a lot. The signs were inconclusive.

CAUTION THIS DOOR IS ALARMED.

He didn't consciously decide to pull the handle and step inside. But that decision was made.

The fire alarm went off.

Fuck.

Think think think.

Sol closed the door and took a big step away from it and just stood there, staring at his phone. Professional-looking people started to filter out of different offices, some pulling on high-visibility tabards over their clothes. One of the hi-vizzers had a megaphone:

"FOLLOW ME PLEASE, STAY CALM AND FOLLOW ME."

Employees started following her. They walked slowly, some giggling and chatting, some groaning, a couple with worried expressions. They streamed past Sol to the fire exit stairs. Nobody paid attention to him. He didn't see Mona Trent-Mach in the crowd.

Then a woman in a wheelchair moved around the corner. She had red hair and glasses. A hi-vizzer clocked her and made a tick on her clipboard and they had a conversation. The company obviously had a protocol for getting her down the stairs. But not a very good one, it seemed: The woman in the wheelchair wasn't looking happy, and the more the hi-vizzer talked, the less happy she looked.

Then the hi-vizzer pulled a piece of equipment out from behind the fire door, and Sol understood the problem. This wasn't one of those special wheelchairs for stairs with the triple wheels at the bottom. It was the budget option, something like a sledge with a sleeping bag strapped to the top of it.

Sol examined the woman in the wheelchair, trying to work out whether she was Mona Trent-Mach. If so, his job was almost done here. He could simply give her the cylinder, run down the stairs, go home, and die of shame.

Then the woman asked Sol to help.

"Of course," he said. Sol and the hi-vizzer lifted the woman into the sledge and buckled her up. He tried not to touch her body too much. She kept apologizing, but she was clearly more angry than sorry. Then they slid her down the stairs. The hi-vizzer went first, standing at the bottom of each flight while Sol lowered her down like a piece of luggage. Ten flights.

"This is shit," the woman said, after the first two flights. The hi-vizzer only nodded grimly. "This is really shit. I've spoken to Troy. Three times." There was silence down the third flight. "What do *you* do then?" the woman asked Sol. "You new?"

"Consulting," he said.

"Consulting for what?"

"I'm not sure I can tell you."

"Ha! Tell me it's another restructure."

Sol still couldn't work out whether she was Mona Trent-Mach. In this moment he couldn't remember what the photo looked like. They maneuvered around another corner. He tried not to touch her body. Impossible.

"What do you do?" he asked.

Maybe her job description was in the file he'd skimmed. Maybe she'd say something and jog a memory.

"Insights," she said. It meant nothing to Sol. "Is Insights going? In the restructure?"

The hi-vizzer made a face.

"Oh, come on," said the woman. "I'm messing around. He can take a bit of joshing for £600 a day."

"Easy . . ." said the hi-vizzer.

"It's fine," said Sol.

"It's fine!" said the woman. "He says *it's fine*, Liz."

Liz, the hi-vizzer, snapped.

"We don't *have* to do this, you know," she said. "Legally, we're not even obliged to provide a sled anymore. Things have changed. So if you're waiting for a special chair to get down the stairs, you can keep waiting. Or you can be grateful for what you get."

The woman went white and trembled with rage, but said nothing. It took them twenty minutes to get downstairs, and if there had been a fire they'd have been burnt to cinders. Outside, everybody was shivering in the drizzle without their coats on, and they looked annoyed at having to wait for the disabled person, and ashamed of being annoyed. Then, after stretching her back for an unhurried minute, Liz went back upstairs for the wheelchair so the woman wouldn't be lying in the street in the rain. People kept murmuring the word "shambles."

Sol still had the cylinder in his pocket. He decided he couldn't do it. If this was Mona Trent-Mach, he couldn't bring himself to fuck up her day any more than he already had. He backed into the crowd and started moving away, drafting his resignation letter in his head. It was a relief, actually. He knew this was a silly idea—a vainglorious, guilty idea, to prove his worth against the worst firm he knew—

Then he bumped into Mona Trent-Mach.

"Excuse *me*," she said, and she tutted, even though it was she who'd meandered, crabwise, into Sol's path. Staring at her phone like she was the only person on the street. She had red hair and glasses. She looked well-groomed and tired and white. It was definitely her.

"I'm sorry," Sol said, "are you Mona Trent-Mach?"

She nodded. And when he didn't say anything, she rolled her eyes. She was making it easy.

Sol offered her the subpoena.

She took it.

* * *

Donaghy loved it. She cackled and snorted and insisted on taking Sol to the pub for lunch. She couldn't wait, she claimed, to tell the boys in the office. But Sol would have to tell her all over again how it happened. So Sol did.

"Why would you set off the fire alarm? That's weird. You're weird."

"It wasn't the right decision."

"No shit."

"But I . . . It was a gamble."

"You're going to get a reputation."

"Well. That's down to you, isn't it?"

"Nothing to do with me. And I'm not completely against your methods, you know. Saved yourself a bit of time, in a way. Next time, why don't you just start a real fire?"

"All right. It was a mistake."

"Get me a drink and I'll think about not telling all the boys on the floor."

Drinks appeared. Donaghy was thirsty. Sol felt safe to ask a few questions.

"What will happen to Mona Trent-Mach?"

"Good question. She'll have a chat with Enforcement soon enough, I think."

"What do you think she has?"

"Don't know. Don't care. Not our department."

"Really?"

"All right, I do care. But it isn't our department. And the fact is, Joe, it's really hard to find these things out."

"Who does know?"

"Look at you. All questions, aren't you."

"I'm interested. I've read a lot about *In re: Albatross Hung*."

"And you still wanted to work for us?"

"I'm a realist. I think GMM got a bad rap. The whole world was going that way, and GMM just happened to get there first."

"Going what way?"

"Well. You know."

"I want to hear you say it. Look, I'm pretty open-minded. I recommended you because I actually *like* diversity. Real diversity, that is. I think it's good to hear a different perspective on things. But you should know I'm a GMM loyalist, and I believe in the values GMM upholds."

"Which values?"

"I believe in family values, like I told Higgins. I'm not ashamed to say that. I don't think the government should be poking its nose in everybody's business. I'm proud of our country."

"So *In re: Albatross Hung*, to you . . ."

"It's not that big a deal. It allows private companies to make the same decisions they've always made, but it keeps the government out of things. Now it's your turn. Tell me what you really think. No filter."

"I'm still learning, Donaghy."

"My name's Jennifer. You can call me by my first name, this isn't *The X Files*. And I get the feeling you've already learned quite a lot."

"Okay. I know that *In re: Albatross Hung* was unprecedented. I know why people get upset about it. Like, the Enforcement team—aren't they basically going to *detain* Mona Trent-Mach?"

"That's strong language. But you're not completely wrong."

"They're going to search her house, too."

"Yes."

"And it's legal—they don't need the police to be involved."

"The police might provide protection for them."

Sol sighed.

"Just a few years ago," he said, "I would have said that was really shocking."

"Things are changing, I agree—but that doesn't mean they're getting worse."

Sol drank.

"What about the disabled woman in the stairwell?" he asked.

"What about her? Come on, it's not like GMM broke her legs or whatever."

"Her colleague told her that legally, her company didn't have to provide any way for her to get downstairs anymore."

"Oh. Yes."

"When did that happen?"

"Not long ago. Pro-business incentive to cut red tape. And look, they still did it, didn't they? They did the right thing. They usually do."

"Can I ask you a question?" Sol asked.

"Go on."

"How did you vote in the Immigration Emergency Referendum?"

"I knew this would come up."

"Did you prepare an answer, then?"

She nodded, her fingers pressed together, like a benign judge passing sentence.

"*On this occasion*, I voted yes. I thought it through *very carefully*. It's not like I don't have compassion for these people. But enough is enough. The government had enough time messing around in Parliament—all this party politics bullshit—and they hadn't fixed it. It was pretty clear to me—and a lot of other people, Joe—that we needed to suspend Parliament. So to fix the problem, I voted yes."

Sol said nothing.

"What? I knew you'd react this way, you all do. Listen, I'm happy enough to hear other people's points of view, the least you could do is afford me the same respect. It's not like it's going to last forever, is it? Once everything's fixed, we'll go back to the way it was, they'll wind down the Emergency Cabinet, your MPs can go back to taking backhanders and claiming expenses—but *we'll have sorted it out*."

"Hear, hear," some nearby drinker saluted.

"*Emergency Cabinet?*" another interrupted. "Cowards don't have the stomach for what this country needs."

Donaghy blushed.

Sol drank his pint. He looked around the pub. It was a typical sports bar, but there were a few more British flags than he'd have expected, and the big-screen TVs weren't exclusively playing sports feeds. One screen was dedicated to a nationalist news channel. Another was live-streaming a broadcast from a man in a yellow kimono who was orating mutely over inset graphics of pyramids, cockroaches, test tubes, and blood.

"You're missing the bigger picture," Donaghy told him in a quieter voice. "Governments don't run the world, *people* do. People in companies like ours. You wouldn't believe some of the things our partners are doing. I attended an away day at the Xanthic Spectrum campus up north. Did you know the entire campus is off-grid? And they don't have any solar panels or turbines or anything—they have their own generator that's *basically nuclear fusion*. And guess how much government money went into developing that? None. Private companies do it better, Joe, if you leave them to it. That's just a fact."

"What does GMM have to do with Xanthic Spectrum?"

Donaghy counted off her fingers: "Patents, secrets, intellectual property . . ."

"Well . . ." Sol tried to think of something more to say.

"I'm sure there are plenty of things we actually agree about," Donaghy said.

"I expect so," said Sol. "But . . ."

"But what?"

"My father was tortured by the junta in Argentina."

"That's terrible."

"He was a bastard."

Donaghy broke the silence that followed: "That's not happening here, you understand? The whole referendum thing—it wasn't so we'd end up like some tinpot dictatorship. It's temporary."

"I hope so."

"It may surprise you to learn, Joe, that we're actually the good guys."

"Is that why you wanted Higgins to hire me—so you could convert me? Is this, like, a challenge for you?"

She laughed. She'd finished her pint and looked excited about the prospect of the next.

"Yeah, maybe. Sometimes I like to set myself challenges. Test myself against something, to see whether I'm really worth what I think I am. You know what I mean?"

M. Carrette didn't seem surprised to see me, although twice he called me "Judith." He looked as haggard as Judith. He immediately took me up the narrow staircase into the flat, as though we'd already agreed that I'd witness the strange shape his life's work was taking.

The flat was long, narrow, and poorly lit. The walls held those sad framed photographs of New York City found in short-term leases. The lounge resembled a sleeper cabin, with two mean sofas facing each other beside a window. I sat, and Carrette disappeared into the shadowy kitchen. I heard a kettle slowly boil. I fingered the package at the point where its flap was gummed down. The activity soothed me, and I forgot myself, and got involved with peeling strips of gum away from the envelope.

"Desist, friend," Carrette murmured. He was standing above me with two cups of some herbal infusion. There was no coffee table, so he deposited them on the windowsill, and turned to the package.

I won't say Carrette looked at the package *greedily*, but he wasn't unmoved by its presence. He relieved me of it with firmness and intent, placing it on the floor—closer to his seat than mine—and his eyes returned to it from time to time.

I looked out the window. The street was busier than before. Several of the "activists" had taken up station on a corner opposite. They seemed to be pamphleteering. I felt like they kept looking up at us.

"Monsieur Carrette, have you had any run-ins with those characters outside?"

Carrette scanned the street. Then he huffed, in a satisfied way, as if he'd identified and marked the types and needn't bother himself further.

"Fanatics," he spat. "Empty men. They have always tried to trap me. Giovanni, Metti & Metti will have to work harder if they want to fool Cléophe Carrette."

"I'm sorry?"

"The GMM men, they follow me. They are desperate to get a piece of the deposit. But you know this, do you not?"

"I knew that. But these people claim to be part of a group. Like, a political group. Monsieur Carrette, I suspect they're racists."

"Did they bother you?"

"They stopped me, yes, but they didn't bother me. Racists wouldn't bother me, Monsieur Carrette, you see. But, um, as for *you . . .*"

"Did they want your package?"

"They seemed to think I'd stolen it."

"Ah, this is a ruse. A classic ruse. They would have taken it from you, if they could. They wear costumes and they try to fool you."

"But Monsieur Carrette, I recognized one of them. He used to be a real *waster*. A person who used drugs. I can't imagine him working for a law firm like GMM."

Carrette narrowed his eyes. He leaned close to the window and looked again. Condensation dripped from where his fingertips touched the glass.

"Perhaps they are real," he murmured.

"I fear so," I said. "But they haven't accosted you, or anything?"

Carrette shook his head.

"Fanatics. Empty men."

This was the second time he'd used the term "empty men." Something about the phrase niggled me. I smelled the fusty smell of the Pentorgan House seminar room, dust burning on old radiators.

"Ciphers," I said.

Carrette flinched.

"*What* did you say?" he hissed.

"Well . . ." I floundered for a while. It had been quite unconscious, a simple word association: from "empty" men to "Ciphers." But how could I explain the minutiae of my thought process to M. Carrette without also explaining the details of Bredsky's Cipher Theory, and where and why I learned about it? I couldn't expose my past to this eminent man.

"Did you say *Cipher*?" Carrette insisted.

"Yes. I was thinking about Cipher Theory . . ."

"Which is?"

I started recounting some of the details of Dr. Bredsky's theory, of how consciousness was a self-perpetuating narrative machine, a process, a kind of *inflowing* . . . But the words sounded false and I got lost. The more I tried to recall the details of Cipher Theory, the more elusive it seemed. Was there ever an actual Cipher Theory? Nonetheless I felt compelled to explain as Carrette stared on, incredulous.

"Did you say, you are a *Cipher*, or I am a *Cipher*?" he finally interrupted.

"We are, um, all Ciphers . . ." I mumbled.

Carrette looked suspiciously at me. "What you call a *Cipher* is not what I call a *Cipher*. I have never been called a *Cipher*."

He looked offended.

"I'm sorry."

"Where did you hear this?"

"I was on a course. A self-help course. We learned about Ciphers and *Kataluins*—"

At this, Carrette gaped. His eyes were wide.

"It's just a funny word I've picked up," I said lamely, in answer to the question he was too shocked to articulate.

"What does it mean to you?" he finally croaked.

"Interloper. A person who shows up and sends all your plans sideways."

"And where did you learn that?"

"The self-help course."

"A *Kataluin* hastens and intensifies change," Carrette murmured.

"Yes."

"But a *Kataluin* is not a person."

"Well, no, it doesn't have to be . . ."

"It is a demon. It is a messenger of Carcosa."

16

Nadia Eze's exposé of *In re: Albatross Hung* called it a monster. The case was, more precisely, a hydra. Its consequences multiplied in ways unpredicted by the litigants, misunderstood by the judiciary, and largely hidden from the wider world of people who might fall victim to it. These were Eze's words. Her long-form essay listed the stripping of human rights that the case had precipitated. Never before had private firms been given such unrestrained power to monitor citizens, seize their property, proceed against them in closed, private courts without their presence or knowledge—the list went on.

How exactly does In re: Albatross Hung *work? As I embarked on my research, I feared I'd never answer this question. Although at first glance it appears to simply allow companies to seize people and their property, the more I looked, the more intricacies I discovered, until the contradictions and complexities seemed insurmountable. But now I've come full circle, and I've come to suspect that beneath the camouflage, the answer is devastatingly simple.* In re: Albatross Hung *does whatever you want it to do. It's a panacea and a get-out-of-jail-free card, empowering a company to do whatever it pleases, so long as it has the resources to defend its prizes. If this interpretation is even halfway true, the consequences will be worse than we imagine.*

Recall Civics 101—responsible, restrained government rests on three pillars: executive, legislative, and judicial. In re: Albatross Hung *undermines the judicial pillar of government. Since such extraordinary powers have been granted to private companies, our judiciary has essentially been sidelined. A shadow state has arisen within the visible state, dominated by oligarchs and the corporations that serve them, and governed according to the law of* In re: Albatross Hung*—that is, the law of "I will take what I can."*

We live in a hollow shell of a country. Our corrupt and craven executive pillar has conquered the judiciary, and law is the plaything of corporations. Justice is now unattainable by the ordinary person. In this era of great beasts, we scurry between the stomping feet of giants, looking for shelter, finding none.

This continued for some pages. On the strength of Eze's political convictions, Sol had always regarded the article with respectful skepticism. Still, he drafted a message for her after his very first day at GMM. An introduction, an invitation, a testing of the waters between them. After a moment's deliberation, he sent it. No reply.

The next month or so was busy for subpoenas. Many people's lives were invaded in the name of *In re: Albatross Hung*. Sol and Donaghy were so good, they got a budget for props and costumes. Sol dressed up as a pizza delivery man, Donaghy a security guard. They got temporary decals for the van: grounds management, pest control, plumbing, butchery. They served office managers and parking wardens, renters and freeholders, mothers, churchgoers, anglers, and Sunday football referees. They engineered ambushes with stalled vehicles, talked their way past guards and spouses, pounced from bus shelters on rainy days.

Sol wrote down the names of the people they served. That's as far as his research went. He didn't inquire after them in the office. He didn't even talk about them with Donaghy, nor did Donaghy want to. They weren't acting like assassins, exactly, but there was this finality after each deed, the gravity of which neither of them wanted to articulate.

Meanwhile, the atmosphere in the city soured. Sol remembered the first raids and riots after the Immigration Emergency Referendum; these had passed quickly and—to Sol, at least—felt somewhat abstract. Now violence erupted every other day. People were banding together to protect or denounce their neighbors, for all sorts of reasons. Vigilante groups became a factor to negotiate. Donaghy dealt with this, through her contacts in the office.

Finally Eze replied. She'd be happy to meet up. They arranged a face-to-face in the train station coffee shop. They'd never met before, but they exchanged physical descriptions, and after her train got in—late—Eze came through the ticket barriers and straight to his table and sat and sighed like someone running into an old friend after a tiresome journey. She was perhaps his age, tall, with narrow eyeglasses and a piercing gaze. She was wearing a two-piece jogging outfit in green, hood up. She was, Sol noticed, the only Black person in the station. This detail sat uneasily with Sol. He felt sure it hadn't always been this way, the city hadn't always seemed so homogenous.

"I hope you didn't call," she said. "My phone's off. Yours should be, too." Sol nodded. He was wearing jeans and a band T-shirt that no longer fit him. A surgical face mask. She grabbed a used coffee mug from a nearby table, cupping it in her hands as if it were still warm. "Guess why the train was late," she said. "There was a fake conductor on it."

Sol cleared his throat.

"What?"

"A fake conductor. Someone was trying to take down people's details, pretending to inspect tickets, but he kept asking where people were going and what they were doing."

"Police?"

"No. And not GMM, either. It was some so-called activist looking for illegal immigrants. Wearing a uniform and everything, part of a group called the Hasturian Guard."

"What the fuck?"

"I'd heard of them before, out in the country, but you don't see them back in Lewisham. He didn't get to my part of the carriage before the real ticket inspector came from the other end. I thought they were going to have a fight. The conductor decided to chuck him off at the next station, but he obviously tipped off his mates, because they were waiting there, and they pulled the conductor off, too."

"What? Did you call the police?"

"Somebody did. Fat lot of good they were. Then some passengers got out, started picking sides. There was just this big fight going on, on the platform, with the conductor in the middle of it. The driver locked the doors and we left."

"I can't believe it."

"Don't look so surprised. This kind of stuff happens all the time these days. When's the last time you were in London?"

"A few years, I suppose."

"They're building walls. Around the neighborhoods, between the boroughs."

"Why?"

"They call them 'peace walls.'"

Sol blinked. "Is this, like, after the riots?"

Eze stared at him. "Riots. Are you talking about the protests after the referendum," she said, her voice betraying a deep well of emotion, "or are you talking about the time they burned down Forest Grange?"

"Um . . ."

"They're building walls. Walls to keep us *safe*."

"Well, I guess it kind of makes sense . . ."

"No, it doesn't make any sense!" she hissed. "It's a lie . . ."

"I'm sorry. I just wanted to talk about GMM."

"Don't you see these things are connected?"

Sol stared at Eze. Her eyes looked tired. As if she had been up all night looking at strange data. He began to feel doubt about the meeting. She produced a piece of paper and unrolled it across the tabletop. There was a list of names, connected with thick black lines. Sol was dismayed to see how crumpled and stained it was.

"Remember the name you gave me, your boss at GMM, Higgins? I made a list of companies he's had a stake in. Then I made a list of companies that *those* companies have partnered with at least twice. The list is small but consistent."

Sol looked. The names meant little to him.

"Explain, please," he said.

Eze pointed at the top name on the list. Her finger was trembling.

"Prism Consultancy. Remember the Immigration Emergency Referendum? The one where we voted to suspend elections until the 'immigration emergency' was fixed?"

"Of course I remember. And I voted against it, you should know."

"Well done. Guess who ran promotion on the pro-Emergency side?"

"Prism?"

"Prism Consultancy. They do market research and policy influence work all over the world. Targeted ads, focus groups. It's one of those post-hippie psychobabble firms, dark side of the Summer of Love. They used to run therapy courses for soldiers with PTSD. Then they got into advertising. Now they tip elections."

"Spooky."

"Now look at this one: New Ministries Holdings. This one has been channeling money into fringe groups for years. A lot of new nationalist movements, and anti-progressive movements, and a couple of far-left conspiracy movements. I don't know about the Hasturian Guard. It certainly seems like the kind of thing they'd finance. Then there's Crown Leviathan. You should know them. They build missiles." Sol nodded. "PanOp Insights is a camera surveillance company. They got in the news recently because of the concentration camps. This is where it gets odd. This company is called Xanthic Spectrum, and it specializes in alternative sources of energy—mainly renewables, but also nuclear. Fusion, I mean."

"I know them," Sol said. "My line manager was raving about them, about how they're the future of energy."

"Uh, huh," Eze continued, running her finger over the longer list on the right-hand side, "and these other companies are all subsidiaries, or contractors, or collaborators with this first list. And GMM sits at the middle of it."

Sol stared at the list.

"I'm not sure what to make of this," he said. "Companies trade with other companies. That's how they exist. Connections aren't necessarily conspiracies. I came to you with a concrete thing: *In re: Albatross Hung* writs. Now, I've been keeping the names of the people we've been serving subpoenas. We could *prove* that GMM is detaining people, you understand?"

Eze shook her head.

"We're past that now," she said.

"What do you mean?"

She shrugged. "They're obviously not the only people carrying out kidnappings anymore."

"But what about *In re: Albatross Hung* writs? What about the law? GMM has been using these subpoenas to wield incredible power. They've taken the law and twisted it so they can do nasty stuff for nasty people. Including the companies on your list, right?"

"Yes, thanks, I do remember the article I wrote."

"I'm offering you corroboration."

"Yeah, thanks—for whom? A few years ago, when I wrote that article, it could get published in a newspaper and somebody sympathetic—a judge or an MP or something—might read it and be able to do something. Don't you see that's impossible now? No MPs, no Parliament, no debate. Judicial system's fucked. I can't even get my stuff out on the Internet because of the fucking National Firewall. It's over for me. There's nowhere to go. I stay in my house in my little sanctuary zone and do digital shitwork for a subsistence wage. So thanks, thanks for reading my article—but how do you think, out of everything that's happening, we can fix *In re: Albatross Hung*? Where have you been for the last few years?"

Sol was at a loss.

"I've been dealing with some personal issues," he said eventually.

"I'm sorry."

They stared at each other for a while. The train station was quiet. A pair of footsteps approached from behind Eze, and she drew her hands into the sleeves of her hoodie. When a couple walked past, holding hands, she breathed an audible sigh of relief.

"I have to go. No offense, Mr. Sol, but I don't feel safe up here."

"I really doubt people know who you are," Sol said.

"You still don't get it, do you," Eze said. She rolled up her sleeve and pointed at the skin on the back of her hand. "I can't hide *this*, can I? I'm not going to feel safe until I'm back in Lewisham. Behind my big wall."

She stood up. They pretended to hug.

"I'm sorry," Sol said, for want of anything better to say.

"You know what I'd do, if I were you?" she asked, after some thought.

Sol shrugged.

"I'd look at the Archimboldi Deposit itself."

"But I thought it was just a vehicle to change the law."

"So did I, for a while. But I've been rethinking things. Here's the issue, Mr. Sol: GMM filed *In re: Albatross Hung* while they were chasing the Archimboldi Legacy in the nineties. Thirty years later, the country's gone to hell and *In re: Albatross Hung* is one of the causes. If they just wanted to change the law to grant themselves more power, it would be mission accomplished for them, right? With all the citizens' rights and workers' protections gone, with all solidarity destroyed, everybody scrambling, everybody panicking, falling back on old prejudices, ready to believe any lie you tell them, they're surely free to make as much money as they can, or remake the world based on whatever fucked bigotry drives the rancid little goblins in their heads they call ideology. Playing soldiers with skinheads, the fucking *Hasturian Guard* . . ."

Eze stopped. She breathed deeply, eyes shut. Sol realized how shaken she was. The experience on the train must have hit harder than she let on. Sol wondered whether, despite the fearlessness of her writing, Eze hadn't fully apprehended the reality she faced until today. He felt an impulse to tell her it would be okay. He didn't want to lie. He said nothing. Eventually she collected herself.

"Listen," she said. "The point is, shouldn't they have stopped chasing the Archimboldi Legacy? Yet here you still are, issuing *Albatross Hung* writs in exactly the same way they were originally intended."

"I'm told they're caught up in a legal bind. There's something called the Archimboldi Fund that they can't release until they've destroyed all the pieces of the legacy."

"Oh, really?"

"I'm told this is the inside scoop."

"Does it sound very realistic to you?"

"I honestly don't know. I don't have experience with these things."

"I have some experience, and I can tell you it sounds like a load of bollocks. Follow the legacy. There's something in it that they really, really want. And you can mark my words they aren't destroying it. Whatever Archimboldi wanted when he wrote his will, GMM stopped following his wishes long ago."

I believe I underestimated the cumulative effect of the strange events I'd experienced that day. The man (was it a man?) in the alley; the racist "activists" in the street; now M. Carrette seemed to be reaching into my memories and pulling out yet another squirming, untrustworthy thing: that word, Carcosa.

A Kataluin is a demon. A messenger of Carcosa.

I wanted to cry. Sweat dripped down my back.

"Is there some kind of translation problem, perhaps?" I asked in a quiet, strained voice.

"Oh? Perhaps I mean, uh, *Geist.* Spirit. A totem or a portent of power to come."

I nodded. I still wanted to cry. But I did something far worse: I talked. I just talked and talked at M. Carrette, in a clever-clever know-it-all tone, about signs and portents, all the while watching myself with horror, unable to prevent the next spillage of pseudo-academic sludge from between my lips. Worst of all I explained—for shame—I *explained* Archimboldi to Cléophe Carrette.

And M. Carrette listened, with the expression of somebody who'd resigned himself to the mediocrity of the intellects he met on a daily basis. I knew at that moment where I stood in relation to this man. If this had been an audition to work with Carrette, I'd decisively failed.

At last, my words ran out. The package was resting on the floor between us. He'd been eyeing it the same way my precious few dates had eyed their phones throughout our dinners, hoping for deliverance. Finally, I'd nothing left to say to prevent him from picking it up.

"Will you open it?" I asked.

"Not here."

"Is it a secret?"

"I am afraid so. I must move it to a safe place, if you will excuse me. Perhaps you'd like more tisane?"

My tisane was still scalding hot. Nonetheless, he left me. Behind the condensation on the windowpane, the streetlights flared and wavered like torches.

From the corridor down which M. Carrette had disappeared came the softest exhalation. I'm unsure whether I heard it or felt it. But I knew at that moment that M. Carrette—in his kitchen, perhaps—had opened the package.

Breathing slowed. Everything went still.

There is a moment in Chambers's "The Mask," in which the narrator falls into a fever and tours the realm of Carcosa:

I saw the lake of Hali, thin and blank, without a ripple or wind to stir it, and I saw the towers of Carcosa behind the moon. Aldebaran, the Hyades, Alar, Hastur, glided through the cloud-rifts, which fluttered and flapped as they passed like the scolloped tatters of the King in Yellow.

Aldebaran, the Hyades, Alar, Hastur: I could get lost in these exotic proper nouns. They're real places, you understand. Not places we could visit, without being annihilated: they are stars.

In that long, quiet moment, I felt a sense of peace.

Not peace—calm.

Not calm.

Control.

I don't know exactly how long I stayed in Carrette's flat. At a certain point my tisane became cool enough to taste (it was revolting). At a certain point it became cold. Carrette remained elsewhere, arrested by the contents of the package. I tried getting up. The air felt soupy. I plodded toward the corridor like a deep-sea diver. The atmosphere in the entire flat had become concentrated, perhaps treacherous. Part of me wanted to *dig it.* I was making swimming motions while I walked.

Then the feeling of heavy control came on stronger: I felt a sense of being in more than one place at one time. As if the surfaces—the neatly cut geometries of domestic architecture—were as paper-thin as the blueprints that had preceded them. A picture of a living room, through which we might see the picture of another living room, and another. Through transparent walls I believed I might perceive the House of the Dead Man, with roots and boughs breaking the architect's designs; these too could easily fall away to reveal the lines of the ALI's cold room; through these were the traces of Dr. Bredsky's office in Pentorgan House; and through these, the busy streets of a South American city . . .

Underlying this was a palpable sense of nostalgia, a solvent nostalgia strong enough to thin the surfaces of the present world, dull the apprehensive senses, and make visible remembered realms. And the feeling in which I was immersed was not my own; nor was it Carrette's. It came from elsewhere. We were like deep-sea divers, wavering in the blackness, subject to currents that served intelligences far beyond our ken.

Now I felt afraid. By force of will I hauled myself free of the current and reeled back to the window, and squeaked a wet little hole in the condensation. The Hasturian Guards had departed, leaving a heap of trash bags at the side of the road. It was dark and quiet on the streets of our town, perhaps a hundred thousand miles away. I had to get out, get home somehow.

It didn't occur to me at the time that I was abandoning M. Carrette. I was guided by instinct: wading through this static, trying to make my way to shallower drifts. I reached the stairs, and discovered that with every downward step things became a touch easier. The free-floating layers of memory-space fused back together; opening the front door was like stepping back on solid ground; and when the full force of Earth's gravity hit me it came with a wave of nausea, and I vomited expansively across the pavement.

In that moment I'd forgotten Carrette. But it played on my mind afterward, to recall that I left his front door wide open; and that as I staggered away, I sensed the presence once more of what I called the Corpse Man, the thing from the alley making his inexorable progress up Sanderson Drive; and that I knew his trajectory was toward that open door; and that in a moment of intuition I accurately named the entity: *Kataluin.* Arbiter of change. Messenger of Carcosa.

I won't repeat the jaundiced rumors about what the popular press called "the Carrette misadventure." It is worth, however, dwelling on the evidence I've seen shared on a few morbid websites. One photograph in particular, leaked from the office of the county coroner, is worth describing.

It's of Carrette's kitchen. The room is long and narrow. To the left are the white goods, the counter. Nothing special. On the right is a small low window.

But a viewer is unlikely to look at the window. The subject of the picture sits on the linoleum in the center.

It's a monochrome substance. A mass. It looks like a photocopied caterpillar; or perhaps driftwood; or a distant ridge of mountains. Black, white, and grey. A landscape in the aftermath of a volcanic eruption.

Sulphurous fumes, buried lives, rivers of choking mud. Such are the images that come to mind gazing on the last mortal remains of M. Carrette.

I learned of Carrette's death the same way most others did: from the news. I was at home. After stumbling back from Sanderson Drive, I'd collapsed into bed and dreamed a lifetime's worth of nightmares in fourteen hours of sleep. The headlines I awoke to were unpleasant but unsurprising, confirming a likelihood I'd already intuited.

The press called Carrette's death a "mystery" and hinted at "misadventure." I felt no doubt there'd been foul play. As to who was responsible, possibilities collided in my mind. Logically, I knew M. Carrette had enemies: Academics envied him; GMM goons were following him; he would have been a target for the Hasturian Guard—or any other of the horrible gangs cropping up in our benighted country—by virtue of his ethnicity.

But instinct told me none of these people were responsible for what happened to him. I became fixated on two things: the package Judith Bea had me deliver to Carrette, and the *Kataluin* that pursued it.

17

After he passed his probation, Sol was treated to a team-building weekend with the GMM boys. They hiked over peat moors with an old-fashioned map and compass. They sheltered from the storm together in a cabin. Blowing on hands and stamping. Once they reached their destination, the Team-Building Guide directed them to salvage wooden planks and build a bridge across some marshy land. Once this construction was complete, they each walked to its midway point to perform a trust fall into the waiting hands of their colleagues.

Sol learned the names of these people, and after whisky in the bunkhouse he found himself wanting to believe what the Team-Building Guide asserted: that they were, in fact, brothers-in-arms, parted by the vicissitudes of fate but reunited now in the benign embrace of their firm.

Once people were drunk enough, they started reflecting more candidly on GMM's reputation. It was generally felt that GMM was unfairly singled out by bleeding-heart activists with axes to grind. Somebody brought up Nadia Eze's exposé, and the atmosphere grew tense, since it was suspected Eze received insider help. As such, people were especially quick to condemn her social justice warrior bullshit and anti-white posturing. It was prejudice of another kind, one man asserted: anti-Catholic. It was pure sectarianism.

Little wonder, commented another man, *given where she comes from.*

She should be grateful she's here and not there.

Don't get me started.

Coming over here, somebody said, joking and not joking.

Then someone said something that tightened Sol's focus:

"Is she on the list?"

"Shut up," someone else said.

"Well, is she?" the questioner repeated. He seemed to be asking an older man with a chinstrap beard.

Chinstrap shrugged.

"I don't keep the list," he said. "That's Guard business."

"I can't believe those weekend warriors keep up-to-date paperwork," said some new wag, and the chat degenerated again:

Hasturian Guard Neanderthals.

Hey, those are our Neanderthals you're talking about!

Shut up—this is sensitive stuff.

We're all brothers, aren't we?

* * *

Sunday night, at home, Sol wrote all their names down. In a second column he wrote down their positions in the company, locations, responsibilities. He didn't know what he'd do with this information. He didn't want to believe nothing could be done. He encrypted the folder in which he kept the list, encrypted his backup hard drives, enabled multi-factor authentication for his phone. He removed himself from the national register.

Around midnight, impulsively, he called his ex-wife, Dulcie. She didn't answer the phone, and he didn't leave a message. Unsatisfied, he decided to call his sister instead. His anxiety grew as the phone rang, and by the time Sara answered he could taste blood from his chewed lip.

"Hello?" She sounded half-asleep.

"Sara."

"Joe. Christ. What time is it?"

"What time is it where you are?"

"I don't know. Night time. What's wrong?"

"Have you spoken to Dulcie recently?"

He heard a familiar, frustrated groan.

"Joe, whatever's going on, I don't want to be involved."

"It's not like that. I'm just checking in."

". . . She's fine."

"Where is she?"

"Joe . . ."

"Is she still in London?"

"She met a guy. A Swiss guy."

"Oh."

"It's been a year now, you can't be surprised."

"No. I'm glad. So she's there? In Switzerland?"

"I guess so."

"And you?"

"I'm fine. Still here, out in the bush. And Sven is fine, too, thanks for asking. He got a promotion, actually. He's practically running the mine now."

Sol had no response. He disliked Sven. But Sven would keep Sara safe, in the way she needed. In moments like these he appreciated the value of that.

"What time is it there?"

"I told you, it's the middle of the night. Joe, what's going on? Are you worried? Sven says it's a storm in a teacup. The Emergency Cabinet will never bend to those crazy bastards' demands. It doesn't make economic sense. The country needs investors. Stability. Not chaos in the streets. And Sven should know, you know."

"What demands?"

"The strikes? The roadblocks? Joe, you should pay more attention to the news. It's a big story, even here."

"Well. I love you, Sara."

He knew exactly how she'd react. But it needed to be said.

"What's *that* supposed to mean? Do I have to worry about you now?"

"I'm just saying. I miss Mom."

"What am I supposed to do with *that*, Joe? It's the middle of the fucking night. Christ, Dulcie was right about you. I don't know how she stood it as long as she did. Go to bed."

He didn't go to bed. Instead he went out and withdrew money from his account. He placed it in a roll-on suitcase with a change of clothes, a toothbrush, some toothpaste, some foot powder. His wedding ring.

The news of Carrette's death hit the ALI hard. Management were cloistered in endless meetings and everybody else was circulating between the kitchen nook and the bathroom. Ceaseless cups of tea.

The moment Judith arrived, late and rather haggard, Mr. Holmes swooped downstairs and pulled her into a reading chamber to debrief. When she stumbled out, her colleagues descended on her for endless commiserations. Finally she was left alone to pack a few documents away and cry at her desk.

It was confirmed to me then that Carrette's flat on Sanderson Drive was a secret. There was a close moment: Someone was reading out the latest update from their phone and mentioned the address. Judith caught my eye. She gave me a look, like she needed me to keep quiet and follow her lead. So I did. I watched her very closely, in fact, as every new detail was read out.

The most instructive moment came when we learned the detail of Carrette's discovery by a delivery driver. This fact Judith seemed to accept, at first, as straightforward and unsurprising. Then her eyebrows narrowed as she seemed to process the implications. Then the color drained from her face.

I caught up with her on her way to the smoking bay. She acknowledged me without speaking and swiped the lock to open the exterior door. A breath of outside air met us, smelling of damp and shadows. Judith sucked it in like a swimmer on the shore. She was shaking.

"Thank you for not saying anything in the office," she said eventually. "Please, don't tell anyone you've been to his flat. I never should have got you involved."

"What were you doing with him?"

"Nothing like *that.*"

"I know that."

"I can see the way the papers are taking it."

"That's just the papers."

"It's not fair. He was such a lovely man."

I didn't say anything.

"He was interested in facts. The truth."

"Judith," I said, "what was in that package?"

She stiffened.

"You know I can't tell you."

"I was followed."

"What?"

"I was followed to Monsieur Carrette's flat. There's this man who appears sometimes. Only he's not a man. He's come here before. And yesterday, he followed me. He followed the package." Judith gulped, like her throat was dry. "There's a word that Monsieur Carrette used," I pressed. "The word is *Kataluin.*" I watched her carefully for signs of recognition. She gave away nothing. She seemed petrified, in fact—her face a mask. "The *Kataluin* did this, didn't it, Judith?"

Finally she snapped.

"*Kataluin* can never act alone. They are drawn to his power. If you see *Kataluin*, it means the King is trying to break through."

She seemed to regret her outburst quickly. She covered her face and turned around, all the way from me. I heard her muttering into her hands. "Fuckfuckfuck," she was saying.

"Which king?" I asked.

She ignored me. After half a minute the crisis passed. She pulled a huge spliff out of her handbag.

"This was for later," she explained. I grunted. I didn't approve. I knew that every inhalation would take her further away from what she'd been about to say.

"What king?" I tried again.

She inhaled.

"This is fucked," she said. "I feel like he's still alive. I'll head inside and he'll be there in the reading room, ready to give me my assignment. But that won't happen, will it?" She stopped. Her joint had gone out. She cupped the lighter and inhaled, and I saw the damp strands of cigarette paper sticking to her lips as she mumbled. "I'm still here, though, right? I'm still here. This is me." Suddenly she stopped and stared at me. "Tell me something I don't know," she said.

"Um."

"Tell me something I've never heard before."

"Salvatore Archimboldi . . ."

"Not about Archimboldi! I *know* Archimboldi, you cretin!"

"I was born in 1984 and I have no phobias."

She took a moment to evaluate what I'd said.

"Fine," she said, eventually, shaking her head. "Fine, I guess I'm still here. Still awake here. It was a *Deferral.* He's gone."

There was that annoying word, *Deferral.* How did Judith come to utter it? Hard to imagine she'd undergone treatment at Pentorgan House. And the way she used it was off. I recalled "Deferral" meaning something like a psychic tantrum, the kind of blowup that might tempt someone to relapse. But was my memory right?

"Do you know how Monsieur Carrette died?" I asked.

"I know what it looked like from the outside," she said.

"What did it look like?"

"Light. Heat."

"An explosion?"

She nodded.

"I don't understand. Why do you say *from the outside*?"

She stared at me with lazily dilating pupils.

"We can never know what he went through."

"Except he *blew up*. You know that."

She shook her head.

"Nobody can travel a Cipher's bridge but the Cipher itself."

I felt sick.

"You're making me feel like I'm back in therapy," I said.

She gave me a long, steady stare.

"I'm sorry. I never should have involved you."

"What was in the package you gave me yesterday?" I asked, one last time.

She shrugged in a despairing way.

"It must have been *The Truth of Carcosa*. We found it. Well done, us."

She shut down then, and I returned to work. Twenty minutes later she weaved back into the office and made straight for the cold room. She came out with a box, and waved it in front of me long enough for me to read the label: CORRESPONDENCE 1984.

Twenty minutes after that, she was caught photocopying sensitive documents in the reading room. The Institute uses a system whereby the scanner-photocopiers send electronic versions of everything you put through them to the offices of the lawyers upstairs. Judith was escorted from the ALI by security. I never saw her again.

* * *

Let's do a little recap. Call it revision, drawing together a few key points. Not so much reaching conclusions as standing at the door behind which conclusions hide, wondering whether to finally push that exit bar. CAUTION. I pull out my notepad, a big black marker pen, and open up a double page.

Known terms:

Carrette

Judith Bea

Archimboldi

1984

Known facts:

- *M. Carrette was writing the biography of Salvatore Archimboldi. In so doing his research took him to a certain year in Archimboldi's journals: 1984.*
- *Judith Bea helped Carrette research this same set of documents. And both Bea and Carrette became sick, over time, while carrying out this task.*

But how important is this detail? Unclear. People get sick. People get strange. The unelected leader of our country holds regular rallies across the country in which he denounces shadowy cannibalistic forces subverting society.

- *Carrette's death is a nationally reported event.*

As to the nature of his death: Whatever Judith Bea had to say about it, all we have is speculation. The photographs give us little to go on; just because his body was incinerated, doesn't mean he died a legally suspicious death. People have been known to keel over while cooking or smoking and subsequently ignite. Nonetheless:

- *Immediately after this catalyzing event, Bea attempted to make copies of the same documents (1984) that had been central to their exhausting toil for so many months. She failed. Then she disappeared.*

Now to assimilate some less concretely factual elements into our mental map. Again I retrieve my marker pen:

The House of the Dead Man

The Truth of Carcosa

Dr. Bredsky

To repeat: In my untrustworthy youth I spent time in a derelict house, which I called the House of the Dead Man. Here, I encountered a book called *The Truth of Carcosa.* Given that I barely remembered the book, it was reasonable for me to regard it as a drug-inspired fantasy—which I did, for many years. I believed my own therapist, Dr. Bredsky, encouraged this understanding. Thinking back, however, I cannot recall her ever telling me "there is no *Truth of Carcosa.*" And Judith spoke the words "the truth of Carcosa" to me after she first accessed the 1984 documents, and again after Carrette's death. Indeed, she told me I'd actually delivered the *Truth of Carcosa* to Carrette's flat on the calamitous day in question.

Let's accept that *The Truth of Carcosa* was a real book. We might then assume that the book has been suppressed. Which means we must introduce another factor, the erstwhile destroyers of all Archimboldi texts:

Giovanni, Metti & Metti, LLC

Might we posit that Archimboldi wrote this book in 1984? That that year's correspondence contains clues to the whereabouts of any remaining copies?

If so, we can start pulling things together: Given the whirlwind of interest circling Archimboldi's existing corpus, and the principle that scarcity determines value, we might assume that any remaining copies of *The Truth of Carcosa* are very valuable indeed. We might posit that Carrette and Bea, searching for a rare manuscript, attracted the attention of outside forces. Carrette was killed for a valuable artifact.

This version of the story makes sense, and might satisfy an outsider; however, I know it to be false.

Why? Because GMM agents would never have done this. They act within the bounds of the law (don't they?). And what would those illiterate goons in the Hasturian Guard have known of *The Truth of Carcosa*? Then there is the Corpse Man. I must write its true name:

Kataluin

According to my (increasingly muddy) memories of Bredsky's teaching, a *Kataluin* is an interloping spirit, a bobble in the sober weave of one's life. But why should Carrette's interpretation—that it is a demon, a messenger—not also be true? What if Dr. Bredsky's cosmology of powerful words denoted not metaphors, but *real things*?

Cipher

Deferral

Accession

Recall, please, how I defined certain words as signs (simple, communicable) and certain words as portents (personal, powerful), and understand that these words above are portents for me, that my sobriety and stability demand they be understood as metaphors, not realities.

Yet my hand wields the pen once more:

The King in Yellow

And it returns to me that the Carcosa named in Archimboldi's book is the home of an entity called the King in Yellow, an entity found within the eponymous work of fiction Dr. Bredsky encouraged me to read during my recovery in a beautiful hospital that might once have been a castle:

Pentorgan House

And I am back in that strange clinic, and the good doctor—a sweet-scented mummy, a rictus-bearing flap of old flesh—is asking me to visualize, if I can, the Palace of the Yellow King in far Carcosa. What does the lake of Hali look like? she asks. What damp scents does it exude? Do visitors arrive by boat, stepping aboard a sturdy wooden jetty hung with banners and pennants—or are they required to pass beneath a grand stone arch? What rich pollens flow from the flora of Carcosa?

She doesn't ask me to narrate my imaginary journey, for as she has explained, my bridge to Accession is mine alone. Indeed, she observes my meditation with a kind of wonder, as if I am displaying an extraordinary talent just by thinking, the process of traversing (and building) the fabulous maze, and I feel so very special—such a good Cipher—in this memory, that returning to the present moment feels like coming up for air in a cold, cold pool.

Oh, my head aches. I cycle in my ruminations between different understandings of the signs and portents that shape my life, and while my interpretations change, the poles they orbit remain fixed. *The King in Yellow* is a book is a play is a personage to be feared to be loved. *The Truth of Carcosa* is a book and a bomb. I seek comfort in the same words that unnerve me. I barely get any work done. I take longer and longer to return from my mandated breaks. Jan no longer looks me in the eye.

I spend my time here in this stale little staff room where nobody ever comes. I have started to linger after hours. Thinking. Dreaming. Staring through the window at the progress of the shadows on the spackling. It was on one such extended break it struck me that I had a duty, if the intuition growing in my belly were true, to warn others. But of what, exactly? And how could I persuade any reader that I wasn't a lunatic?

I produced a notepad not unlike the one described above and wrote the following words:

In fact, I am quite sane.

18

In the clearing, Scottie places the final page of the Special Report face down in the left-hand pile. It's past midnight now. The fire's going strong, and fuel is plentiful. Scottie isn't tired. But he's not sure he's ready for the next stage.

He stares a while at the pile of papers before him. Then he rotates the whole manuscript 180 degrees.

The paper is covered with scrawled handwriting. Where the printed report ended, the author flipped the manuscript over and continued with a pen, moving back, page after page, to the beginning again.

Scottie reads.

Everything has changed in the last ten days.

Excuse my scrawls. I haven't the equipment to type up my notes. But I barely notice the limitations of the medium; my pen flies across the page, ink turning psychic somersaults as I write: Where once I felt doubt, now I have certainty. The "linguistic fact" of loneliness has been disproved. I've never felt more elated, more shaken to the core, as if I could twitch my shoulders and my skin, my flesh, might slough to the ground as I soar toward my destiny.

Certain practical problems remain. I've enough canned food and bottled water to last, but my supply of pens concerns me. My immediate goal is to record these last critical weeks, both for providence and to clarify the thoughts rushing through me like a mainline charge.

I have been learning of Carcosa. The lineage of Carcosa.

My research began weeks ago, when I was still employed and the city wasn't on fire. It began with a simple Internet search. I'm not sure why I hadn't done this earlier: Why, after weeks of wondering at the reappearance of curious signs and portents in my life, I only then tried feeding one into a search engine. Perhaps I feared what I would find. In truth, I had reason to.

First I learned of the extent of the Yellow Mythos. From Chambers's The King in Yellow a whole world has sprung, dedicated to the Yellow King, to Carcosa. The closer you look, the more you see these words appearing in novels, films, games, shows: They weave a collective alternate reality for thousands of enthusiasts. I discovered forums where fans gather to discuss their interest in this alternative reality. I was heartened, fascinated—and ultimately disturbed by what I found there.

Some crossover has occurred between the fandom and the rising tide of intolerance subsuming our nation. It seems du jour for certain members to espouse the most violent opinions when confronted by facets of the world they don't like—foreigners, mainly, and women. Here, the significance of the name "Hasturian Guard" finally hit me. Hastur, the star in the sky of Carcosa. A floating sign in the mythos. And now, the name appropriated by a pack of thugs.

Do they read, these bullies and brutes? I suspect not. Chambers's original stories seem nuanced and ironic, hardly a rallying cry for national chauvinists. But they can look at pictures, I suppose. Perhaps they've been seduced by a retrograde aesthetic, believing that enjoying the vision of the fin-de-siècle world means embracing its popular prejudices. Or perhaps there is no rationale. Perhaps the madness of this rabid demographic is simply madness, unreason, a nervous response to some hidden external stimulus. Pure mimesis.

Consider the virus. A virus is not truly alive; it lives through the processes of others, injecting its DNA into its host. Consider that a word is like a virus. Infinitesimal, it flies through the void between membranes and tissues. The sky that enfolds it is gigantic and black. The cell walls it penetrates are like asteroid belts. When it lights upon a new planet, it will remake it for its own purposes.

The word "Carcosa" flies through the void. From Robert W. Chambers to a thousand other lonely scribblers; and ultimately to some shaven-headed oik who gathers his violent friends together and calls them "the Hasturian Guard"; to the editor of the Aldebaran Gazette, a particularly rabid website full of Nazi propaganda dressed in the costume of Romantic science fiction; to a certain gentleman in Kentucky, who dresses in a kimono and spreads Carcosan truths leavened with antisemitic conspiracies on a popular weekly livestream, calling himself (oh, the audacity) the Yellow King.

But here's the question: Does the virus live? Does the livestreamer appropriate the King's name, or does the King appropriate him?

19

Sol asked Donaghy what she thought of the Hasturian Guard. She said she didn't know much about it, but she couldn't endorse violence except in extreme circumstances. However, she saw where people were coming from, banding together when the government didn't have their best interests at heart.

"But mainly," she said, "they're a nuisance, aren't they? It's just an extra factor to negotiate when we serve our subpoenas."

"You seem to have a good idea where they're going to be."

"Yeah, I get updates from our community outreach teams."

"Ah, right," Sol said. He yawned. They were working a late shift, waiting outside a target's house. The target hadn't been home in three nights. They'd been tipped off, Sol suspected; gone to ground.

Donaghy had worked hard to convert Sol to conservative principles these last three nights. She professed to believe in the power of debate, so she got frustrated by Sol's most recent defensive strategy, which was to simply agree with everything she said.

"Next you're going to tell me these people don't *have* a community. Too white, I expect, to count as a community in *your* eyes—"

Then her phone vibrated. She took it out, unlocked it, and forgot all about her racial grievances.

"Huh," she said. She stared at the screen. "Huh."

Then she pulled out the briefcase and programmed the label maker, printed out a name and read it over twice before handing it to Sol to stick on a subpoena. The name was Cléophe Carrette.

⁂ ⁂ ⁂

They parked opposite a closed chip shop on Sanderson Drive with a bleached LEAVE MEANS LEAVE poster on the window. The street was dark, surfaces slick with rain. Donaghy stared up at the windows. She checked out a narrow plyboard door, just left ajar by a departing figure that they quickly assessed wasn't Carrette.

"You dressing up?" Sol asked.

Donaghy nodded. Sol handed her a jacket with delivery service livery. It was very similar to the American postal uniform. He'd never seen anyone in England wear anything like it, but people accepted its cinematic reality.

Donaghy wriggled it on and then pressed her hand to her chest. She made a gulping sound, like the enormity had just hit her. Cléophe Carrette was in that building, just over there—and she was allowed to catch him.

"You okay?"

"I'm okay."

Sol waited for her to go. She didn't.

"You'll be fine."

Donaghy scowled at Sol, but nodded, left the van, and walked up to Carrette's entranceway. Sol watched her prod the door open and disappear inside. Open doors meant legal right of access, according to the GMM rulebook, but it made Sol a little uneasy. What if Donaghy was walking into something—a party, or an altercation?

He scanned the deserted street. The streetlights illuminated a heap of garbage bags on the pavement; evidence of one of the Hasturian Guards' heart-and-minds litter-picking exercises.

What if the guards were in the flat right now?

The question bothered him. He didn't fear for Donaghy's safety, but he disliked the idea that the guards and GMM were colluding to detain Carrette. He wouldn't want to be culpable for whatever the guards were doing to the man.

He pulled on the second American delivery jacket. He counted to ten, watching the door, uncertain whether the counting was merely a sop to cowardice. Finally he got out of the van. The rain misted down through his thinning hair as he crossed the street. The district's streetlights flickered, all at once. He paused. He took another step, and the nearest lamp exploded in a shower of white sparks.

Darkness.

Ahead of him he saw a flickering shape; it was the size of a person, yet his confused senses first mistook it for a moth—a desperate, thoughtless thing, battering against a bulb. The shape—it *was* a person, he realized—flitted out of the curbside shadows and toward Carrette's flat. It moved with impossible speed. He barely had time to register a limb, a vaguely human profile, before it had disappeared into the narrow doorway.

Sol followed. He found an empty set of stairs beneath a yellowish electric bulb. No footsteps, no trace—as if a ghost had just passed through the door ahead of him.

The creaking stairway was short, but by the time he reached the landing, Sol was gasping for breath. The air felt rarefied. The door ahead of him was half-open. Sol stood there and listened. He heard a thumping, a *thwub-thwub* sound, that might have been his heartbeat. He heard Donaghy's voice. Donaghy was just behind the door.

Some kind of negotiation was going on. Sol considered returning to the car, but couldn't bring himself to set all the steps creaking on the way back down. Just the thought of those creaking stairs awakened a sense memory that gripped his stomach and provoked his gag reflex. He thought of wooden hulls trapped in ice, fingernails bent back, plastics deformed into the shape of an irrupting force. He stood there, holding his breath, listening.

He couldn't tune into what Donaghy was saying, but it seemed she was asking questions, playing a hardboiled cop getting a confession from a perp. But then everything twisted, and Sol realized it was Donaghy who was confessing. Yes. Donaghy was weeping. He started to perceive the weight of Donaghy's guilt. The slimy, nasty things she'd done. Racist. Liar. Litterbug. Sol found himself thinking, *don't give away any more*. Donaghy was being misled. Whoever she was confessing to, they weren't going to forgive her. They were listening and making notes. They would punish her.

Then Sol realized he hadn't been listening to anything at all. The room next door was silent. His heartbeat was going *thwub-thwub* in his head.

He was afraid now.

He didn't move, but the door in front of him crept open. It made the tiniest *zipping* sound, like stiff little fibers snapping. He looked at the floor, appearing behind the swinging door. It was linoleum. Yellowish. The doorway was clear now. Sol tried to look up. He couldn't move his neck, so he forced his eyes. He saw the skirting board, marks in the floor. Then finally he got the message through to his neck and his neck responded. His head moved. He heard the popping and crunching of muscles and tendons. That was his body, going *pop pop creak*. He was looking around. The room held two sofas, a pile of newspapers, photos of New York on the walls. Everything was normal. But the walls were sweating, and there was a heavy vibration running through everything, like a disconnected bass amp. Sol felt sick. A bright white light was shining out of a corridor to the right. Bright as a halogen lamp. A grow farm? No.

Sol kept looking at the mark on the floor. It was a gouge. It was part of a scraped line, like a drag mark, leading down the corridor.

He was moving now. His feet took him across the room, toward the light. It was blindingly bright, and something smelled bad. Hot tar. Fireworks. Barbecue—*bad* barbecue, the worst of barbecue.

The corridor was narrow with blazing light at the end. Sol shut his eyes and his eyelids throbbed pinkish-orange. The light was hot. The smell was acrid. There was his heartbeat again. Donaghy's voice came and went. Looping around and around: questions, answers, crying, laughing. Sol took a single step forward. Blinked his eyes open a couple of times. He was staring into an explosion. Just hot light. Roaring light.

He kept thinking about Donaghy. He saw her like a cartoon, drawn with light. A strobe or a laser. She was progressing down narrowing corridors, running between linear indications of perspective. The lines kept shaking and wriggling. He saw sketches of soldiers. Hooks, wires, straps. Donaghy was on her knees. She was bowing to something. Higgins. No. Somebody. A king. In a crown. He smelled sulphur. Flashes. He felt a burning sensation in a spot on his arm.

When Sol opened his eyes again, he saw the outline of a door on his right and a nautical themed sign that said "Bathroom," and it acted like a signal for his guts. He pushed through the door into a darker space and purple streamers floated over his vision as he found a toilet and puked.

This puking went on for a while. Then he dropped off the toilet bowl and the bathroom floor folded around him. It was made of electricity. When his heart beat, the colors in the room changed. Every color in the rainbow. Red. Orange. Yellow. Gave battle in vain.

Nothing.

Eventually the shape of the room pulsed together again. There was a toilet and a tub. Medicines on shelves. Sol was on the floor, but he could get up again. The door was open, framing Donaghy in her foolish postal uniform, holding her subpoena like a broken sword. There was no light behind her. Everything was cool and dark.

"Carrette's dead," she sobbed. "We have to call the police."

Virology and mimesis occupied my mind as I trawled the web for Yellow Signs. This wasn't idle research: wherever I found references to Carcosa I would look for connections to the ALI, to Carrette, to Judith Bea. I was convinced that something awful had happened to Judith after she was hauled off campus. She'd disappeared. Her phone was dead, her social media selves evaporated. I wandered down the shady lane to her house one evening to find it empty.

I left messages where I could: posts in forums and chat threads. One such forum, the Aldebaran Gazette, was made up like a 1920s newspaper and when you posted comments, they appeared in the "Letters from Esteemed Readers" column in a newsprint typeface. For a fee, you could post a message in the "Classifieds" column. My message for Judith read: "I want to know The Truth of Carcosa. DM me JB. Louis."

I camped out on the Aldebaran Gazette after posting there, engaging virtual passers-by with questions. I learned little about them, besides the fact that they believed immigrants were pedophiles, but I was surprised at how interested they were in me. Hard to admit I was flattered. But loneliness has been a consistent theme in my life. In the chatrooms of the Aldebaran Gazette I found people who were curious about me: my linguistic ideas, my philosophies—and, frankly, how I was feeling.

I was feeling dreadful, of course. Confused, frightened. I didn't share the nature of my fears online, but my correspondents—these grotesques, these brutal subhuman fools—actually seemed to notice my anxiety, and offered what comfort they could.

I entered into a lengthy discussion with a user named "Yellow_Sp1der" whom I soon suspected to be my old friend Spider (or "James") himself. His spelling hadn't improved, and his opinions had certainly deteriorated, but something in our discourse reminded me of why we'd spent time together in the past. Despite his bountiful flaws, I cannot deny the rush of warmth I felt when I saw that Yellow_Sp1der was online.

Not that either of us removed our masks, so to speak—our aliases remained intact. And not that I was suborned into the Hasturian Guard's fetid schemes. I am NOT a racist. But. I began to perceive a complexity—and an opportunity: Worthless sacks of skin as the Guard may be, they aren't entirely without use.

20

Sol and Donaghy's debrief took place in a warehouse. A senior manager named O'Dowd conducted the interview. He was older, with an officer's mustache, but his speech had a modern-professional veneer, calculatedly informal and full of subtly threatening phrases like "going forward." The warehouse seemed to be O'Dowd's personal fiefdom. There was a bay full of vehicles and tarp-wrapped machinery, and a raised loading area with a glass-walled office. The office resembled a bunkhouse, with a daybed alongside the computer suite. Sol guessed O'Dowd worked in Enforcement.

"And what did you see on your way out?" O'Dowd asked. He was sitting on a swiveling office chair; Donaghy and Sol were on folding camp chairs, drinking tea—hot and sweet, for shock.

"Nothing," Sol said. "Everything was back to normal."

"No traces?"

Sol remembered seeking out the source of the light. He remembered what he saw in the kitchen.

"Ash. There was ash on the kitchen floor."

He remembered the feeling of relief that washed over him after the light and sound stopped. Like when a big piece of machinery that had been running long and loudly shut off without warning, and in that yawning silence you went, *Oh. So that's what the world sounds like*.

"Thanks," said O'Dowd, making notes.

"It was Carrette," Donaghy said.

"What do you mean?"

"He was burned up."

"Are you sure it was him?"

Donaghy took her phone out and showed a photograph to O'Dowd. O'Dowd took the device between his fingertips. He peered at it.

"Are you sure it was him?" he repeated. "Think carefully."

"Yes."

"How sure?"

"On the balance of probabilities."

"Did you see him die?"

"Perhaps."

"Oh, dear. This isn't very helpful."

"I think they were using some kind of sound gun," Sol interjected. "To confuse us. Maybe light, too. Some kind of sensory overload, to incapacitate us."

"Interesting. They? Who?"

"I don't know. Do you?"

O'Dowd made a note. Donaghy looked away.

"Miss Donaghy."

"Jennifer."

"Jennifer, quick question: Did you *serve* Mr. Carrette before this incident occurred?" Donaghy pulled the subpoena from her jacket pocket. The plastic case remained untouched, the seal unbroken. O'Dowd groaned. "Please answer, Miss Donaghy, for the record."

"No."

O'Dowd stepped out onto the loading area to take a call. Sol started to feel uncomfortably warm, and unwrapped himself from his emergency reflective blanket. Sol and Donaghy looked at each other. Sol felt suddenly icky about Donaghy. Something to do with the intimacy of the experience they'd just shared. Like a one-night stand. Sol wanted to get away, take a shower, forget all about her, but he knew that the knowledge of her would stick, like an unscrubbable scent.

O'Dowd re-entered.

"Do you know who it was, then," Sol asked, "who did this to us? To Mr. Carrette?"

O'Dowd ignored him. He was holding his phone like a pistol recently discharged.

"Jennifer," he said, "I regret to say you've been placed on performance review."

"What?"

"I'm sorry."

"Oh, *come on*!"

"Heads are spinning in the office, Jennifer. They'd chew my ear off for an hour if they could. You *almost* had him, that's the issue. You *almost* cracked the ALI wide open. But you didn't deliver."

Sol was unnerved by O'Dowd; he couldn't place his authority.

"Who *are* you?" he asked.

"Mr. O'Dowd, for now."

"What's your job title?" No answer. "Do you work in Enforcement?"

"I have a roving brief."

"Yes, yes," Donaghy shouted, "he works in fucking Enforcement. Look around you, Joe. He's got crossbows on the fucking walls."

"Jennifer."

"What are you going to do," Donaghy snapped back, "put me on review?"

Sol looked around. There were, in fact, two crossbows mounted on the office wall. One was old and ornamental. The other was new, made of some slick carbon fiber material, and looked deadly. While

Donaghy and O'Dowd argued about Donaghy's job prospects, Sol paid attention to the other kit lying around in the office space. Gym bags and duct tape. *This was it*: a black site. This was where GMM Enforcement teams took the people they served.

And where exactly was he? How did he get here? He attempted a mental map: the route out of the city on the main road, then the loops of the commercial estate, the rows of parked trucks, the intruding vines, the flooded wetlands, lit up by headlights. His phone could map everything out for him, of course; but O'Dowd took it before driving them to the warehouse. And O'Dowd hadn't returned Donaghy's phone, either.

Black site. Incommunicado.

"Mr. Sol," O'Dowd said now, "I want to backtrack now to a comment you made earlier. I'm interested in what you said about, uh, *sonic weapons*. Why would you say that?"

"There was a sound," Sol said.

"Did *you* hear this sound?" O'Dowd asked Donaghy.

"Maybe. I don't know."

O'Dowd turned back to Sol.

"What was the sound like?"

"A hum. A vibration."

O'Dowd noted it down.

"Anything else?"

"It was a . . . confusing vibration."

"Confusing how? Be specific."

"Multiple sounds in one. Like you'd think it was one sound, but it was another."

"*Confusing*. What about you, Jennifer?"

"I don't know."

Back to Sol.

"Multiple sounds, like listening to the radio between stations, by any chance?"

"Yes. A bit like that."

"Music or talk radio?"

"Talk radio."

"I see. Jennifer?"

Donaghy didn't know.

"A voice you recognize, Mr. Sol?"

"Yes."

"Thanks. Whose voice?"

Sol pointed at Donaghy.

"Hers."

"That's bullshit," Donaghy shouted, "it was *your* voice! It was his voice, not mine! Saying all these fucked-up things."

"What things?"

"Talking about *me*."

O'Dowd made a note.

"What are you writing down?" Donaghy demanded.

"I am writing that Mr. Sol heard Jennifer's voice, and Jennifer heard Mr. Sol's voice. Is that accurate?"

Nobody said anything for a while.

"I want you to call me Ms. Donaghy from now on," said Donaghy.

"Of course."

"What does it mean?" Sol asked.

"It means we're going to have to extend the debrief."

"What does that mean?"

"It means we're stuck, Joe," Donaghy said. "It means we'll be bunking up for a night or two."

Black site. Incommunicado.

O'Dowd tapped his pen on his clipboard.

"This is one of those moments, Mr. Sol, where GMM requires a little flexibility from you. I hope you didn't have any weekend plans."

Sol considered this.

"No, none."

"We've got a bit of a knot to work out, you see."

"I'm happy to pitch in."

"There's a good boy. I knew we could count on you."

My search for Judith Bea ultimately took me to the Berryman. Other than the ALI, it was the only place I'd seen her. I frequented the pub for a week, and Judith didn't turn up. Since I was now in the pub every night, I got to recognize the regulars. Old white blokes, mainly, upset about the world. Every night a Hasturian Guard would come in and scan the local notices to make sure nothing seditious was getting posted on the walls. This was new and unwelcome to most drinkers. Another regular customer caught my attention. He, too, was old and white, but not so old as most. He had salt-and-pepper hair and a mustache. He looked like a PE teacher: lean, with mean black eyes. His left arm was in a sling.

The PE teacher knew nobody. He drank alone, and slowly, and never got drunk.

I usually leave pubs before closing time. There's an intensity to those last fifteen minutes that makes me feel uncomfortable. But one night I must have gotten caught up with scrolling through the Aldebaran Gazette. It felt like I'd just picked up my phone, but before I knew it, the landlord was running a broom over my feet. I missed my usual bus, and had to wait outside for the next one, which was how I saw the PE teacher leave.

He was the last to exit the pub, but he wasn't weaving or swaying like the other regulars. He strolled out, looking neat and tidy as ever, left arm still wrapped in its neat bandage, and got into a waiting vehicle. A van painted imperial blue. When he opened the passenger door, the interior light came on and I got a glimpse of the driver: a priest. He was wearing a dog collar, and a cassock, and everything. But I felt instantly convinced that the priest outfit was a disguise. It didn't fit the man: He was too muscular and dense-looking, and his haircut—I thought—resembled a soldier's crewcut.

I watched the fake priest exchange a few words with the fake drinker. Their interaction confirmed my suspicion: These were GMM men, and they too were searching for Judith Bea. Then they shut the passenger door, the light went off, and they drove away.

21

"You didn't play that quite right," Donaghy said. She stretched out on her bunk and tapped her fingers against the wall. Steel resonated. The chamber—a shipping container—echoed.

"What are you talking about?"

"You didn't look shocked enough. Your average fellow doesn't just accept he's getting kidnapped by the boss. O'Dowd will figure you already knew something about his methods."

"How much did *you* know?"

"I knew they kept people sometimes. I didn't know they did it in shipping containers, but I probably should have guessed, hey?"

"Who do they keep?"

"Not everybody. This might not just be about the Archimboldi Deposit. There are other contracts. There's overlap."

"How do you know?"

"I've been working for this firm for fifteen years. When we got the Xanthic Spectrum contract a whole new department was set up, with new training, a separate office, the works. Once in a while someone would come by who you didn't recognize and who looked—well, a bit like Mr. O'Dowd. And there were whispers, you know."

"Whispers?"

The door unlocked and opened. O'Dowd's head bobbed in.

"How are you lot holding up in here?"

"Great."

"Good stuff. Sorry we took so long. We're rushed off our feet. I've got another training I want to run through with you, though. If you have a minute."

"I think we have a minute."

They left the shipping container and inhaled the marginally fresher air of the vehicle bay. It was brighter here: The whitewashed, windowless walls reflected more light. O'Dowd led them up the ramp to the office.

Inside, the two camp chairs had been drawn up in front of a TV set on a wheeled frame. There was a little table nearby with a coffee press, sealed plastic jugs of milk, and stained mugs. One of the mugs said BEST DAD EVER.

They sat and O'Dowd turned off the overhead light.

"I expect you're wondering what happened today and why we're so keen to keep you with us right now. I could tell you straight up, but I'm fairly sure you wouldn't believe me. So we've got a presentation prepared. There are two videos. I'd be grateful if you'd save your questions until you've watched them both."

* * *

Video one was a piece of VHS footage. The resolution was vibrant and grainy, the date stamp in the corner read 06/04/1994. The action started in the back of a van, where the camera operator trained the shot on two men pulling equipment out of a lockbox. Both men acted with the professional nonchalance of tradesmen about to start a job, but they were dressed as priests: one in a long black cassock, the other in a dark jumper and dog collar.

Both priests jumped out of the back of the van and started walking with purpose up an overgrown country lane.

Cut to a close-up shot of an old gate slamming shut.

"Why would Bredsky leave that open?" Jumper Priest asked. It seemed to be a grand gate, perhaps the threshold to some country estate. Jumper Priest bolted it and led the party onward beneath swaying trees.

"Somebody else is here," Cassock Priest said. The camera followed his pointing finger toward an ambulance. The priests picked up the pace, and it was all shakycam and footsteps, brogues on gravel and lawn.

They stepped into the shadow of some large old manor house and the picture resolved into two paramedics in green polo-neck shirts, one carrying a bulky backpack.

Now the paramedics were walking single-file on a slate-topped wall between grass and a still body of water. The priests followed the paramedics. One of the paramedics was sure-footed, but the other kept stopping and tensing up as if about to fall.

Cut to a set of wet slate steps in deep shadow.

"Listen," Cassock Priest told the paramedics, "we'll go in first. See what the situation is. We'll let you know."

Fumbling with keys, Jumper Priest was working on a lock in a trapdoor at the base of the structure. Then a loud CLANG and—swing back—the door yawned open, a shadow containing the glints of bottles in a row. Cassock Priest pulled out a floor plan in a polythene pocket. He switched on the headlamp on his forehead.

"Bredsky?" he called out timidly. "Bredsky?" he said again, even quieter. His eyes were wide. "Come on then," he said to Jumper Priest. The camera followed Jumper Priest between dusty rows of wine bottles, then up a set of stairs into cleaner corridors, similarly unlit but with daylight illuminating the carpet beneath unshuttered windows. Grey institutional carpet; green institutional walls.

The priests hustled. The camera paused on a door labeled CONSULTATION ROOM 4, which had bars over its peephole window.

"Bredsky?"

The priests were in an office space, with filing cabinets and boxes of papers, a fax machine, phones, and a chunky computer. Cassock Priest whipped out a tool bag and unscrewed the back of the computer. Jumper Priest wavered a little, then pulled a wastepaper basket out from under the desk and started filling it with paper out of the printer and the fax and specific drawers.

Now the camera operator walked away from the priests, down the corridors. For the first time, the camera operator spoke: "Bredsky!" It was O'Dowd's voice—younger, perhaps; a little more melodic. O'Dowd clumped up carpeted stairs. The higher he went the dimmer it was, and the more muffled his voice became as he called out. The stairwells were steeper, fit now only for single-file traffic. The windows were tiny and fogged with condensation. The camera showed O'Dowd's hand pressed against the wall. Another set of narrow stairs. Another tight corridor. O'Dowd was breathing heavily. Something was scratching at the porthole window.

"Bredsky?" O'Dowd whispered.

A distant thumping sound.

The camera whipped round. Down the stairs again, two at a time, heavy breathing.

"Russo!" O'Dowd shouted. "Russo, where is she?"

Wisps of smoke drew through the frame.

Back in the office, everything was still again. The metal wastepaper basket contained a blaze of papers. In the center of the room, a desk had been pulled out of place. Kneeling beside it, his head in his hands, was Jumper Priest. On the table, a disabled fire alarm came into view, its batteries lying beside it, and a muddy footprint. Now O'Dowd panned up to the ceiling, where a square hole led to some crawl space.

Jumper Priest groaned. O'Dowd shouted, "Russo!"

In the square above, smoke was briefly visible.

The camera retraced a path, from the flaming wastepaper basket, to the fire alarm, the footprint on the table, the trapdoor above, Jumper Priest on the ground below.

"You fucking clowns," O'Dowd said. "You smoked yourselves out, you idiots." On the floor, Jumper Priest shook his head. Above, the smoke skeins moved again. But something was strange: The smoke in the crawl space wasn't like that rising from the fire. It seemed an entirely separate smoke: paler, thicker, like mud roiling at the bottom of the ocean.

O'Dowd clambered onto the table beneath the trapdoor. The camera was lifted, tilted, and placed just inside the lip of the trapdoor frame while O'Dowd started hauling himself through the gap. As the lens aperture adjusted, the shapes of boxes emerged out of the shadows. Something else, too, resolved slowly into form: a crouched figure, and the back of a pair of hands covering a face.

O'Dowd gasped. Everything creaked. The hands were the Cassock Priest's hands and they were covering his face. Something awful had happened here. The camera tilted and O'Dowd was falling backward. He grabbed one of Russo's arms. Russo didn't react. Russo's raised arms were stiff, like a mannequin's arms, and didn't leave his face. They were clamped. Glued. Elbows scraped against the wood, and after a second of strain there was a wet tearing sound like sticky tape unrolling, and the hands came away from the face—no, the face was actually peeling away—*sluurrp*—ripping from the skull like a rubber mask—and for a few frames a sad, empty-eyed visage of gore and teeth filled the screen, and then O'Dowd dropped the camera.

That was the end of the first video.

Sol sipped his coffee. It was cold. His arm itched a little. He looked at Donaghy, who glanced at him but remained largely focused on the AV setup, where the present-day O'Dowd—aged, it seemed, by the things he'd seen—was starting another video.

22

The second video had an interview room setup. Bare walls, electric light, table center and forward, an interview subject seated, addressing the unseen interrogator. The date on the tape read 07/04/1994. The subject was O'Dowd.

"The very beginning?" he asked the interviewer. Then he nodded. "I met Bredsky the same day I first met Archimboldi. Archimboldi had just got his prognosis, and he got Bredsky to call us first. The assumption was, Bredsky was his agent. But she seemed a bit more than that. Call it a guru-student relationship. Archimboldi trusted her implicitly. She was in the house every day, supposedly putting affairs in order.

"Archimboldi was in this big suburban house out in Bromley. Full of paintings and antiques. Bredsky met us at the door, took us into the parlor, gave us coffee. She was definitely trying to sus us out. Asked a few casual questions. I think she was priming us, in a way, for what we were going to hear."

[Question, inaudible.]

"She wanted to know whether we were going to run out the door when Archimboldi told us what he thought was going on. We weren't going to do that. People have all sorts of reasons for setting up their wills how they want them. We don't have to believe everything they believe. It's a transaction, in the end. Business.

"Once she'd decided we were up for it, Bredsky led us into a room set up like an oxygen chamber. Plastic all over the walls and this inflatable soft airlock to get in. Walls lined with gas canisters hissing all the time. And Archimboldi inside. He was lucid half the time. The rest of the time he wasn't exactly ranting and raving, but he wasn't well."

[Cut. The scene returned virtually unchanged, except O'Dowd looked more serious.]

"He thought he'd brought a curse into the world and the only way to rectify it was for us to destroy everything he'd written. That's it in a nutshell."

[Inaudible from the interviewer. O'Dowd rolled his eyes.]

"You don't have to believe it, what's important is that *he* believed it. He was a writer. He thought he'd written a genuinely evil book. It was like the *Necromunicon* or something. How do you say it?"

[Inaudible from the interviewer.]

"An old evil book out of a horror movie. I thought it was strange, yes. But not *that* strange. He was writing, and what he wrote was important to him, so if he felt any paranoia, it makes sense that it would focus on his writing. If he were painting pictures, he probably would have asked us to destroy his pictures. You understand? Because it ultimately related back to him, you know? That's what paranoia is, it's inflated self-regard. I mean *non-pathological paranoia*, you understand.

"He said that ten years ago he'd been subject to a spiritual crisis. The only person who could reach him in this dark period was Dr. Bredsky. He held her in this incredible regard, as if she'd saved his life. But before Dr. Bredsky rode in like a knight in shining armor, he said, his madness had caused him to produce a terrible piece of work. A manuscript called *The Truth of Carcosa*. After he sent this manuscript to the publisher, terrible things started happening. His publisher killed himself. The printing press burned down. You know already that these events actually occurred. The writer saw what was happening and called for Dr. Bredsky. Thanks to her ministrations, Archimboldi realized that for months now he'd been reading and working in a dream, producing a body of work that he now understood to be purely evil. So he burned his notes. He ordered his new book be recalled. Most copies were pulped.

"But a few remained, he said. They needed to be destroyed. That's why he needed help. And if we didn't believe him, he said, we should look at his hand, this mark on his hand. He showed us his hand. He said, *do you see the yellow sign?* I didn't see a thing. I said, yes, I see it, let me draw you up a contract."

[Inaudible from interviewer]

"Why argue with a man who's dying? A man who's grieving, guilty, wanting to make amends? And anyway, he *did* keep scratching his arm. And I sent the draft to you, didn't I? I haven't heard any complaints about it so far. Seems I did this firm a service."

[Cut. Slight change in light. Perhaps a door had closed. Perhaps the sun was setting.]

"Bredsky? No, I didn't hear anything more from Bredsky after that day. I went on other projects until the writer died. Then the contract came into effect, and we started gathering up his possessions. I wanted to consult with Bredsky, since I thought she had a kind of official status as agent or something. But we couldn't get hold of her.

"Now there's very little publicly known about Bredsky. I started digging. I determined that Bredsky was the director of a marketing company called Prism. The registered address was a warehouse, a shell address in Kent. I wrote up an inquiry, specifying Bredsky and Prism, and ran it up to Comus, and they sent it out on InterLaw for all the branches and partners. That's when we got a hit from Russo.

"Russo wasn't on the books, you understand, but he was on the InterLaw network, so we must have worked together at some point. He said he knew Prism and he'd met Bredsky; they weren't actually in Kent, obviously, but this great big castle in the West Country. Pentorgan House.

"Russo didn't have the exact address but he'd been there, and he could find it in person, and since he was in some old priests' home in Somerset I could pick him up on the way to the South Hams. That's what I did. He brought along someone from his organization, a younger fellow, while my partner couldn't make it, so, as per protocol, since I was alone, I brought the camcorder. Russo navigated. Once we got there, I started filming."

[Inaudible from interviewer]

"Yes, that's where the tape starts. We didn't get straight to Pentorgan House, since Russo didn't remember so precisely where it was. You've seen the tape. We walked for maybe an hour. And when we got to the house, we weren't alone.

"Apparently Bredsky had called an ambulance. We never found out what for. It was awkward, since we had no right to be there, but Russo did the talking, and the paramedics agreed to let us tag along. You'd be surprised what you can get away with in a cassock."

[Inaudible from the interviewer. O'Dowd smiled.]

"Russo, I'll admit, he jumped on the opportunity. You'd expect a little more circumspect attitude from a priest, I suppose! But really, he had his own job to do. They gained entry to the cellar and I followed them through to the office. They started looking through files. I started looking for Bredsky."

[Inaudible from the interviewer.]

"It became clear to me, after I heard a sound, that the following events had occurred: Russo's partner was disposing of files using a kind of makeshift burner. To do this, they'd disabled the fire alarm. And apparently in so doing they'd discovered the trapdoor to the crawl space above the office. And apparently Russo had gone up there. Then whatever happened, happened."

[Inaudible from interviewer. O'Dowd shrugged.]

"There'd been a fire or shock hot enough to fuse the skin together. I'd heard that could happen with lightning strikes. So. His hands were raised like *this*, so I assume he tried to protect himself. He was on his knees. There was some atmospheric evidence. A little smoke, vapor, a smell in the air like . . . *tar*. As well as the smell of, you know, cooking. There were about fifteen boxes in the crawl space. The labels said they contained proofs from Archimboldi's publishers, but what was really in them I never investigated. They were mainly intact, but one had a burn on it. That's as much as I investigated. I figured this was outside my realm of expertise. So I put out the urgent call. My responsibility ended when the cleanup team arrived."

[Inaudible from interviewer. O'Dowd flinched.]

"I informed the paramedics that Bredsky wasn't on the premises. They treated it as job done. Relieved to get out. And to be fair, we didn't find Bredsky. Did you find Bredsky?"

[O'Dowd grinned. A shit-eating grin. Cut.]

For some time the Emergency Cabinet had been warning us that the will of the people couldn't be constrained much longer. Their every concession to the patriots leading the strikes in the docks and power plants had been derailed, it seemed, by weak-willed holdovers of the liberal regime. Enemies within and without continued to defy calls for patriotic action. Now came a special announcement, delivered by somber officials in sharkskin suits. The Cabinet was reaching the end of their tether. They were very close, they warned, to washing their hands of it. If those who made themselves targets for England's righteous fury couldn't exercise self-control, couldn't rein it in a little, couldn't make themselves less visibly aberrant, then the government could no longer guarantee their protection.

The next day the Hasturian Guard annexed a housing estate in the north of the city. A week later, a mob conducted a lynching on the grounds of the municipal sports center, and journalists were instructed not to report on it. The next day, three journalists disappeared.

Life continued, sketchily. People worked and stockpiled. I felt impelled to post inspirational analyses of The King in Yellow on the Aldebaran Gazette. They were well received. In the evenings, I walked streets enervated by frightening possibility. My route led to Hourglass Lodge, and the road on which the House of the Dead Man sat. I walked up that street and scanned the houses—ordinary-looking terraced homes with bay windows and comfortable lives inside—and tried to remember which spackled facade hid my house from me.

And I couldn't.

But at that very moment I received the first important response to my ad in the Aldebaran Gazette. It came in the form of a voice message—just two words: "Hello, Louis."

It was Judith's voice.

"Where are you? Are you okay? Do you need help?"

She was safe, she replied. But yes, she did need help. Would I be able to provide it?

"What do you want?"

"Nineteen eighty-four."

My apprehensions were confirmed. Nineteen eighty-four: the year Archimboldi wrote The Truth of Carcosa. She was after the book.

"The files from 1984, in the cold room?"

"Yes."

"What do you want it for?" I asked. I was walking. The sun had set and the people in the street had fearful eyes. They crossed the road to avoid me.

"It's . . . important."

"I can't just go there and grab it out of the archive," I said. But as I said so, I knew I could. Still more, I wanted to. Burgling the cold room had the romance of a signal crime, the echo of a door closing forever.

"You're clever. You can."

"Why?" I repeated.

"I'll tell you later. In person."

I felt slightly offended by the teasing way she pronounced "in person," as if she were trying to tempt me, had mistaken me for a far lonelier and less intelligent person than I am. Nonetheless, I can't deny my agreement was secured.

"Where do you want me to bring it?"

"The Berryman. Two days' time. Please, Louis, call it another favor. I know it's not fair, but I need this."

23

Same interview room setup. Same bare walls, same electric light, table center and forward, an interview subject seated in front of a thin pile of papers covered in handwriting. The date on the tape read 08/04/1994. The subject was the priest who wore a jumper in the first video. He was now wearing a freshly laundered set of exercise gear. His hood was pulled tight around his face. He looked younger without his religious getup. More innocent. He read from the statement in front of him.

"My name is Bruno Schultz. I accompanied Father Russo to Pentorgan House with Mr. O'Dowd on April 4, 1994. I was in the office with Father Russo when the accident happened. Mr. O'Dowd was not there and neither was any other employee of Giovanni, Metti & Metti LLC."

[Schultz scratched his arm.]

"I first became aware of the accident when I heard a noise in the crawl space above. Russo had gone up there to find some documents."

[Inaudible from interviewer.]

"The documents pertained to a legally privileged matter."

[Inaudible from interviewer. Schultz took a breath and returned to his prepared statement.]

"I first became aware of the accident when I heard a noise . . . I looked up to the trapdoor and called Russo's name. Then I was knocked to the floor."

[Inaudible from interviewer. Schultz scratched his arm while answering.]

"It was a loud noise. If I had to describe it, I'd say it was . . . mixed. And loud. Like lots of different noises together."

[Inaudible.]

"Not like an explosion. Like a wave. I actually went up to the trapdoor because I thought Russo was calling for me. I had this weird feeling."

[Cut to:]

"No it wouldn't be right to call it an explosion. Or I didn't realize it was an explosion until after it was finished. I could hear Russo talking to somebody, and I . . . I was jealous."

[Cut to: Schultz was scratching his arm. The puckered edges of his hood were dark with sweat.]

"It doesn't matter what I was thinking, though, does it? In the end what happened to Russo wasn't about me. It was about whatever was in those boxes up there, wasn't it?"

* * *

Cut to the same scene, but with the screen divided in half.

The left-hand side showed Schultz attempting to sleep on the interview table.

The right-hand side displayed a similar space, but with an empty table.

In the left-hand feed, a shadow passed the frosted glass of the door behind Schultz.

In the right-hand feed, a door opened. A person in a full protective biohazard suit entered carrying a cardboard box. They looked like Gumby, the rubbery, stretched cartoon character with a square head. This Gumby person laid the cardboard box on the table, then unrolled a canvas roll full of tools. They selected a fat scalpel and moved the blade quickly and smoothly through the taped-up lid of the box, and stepped neatly back, waiting for something dramatic to happen.

In the left-hand feed, Schultz twitched.

In the right-hand feed, the Gumby person opened the cardboard flaps and illuminated the oblong objects stacked within the box. Books. The Gumby person gestured to the camera. Frustrated shrug. They retreated to the door. It closed behind them. Stillness.

In the left-hand feed, a shadow passed the window behind Schultz. He scratched his arm. Slowly, like a cataract forming on the screen, a tendril of smoke appeared, rising from his hood. Schultz's hands started moving over the table. Rubbing and wiping. Like he was trying to clear something invisible off the surface. Trying to scuttle through the silt at the bottom of the ocean. His head remained pinned to the tabletop. The smoke stream intensified. Schultz's movements sped up until he was unmistakably *writhing*. The smoke was dense and opaque, rendering the soundless footage surreal; it was a plume dividing the feed neatly in two, a weird irruption with scrabbling claws.

In the background the shadow reappeared in the window. The door flew open, and the Gumby person was there, gesturing shock and confusion. Then they disappeared from the doorway, and reappeared seconds later in the right-hand feed, edging that door open and peering around the corner to see that nothing, absolutely nothing, seemed to be happening.

Finally, after a long delay, they moved forward and grabbed the table on which the box was sitting. The box on top slid toward the table edge. Then the Gumby person pulled clumsily, too hard, and the box toppled over, and a single book tumbled onto the floor, where it slid faster and further than natural toward the foreground.

The left-hand feed went black.

In the right-hand feed, a silent shock wave sent the Gumby person sprawling. The fallen book was now faintly smoking. Another figure in a Gumby suit appeared, seized the box with its remaining contents, and exited at speed. The fallen Gumby person pulled themselves to their feet. They were perhaps ten feet from the book. The pages were lifted by some unnatural breeze. The Gumby person edged toward it. Eventually they crept close enough to the book to grab one corner with clumsy, heavily gloved hands. They gingerly slid it back across the floor and out the door. When they were halfway across the room, the left-hand feed reappeared.

The space that Schultz previously occupied was empty: empty table; empty, overturned chair. No smoke, no ash, no soot. For a few seconds both feeds were still. Two empty rooms. Then a Gumby person edged open the door to Schultz's room. They stood in the hallway. Their black square visor showed nothing. But their hands shook. They stepped forward, once, then immediately retracted their foot. And from underneath Schultz's table, slow as wax, something pale started to emerge.

End.

24

"The incident you just saw occurred in 1994. Yes, I was there, that was me."

"You used to be a real firecracker," Donaghy said. O'Dowd blinked.

"What was actually in those boxes?" Sol asked. "Looked like books to me."

"They looked a lot like books to me, too: proofs of a book Archimboldi wrote, named *The Truth of Carcosa*. And they *were* that. But they were also something more."

"You believe what the old man said about a curse?" asked Sol. "Evil books?"

"Not for a second. But the evidence shows that they were hazardous."

"Hazardous like a weapon?"

"Hazardous like a hazard. It's speculation to go further than that. The footage looks strange, I acknowledge. A little spooky. But ultimately we treat it like what it is: evidence of exposure to hazardous materials."

"What happened to the young priest?"

"He died. Eventually."

"How?"

"His body suffered burns, similar to those on Russo's body."

"Radiation burns?" asked Sol.

"Good guess, but no. There was no evidence of radiation anywhere in Pentorgan House or the holding facility."

"Chemical weapons? Biological?"

"No evidence of known chemical or biological agents were discovered."

"What *was* discovered?"

"Marks. The bodies had marks on them. They were hard to identify, given their state, but we determined that they weren't abrasions, burns, or tattoos."

O'Dowd turned the TV back on and navigated through the *GMM Intranet* interface until he found two image files, side by side, labeled RUSSO and SCHULTZ. Both images were zoomed in tight on the subject's skin, close enough for pores and charred hairs to be visible, with the mark—not an abrasion, burn, or tattoo—centered. Each mark was similar, but distinct. The rationale to their composition escaped Sol. They looked a little like abstract hieroglyphs or QR codes.

As if on cue, though, he scratched his arm. Donaghy, too, scratched her knee. O'Dowd clocked it.

"Whatever the substance was in those boxes of proofs, it didn't act in a simple way. It wasn't like anthrax, where you get one whiff of the powder and then the disease takes its course; or plutonium, where you get exposed for a certain amount of time and get correspondingly sick. None of the technicians got sick, even though they were as close to the boxes as anybody else. Nor did they receive marks on their skin. So we started operating on two assumptions. The first was that some set of catalysts was at play here, activating the previously inert material. The second assumption was that the mark on the skin was an indicator of activation. This substance doesn't affect everybody equally or predictably, but these two assumptions haven't been disproved yet. Not in thirty years."

"What are the catalysts?"

O'Dowd stared at Sol. Then he decided to keep talking.

"It's weird," he said. "These are *books*, like you pointed out. And the first catalyst is that somebody has to read some part of them. When the cleanup team pulled the crates out of Pentorgan House, one of them had been opened, and one book removed, and it seemed that the Cipher—sorry, Father Russo—had started looking through it. But from what we can tell, Father Schultz didn't even touch the books. So just by reading the book, Father Russo seemed to have activated something that didn't then stop."

"So Carrette . . . ?"

"We can assume he had a copy. We can assume he started reading it."

"What are the other catalysts?"

"Hard to say. Affected parties claim to have seen . . . disturbances . . . shortly before Deferrals occur."

"*Deferrals?*" Donaghy asked. She seemed incredulous, as if she'd heard the phrase before in a completely different context.

"Sorry. Explosions. Reactions."

"Disturbances . . ." Sol murmured. He remembered the shadow he glimpsed entering Carrette's apartment, just before the whole reaction (Deferral?) went down.

"Did you see any disturbances?" O'Dowd asked Sol.

"No, nothing," Donaghy interrupted. "Absolutely nothing, and thank you, Mr. O'Dowd, for this, this training has been very helpful, but really, I think it's time we got back to work, don't you?"

"Well, Ms. Donaghy, not so fast. It's best we wait. As I said, this phenomenon doesn't emerge in a linear or simple way. It tends to manifest in clusters. When one incident occurs, we can expect more to follow—at least, in the short term. So we wait, and watch."

"Watch what? What are we watching?" Sol asked.

"It's us," Donaghy replied. "He wants to see whether we've got the marks. That's why he's keeping us."

"Your participation in the observation process is valued," O'Dowd said.

"He's wrong, though, because we don't have any marks. He's wasting his time. He's going to be embarrassed."

O'Dowd got up. Donaghy flinched. Her body language had become tense and stiff, her arms crossed over her chest. O'Dowd seemed tall now. The ranginess of his limbs beneath his pseudo-military getup seemed suddenly important. He handed Donaghy and Sol each a clipboard with photocopied pages and a felt-tip pen.

"At this stage in the observation," he said, "we're going to rely on self-reporting."

The front sheet featured an outline of a human body and some check boxes. Sol's arm was itching. He worked hard not to scratch it.

"There's nothing to report, actually," said Donaghy. "So you can stop wasting our time. Since I'm going on performance review, I wouldn't mind getting a head start on my real work."

"We need you to do this."

"I need you to call Higgins."

"I've spoken to Higgins."

"I need to speak to him myself. I don't care what you think he said. Everything changes once I've had a word."

"I'm sorry, Ms. Donaghy, Mr. Higgins won't have time to talk to you."

"If you want me to cooperate with this self-reporting bullshit, you'll get Higgins down here. Now."

O'Dowd sighed.

"Trust me," Donaghy said, "you'll regret *not* bringing him down. I don't think you know what you're doing, frankly. You'll be glad we can get this sorted nice and quick. Painless."

"I think you should do as she says," Sol added. "He is her mentor, after all."

* * *

They were to wait in the shipping container. They sat in opposite ends. Sol felt certain the itch in his arm intensified when Donaghy was nearby. He didn't mention this to Donaghy. If they didn't talk about it, perhaps it wouldn't be a thing.

They didn't talk at all.

Sol examined the medical questions that accompanied the diagram on the self-reporting sheet. They weren't very systematic. They listed symptoms like bloat, headaches, nightmares, and confusion. Some symptoms were strangely phrased ("monkey laugh") or frankly confusing ("sleepiness, sleeplessness, exhaustion, sleep apnea, sleepwalking, uncontrollable sleeping"). It seemed they'd been copied verbatim from subjects' self-reporting forms. Itching dominated the list: *creeping, crawling, prickling, raw . . .*

Sol dropped the form. He lay down on top of his arm, focusing on the relief brought by the pressure on the limb, the slow deadening of sensation as his circulation was constricted. Projecting himself into a cold, distant place.

Eventually they heard footsteps outside the container. The door had been open the whole time, and they wandered out, half expecting a platoon of armed guards, but there was only one other employee, a young man standing ready to operate the outer shutter. At a signal from O'Dowd, he pressed a big green button.

The shutter rolled upward and a luxury car slid through, easing into place before the shipping container. A back window wound down. Higgins appeared, a look of vague concern on his wrinkled face.

"My girl," he said, "what a conundrum we find ourselves in. What a pickle."

"Can you talk to this man, please, Mr. Higgins?" Donaghy asked, pointing at O'Dowd. "He's preventing me from getting back to work."

Light tone. Making a joke of it. Please let it be a joke.

"Yes, yes, we have spoken. Oh, Jennifer, they tell me Carrette was in your hands."

"It seemed that way for a moment."

"For a moment. Carrette, and the whole ALI. How did it feel, my girl?" Donaghy seemed unable to respond. Unable to do anything at all. Pinned down, in her place, by his vampiric concern. "Yet it all slipped away. I sympathize, I really do. I've seen a lot of young talents come through my office and I've tried to nurture them all. I want to give you succour, my dear, in your moment of weakness. If I could see any route forward for you, I would. Give it. *Succour.*" He sighed.

"What do you mean?" Donaghy murmured.

"I've been working hard to make sure you're kept comfortable. Are you? Is there anything more we can provide to keep you comfortable?"

"Mr. Higgins, I . . ."

"Yes, my dear?"

"I'm sorry . . ."

Donaghy's lip started to twitch. She swallowed—one of those huge, painful *gollums* you make before you break out bawling.

Her transformation into a little girl was almost complete. It was too much for Sol to bear.

"Let us out, you old fuck," he snapped. "We're being held here against our will. Let us out."

Higgins laughed a smoker's laugh. He seemed genuinely delighted, for a second—then his expression hardened. The window rolled up. For a moment they stared at the reflection of the loading bay, with the monolithic shipping container and their tiny silhouettes against it; and then the car smoothly retreated, and the shutter clashed down.

"Why would you say that?" Donaghy hissed at Sol. "You ruined it. You chased him away."

"I'm sorry."

"He was going to help us."

"He was never going to help us."

"I could've persuaded him. I almost cracked it for him, understand? He values me. He would've listened eventually."

"He wouldn't."

"You called him an old fuck. *You're* the fuck!"

"I'm sorry. He's been lying to you all along."

"Fuck you."

"There's no Archimboldi Fund. Don't you see? They want the manuscripts. Whatever power those books contain—that's what they want."

I spent another day typing up my report. I wasn't entirely sure of its purpose, but I supposed it might serve as an explanation of sorts for my colleagues. I printed the report the evening before the heist. The following morning I made sure to arrive at work on time and complete my assigned tasks conscientiously, as if it were an ordinary day. This was easy to accomplish, since I still largely disbelieved I'd go through with the crime. It still had the veneer of the romantic something to idly imagine doing during a tiresome task.

I took my lunch in the smelly, deserted staff room that had become my retreat. I had my rucksack with me, with my Special Report inside. As I ate my sandwich, I pulled it out and started to read.

It quickly struck me that I'd gone horribly wrong. This was insane. These were the musings of a lonely, unhappy person who needed to go back to therapy. I couldn't commit a theft like this and leave this half-baked dross as my confession and testament. I couldn't—I realized—commit a theft in the first place. A cascade of resolutions followed, ushered and attended by the relief of submission to my ordinary fate: I'd return to the office after lunch; on the way, I'd slip the damned report into the confidential paper disposal trash can; I'd do my work properly and perhaps even hang onto my job; I'd practice my meditations on the Cipher and renew my mantra chanting, call my parents, see how they were doing, if they needed something, would they like to see me.

Having thus rid myself of my burdens, I felt elated and exhausted. I decided to take a power nap. Just in time, I remembered to pull my housekeys out of my pocket and clasp them before me as I settled onto the sofa. Waves of waking dream substance washed overhead, and I felt my hand tense then relax as my body fought then accepted sleep. I felt the cold keys hang off my heavy fingers. I felt the cold, and the heavy, and the fingers and the keys all disembodied and disconnected, as my palm opened and the keys detached to accelerate into limitless space, infinite time . . .

The sound of the keys hitting the floor woke me. But I was in darkness. With open eyes I saw nothing. What I'd always feared had actually come to pass: I'd overslept in the staff room. I'd slept through the working day, and night had overcome me, and I was alone in the bowels of the Institute.

Instinct warned me not to turn the light on. Instead I used what little moonlight entered the window to help me scan the floor. I found the housekeys (a fish scale winking in the deep) and my bag (a predatory shadow); I groped to the door.

The corridor was lit with low emergency lights that intensified the silty green tones, and I knew I was going to rob the cold room. The knowledge was a thrill—a deviant, sexual thrill—and acknowledging this, knowing I could just as easily ejaculate over the walls or curl out a turd in some corner as break into the cold room—calmly knowing that these outrageous outcomes were equal possibilities sealed my determination to commit the theft.

In this feral state of mind I followed the corridor. I opened doors with my key card. Diddly-dee. Inside the office I paused to finger the clothes on the coatrack. I recognized by scent my own jacket and the shawl Jan wears in the cold room. No other coats hung there; I was alone. The darkness held an archipelago of faintly illuminated desks. I cruised between them. The cold room was one sealed door away.

The door was heavy. I swiped my access card on the reader. It stayed silent, its operation light a stubborn red color. I waited. I thought I heard a sigh, or a whisper, somewhere close by.

Then the operation light flashed green, and the happy little charm inside piped up: diddly-dee.

The magnet lock disengaged. I seized the handle. Cold air escaped and warm air flowed through, and I stood within a miniature vortex before stepping through the threshold. As the air-conditioning unit turned on automatically—click, thunk, whir—so too did the fluorescent lights, in staccato flashes of white, before something went awry in the circuitry, and several strip lights failed at once.

I walked between shelves stacked with brown cardboard boxes. I smelled bleach, glue, and infinitesimally slow decay. I remembered how many people dreamed of entering this sanctified space to witness the glory preserved therein. I remembered the first day I opened The Truth of Carcosa and I remembered fire; I falsely remembered nothing but fire, sparks, and flames and billows of smoke rising from the book in my hand.

The box before me was labeled "1984." Inside were two folders. The first, slimmer folder was labeled "Item Descriptions, JB & CC"; the second fat folder read "SOURCE."

I took them both.

I headed back to the door. The stochastic pulsing of the failing lights traced strange routes between the aisles, as if something were moving around me. I could feel my heartbeat. At the door I pressed my palm against the release bar and discovered an unexpected resistance, but still—clack—it opened, and a strange yellowish light fell through the crack. Only then did I look down and notice the sign, CAUTION, affixed to the bar.

CAUTION. FIRE EXIT.

The alarm went off.

Robert W. Chambers's "In the Court of the Dragon" occurs in nineteenth-century Paris. Our narrator is attending a church service. Having spent the night reading The King in Yellow, he is exhausted and ill; he doesn't recognize the church organist, a slender man whose face is "as white as his coat was black," but is repulsed by the heavy, malevolent music he plays. Our narrator starts to interpret in this cacophony a narrative of flight and pursuit: "Up and down the pedals chased him, while the manuals blared approval. Poor devil! Whoever he was, there seemed small hope of escape!" Exhaustion overcomes our narrator—he falls asleep and dreams of being pursued across the city by a malign figure he half-recognizes. Finally, at the moment when he's cornered, our narrator wakes again, back in the church. He remembers the identity of his dream pursuer: the King in Yellow, whom he had wronged in some past crime. But has the dream truly ended, or has he awoken into further nightmare? Lo, the church walls fall away, and our narrator finds himself in Carcosa, in the King's merciless grasp, awaiting punishment.

Reading this story, I recalled The Cat Concerto, the 1947 animated short in which Tom and Jerry chase one another over a grand piano while performing Liszt's Hungarian Rhapsody No.2. Jerry is trapped in the piano, being knocked about by the felt hammers that rise and fall as Tom plays the keys. Tom plays a glissando, and Jerry is obliged to outrun a wave of hungry felts, like fat white teeth. Pursuit in music.

Easy enough, with the help of Tom and Jerry, to imagine the same labyrinth as our Carcosan narrator. Here is a cartoon minotaur; it has been drawn, in thick black lines, by a pervert. The bass rumbles. The minotaur bellows. The lines wriggle and crawl. Its genitals are gigantic, moving with a life of their own. An obscenity from a suppressed reel.

I have a headache.

Where was I?

CAUTION. FIRE EXIT.

Yes, I remember after I closed the cold room door I was in an open space beneath concrete walkways, with service roads and docking stations. Electric lights illuminated misty curtains of rainwater in dirty yellow. The wind was cold but carried something redolent of decomposition.

I was almost too surprised by my unaccountable mistake to move. The alarm was blaring from behind me, and I saw flashes of red and blue in the distant darkness. One such set of flashing lights quickly resolved into a vehicle: one of the golf carts the Institute's security contractors used.

I ran. I'm not sure how long for. It felt interminable. I followed walkways and stairways, crossed grassy courtyards and plazas, ducked under subways and leapt gates. Several times I lost my pursuers by crossing rough ground or changing levels like a hero in a platformer game, but then another guard would appear, and I'd be forced to double back or jump some gap between causeways, and inevitably I'd see vehicle lights rounding on me, the irreversible side scroller forcing me forward.

I gripped the folders to my chest as I ran, the wind and motion kept jogging pages out of the binding, and I'd waste time trying to square everything back into the folders. I remembered the rucksack on my back, but when I slowed and slipped the bag off my shoulder to stow the folders away, I realized almost too late that the guards were almost upon me, and the seconds I spent prevaricating—nightmare paralysis mode—made completing the operation impossible, so I had to dash forward with the folders in one hand and the bag in the other, pages flapping in the wind.

After that timeless period in the labyrinth, somehow I found myself running on the grass between the ALI and the river. The cart behind me couldn't traverse this terrain, and it zoomed away in a likely effort to head me off elsewhere. I ran, but I remained mindful of the rabbit warrens riddling that area, so without slowing down too much I tried to lift my knees and step vertically to avoid spraining an ankle in some hole. Two guards followed on foot. I could hear them breathing, feel rain soaking through my clothes. Several times I perceived a gap beneath my questing toe, and I half-skipped, half-hopped, and danced past the burrow without injury.

Then I heard behind me the sound I'd been hoping for: a pop, a crump, and a whimper. One of the guards had stepped into a rabbit hole. He'd chase me no further tonight. His companion doubled back to help, and I was alone, skipping over the shadows in the darkness.

Hearing the river ahead, I felt a wave of foolish relief. There was an odd dip before the bank, and it concealed until too late the trap waiting at the riverside: a security cart, with two guards beside it.

I was tackled before I could change course. Hitting the ground knocked the wind out of me and I lay quietly on the turf while the guards retrieved my folders and pulled the rucksack from my hands.

Nobody spoke. Radios crackled. The guards seemed decent enough. They bound my hands with plastic ties and placed me in the back of the cart.

We trundled along the riverbank on a circumferential route back to the Institute. The electric motor whined. The headlights lit up grass tufts and rabbit tails. I was wet and cold, and I very quickly returned to that state of quiescent relief I'd felt in the staff room before I fell asleep. I was going to the police station again (foolish, I realize now, to imagine that police stations were functioning). I would confess to the crime I'd committed. I would tell the nice officer what I'd been thinking, in these last strange days, and they would judge me unsound of mind. I'd hand over moral authority entirely to the waiting arms of the state, in which—despite all evidence—I still held faith. I'd stop believing in The Truth of Carcosa. Somebody else could take charge.

I heard a combustion engine moving somewhere near. A police van, perhaps, come to meet the guards. The radio crackled.

A pair of headlights appeared in front of us. Full beam. Not slowing. Impossible angle. Some mistake, surely—

The driver yelled, and twisted the wheel, and the impact of the oncoming vehicle—an SUV—shunted us sideways and up the bank. The SUV barely slowed, grunting forward, its muzzle dark and angular, until the cart had pitched sideways, and I watched the guard in the passenger seat fall behind the roll bar, then beneath, and I saw his body disappear into shadow, but his limbs wobbled, like a doll's limbs.

The cart's engine was still whirring away, one wheel spinning, flicking up a spray of dirty water in the headlights. The SUV had finally stopped, but the engine continued to chug along, its vibrations agitating the puddles beneath. Two figures exited the vehicle: I recognized the PE teacher and the fake priest from the Berryman. They were wearing camouflage gear now.

The pair ignored the cart and its stricken passengers; instead, they scanned the muddy ground, searching for something.

My bag and the folders had been stowed in a trunk on the back of the cart. The trunk was now empty, broken lid wavering in the wind. On the grass I saw my rucksack; a few feet away a folder lay half open, releasing its pages, white scraps flitting and loping off into the shadows.

I rolled over and let my head hang over my knees for a second. I felt strange. Out of the corner of my eye I saw the PE teacher stooping over another spot on the ground. The second folder. Trying not to attract his attention, I grabbed my rucksack. I crawled to the closest folder and started collecting the wayward pages. I squinted to read the label on the folder, and a flash of blue light illuminated the words: "Item Descriptions, JB & CC."

A siren whooped. The police were finally here.

They pulled up beside the SUV and three officers spilled out, looking serious. I believed, for a second, that they were going to help the stricken security guards, or arrest the perpetrators of the attack. Or arrest me (please!).

But they didn't. One of them approached the PE teacher, whom he recognized, and the PE teacher handed him a clear plastic tube containing a rolled-up piece of paper. The officer read, nodded, rounded up the other cops, and they piled back into their car.

The car sat there, lights flashing impotently.

The PE teacher resumed investigating the spoils. He seemed to home in on something—the other folder, I surmised—when I heard a shout, and the electric whine of another cart, and reinforcements from the ALI crested over a nearby hillock, fronted by Mr. Holmes from the legal department.

"Cease and desist!" he cried, or something similar, and he charged down to meet the PE teacher in the grassy hollow.

Goons in ALI uniforms swarmed over the ridge and a standoff ensued. At the center of attention, the PE teacher cleared his throat. He spoke loudly and clearly.

"My name is Francis O'Dowd, and as a representative of Giovanni, Metti & Metti, LLC, I am empowered under the precedent of In re: Albatross Hung to take possession of this document."

He nodded back toward the police car. The officer waved.

In response, Mr. Holmes extended his bony hand to direct a couple of guards to the police car. Without rolling down the window, an officer pressed the document against the pane for inspection.

Mr. Holmes wasn't going to roll over—I would never expect such from him—still, his next move shocked me. He made as if to retrieve a document of his own from his pocket . . . then he headbutted Mr. O'Dowd.

I don't know what would have happened next, had events followed their natural course. A few punches were being thrown—a few shouts, and shoves; the fake priest was about to land a streetfighter blow; but then something truly weird happened.

The Corpse Man appeared. The Kataluin.

It emerged, not from over a hill or riverbank, but from the shadow cast by Mr. O'Dowd. He seemed to rear out of it—the minotaur, the vibrating monster—and knit together into steaming black cloth and rubbery white cheeks.

The Kataluin extended greedy, crawling hands toward O'Dowd. O'Dowd seemed not to notice.

There was a flash.

I saw a sinuous volt of bluish light, like a vein or root, emanating from the Kataluin's hand; a moment later the volt was a scar on my retina, the Kataluin was gone, and O'Dowd's face was alight with strange fire.

Pages fell to the ground, dissolving into sparks and cinders. Smoke billowed like silt. Security guards and lawyers scattered and ran. The tires of the capsized cart set on fire. O'Dowd turned his mask-like face to me, and I looked for his eyes, and couldn't find them. His suit was aflame.

I stuffed one last handful of papers in my bag. Another arc of lightning wrapped O'Dowd's hands. At his feet, blades of grass flared and burst into scratch-shaped progressions of sparks. Somebody was shouting panicked orders. The police car reversed and accelerated away. The burly fake priest pulled some kind of protective mask over his head. I turned and ran, and whiteness exploded behind me like a strobe, and my giant's shadow stretched across the river, its windmilling arms making the pines sway.

25

Sol and Donaghy, back in the container. Alone together. Hostile. Itching. Sol his arm, Donaghy her knee.

Sol stayed his hand. He studied his fingernails. He decided where to start.

"Jennifer, did Higgins ever tell you anything about this?" he asked.

"*This?*" Donaghy's voice dripped with contempt.

"This place. This . . . danger. These videos."

"No, Joe. Thanks for asking and reminding me."

"I'm sorry. I wasn't trying to get at you." More silence. Donaghy read over the symptom list O'Dowd had provided. She scowled. She trapped her hand underneath her thigh. "Jennifer?"

"What?"

"Do you believe what you saw in that video?"

"Yes."

"Do you believe what O'Dowd told us?"

"Yes."

"How does that fit with what you heard before, about the Archimboldi Trust?"

"What do you mean?"

"I mean, if the Archimboldi Trust is so big, and GMM is looking for a way to unlock it, and they want to persuade people to give up their letters and scraps, then why wouldn't they just let people know that the Archimboldi Legacy is really dangerous?"

"People could still want a slice of the trust. They might still use the legacy materials as leverage."

"If I had a piece of radioactive plutonium in my garage, I'd feel quite positive about getting rid of it. Honestly, I'd pay."

She shook her head.

"I don't know."

"And that stuff about persuading a judge to approve the release of the fund—wouldn't a good lawyer just focus on finding the right judge?"

"Joe, what would you know about this?"

"Probably less than you, Jennifer. But the fact is, I'm less invested in the knowledge that I have."

"Higgins said . . ."

"How much did Archimboldi really have when he died? How the fuck could you invest one man's fortune and then ten years later it's big enough to provoke a lawsuit that's so big and serious it ends up changing the law of the country?"

Donaghy squeezed her face between her hands. She rubbed her cheeks up and down and stretched them back and forward.

"Fuck," she said. "No. From an outsider perspective it doesn't make that much sense."

"No."

She sighed.

"So what's your theory?"

"It's a weapon, Jennifer. They're not destroying the Archimboldi Legacy at all. They're collecting it up. They want to use it."

"Oh, right, here it comes. Here comes the hippie bullshit."

"Think it through, Jennifer."

"You've been a rat the whole time, haven't you? Spying on GMM for your democrat friends."

"Don't turn it on me. We're in the same boat here."

"We are fucking not. You only just passed your probation. I had a future in this company. I had a mentor and a pension. And a big fat mortgage."

"I'm sorry."

"And I almost got Carrette. I almost sealed the deal. But I didn't. And they put me on a *fucking performance review*."

"I'm sorry."

"If I lose my job I'll be a civilian, and they do whatever they want to civilians, don't they?"

"I'm sorry."

"And Carrette burned to a kind of ashy goo and I got exposed to toxic waste and everything my mentor told me before was bullshit and they're keeping me in a shipping container, waiting for me to burn up, too."

"I'm sorry."

"*It's a lot*, Joe."

Donaghy scratched her leg. Sol scratched his arm.

"What should we do?" Sol asked.

She shook her head.

"I've got nothing for you. I'm spent. I just want to sleep."

"Okay, let's sleep."

"Okay, Joe."

They lay for a short while beneath the glaring light inside the shipping container. Sol pulled the cover off his thin pillow and wrapped it around his head. Donaghy did the same. Yellowish light filtered through the fabric.

"Jennifer?"

"Yes, Joe."

"Did you look at the list of symptoms?"

"Yes, Joe."

"That's a lot of self-reporting. How many people do you think they exposed?"

Donaghy pulled the homemade blindfold back off and consulted the form again. She recited: "*Do you hear words. Do you see words. Do words appear on your skin. Do the words change. Does your skin feel hot. Do you experience prickly heat. Does it tickle. Visions. A sense of impending doom.*"

"A sense of impending doom?" Sol scoffed.

"Impending doom is a symptom. People get it when they're having a heart attack."

"I didn't know that."

"My mother died of a heart attack."

"I'm sorry."

"Fine."

"Jennifer–"

"Bit late to start making friends now, isn't it? Let's keep it professional."

"I'm sorry."

"Stop apologizing."

". . ."

"Do you know something, Joe?"

"Go on."

"All the time I've known him, I've only ever seen Higgins smoke straights."

"Huh."

"Why would someone who only smokes ordinary cigarettes keep a humidor in his office?"

"Special occasions?"

"Maybe. Very special occasions."

The lights in the container turned off. There was pitch blackness, then a dim light came on. A night light, to keep away the jitters. Sol was grateful.

* * *

"Jennifer?"

"Yes?"

"I'm divorced. Just a few months ago."

"I know."

"How?"

"It's written all over you. You're not going to hit on me now, are you?"

"No."

"Phew. Thank fuck."

"Alright."

"I wasn't looking forward to *that* conversation."

"Yeah, yeah, okay."

Silence for some time.

"Well, is that it? Is that all you wanted to tell me?"

Sol felt an impulse to give Donaghy some version of himself. Despite everything unpleasant about her, he wanted to share and feel accepted. But there was nothing in his own story he could bear to expose to her gaze.

"Do you have a mark on you, Jennifer?" he asked instead.

"No," she said, without checking.

"Nor do I."

They lay on their bunks willing sleep to come. They scratched the prickly delineations, slowly forming, on their limbs, in their dreams. They scratched, stretching off into dream space, uneasy.

The next thing I knew I was at the city limits. I didn't feel afraid, exactly. If some soul technician had asked me, how do you feel, I would've said "feeling" was a distant satellite to me, adrenaline alone was my cold carapace on my journey through the night. I didn't dare go home. I followed the old London Road halfway into town, to a homeless shelter where the night manager—a man I knew from long ago—allowed me to sleep on the sofa.

I sweated a couple of hours' sleep into the couch, and left before dawn, moving in a roundabout way toward the Berryman. I ate something mushy and cold from a corner shop. I checked my phone for news about the break-in or the fight or the fire. There was none. In fact, there was no news. All reputable news sites had shut down. The only communication came from the buzzing and frothing of social media and conspiracy sites. Last night's rain had never really let up, and I had to keep moving to stay warm. I circled the block around the Berryman until it opened its doors.

Inside, like a fantasy made real, was an open fire. What was more, beside it a comfy chair was free, just for me. I drank—savored—a glass of sweet lime and soda. I tucked my knees beneath my chin. I discovered (o, pleasure!) a copy of Archimboldi's Mulberry Sands in my rucksack and placed it on the armrest to signify propriety. Thus posed, I spent the rest of the day in a state that looked a lot, outwardly, like rest.

As I dozed, my mind settled upon a half-finished essay I'd been posting in fragments on the Aldebaran Gazette. My subject, Chambers's "The Yellow Sign," concerns a painter, Mr. Scott, who lives in proto-fascist 1920s New York, and runs in the same circles as Hildred Castaigne, the Napoleonic lunatic from "The Repairer of Reputations." Scott is concerned about the strange music emerging from a neighboring church. This church is haunted by a figure known as "the watchman" (clearly corresponding to the black-clad organist of "In the Court of the Dragon"). At the story's opening, Scott looks out his window and he and the watchman happen to glance at one another. For Scott, "the impression of a plump white grave-worm was so intense and nauseating that I must have shown it in my expression, for he turned his puffy face away" like "a disturbed grub in a chestnut."

This watchman's pale skin is swollen, with a grotesque invertebrate milkiness; he is a composite of corpse and corpse-eater; indeed, Scott's first sighting of the watchman causes him to ruin the painting he's working on. Without realizing it, he starts to apply a "sickly color" to the study; he attempts to remedy it, but the more he scrubs, the more the "gangrene," "disease," "infection" seems to spread. We never learn whether the sickness Scott paints is a consequence of inner or outer infection—that is, whether he is a source or mirror of evil. This point resonated with my readers on the *Aldebaran Gazette*, who are more apt than most to seek signs of infection, whether ideological or racial (grotesque—but is it my responsibility to govern the responses of the only readership I have?).

As yet unwritten was my analysis of the second half, where Scott falls into an affair with his model, the young and innocent Tessie Reardon. When the pair spend a rainy day in tempting idleness, disaster strikes: Reardon discovers a foolishly misplaced copy of *The King in Yellow*; ignoring Scott's warnings, she snatches the book, dashes off to some secret nook to read it, and falls into a stupefied daze. Upon discovering his befuddled lover, Scott, too, becomes absorbed with the text, which seizes his attention before he can stop himself. Once the reading is complete—*fait accompli*—the couple lie back in a post-book stupor.

Jaded, no longer virginal, Scott and Reardon fall to talking. They talk in a "dull monotonous strain" of the King in Yellow and the "Pallid Mask" long after midnight sounds: "We spoke of Hastur and Cassilda, while outside the fog rolled against the blank windowpanes as cloud waves roll and break on the shores of Hali."

Something clever in the writing here echoes the earlier playful confusion of <u>sources</u>—of infection, inspiration, influence—as though the sounding of midnight mightn't have been an external sound, but a topic of discussion by the afflicted lovers; as if the spires, fog, and tolling bells were conjured out of words; these doomed people <u>told</u> the world and made it so.

Dozing in the Berryman that afternoon, with half an intention to compose the second part of my essay, I recalled how this reading had impressed Dr. Bredsky. She'd told me it aligned with Cipher Theory and we spent a fun hour fleshing it out. She'd never had a client learn so quickly, and she hoped that with these new theoretical structures I'd be equipped to walk the path to Accession such as nobody had achieved before.

These memories flashed before me. A fever heated my forehead, and strange certainties started to crystalize.

26

A sense of impending doom woke Sol. He was alone. The door to the shipping container was ajar. He heard a thud outside. Something was awry.

Sol crept out. He could smell the fustiness of his clothes, the eggy reek of his breath. It had been over a day since he washed, and there was a waxy film on him. Outside the shipping container everything was still. A steaming coffee press sat on a tray beside the door, with two mugs: one upright, one on its side, displaying the cropped legend EST DAD EVE. There was a mobile phone on the tray.

Quiet.

Sol looked up at the office. O'Dowd was standing in there with his right hand pressed up against the window. Sol waved. O'Dowd spread his fingers in reply.

Sol walked up the steps to the platform. The door to the office was closed, a set of keys hanging out of the lock. Sol realized O'Dowd's left arm was hanging awkwardly, blood trickling down his finger.

O'Dowd watched him. He didn't ask Sol to open the door. He didn't even approach the glass. He was, it seemed, frozen in a moment of tactical immobility, hoping perhaps that Sol wouldn't realize his own advantage. Hoping, perhaps, that dumb social impulse would impel Sol to release him.

Sol smiled. O'Dowd smiled back. Social impulse. Sol walked back down the stairs. He poured coffee into the BEST DAD EVER mug and drank. It was good. He wondered briefly what tactic Donaghy had used to lure O'Dowd into the office space and shut him safely inside. Then he picked up the mobile phone on the tray.

It was Donaghy's. He could think of no reason why she left it there, if not for him to find. In fact, the identity lock had been disabled, and an app was already open in the device, ready to discover.

It was Donaghy's inbox, open on an email received some months ago. The subject of the email was "To our Partners: The Art of the Possible." It was from an address within the energy company Xanthic Spectrum, who had apparently attempted to recall it. *Sent in error*. A document was attached to the email.

Sol looked up at O'Dowd, whose smile died slowly. O'Dowd slammed his fist against the glass, but the impact was muted. Reinforced glass. He said something Sol couldn't hear.

Sol opened the file and skimmed through what seemed to be a marketing document: text, images, embedded videos. He clicked Play on the top video, labeled RESTEVO, 1978. It showed grainy aerial footage of a slow-moving river of sludge, perhaps mud, ash, or oil, with black specks and dregs and stick-men emerging and submerging in a chaotic flow. Sol found the movement nauseating, and stopped the video after only a few seconds. He read the accompanying text.

Perpetual Deferral: The Art of the Possible

The horrors of Restevo Linguistics Conference are long behind us, but we'll never forget the lessons it taught. In the years following the disaster, we learned many things, the most important being just how close Earth came to experiencing a full Accession on September 3, 1978.

But research and development is a chain of collaboration. It means we build on our past mistakes and pass our successes on to our partners.

Our collaboration has endured many decades. In partnership, important landmarks such as the Accession Mapping and the Node Cultivation Project have been completed. We have formulated the physics of Accession and Deferral, and established the conditions that prevent full Accession.

But with the arrest of Dr. Adriana Bredsky and mothballing of Prism Consultancy, the consortium has reached a crossroads.

Beneath was a second video. Sol pressed Play. Clippings from newspaper articles faded in and out of the screen. Headlines read "Twelve Dead in Corporate Bonding Ritual Gone Awry"; "Marketing Guru Sought over Sweat Lodge Deaths"; "Who Is Adriana Bredsky, Consultant to the C-Suite?"; "From Casino Arms Convention to 'Roiling Inferno': What Went Wrong?"; "Nevada DA Vows Justice in Sweat Lodge Tragedy"; "Survivor Describes Sweat Lodge 'Hellmouth'"; "Bredsky Hunted"; "Shady Quack Pinched in Sting." Images were of a tarpaulin structure featuring the Prism Consultancy logo, partially collapsed into the desert; rows of ambulances and police tape; officials in bolo ties and Stetsons giving press conferences; piles of emergency blankets and medical packaging; an elderly woman in large, square, thick-rimmed glasses being led from a motel to an official car by Texas Rangers.

Bredsky's arrest presents a challenge to the consortium. Analysis suggests full access to Prism Consultancy's

> assets may be delayed by up to three years. Indeed, we can't yet guarantee their acquisition at all.
>
> But this consortium has always benefited from flexibility. We've welcomed and farewelled partners and collaborators in the past.
>
> Now it's time to outline what is needed to meet this new challenge. But first, we want to remind you, our partners, of exactly what is at stake.

Beneath was an illustration: a utopian landscape of productive fields, factories, and neat modern cities surrounded a futuristic power plant featuring the Xanthic Spectrum "XS" logo, backlit by a setting sun. Each building glowed with light from within.

> Cheap, clean energy. It's been a dream for centuries. The disadvantages of our competitors' sources—be they polluting fossil fuels or unreliable renewables—are many and obvious. We alone are in a position to look beyond our nearest star, to a source of energy unimaginable by most.
>
> Perpetual Deferral is not a pipe dream, but an achievable reality. Perpetual Deferral could generate the energy needed to power four Earths. Whoever achieves Perpetual Deferral achieves the ultimate strategic advantage. But how does it work?

The final video was labeled ACCESSION/DEFERRAL DYNAMICS. Its motionless first frame showed a three-dimensional square grid stretched toward a distant horizon in a sea of infinite blackness.

Sol hovered over the Play button, but some sense of foreboding prevented him from clicking it. Instead, he read on.

> Underpinning the world we occupy—our workplaces, our homes—is a stretch of space-time.
>
> Accession is the passage of an entity from one vector of space-time into another. The presence of the irrupting entity generates tremendous energy, focused on the Cipher that marks the entity's target.
>
> In an Accession, this energy would be spent granting the entity ingress into this plane. An Accession must never be permitted to occur. In a Deferral, the Accession fails. But the generated energy has to go somewhere.

Finally, Sol's curiosity overcame his instinctive reluctance, and he played the grid video. A yellow form coalesced beneath the grid. The grid, consequently, started to deform. It bulged upward, creating a mound-like protuberance in the plane. The protuberance grew to obscene proportions, then the lines of the grid snapped and curled away like clipped wires and the yellow form erupted across the plane, coating the white gridlines with dirty yellow, forming chaotic patterns around the rupture like a claustrophobic fever dream.

Observing the unnatural movement of the forms, Sol involuntarily recalled the interrogation of Father Bruno Schultz: Schultz's face pressed against the surface of the interrogation table, smoke billowing from beneath his hood, lights flashing, limbs crawling. Sol's stomach churned.

Xanthic Spectrum possesses the capacity to harness Deferral energy. Xanthic Spectrum has studied the conditions that limit Accession and preserve the safe boundaries of Deferral. Xanthic Spectrum is a trusted partner in the quest for Perpetual Deferral.

WHAT DO WE NEED FROM YOU?

- ❑ **Reliable supply of nodes and Ciphers**
- ❑ **Enhanced access to PRISM R&D results**
- ❑ **Forward-looking commitment**

As a partner of Xanthic Spectrum, we seek enhanced cooperation for maintaining our supply of nodes and Ciphers. Our work cannot continue without materials, and the pool of available nodes has decreased almost to choke point. Nonetheless, we are confident that 5 to 7 percent of untapped nodes can be located using existing methods, while "ring-fenced" nodes may come under our purview with the correct pressures applied.

Of course, these nodes cannot last forever, and in the medium term, a second Node Cultivation Project is no doubt necessary. In the absence of Prism Consultancy's active assistance, we seek enhanced access to their R&D results.

Which brings us to our last requirement: forward-looking commitment. We're building a new world with our research. We invite you to join us. The partner that can supply the resources we seek reliably, quickly, and discreetly will be assured of a place at the table in the glowing future Xanthic Spectrum predicts.

Sol drank a second cup of coffee, scanning the document again. He paid attention to the strange words: Accession, node, Cipher. Occasionally he looked up at the office, where O'Dowd was heaving an office chair uselessly against the plexiglass. Sol looked toward the exit. Donaghy had left the door ajar. Sol followed, taking the phone with him.

It was wonderful to be beneath the sky again, but the spitting rain and his whirring thoughts suppressed any elation Sol felt on regaining his freedom. He passed through an industrial estate beside a low stretch of wetlands, all of it half remembered from the shell-shocked journey from Carrette's flat. He realized what made the illustration of the power station in the document look so familiar: It resembled the humidor in Higgins's office—right down to the "XS" logo.

Sol made a mental inventory. He didn't have his own phone, but he did have his wallet. And he had a decent jacket, and his shoes were comfortable. He didn't know exactly where he was, but he could guess where Donaghy had gone, and getting there himself was just a logistical problem to solve. And it was solvable. He found the main road. He started to walk.

When I awoke in the evening, my throat felt raw and the atmosphere in the Berryman had become oppressive. Not that anyone was upset. The problem was quite the opposite: People seemed far too cheerful to me. Drinkers piled into the pub like happy funeral-goers. An obscene image popped into my mind but was gone just as quickly, and afterward I couldn't recall its details: some fetish item, around which clammy festivities were planned. Something all folded up. The lights started to pulse. I checked my forehead—I was burning up.

My phone buzzed. It wasn't a message for me, but a newsflash. The major news sites were back online, nothing had happened, things had got better, actually; the news was going to be good from now on. People in the pub were staring at their phones, shaking their heads. I wondered whether Judith was here. I scanned the scrum, and was momentarily sure I'd spotted her; but it was another woman I saw, a fleshy woman in a low-cut floral dress, giggling and jiggling her way back from the bar like an illustration of a wench at an ancient festival. Flowers in her hair. I felt lonely.

My phone buzzed. A government warning: shelter in place, the Emergency Cabinet had been dissolved. It buzzed again: disregard previous instructions, everything was fine, the Hasturian Guard would be holding a press conference soon.

Buzz.

Not an announcement, this time. A voice note for me.

I pressed Play and heard Judith's voice, calm, sweet sounding: "Louis, are you safe?"

She sounded like she really cared. I replied with a voice note, stating that I was safe.

"Did you manage to get the files?"

I said I had. I said I was at the pub, where was she, what was happening? It was frustrating to be messaged this way when I'd spent the whole day waiting for her at our agreed-upon rendezvous.

"The road is blocked so we can't come into town. We can't meet you. You probably know better than we do what's going on, but . . . maybe you should get out. Come to us. We're at the Greenwood Community."

<u>We're at the Greenwood Community</u>.

<u>We</u>.

I sighed. I wasn't so much surprised as disappointed with myself for not predicting it: Judith must have run to Scottie. The two were together, up in the woods, in the hippie commune. Of course.

Hard to explain what went through my mind at this point. At this critical juncture in history it might seem incredibly petty to feel <u>rejected</u> in the way I did then. And yet. Why couldn't she even <u>tell</u> me? Did she think I couldn't handle the truth? I found myself recalling the way Scottie's ex Hattie had tried to keep me out of the House of the Dead Man. As if she should be the gatekeeper of knowledge, the one who knew my limits, what was best for myself and the world, when history was proving to me that not only can I handle the truth, that same truth is <u>I have no limits and I belong everywhere</u>.

I stared at the package in my hands.

The very label, "Correspondence 1984 <u>by Judith Bea and Cléophe Carrette</u>," signified exclusion. They were the chosen ones, the clever ones with their names on the file. But, I reminded myself, only because they put them there.

Rebelliously I opened the folder. I wanted to know what could possibly be so valuable to this pair. There wasn't much to it, at first sight. Just a printed document of notes, Judith's notes, made while she read Archimboldi's letters.

I didn't exactly think hard about what I would say next. I gave the appearance of thinking, but actually I was savoring the moment—the <u>devilry</u> of the moment—where I finally turned on Judith.

"What's it worth?" I pronounced into my phone.

I received no reply. Eventually I followed up with another voice note: "I know you've been looking for The Truth of Carcosa."

All the while I was scanning the notes. The file wasn't particularly well written; no genius insights flashed off the page. I couldn't see what special talent Judith had that I'd lacked that made her the more appropriate bearer of the Archimboldi Chalice.

Impatiently I flicked through the pages. My hand slipped and a page opened before me that caught my attention.

My phone buzzed. Judith had sent a long voice note. I pressed Play.

"You're right. We were looking for The Truth of Carcosa. I'm sorry we could never tell you about it."

I heard Judith's voice but my attention was riveted to the printed page before me, which was familiar and strange and terrible, and unfolded like the revelation of a personal nightmare.

"We found a copy," Judith's recorded message continued. "You delivered it to Mr. Carrette. And again, I'm sorry: I'm sorry I put you at risk."

Her voice was quiet and far away. My face was uplit with the pale glow of the jewels, the bleached bones, the furnace before me.

"The Truth of Carcosa isn't just a book. It's a tremendously dangerous thing. It's a source of power that terrible people want to use. It's a gateway for the Yellow King. It allows him to build a bridge, from his world into this one."

Everything she told me I already knew. Had known for years.

"You see, what happened to Cléophe was terrible—but it could have been so much worse. The Accession could have succeeded. Then we'd all be sharing our world with that . . . thing. We got lucky this time. But we don't know if there will be a next time."

She was right, but she was wrong. She and Carrette were clever, but I was cleverer. With effort I pulled my eyes away from the page, folded up the papers, stuffed them in my bag.

"Louis, we don't think there are many copies of The Truth of Carcosa left. But I don't dare hope there are none. The information we need, to find the remaining copies, is in the Correspondence 1984 folder. We must finish what we started: We must find whatever copies remain and destroy them. Please help us, Louis. Please bring it to us."

I got up—lightheaded—fought my way to the bar and ordered a double measure of vodka.

I drank it in one gulp. As the diesel burned my throat, I recorded my final voice note for Judith:

"I'll see what I can do," I said. I meant it. I soon would see exactly what I can do. And so would the King.

27

Sol had the whole journey across town to reflect on what he'd seen in the Xanthic Spectrum presentation. It seemed they were using a whole different language at times, yet the terms weren't alien to him, nor was the way it was deployed: This was a new corporate doublespeak. Deferrals, nodes, Ciphers—they were sanitized words for explosions that ripped out of Archimboldi's book and killed people. But the ultimate energy source—the entity lying beneath their plane of space-time, trying to provoke something called "Accession"—this was beyond Sol. Still, he recalled, certain physical processes did act as if they had will. The exponential acceleration of a nuclear fission reaction, when two uranium rods were pushed together—from a certain perspective, couldn't you start to believe that something in them *wanted* to explode? Was this what they meant? His mind cycled in widening gyres but returned to his immediate task: follow Donaghy's footsteps; discover what she wanted to discover; persuade her to join him in escaping with whatever evidence they found; take that evidence to Eze.

His feet were blistered when he reached the commercial estate containing the GMM office. The estate had a grey, buzzing aspect under a keen wind. The sky was a uniform off-white color like cheap paint. He reached one of the side doors to GMM without meeting anybody. In fact, the whole campus was deserted, which was odd, since it was only Tuesday. Perhaps, Sol thought, there was another disturbance going on.

He used his swipe card on the door—*diddly-dee!*—and was relieved when a light flashed green and the PanOp Insights security mechanism unlocked. He wondered whether he should jam the door open. He stood undecided for a while, thinking about sticking a fire extinguisher in the gap; then movement in the distance caught his eye.

Somebody was coming. They were moving directly toward him across the estate, heedless of obstacles. There was something inhuman about the way they were zeroing in on his location—or was it the wallowing gait that he found unnerving?

He released the door handle. The glass and steel construction swung closed at a leisurely pace—so slowly that despite the fact the figure was fifty feet away, Sol started to panic and push it closed; but some pneumatic mechanism resisted him, so he heaved his entire weight against the panel, and for a few nightmarish moments he felt he was caught in a dream loop: the indistinct figure threatening but never arriving, the door slowly moving but never sealing, panic rising but never resolving.

Then, at the moment the door clicked shut, a fully realized man materialized on the other side and slammed his body against the glass. Sol first assumed it was some goth-punk wearing white corpse paint: The clothes were black, the skin yellowish-white like wet bones. But this was no costume. The man's flesh was swollen and loose, as if he'd lain submerged in dark water for a season; his suit was filthy; his face was an indistinguishable mass, a pallid mask with holes for eyes; and his limbs moved with impossible speed, in a flurry, like the scratching appendages of a poisoned moth, his fingernails splitting and shedding like dead leaves as he tried to get in.

Sol fell back, floored by a wave of nausea. The sickness rippled through him like a shock wave, terminating in the itchy spot on his arm, which continued to thrum after he staggered away with a high-note afterglow, somewhere between pain and sickened pleasure. The thing, the Corpse Man, remained outside the glass door, scrabbling and smearing without method, jabbering without reason. Sol made his way to the stairwell.

The door onto his own floor said CAUTION and ALARM, but when he pushed it open no alarm sounded. He entered the open-plan area where he'd carried out his training assignments. Neon signs, stylized as handwriting, continued to express motivating sentiments.

REACH FOR THE STARS.

He crossed to the central zone where meeting rooms and senior offices were concentrated. TAKE INSPIRATION FROM AFAR. Higgins's office, he remembered, was of a heavier, more solid material than the rest of the building. He was beginning to intuit why.

SUCCESS IS A JOURNEY.

He found the door to the office—heavy, indeed; heavier even than the solid oak it resembled—and pulled it open.

Judith's motives were good, in a conventional sense, but she was wrong—dead wrong—when it came to Accession.

Accession is a meeting and melding of minds; it is the point of True Communication, where the portents of One become the portents of Another. It is the end of loneliness. What is there to fear?

For the first time in years, I clearly recalled Dr. Bredsky's catechism the afternoon she accompanied me on my own tour of Carcosa. I had taken her from Lake Hali Harbor to the Promenade of Wire to the Portal and through the various Tollgates (of Chafing, Wind, Oil, et cetera) that mark the path to the Chamber of the King. Please don't read too much into the names I gave each waypoint; they were off-the-cuff inventions, inspired by whatever sensation the LIN probe happened to be provoking as Dr. Bredsky moved it between pressure points. She asked me, in a breathless, ritualistic tone, where I was going, what I could see.

There was nothing sinister about the process or the goal. Indeed, I felt a blend of comfort and elation. My own map of Accession was being produced—my very own; and Dr. Bredsky consistently praised the ingenuity of my designs. Furthermore, it was clear that Accession was a reward for genius. Other clients had come and gone from Adriana's chambers; none had matched me—she vigorously asserted—in terms of the potential I presented. So while we understood that Accession was technically impossible, we both indulged the notion that for somebody special it was a genuine possibility; and the tacit understanding arose that I might be that special person.

Of course, no Accession was reached in these proceedings. After a few hours of the practice, I left Dr. Bredsky's office feeling pleasantly relaxed. The world didn't end. Now, I didn't understand why Judith would attach such monstrous import to a word that I knew to be purely positive.

She was happy that her friend and colleague M. Carrette had burned to death, instead of achieving True Communication?

I understood, there in the Berryman, that Archimboldi needed me to read his opus. He needed me—a Cipher of genius—to complete his most daring project.

Judith and Scottie were now firmly positioned in the enemy camp. I had to thwart them by whatever means necessary.

Meanwhile, the Berryman had become even more crowded. Brutal music was playing and people were dancing. I wanted to get out, but the route to the door was clogged with ruddy-faced drinkers. I navigated tables and wildly swinging limbs and a disconcerting conga line that pounced from nowhere and snaked away with a beery slipstream and a thunder of shoes. Somebody grabbed my hand. I was swept forward through a series of arches formed from interlinked hands, and deposited back by the fireplace where the stuffed cat had come alive weeks before.

I decided to leave by the back door.

The moment I stepped into the rear parking lot I was seized by the shoulders and a hand covered my mouth. Two black-clad members of the Hasturian Guard hustled me directly into the back of a van.

The interior was dimly lit and smudged with grime. A single glum policeman sat with three masked guards. My hands were bound, my mouth gagged, and I was forced to kneel while a guard emptied my pockets.

"Name?" the policeman asked. He was holding a clipboard.

A guard wearing a wolf mask emptied my wallet onto the bed of the van and poked around the scattered cards.

"Louis Barrow," he pronounced eventually. "Is that French?"

"Right." The policeman noted the name, and started reciting, "Louis, you are detained under the Emergency Powers Act, and there are no rights to read you—"

"Hold on, what's this?"

Wolf man held up my "Trusted Citizen" card. He passed it around.

"Could be a fake," another guard said. "Check his phone."

Wolf man unlocked my phone with my finger and started scrolling and swiping through my open browsers.

"You've been on the Aldebaran Gazette a lot?" he asked. I nodded. I watched his eyes. I felt quietly confident, but I didn't anticipate the expression of open admiration that came over him.

"Those articles about the King—that's you? You're the Yellow Mythos guy." I nodded. He was referring to the posts I'd been making about The King in Yellow, and a few nascent theories of Accession and the like, which I'd started writing in response to user queries on the Aldebaran Gazette but which, it seemed, had taken on a life of their own.

Wolf man hurriedly pulled the gag out of my mouth and cut my wrist ties. He said, for the benefit of the others, "He's the real deal, this one. True believer. Cross his name out." This last instruction was for the policeman, who meekly obeyed.

My belongings were respectfully returned to me. Wolf man shook my hand. He looked bashful.

"I don't normally read much," he said, "but you've inspired me. I've been learning all about the Yellow Mythos, and it's . . . kept me going. Thank you. Keep up the good work, sir."

Honestly I had no idea what he meant by inspiration. It had never been my intention to encourage these buffoons; I was just grateful for an audience. But I accepted his help out of the van and we stood together in the parking lot, looking back at the Berryman.

Things had changed there. The door through which I'd left was now barred, and the patrons had spilled out the front door. I suspected they'd launched an impromptu street party until I saw the parked police car and ranks of Hasturian Guards surrounding them. Then I understood the nature of the shouts, the crunching that I'd mistaken for music. This was no party: It was a raid.

The Guard had the revelers contained in a kind of wedge around the smoking area. They had riot shields and clubs. I heard a collective yell and saw a mass of people try to burst out of the Guard line—but the line held firm. I saw people fall beneath their blows and kicks. I saw snatches: a thin wrist folding the wrong way; fingers beneath stamping boots. I heard breaking glass and snapping bones.

"We're clearing it out," Wolf man told me. "It's been a long time coming. Lots of libs use that place as a kind of indoctrination center. Pedophile rings. Blood harvesting. That'll stop now. I don't know if you saw the news, but we're in the Emergency Cabinet now. The brakes are off."

I nodded. A woman in the crowd started wailing. I didn't flinch.

"It's about time," I said. "Best we get the whole place cleaned out."

28

Higgins's office was wrecked: Oak paneling had fallen away to reveal the concrete wall, and while some of the panels were charred, others were splintered, and still others appeared to be chemically bleached.

The overstuffed leather furniture was tumbled and split and splayed. Higgins's desk had been crippled. The Xanthic Spectrum humidor was open, and the glow from within was the only illumination in the room. The source of the glow was a book—something very similar to the books in the video footage, but alive with internal light.

Donaghy was lying prone on the floor. A long black wire led out from beneath her chest, snaking across the ground and back up to a device in Higgins's hand. A stun gun? It had a bright red plastic trigger, and dials and switches. But it also had a cable running back out to the humidor. And another cable connecting to something like a collar around Higgins's neck. There is something unfinished about the design of the equipment. Like a prototype or low-budget prop.

But when Higgins squeezed the trigger, both ends of the cable *popped* in tandem and Donaghy jerked into a fetal position, grunting, and a kaleidoscopic aura appeared around the humidor, and a wave of sickening power hit Sol, too, so that he stumbled, but didn't fall, nor stop watching light creep like a cinder spark back up the cables toward Higgins, watching the collar around Higgins's neck pulse, his lips quiver with pleasure, some unnatural emanation leaking from the thin white hair on the back of his head. He sighed. It was an unmistakably sexual sigh. He squeezed the trigger again.

All the while, Sol was buffeted by sound. The manuscript in the humidor was like a wasps' nest, buzzing and growling in waves of static. Sol couldn't identify words in the torrent, yet also couldn't suppress the impulse to do so, and with cycle after cycle his language center presented him with scraps of words, phrases, floating points of meaning.

The mute part of his brain tracked the flow of power in the room. It came from Donaghy, writhing and smoldering on the floor. It came from the glowing manuscript. He could feel it leaking from himself—a faintly vertiginous feeling, centering on the mark on his arm. It was like the sensation provoked by the Corpse Man's presence—only this was far more controlled. The equipment hitched to Higgins had harnessed and channeled the energy.

This much Sol understood in a moment, recalling the presentation on Donaghy's phone: happy power plants radiating energy out to happy consumers in their homes and factories and farms. This device was some early version of the Xanthic Spectrum model; here was a node (pages flapping); here was a Cipher (writhing on the floor); and somewhere behind it all, radiating madness, was the entity behind the plane.

A moment later the tableau fell apart.

He heard the approach behind him: the scurrying sound of many footfalls. A dry creak as of a door opening to a room in the back of his mind. The Corpse Man was here.

Sol turned and momentarily glimpsed the figure accelerating across the office space, furniture skidding off before him and tumbling in his wake, his shoes flying off after one step, the flapping jacket disintegrating after another step, his scalp flapping open above the mask of intent below.

He advanced, and Sol quailed, but the Corpse Man never reached him. Before he was three steps away the lines that defined his form splintered and wriggled free. The shadows between his folds of flesh lifted as worms and tails and oil trails, the whole deconstructed mass spiraling past Sol to the device in Higgins's hand. Sol felt a tickle. He smelled burnt hair.

Higgins's equipment sparked. The humidor flickered. Higgins became, for a strobe's flash, an entirely different man—grave and bony and eight feet tall in a yellow patterned robe—but then the humidor's light regained its full power, and Higgins returned, charred and doll-like, with smoke pluming from his eyes; and one of the cables first melted then squirmed away, and from the floor Donaghy started at last to scream.

Not a scream of fear or pain. A scream from that bright white space beyond agony from which no comprehensible messages return. The scream, Sol recognized, from footage he had witnessed as a lawyer, of somebody burning alive.

Sol moved then, out of the room which was suddenly full of choking black sausagey smoke and out into the office, which had a fire extinguisher. Just as he grabbed it, a door opened, and in walked somebody in an outfit Sol recognized: the Gumby person suit.

Sol could have taken the fire extinguisher and tried to reach Donaghy before the Gumby person reached him. He could have tried to put her out.

Instead, he smashed the Gumby person over the head, and ran, and saved his own life.

* * *

"Nadia, I need your help. I've found out something about the Archimboldi Legacy. It's crazy. It's horrible."

"Where are you?"

Sol was at the bus station. He was using a burner phone from his go-bag. He had no time for details. Panic was speaking for him.

"It's about technology, Nadia! Technology and power. Did you read the file I sent you?"

"Come to London."

"You were right—all those companies working together. It's a conspiracy!" The line broke down into clicks and static. "I can't hear you," he said. He paced around, holding the phone aloft, chewing his lip.

Finally:

"Mr. Sol, you've got to get out. Get to London as quick as you can. Things are about to go . . ."

Gone.

"Nadia?"

Eze's voice came in snatches between waves of interference.

". . . sealed off the barracks and . . . OSINT . . . lines of trucks in the rest stops . . . general mobilization . . . can you hear me?"

Sol ended the call and boarded the next bus with two dozen other anxious, overladen passengers.

They got as far as the highway.

Sol first assumed the uniformed youth waving down the bus was a police officer. But his black fatigues had no insignia, and he was carrying an old-fashioned shotgun. The vehicle pulled up.

The guard jumped aboard. He was very young. He spoke to the driver and the driver announced cheerfully, "Wallets and IDs please, ladies and gents!"

People started muttering but complying, as if this was normal, or they didn't want to believe it wasn't normal. Sol took out his wallet and considered his options. GMM worked with the Hasturian Guard. Could they have handed over his details? Couldn't he just refuse to hand over his wallet?

His hands were shaking.

At that moment he noticed the woman in the seat opposite his. Her hands were shaking, too. In fact, she was rocking to and fro, clinging to a garbage bag full of clothes, her knees tapping uncontrollably. Sol realized two things: First, she was the only dark-skinned person on the bus; second, he knew who she was.

Judith Bea. ALI employee, colleague of Cléophe Carrette.

People were passing their wallets forward now. Sol could see a handful of guards outside, peering through the windows.

Think.

He pulled his rucksack open and surveyed its contents. Clothes, toothbrush, medicine.

Think.

His toothbrush was packed in a plastic cylinder. He pulled the contents out. He took the information sheet from a packet of pain-killers, unfolded it, and rolled it into a tube. Inserted it into the cylinder.

The woman, Judith Bea, was watching him.

Her eyes went wide as he fished out his GMM lanyard and let it hang outside his jacket.

He leaned over to her. He spoke as calmly as he could.

"My name is Joseph Sol," he said. "I know who you are, and I'm on your side. I need you to do something brave. I need you to trust me."

He watched her calculate her options, silently, before finally giving the slightest nod, her eyes still full of suspicion.

He stood up, gesturing for Bea to stand behind him. With the toothbrush cylinder and GMM swipe-card outstretched, he walked down the aisle toward the guard.

"Good morning, brother," he said, working to suppress the weakness in his voice. "I'm on *In re: Albatross Hung* business. I hope this isn't going to take too long. I'm escorting my target to the rendezvous."

He indicated Judith. Out the front window he could see the chrome plating of the diner, just down the road. He pointed at that.

"I don't want to miss the pickup window," he said.

The guard stared at him. Sol knew it was a gamble. He needed the guard to be familiar but not intimate with the relationship between his group and GMM. He needed him to recognize the cylinder as a Silver Bullet, to treat it as a totem of power and not think to look closer.

The guard didn't look at the cylinder. But he didn't move from Sol's path. He peered over his shoulder, looking Bea up and down.

"What did she do?" he asks.

"Not my department. I just deliver the subpoenas."

"They've all done *something* . . ." the guard said. Bea's eyes were glued to the floor, hands shaking as she endured the man's gaze.

Sol shrugged. He tried one last gambit.

"My colleague Jennifer Donaghy normally does the outreach stuff, you may have met her before."

"Oh, Miss Donaghy, yeah, I know her."

"I don't want to keep her waiting, if you don't mind. Got a lot more to deliver today."

The guard stood aside with exaggerated courtesy. He leered at Bea.

"Keep up the good work," he said, winking at Sol.

They got off the bus and hustled up the road, feeling the eyes of the guards on their backs until they entered the diner parking lot and ducked behind a building, where Sol threw up.

He sat a while with his head between his knees. Bea stayed alert, still gripping her garbage bag, listening to the bus engine slowly grind away.

"What's your name again?" she asked.

"My name is Joseph Sol. We've got a lot to talk about."

And now we are here, at what I sense will be the end. I've a few threads to draw together before I conclude my report, and I only hope this fever lets up long enough for me to maintain focus. Just now I paused for what I understood to be the briefest of breaks—a key-drop nap, if you will—but came to consciousness in the bathroom, rainbow streamers pulsing in my vision. I fear my strength is failing.

I'd wanted to end my report on a purely triumphal note, but the situation is more properly mixed.

The good news—fantastic news, really—is that I've completed my reading of the *Archimboldi Correspondence 1984*. It has confirmed the theories I've developed these last weeks. It provides all the clues I need to locate more copies of *The Truth of Carcosa*, just as I intend to do.

The prospect of Accession has never been so close. And while I want to raise my arms like a marathon runner reaching the finish line, while I want to sing and shout, to let the world know that *I Am Not Alone Anymore*, in gloomy moments doubts I thought conquered reappear.

Like, what about Judith Bea?

I don't mean I'm concerned for her welfare. I'm concerned about the position she takes in my personal cosmology, the role she's played in revealing all these important truths. I feel obliged to assert that I *did not fancy* Judith from the moment I met her. My actions in the last few weeks *haven't* been motivated by unseemly desire, prejudice, or jealousy.

To the skeptical eye, the timing of Judith's first utterance of the word "Carcosa" is admittedly suspicious, given that it occurred just after I discovered she'd been intimate with Scottie, an implicit rejection of a host of unspoken and unrequited fantasies; okay, I'll admit it, the *desire* I felt for her, and an irruption of my unwanted past, plausibly triggering the creation of some kind of totalizing alternative schema that recentered my bruised ego, transforming my unattractive sexual desire into the laudable drive to prove my worth, validating my intelligence and thwarted academic *ambition; yes, the introduction of this ludicrous sojourn in Pent Organ House with a mummified kink archetype named Dr. Adriana Bredsky (may as well have called her Doktor Elektra) should properly be interrogated as a nakedly self-serving externalization of all the bad affect in which my consciousness is immersed.*

And yet, I have read the correspondence, a factual document that confirms everything—everything—I have previously written!

Why, then, does some rebel in me rise up and deny what's in front of my eyes? It is, I expect, the same weak party that wants me to return to treatment. The weak part of myself that sees the jaws of success yawning ahead and is frightened, since it's only ever known the comforts of failure.

Let me recount my progress so far.

First, I found this place. It took me awhile. Trolling up and down the street didn't work. The fronts of the houses all look the same now: uniformly well maintained, the interiors shielded with slatted shutters or curtains. I had to retrace my steps through Hourglass Lodge hospice. That place hasn't changed. I found the yew tree in the rear and the garden beyond. It had been tidied up. No more spindly weeds or anaerobic pond. But the basic structure, the bones of the House of the Dead Man, remained recognizable to me.

The same was true for the interior. As I entered the refurbished conservatory and moved into the living room with its expansive sofas and deep shag carpet, I understood that the place hadn't truly changed, beneath its redecoration. The rotten structure existed beneath the clean lines of the renovated house. I could smell it.

Moving up the stairs, the beam from my flashlight illuminated carefully chosen silk-effect paint and family portraits hung in artful clusters; yet when I pressed my palm against the wall, I felt the movement of decrepit capillaries: a heartless pulsing, a poisonous surging, cold and vivid, of decayed corpuscles.

The flick of a light switch behind a bedroom door, a cautious murmur—I was detected. I scurried back downstairs and outside, ducking into the undergrowth at the end of the garden. I needed to collect my thoughts. Plan.

Distasteful as it might seem, I'd been impressed by the speed with which my Trusted Citizen card produced results outside the Berryman. And my interests certainly trumped the inconvenience of whoever had decided to settle in this property. It struck me that I might make use of the Hasturian Guard again, to remove the inhabitants so I could check that no copy of The Truth of Carcosa remained on the property.

I made my secret way to the estate the Guard had annexed. There, at the mouth of a cul-de-sac, a local bureaucracy was operating out of a set of shipping containers. I produced my Trusted Citizen card and gained instant respect and obedience. I was shown into a container divided in half: On one side of a steel bulkhead a clerk was operating a help desk of sorts; on the other side, thuds and groans evinced the machinations of the new state.

Using a bookie pen attached to a chain, I wrote out a short and simple denunciation: Something to the effect that the residents of the address in question were liberal people smugglers. They handed out anti-patriotic propaganda and hosted globalist parties.

I read the note. I screwed it up. It was far too coherent.

I started again.

I would need, I realized, to ventriloquize the paranoid and ignorant whose invective flooded the Aldebaran Gazette comments sections. I wrote in short, incoherent phases, as if trying to communicate truths shrouded in dementia. The result, which invoked blood libel and cannibalism, pleased me. I wondered whether a future in demagoguery might, in fact, be my line. I handed in the denunciation, showing my Trusted Citizen card one more time, and was saluted.

I floated through glass-strewn streets back to Hourglass Lodge, scaled the fence once more just as dawn broke, and scurried back to my yew tree. From the bottom of the garden, I settled down to wait for the household's removal.

I didn't have to wait long. Within an hour I heard hammering on the door. I was relieved to be going inside: My muscles were stiff and my nose was flowing. But the clamor in the house didn't die down as quickly as I expected: Instead of taking the household away with them, it seemed the Hasturian Guards were conducting an interrogation of sorts inside the house. I heard screams, and thumps, and scraping of furniture.

I heard a child's voice.

It occurred to me, as I sat outside listening to the family I'd denounced being tortured in their own home, that I'd achieved a new level of understanding with Salvatore Archimboldi. He'd been a refugee from exactly this treatment when he arrived in our country. And, as his critics had relentlessly asserted, his escape had been facilitated by a certain level of cooperation with the authorities. But he must have perceived the importance of his own fate, the vital work that he would accomplish later in life; otherwise, how could he have lived with himself? It takes a <u>*genius*</u>*—a True Cipher—to appreciate the value of the ultimate goal even in the face of screaming children.*

The wailing persisted for a short time, I suspect—although it felt long—and eventually the family was removed from the property; in the subsequent quiet I entered from the back.

I searched the house, top to bottom. There was no sign of <u>*The Truth of Carcosa*</u>*. In the daylight it was clear that the entire place had been refurbished, and it was unlikely anything from the previous occupancy remained. I looked at family portraits, and doubts assaulted me. But the notion that I might, in fact, be insane no longer held its paradoxical comfort: Given the rapid developments in our country in the last few* *months, no treatment program likely exists that might benefit me. We are all at sea here. And the tumult has only increased: I hear car alarms outside, and cheering, and gunshots. I suspect no police could arrest me even should I request it. All past certainties are lost. The future is mine to grasp.*

I excavated a space beneath the living room floor. I passed through layers of carpet, floorboard, joists. I lay on the living room floor and put my head in the hole. I breathed in the spores and dust, and willed the book to return, to make itself known again to my hands. No sign. Not to worry. I sat in the living room that was once a mash of paper and book spines, and is now pastel and dry carpets, and some blood and knotted cord. I ate cold cuts out of the fridge and drank orange juice.

I read the correspondence.

I know where to go now. I should have known all along, for it will be a homecoming of sorts.

If your path is the same as mine, I will see you there.

Archimboldi Correspondence 1984—
Item Descriptions, JB & CC

Authors: Bea, Judith
Keeler, Jan
Carrette, Cléophe

[Judith—welcome to your probation. Remove confidential/libelous references and replace with "confid." If you have any questions, please put them into square brackets like these and I'll answer them likewise. Do not delete these notes! Once you have passed probation you'll report directly to M. Carrette. Good luck! Jan]

January 1984

Letter from Archimboldi [hereafter, A.] to Jonathan Crew, editor at Albatross Hung, 01/13/1984.

A. discusses editing and proofing his recently published novel The Swordfish Narth. Has complaints and suggestions for improving the process. Mentions specific controversial edits on pages 4, 36, 389, and 393. Defines authorial authority. Invokes freedom of speech in the context of repressive regimes then extant in South America. Criticizes Margaret Thatcher, Ronald Reagan, and Henry Kissinger. Attacks pro-Western myopia of otherwise educated metropolitan British elite. Asks after Crew's family. Ends with a joke.

Letter from Crew to A., dated 01/17/1984.

Crew responds warmly to A.'s joke. Addresses personal family issues [confid.]. Attends to A's criticisms of editorial changes in The Swordfish Narth. Explains his decisions as interventions in spelling, grammar, and clarity. Points out that three-quarters of the edits were punctuation only. Apologizes for Margaret Thatcher's affection for General Pinochet and U.S. sponsorship of Operation Condor. Describes the weather.

[Judith—this is satisfactory. Carrette will take over as your primary supervisor as of today. Jan]

Letter from A. to Jaime Bolo, poet, 01/19/1984.

A. greets Bolo [how? more detail please—CC]. He asks after his family [Judith these men are exiles, are these questions freighted with hidden meaning?]. Describes a recent dinner party hosted by author Cecilia Burton and attended by progressive literary figures [good, but more please]. Discusses loneliness, politics, history, gardening, childhood, and memory. Asks Bolo his opinion on the UK-Southern Cone Artistic Cooperation Movement. Sketches future plans for a sequel to The Swordfish Narth.

[Thank you, this is good work, but please do it again—this time go further and draw out the themes our protagonist is trying to make manifest. I know you understand. With your guidance we can discover the truth in these letters. Carrette]

AGAIN: letter from A. to Jaime Bolo, poet, 01/19/1984.

A. greets Bolo warmly. He asks after his cousins Javier Rojas [living in Mexico] and Benjamin Sepulveda [presence unknown]. Describes a dinner party hosted by Cecilia Burton and attended by Jonathan Crew, Doris Lessing, and Herman Rondo. Describes anticipated arrival of Jag Caruthers, with attendant anxieties, and the relief and vindication when he failed to appear. Discusses the experience of loneliness in crowds, namely the guests at the dinner party, also intellectual loneliness of the sort that comes about when a person is out of step with the cross-currents of the era and milieu; namely, his disinterest in engaging with theoretical discussions about the value of art with untested radicals—people who espouse Marxism but would never venture beyond the Iron Curtain, who detest fascism but whose houses have never been burned down. Expresses the equivalent of a tired sigh. Returns to first principles. Describes the apparent causes of the rightist coups in Paraguay, Brazil, Bolivia, Uruguay, Chile, Peru, and Argentina as elite fear of the masses, bourgeois fear of revolution, and Yanqui fear of Communist influence. States that the true cause wasn't fear but loathing, the exercise of violence for its own sake. States that violence is a substance, mined from a different plane. Describes observing the early days of martial law in his own city. Deploys the metaphor of a mining operation coming into being: machines of men and matériel delving into the city streets to excavate, process, and dump the slag in unmarked exurban pits. States that this description is inaccurate, since to live in the occupied city was to be exposed to its official and unofficial emanations: a reheated mass of old fears and grievances; a confection of rumors, lies, and mistreated truths; and desperate pleas for a return to gentleness; describes, also, days of banality interspersed with concentrated moments of violence. States that violence can never be revisited, since it overloads the nervous systems of witnesses and participants, and its true substance—undigested, still toxic—comes out only in bad dreams, nervous tics, inappropriate laughter, and further acts of violence. Describes the birds in his bird feeder. Lists species. States that in the early days of the coup he wanted only the return of his own petty freedoms: open bookshops and uncensored films in the theater, and the state of full-bellied, narrow-minded complacency, including remaining unmoved, as he previously had been, by the desperate state of the indigenous rural poor. Lists edible flowers growing in the garden. Lists artists and musicians who have disappeared. Asks, what is the value of metaphor. Describes the particular timbre and tone of the barking produced by the dogs kept by A.'s neighbors when he was a child, using interlinked metaphors drawing from natural science, music theory, and gnostic theology. Does it well. States that he was once a child. Asks whether Bolo perceives the plasticity of his dreams of childhood, with their ever-rejuvenated textures, intimations of primary experience. Describes [redacted—confid.] from his childhood. Compares his modest, well-meaning dinners with leftists to the lavish banquets to which certain South American authors, entrepreneurs, artists, and academics have allegedly been invited, at the Cromwell Hotel, Holborn, by Foreign Office secretaries at the behest of the U.K.-Southern Cone Artistic Cooperation Movement (USCACM). Asks whether Bolo regards the USCACM as a trojan horse compromising critics of the fascistic South American regimes, an insidious puppet show legitimizing the UK's support of such regimes, a treacherous scheme monitoring critics of the country's allies, or all of the above. Speculates that the food might be drugged. Signs off with apologies.

[Thank you, Judith, that will do perfectly.]

Letter from A. to Crew, 01/20/1984.

Addresses personal matters concerning Crew's family [confid.].

Letter from Crew to A., 01/25/1984.

Greets A. with formality. Refers to enclosed clippings of reviews of The Swordfish Narth [missing]. Engages in clumsy preamble. Refers to conversations held with [Albatross Hung senior editorial manager] Sidney Grote and [marketing executive] Dea Fenton. Specifies discussion of [Jag Caruthers's autobiographical novel] Backhand. Criticizes Caruthers's insensitive treatment of family trauma. Insinuates that a superior talent could make more of the same material. Relays Grote and Fenton's speculation that A. might break from pattern and risk a more personal approach. Wonders, as if privately and without consequence, whether A. has considered the possibility of an autobiographical novel, since he so eloquently described his experience of the coup in earlier correspondence.

Letter from A. to Bolo, 01/27/1984.

[First pages missing.] Fragment begins mid-sentence with A. asking whether Bolo ever feels guilt for surviving. Apologizes for the baldness of the question. States, without recourse to poetic devices, that only through the mediation of certain cultural signifiers can A. access the emotions associated with their calamitous shared history—and even such access he regards as untrustworthy or mediated, even constructed for his own therapeutic benefit. States that he won't ask Bolo's permission to write about their shared history or homeland, and that he hasn't decided definitively whether to do so. States that he may seek expert advice.

Letter from Adriana Bredsky [C.E.O., Prism Consultancy] to A., 01/27/1984.

[Much is unclear due to blurred nature of the handwriting and content.] Bredsky's greeting suggests intimacy or haste. Describes meeting A. in a recent dream [probably]. States that A. stands before an open channel and a nexus of opportunity. Reiterates foundational principles of synchronicity [largely smudged]. Cites Arthur Koestler and another [indecipherable]. States that she feels obliged to answer A.'s invitation and provide the assistance requested. Refers to an enclosed reading list [missing].

[Judith, how did Bredsky and A. actually meet? We cannot take for granted that our protagonist projected himself into Bredsky's dream! CC]

February 1984

Letter from Bredsky to A., 02/01/1984.

In more coherent terms, thanks A. for his kind words [correspondence missing], and expresses pleasure at being able to help a fellow creative in their hour of need. Professes that she'd be delighted to send more materials, but work commitments limit the time she can spend. Praises A.'s creative abilities, wisdom, and physique. Explains that a formal course can be devised, comprising a dual literary-therapeutic approach with residential supervision. Quotes a sum of £5,000.

Letter from Bredsky to A., 02/03/1984.

Bredsky adopts a more professional tone, although still bright, still playful, in response to [missing] correspondence. Restates proposed fee of £5,000. Breaks down costs with emphasis on rare materials, specialty equipment, and the going rate for therapeutic services. Adds that she'd regret missing the opportunity to work with a writer of manifest genius on a project that could resolve trauma into creative energy for transformational purposes. Details cooperation of PanOp Insights [they make CCTV cameras, no? CC] in new project involving state-of-the-art creative interrogation [? CC]; hints at institutional work with Ministry of Defence; insists she'd rather spend time working with exceptional people like A.

Letter from A. to Bolo, 02/03/1984.

A. greets Bolo guardedly, as if anticipating rebuke. Complains about the financial arrangements between authors, agents, and publishers. Complains about Ronald Reagan. Complains about the weather. States that what he fears most is madness; that madness will have come at the moment he perceives any one object to be what it is, purely, without qualification or condition, with the opacity of the eternal. States that he dreams of a substance whose existence satisfies this specification. States that the substance follows him into waking moments; that it has an aroma, an aura, a tangible presence, a specific luminescence, a resonance, and a discernible impact on the planet's gravitational field. Wonders how long General Pinochet will live. Wonders whom Pinochet will outlive. Describes something that

I cannot describe, because I cannot adjust any element of his tightly wound and precise machine of language without the meaning of the entire structure unraveling, and I must not repeat it verbatim. Describes something. Describes it beautifully. Asks Bolo the date of his own birthday. Apologizes. I want to comfort him.

[Judith, are you ok?]

[Just tired. The longer I spend in the cold room the more likely I am to get a headache. Maybe they should check the paint for lead!?]

[What can you tell me about USCACM? CC]

[There isn't much out there. It was sponsored by the Foreign Office as a soft-power initiative, apparently with the British Council. They put together events and exhibitions with artists in Southern Cone dictatorships, which was pretty innocent, except, as a few people pointed out, the only artists available were the ones who hadn't run away or been killed. Hard to see it not basically legitimizing the regimes—especially since it shut down immediately after the Berlin Wall fell. JB]

Letter from A. to Crew, 02/15/1984.

A. requests updated information regarding his percentage of royalties. Mentions Marx and Engels. Describes encounters in anarcho-agricultural communes in 1970s [confid.]. Describes looking for Jag Caruthers in a seemingly endless party taking place in a labyrinthine repurposed nursery glasshouse. Asks to renegotiate agency commission.

Letter from Crew to A., 02/17/1984.

Reply to the above. Crew mentions Jag Caruthers. Refers A. to copied sections of his contract, indicating an agreed later date for the renegotiation of commission. Terse.

[Judith, let us take a moment to meditate on what has occurred in these months, January to February 1984.

1. The initial correspondence with Bolo is certainly valuable for my biographical endeavors, but not useful for our current research. Agree?

2. The letters to and from the editor Crew appear quite standard business to me. Any theories as to why his mood sours at the end? I quite understand Crew's response.

3. Relatedly, what is your opinion on the items from Dr. Bredsky? Carrette]

[Cléophe:

1. Agreed.

2. Agree with your first point. The cause must be this "course" Bredsky seems to be proposing for A. I looked it up—£5,000 in 1984 is £20,000 today. Hard to understand how an exiled author would come across this amount of money . . .

3. I looked up Adriana Bredsky. She's in prison. There are lots of nasty news stories about what she did to get herself sent to jail (basically a sweat lodge ritual gone wrong, lots of people dead of heat stroke), but apart from the juicy detail that she's not a real doctor, but was, in fact, one of D. D. Linus's patients in the 1960s (looked up Linus—what a rabbit hole!), there's nothing else about her. I have no idea what she had planned for A. I don't know what PanOp Insights could have to do with it, because, as you said, they make security cameras.]

[Judith, I agree Bredsky's intervention appears very significant. But is it true Jungian synchronicity? I should enjoy discussing it with you face to face. CC]

[Let's meet outdoors. I saw a doctor who said I have eye strain. Then my optician recommended a psychotherapist. It's not just headaches—sometimes I get completely exhausted, like my brain's full of cobwebs. I spent four hours staring at the first Bredsky letter—and it's not that long! I don't know where I went. I could do with some fresh air. JB]

March–April 1984

Letter from A. to Jaime Bolo, 03/02/1984.

Greets Bolo excitedly. Expresses hope for an [undefined] scheme to improve the financial returns from his dealings with publishers and agents. States that he's been sleeping deeply, thanks to some therapeutic materials he's received, with a measurable positive impact on his health, but for irregular and sometimes inconvenient periods. Describes a week's sleeping patterns and the consistency and punctuality of his turds. I'm tired, it's like the page is underwater. States that he saw a stranger on the [undefined location] heath that reminded him, thanks to his thin, dark-clad, pale-skinned appearance, of a folk story he heard long ago; that he spent hours attempting to remember the folktale; that on discussing it with his maternal aunt, now in Mexico, expensively telephoned and unhappily awoken, he realized no such folktale existed containing this man; a slender, pale man in black, moving across the grass; floating; perhaps dancing.

[Judith, I shall miss you, but I must recommend you rest a day or two until you can shake this grippe. Carrette]

Three letters between A. and legal firm Giovanni, Metti & Metti LLC, between 03/14/1984 and 03/31/1984.

A. and GMM correspond regarding the possibility of amending or escaping A.'s publishing contract with Albatross Hung. These options are ultimately not pursued.

Letter from A. to Bolo, 04/02/1984.

Complains about the intransigence of agents and publishers. Describes meeting [literary agent] Keira Sassoon outside the Iberico Theatre on Jermyn Street after a musical. Expresses disgust at the falsity of their forced conversation; the voracity and amorality of the gatekeepers of the industry; their professed sympathy with his struggles in the abstract, as a Latin-type expatriate, with all attendant romance; their failure to enact sympathy's practical form; namely, pecuniary justice.

[Judith, I must warn you. You may be approached by persons who claim to know you. They may even come to your home. They may be men or women, of any age, wearing outfits denoting any possible profession. They will do this: Call you by your name. You mustn't answer. Do not say, "yes." Don't say, as if on the telephone, "this is she." The moment you acknowledge them and give away your identity, they'll hand you a package, and without thinking you'll accept it, and then the subpoena will have been delivered, and all our work will be for nothing. GMM's Archimboldi estate ghouls are everywhere. They disguise themselves as postal workers, delivery drivers, street urchins, mysterious lords and ladies. They have no scruples. My phone is being monitored and my mail intercepted. Not a scrap of paper do I allow to leave my hands with my handwriting on it. The stakes are too great.]

Letter from April Bainbridge, Countess Devonshire, to A., 04/08/1984.

Expresses surprised pleasure at being contacted. Mentions a party held long ago. Lists guests including Isobel Crew [wife of Jonathan Crew] and Jag Caruthers. Describes in wistful, disappointed terms something that might have been a literary scene but never materialized. Execrates the 1980s. Expresses fear of the Soviet Union and guilt for underestimating the valor of Soviet subjects. Discusses concepts of peasantry and serfdom. Refuses to loan money to A. Expresses regret at missing him after a recent musical at the Iberico Theatre.

Letter from Col. Samuel D. Lancaster (Rtd), Civil Service attaché, to A., 04/12/1984.

Lancaster thanks A. for his entertaining presence at an informal dinner. Makes light of apparent cultural differences and indicates hopes for a mutually beneficial cultural reset between Britain and the intelligent inhabitants of South America, whom he has pleasure of meeting in his work with the British Council. States that he looks forward to reading The Swordfish North [sic]. Comments as if in afterthought that he will have a word with the Royal Literary Fund and have a £5,000 bursary provided.

May–June 1984

Printed invitation to the USCACM dinner held in Fishmonger's Hall, London Bridge, 05/12/1984.

Fragmentary. Defaced by unknown hand. [This is significant, don't you agree, Judith? His critics would salivate, hearing he sold out his principles and played along with the USCACM. The power of £5,000! Carrette]

[I find it depressing. I'm afraid I won't be in tomorrow. Will try to shake it off at home. JB]

Receipt from Bredsky for A., 06/01/1984.

Letterhead bears logo of PRISM CONSULTANCY and is addressed to Pentorgan House, Devon [remaining address smudged]. Receipt covers £5,000 for psychotherapeutic-creative services rendered. Handwritten [Bredsky's hand] is a request for A. to focus initial meditations on the enclosed texts [missing] as well as the key moments in his flight from his homeland.

Letter from A. to Bolo, 06/01/1984.

Greets Bolo politely. Apologizes for a long absence communicating. Glosses over rumors about himself [plainly the USCACM dinner—CC] as things that Bolo would be too serious-minded, skeptical, and generous to concern himself with. States that he feels an exile among exiles. Recalls the early days after the coup. States that half the poor were paralyzed by fear, and half the middle class by disbelief. Recalls the flavor of disbelief as if it were acid reflux. Recalls casual inquiries about passports and visas and tickets for international travel; jokes about the junta whispered in cafes and recounted loudly at dinner parties; contacts in the ministries quietly groomed with hampers and liquor; sacks of rice purchased and stashed. Describes aircraft tracing routes across the sky; chugging of military engines and stones popping beneath truck tires; clatter of matériel being unloaded; slap of boots on tarmac. States that this digression is neither excuse nor apology for attending the USCACM dinner. States that Bolo and he might be considered brothers, but that the substance that encompasses or enfolds their alleged brotherhood is nothing, in fact, to be proud of; that the true heroic witnesses of the coup are all dead.

[M. Carrette, a man followed me home last night. I have to believe he was real. When I wake in the morning I find it hard to remember I'm not still dreaming. I keep forgetting the security codes but I dare not write them down. I'd never write them down. B]

Letter from A. to Bolo, 06/07/1984.

Greets Bolo as if across a chasm of tempting narrowness but terrible depth separating two promontories on a ridge of rock and scree. Hints at unspoken, mutually witnessed calamity. Describes the weather in heartbreaking detail. Alludes to a heightened state of awareness. Misspells one word in three. Describes being tired and sick, which are two things I know about. Describes working on a manuscript named <u>The Truth of Carcosa</u>.

[Tell me what you know about The Truth of Carcosa.]

[Only what you told me at the start: that it was important, and might have a big role in the biography. I tried to look it up, but the National Firewall blocked me, so I guessed it was related to something sensitive, like the Immigration Emergency Referendum. JB]

[Judith—yes, it is sensitive, but for reasons I haven't yet determined. In fact, it's likely more important than I let on. If we can find a copy of this book, I'd regard it as a great success for our research. The greatest success. Carrette]

Letter from A. to Bredsky, 06/10/1984.

First page missing. Excerpt starts midway through comment about discomfort of the therapeutic process, described like physical pain or interaction with physical restraints. A. thanks Bredsky for her help. Employs new terms, as if A. and she are working together to build some esoteric structure, perhaps architectural, perhaps theological. States that the work has been hard, but great enhancements are imminent.

Letter from Crew to A., 06/16/1984.

Inquires why A. hasn't responded to his letters in three months. Mentions family [confid.]. Argues that A.'s participation in the USCACM dinner shouldn't be regarded as a death knell to his career, but does, in fact, need addressing, given the left-leaning stance of his readership; suggests a newspaper interview.

Letter from A. to Bredsky, 06/16/1984.

Writes in an unfamiliar vernacular. Uses new words liberally, as if testing them out, excited. Agrees that Bredsky's guidance has resulted in welcome improvements. Writes openly about survivor guilt, especially as it relates to [black site under the junta] Villa Monaco. Describes clearly a colonial villa in the unfashionable end of a hilly suburb; paired gatehouses converted into barracks; a long curving driveway through an overgrown garden; an expansive Germanic manor with steep, gabled roofs fitted with quaint dormers; removal of handcuffs in a wood-lined study attended by a sweaty guard; a wait, on one of several benches lined up against the wall; a cup of good, hot coffee; a request to use the toilet, denied; the arrival of an officer and his clerk, both tired and brisk; an invitation to walk with these overworked functionaries of the new state through the grounds, and round a fetid waterway, through an orchard and toward a cluster of outbuildings; a view through the perimeter fence of a startlingly industrial landscape; the sound of gunfire close by. States in plain language the nature of the offer and ultimatum he was given during the stroll: that according to new regulations, corroboration for denunciations of subversives was required from at least two civilian sources; that to maintain the ambitious targets for deradicalization, enhanced cooperation was therefore required; that of the subversives detained on the property, several had already been identified by civilian activists; that A.'s corroboration of the identity of these subversives was a technical step required for the law to proceed to its next stage, and given that he was arrested in the process of illegally fleeing the country, would aid in remedying his own legal position. Describes his first view of La Profunidad. Without recourse to metaphor or obfuscating technical detail, sketches a narrow, square tower, perhaps four stories tall, newly built from reinforced concrete, windowless [does not say, eyeless] and flat-roofed. Describes a single undersized steel door with a tiny letterbox. The whole structure set in a flat glade like an art installation. Describes being handed a list of a dozen names and a children's crayon; being guided through the door [not compared to a mouth]; having the door shut behind him. Describes an impossibly narrow, steep staircase, unlit and windowless, moving in a tight spiral upward; to the right, at irregular intervals, narrow, low steel doors; judas holes on the doors, with electric light emanating from within; the feverish claustrophobia of the windowless unlit stairwell. Analyzes the dislocation of A.'s sense of size: first an ogre, filling all the available space with his breathy shuffling; then a gremlin, slithering around the tight corners of an ever-diminishing world. Describes the contents of the cells visible through each judas hole: coffin-proportioned, with bright electric light in a cage on the ceiling, and a person enclosed, unable to sit, with their bony limbs pressed against the concrete, and a bucket of waste on the floor. States that he recognized many of the inhabitants of the cells. Analyzes the playful imagination made manifest in the design of La Profunidad, from its resemblance to Rapunzel's tower to the child-size proportions of the stairs, the tiny doors; and the fact of its human contents simultaneously hidden and put on bald display. States that he doesn't know how far up the spiral he traveled, but that exhaustion forced him to return to the ground floor, where, in the light emanating through the tiny letterbox, he examined the names on the list and calculated how many he needed to mark with his crayon to ensure his exit from the tower; that he marked the six names unfamiliar to him, then added three more that belonged to people he knew. That upon posting his list back out through the letterbox, he waited for an hour before being released. That his passport was returned to him in the repurposed study and he was granted, at last, use of the latrines.

[There it is, Cléophe. Proof of Archimboldi's collaboration. De Silva would pay a fortune to see this. It proves everything he wrote about the man. I feel sick. JB]

[I too am saddened. But we mustn't rush to judgment. We can guess what was being threatened against A., when he marked those names. Do we know for certain that, if we were in a similar quandary, we wouldn't make the same choice? CC]

[Yeah? But I'm not entirely sure I trust it. This might sound strange, but it's far too clear. I've been reading Archimboldi for months. I'm used to his digressions. I'm used to his lists. But reading this was like stepping out of the woods into a horrible clearing where everything is too bright and the lines are too sharp. It gives me a headache. JB]

[Recall how A. himself equated true clarity with madness. We are in the eye of the storm, here, Judith. I fear what comes next.]

Letter from Crew to A., 06/17/1984.

Crew extends professional greetings, et cetera. Asks whether A. has had time to think about an interview. Requests an update on A.'s progress on his latest project. Asks whether A. has settled on the title Dog Dangerous, and whether Crew can present it to the Albatross Hung marketing department.

Letter from A. to Crew, 06/18/1984.

[Hastily written, sometimes illegible.] A. states that he was never seriously planning to write Dog Dangerous [no work published under that title; possibly Somnolent Angelique, 1989]. States that the project was flawed from the outset, being the product of psychic immaturity, connected with cosmic events outside of A.'s control. Describes a newfound psychic clarity. Refers to extensive reading [subject unspecified]. Makes statements about Crew's family situation [confid.]. Expresses excitement at forthcoming [illegible] event. States that his previous artistic expression cleaved too close to his own sense of personhood. Pledges greater objectivity; expresses desire to disappear into a greater text; expresses terror at [illegible]. Discusses literary theory. Includes obscene sketch. Ends with a joke.

Letter from A. to Bredsky, 06/19/1984.

Starts like a replica of A.'s previous letter to Bredsky, but the previous clarity quickly falls away into confusion. Contains several nested descriptions, of the interior of La Profunidad, the overgrown grounds of Villa Monaco, Avenida Antioquia from which A. hailed a taxi, the airport lounge in which A. was detained as he attempted to leave Cabracion, and a stuffy room full of machinery and electronic devices operated by medical professionals; flits between these descriptions like a blowfly with no concern for narrative coherence. Resembles a prose poem. Between these fabulous outgrowths a figure in black comes to form. Describes him. I can see him but looking back I see no description [Judith, please meet me when you can. CC]. Describes again the journey from gatehouse to villa, but embellishes the gatehouse with alien features and blocks the path with tollgates whose names conjure creaking polystyrene and snapping fingernails, inhabits the grounds with beast-like guards, paints the sky with new stars. Twists the timeline so that our traveler never reaches his destination, but arrives through the gatehouse—a colossal stone arch carved with obscenities—and negotiates with the guards—pig-faced, dog-faced, bird-faced—manning each tollgate, and disintegrates and starts again, but notes the location of each landmark, so that each rehearsal moves a little closer to the tower at the center. Asks, finally, I am nauseated, whether Dr. Bredsky thinks he's ready yet.

[What is this, Cléophe?]

[I can only speculate that this is an early draft of The Truth of Carcosa, or an exercise carried out in its production. What do you think of it?]

[It makes me feel repulsed. I can't hold it in my memory. I don't think my summary covers it, but I can't bring myself to return to the document. JB]

Letter from Stephanie White of Albatross Hung to A., 06/21/1984.

White regrets that personal circumstances have forced Jonathan Crew to scale back his personal interactions with clients, so she'll be A.'s primary point of contact going forward. Expresses excitement to be working with a figure of such reputation as A. States that she's looking forward to hearing more about his progress on the next novel, which apparently promises to address spiritual themes.

July 1984

Letter from Bredsky to Bolo, 07/13/1984.

Bredsky salutes Bolo in formal terms, acknowledging that they've never met. She summarizes her career thus far as a marketing manager turned personal-growth guru, listing her published works on Jungian analysis. Describes the conditions under which she met A.—at a dinner party held in honor of the absent Jag Caruthers [then interned in Algeria]—and summarizes their occasional correspondence, which focused on the subjects of the collective unconscious and violence. Acknowledges that Bolo might not credit the story she's about to relate. States that Bredsky's company, Prism Consultancy, operates out of Pentorgan House, South Devon; that A. appeared at this property in the early hours of the morning of 07/11/1984. Observes that A. didn't know where he was, how he got there, or what he'd been doing for the past three weeks. Relates that A.'s recovery was swift but confusing; he seemed intermittently feverish, sometimes fiercely lucid, always unhinged; he appeared to be carrying out parallel conversations from distinct temporal continuums. Summarizes her own interpretation of events, namely that her recent correspondence with A. had encouraged him to seek her out in a moment of psychological crisis. She regrets, however, that the treatments at her disposal are not suited to A.'s requirements; Prism caters to institutional customers with niche, sometimes coarse, needs; she wouldn't subject so sensitive an instrument as A. to the methods habitually doled out in Pentorgan House. Requests Bolo retrieve A. Instructs him to bring a change of clothing and enough cash to cover expenses incurred in his stay. Explains expenses. Breaks down a daily rate.

Fragment of manuscript by A., undated [likely written in/referring to July 1984].

Narrates the experience of a character named Archimboldi from the moment he comes to consciousness on the grounds of Pentorgan House, Devon. He is hauled from the bushes by a retired officer of the King's African Rifles. Archimboldi is carried into the main house. An electrician in the Royal Engineers, recently rotated back from active duty in Northern Ireland, helps carry him from the reception area into the kitchen; he is supplied with hot sweet tea, then questioned by other therapy participants of an experimental week-long course devised for the Ministry of Defence. There is a barrack-house atmosphere that sours as each participant—rendered vulnerable by recent group therapies—reacts to the sudden appearance of the interloper; yet within the flux of verbal disagreements, brief physical tussles, and sly power plays, a recognizable pattern emerges. Disagreements as to how to treat him resolve into disagreements as to who will "treat" him, following predictable inter-regimental animosities. A character named Dr. Bredsky appears and intervenes before Archimboldi can be trussed into a pressure position. She removes him to the east wing, which is occupied by a private party of society figures carrying out practical experiments in synchronicity. This proves to be a mistake, since the participants mistake Archimboldi's arrival for the result of an extracurricular invocation. Narrates a farcical scene of hysterical shrieking, fainting, and maniacal laughter. Bredsky ultimately finds a berth for Archimboldi in the north wing, which is occupied by suspect priests, all of whom are determinedly asleep, as is their habit at that point in the long night, dreaming their unquiet dreams.

The fragment ends here.

[This reminds me of Somnolent Angelique—the stupid bits, at least. JB]

[Yes, I can see the resemblance. Can we assume A. based his story on his own experiences? His use of his own name is suggestive . . .]

[Ha ha! Now we are being real researchers!]

[Bredsky did, in fact, mention working with the MoD, did she not? Intelligence agencies have used psychologists to improve fighting effectiveness for decades. And we might infer that other institutions made use of Prism Consultancy's therapeutic expertise. Recall that priests accused of crimes against children were typically placed in "retreats" and "hospitals" in the 1970s and 1980s. I think this is a true account disguised in high camp style. As for its reconfiguration in Somnolent Angelique—that is truly a question for Archimboldi scholars. CC]

Letter from A. to Bolo, 07/27/1984.

A. greets Bolo sheepishly. Refers to the return of funds owed and the establishment of moral debt. Apologizes for behaving like a minor character in a farce. States that he feels like a senseless beast scrabbling around in some morass of gruel and feces. States, however, that with every new day he feels small growth of the heroic, fed by the early morning sunlight, which casts things in golden coronas. Lists objects cast in golden coronas. States that the color yellow is more striking than all other colors because it is the Earth's only non-native frequency. Asks after three of Bolo's cousins, all of whom he must know are dead.

[Judith I fear I am becoming gravely ill. Carrette]

[Cléophe, meet me tonight. B]

August–September 1984

Letter from A. to Bolo, 08/03/1984.

Greets Bolo with resentful formality. Requests the return of some books he has lent. Makes noncommittal predictions as to the success of a manuscript he's working on. States that the manuscript has caused him great trouble, and he's looking forward to closing this chapter of his life, one way or another.

Note from A. to Jaime Bolo, 08/04/1984. Unfinished; no envelope or postmark; likely unsent.

Apologizes to Bolo. States that A. has been led astray by the mirage of closure. Describes the pursuit of closure as a species of nostalgia, comparable to the pursuit of the numinous, the butterflies on the veld. Lists endangered species. States that he fears the book he's written; that he believed he could perform alchemy on his memories, transmute his pain into profit; but that the distillation of his experience is a poison. Hints at some torturous, invasive, techno-medical element of Bredsky's therapeutic treatment. Starts to warn Bolo [ends mid-sentence].

[Cléophe, if I understood you rightly last week, you wanted a recommendation: somebody trustworthy in the ALI who could continue our work if we deteriorate. Sorry, there's nobody I recommend right now. There are competent archivists, and they're nice enough people, of course. But what we're doing grows heavier in my heart every day. I wouldn't feel comfortable trusting any of them with responsibility over what feels more and more like my life's work. B]

Letter from A. to Crew, 08/05/1984.

Greets Crew with a warmth that indicates the resumption of ordinary relations. Refers to enclosed [missing] manuscript in coy terms. States that the novel is perhaps more experimental than his previous offerings, but that it has a long lineage. Ancient, even.

Letter from A. to Crew, 09/15/1984.

Adopts a businesslike tone addressing proposed edits and revisions to the [unnamed] novel-in-progress. Systematically rejects 105 out of 113 edits with reference only to page numbers. The remaining accepted edits include five references to punctuation, and the following:

Accepts change of spelling to "Carcosa" on page 167, but states that previous alternative spellings had been intentional, since "cacosa" suggested "shit."

Accepts suggested insertion of the word "epaulettes," commenting that they would make an unusual adornment on the type of Japonaise bathrobe the King typically wore.

Accepts suggestion to rewrite section describing the storming of the compound so as to include character names, cardinal directions, architectural information, and some sense of resolution, including reference to victory or defeat for any interested party. Apologizes.

[Judith—more concrete evidence of the existence of the The Truth of Carcosa: eight minor edits, five of which offer nothing substantive whatsoever. As for the remainder: I see an insulting attitude toward this (assumed location) "Carcosa"; some evidence of the costume worn by the Yellow King, evidently a kimono with military trimmings; and a reference to military action taken against a defended locale. CC]

[These images make perfect sense to me, as if I remember them from somewhere, one of his books perhaps, but I know that can't be true. People keep telling me I need to rest. JB]

October—November 1984

Letter from Crew to A., 10/11/1984.

Crew refers ruefully to recent negotiations regarding revisions to A.'s novel. Avoids naming the text directly. Thanks A. for concessions made; assures him that the changes are intended to broaden the book's potential audience, not through coarsening the material, but by clarifying its meaning. States that not everybody has a specialist knowledge of the esoteric arts. Writes that he's tired [aren't we all?]. Describes his home life [confid.]. States that he feels as though he's about to shed a great burden and feel its absence like a weight in itself and not know what to replace it with. Describes gazing out of his back window at the hospice adjoining his property. States that he sleeps badly, especially since the printers burned down. Describes his dreams, which feature his family [confid.]. States that he values A. as a friend but that he has mixed feelings about the direction he's taking as a writer. Apologizes. Explains that a reader's proof of the text will be delivered within a week. Alludes to difficulties arranging a courier service.

[Judith—thank you for meeting me yesterday. It was a clever suggestion to pursue the lead offered by the printers. The company has gone under, but the insurers who dealt with the fire claim are still operating, and seem quite cooperative. Next week I'll travel to a location where I'm told their pre-digital files are stored. I'm unsure as to the size of this cache, but preparing to stay on-site for a week. Don't worry about me. Carrette]

[Cléophe, I know you can't read this right now, but it helps me to write it. I'm scared for you. I see you, out there alone in the fog, carrying your lantern to those great dark gates. Every night I stagger out of the reading room exhausted as if I've worked my way through a great tome of difficult text; but it turns out I've only managed to read one letter, maybe two. I don't know what I do in there all day. I don't know where I go. Walking to the bus stop the Institute grows and shifts around me like a gigantic machine; I get home, feeling so sick, and throw myself on the bed and think of you, out there. I can't seem to sleep enough—and my dreams . . .]

Letter from Stephanie White to A., 10/23/1984.

Employs snazzy single-word greeting. Apologizes for failure to deliver reader proof. States that Albatross Hung has relocated due to electrical issues in its building. Asserts that the issue is in the hands of the landlord, who is legally responsible, so Albatross Hung remains solvent, operational, and competitive. Recounts the difficulty of locating efficient contractors. Laments a general lack of professionalism. Illustrates with an example of the artist employed to produce the front cover [presumably of The Truth of Carcosa]. Narrates how the illustrator raised superstitious complaints; then requested a revised fee; then simply disappeared, having delivered a passable but unusual sketch via courier. Has fun describing problems in a tabloid style. Alludes to broken contracts and broken limbs. Conjures greedy union organizers and incompetent underlings. God save us from this thoughtless mercenary woman.

[Judith, I thank you for your kind thoughts but really you mustn't worry. My stretch in the insurer's warehouse was in retrospect merely tiresome and frustrating (although I felt some superstitious fears of my own). No concrete results, although I did make a contact who may provide further information. They insist on corresponding by courier—an incredible expense but logical, and the publishers will cover it. But since I returned I've noticed changes in the city. It seems markedly more tense. This political situation is nothing to do with us, of course, but we can't deny that we stick out more than most in this corner of the country. Regrettable that I have to mention this. We must keep our heads down, no? CC]

Fragmentary excerpt of anonymous typewritten manuscript, found in an envelope postmarked 11/02/1984.

The text refers to a presentation made at the 1978 Restevo Conference on Experimental Semiotics [no record of such conference exists].

In note form, it outlines esoteric theories of semiotics that branch into theology, astrophysics, parapsychology, geomancy, metalinguistics, color theory, and political science. The prose is dense and specialized, resisting paraphrase.

[Judith—this is interesting. Can you take a second look? Please don't be cowed by the technical language. You can do it! I may require your help with something else. Let's talk face to face. Carrette]

Letter from White to A., 11/17/1984.

Expresses sincere regrets for the untimely demise of Jonathan Crew. Refers to legacy of good deeds left behind and the necessity of all Albatross Hung employees and partners to maintain good mental and emotional hygiene. Does not mention suicide. Dismisses unreliable tabloid speculation, spooky stories, and crackpot theories. Regarding A.'s work, states unequivocally that his authorial rights will be respected: Reader proofs of The Truth of Carcosa are being recalled and pulped; the first run of hardbacks has already been destroyed, press releases and events canceled, and the offices purged of the artworks associated with the book. Explains that a single experimental print run remains partially unaccounted for. States that efforts are being made to track down the fewer than fifty copies of the book outstanding. Strongly refutes any suggestion that an employee of Albatross Hung would see any value in keeping any text belonging to an associate author without explicit consent. Denies any conspiracy. States that Adriana Bredsky of Prism Consultancy has offered her services to handle the press fallout. Describes meeting Bredsky at several dinner parties, along with Jag Caruthers and Doris Lessing. Expresses enthusiasm for A.'s outline of his next novel [most likely Mulberry Sands, 1986], which she hopes will see a return to lighter themes.

IV

29

"Judy? Judy, wake up now."

Judith Bea fumbles with the switch on her hurricane lantern and peers toward the source of the voice. Weak electric light illuminates Scottie, standing in the entrance of the chamber they've been sharing for the last few weeks. Bea's alarm clock shows three o'clock in the morning.

"What's wrong?" she asks. "How come you took so long?"

"We got back a few hours ago. Didn't Mr. Sol tell you?"

"No, he never came here. I've been asleep. I was so worried, knowing you were out there, I had a cup of Fran's special tea. That tea. I must have passed out."

"I'm fine, though."

"Fucking Fran."

"Judy."

"She's actually a bit of a snake, sometimes, Scottie."

"Judy, listen: We found where Louis was hiding out. It was somebody's house. A family was living there, but the Hasturian Guard took them away. Louis denounced them."

"Holy crap."

"He stayed in their house for a while. Then he torched it. Now he's gone. He left a diary, Judy, and I've read it. I don't know who he is anymore. He thinks he's a genius and a, uh, a *Cipher*. He thinks he needs to read *The Truth of Carcosa* so that he can cause an Accession. *That's what he wants.*"

Bea's jaw hangs open.

"He *wants* to cause an Accession?" she asks.

Scottie nods.

"Why?"

Scottie shrugs.

"He thinks that's what he's been trained to do. He thinks it would be good."

Bea just stares at him.

"But it wouldn't be good, right?" he asks her.

She shakes her head minutely.

"It would be the end of everything," she says.

* * *

Bea climbs up out of the hobbit home. The night air is cool and fresh. She surveys the squat little row of dwellings. They seem so quaint in the moonlight, with the tall trees rising behind. Daylight, she knows, reveals them to be ramshackle and dirty.

Scottie tells her what he saw in town. The rumors they've heard are true, and the Hasturian Guard have revealed themselves. Everything they said before about protecting local communities, about restoring law and order and rooting out criminals and pedophiles, was cover. It's just violence. Racist violence. Although Judy knew that already. Then he tells her what he read in Louis's diary. How Louis wants the Yellow King to come and take him over, take everything over, finish it all.

Bea groans.

"I remember what you told me about how bad an Accession would be," Scottie says. "But Louis, he's got this whole other perspective on it. A whole philosophical idea. The Yellow King is like a god to him."

"That's just what we need."

"But he's not, though, right? This isn't a god, right?"

"I don't know."

"Louis thinks he does. He thinks the clues are in the books. You know, *The King in Yellow*, *The Truth of Carcosa*."

"I think I should read Louis's diary."

Scottie nods.

"I've got it stashed in the clearing. I want Mr. Sol to see it, too, but I think Fran wanted him tonight for some treatment . . ."

"Yuk," Bea says.

They trek along a duckboard walkway down an incline toward another clearing in the woods. Dim solar-powered lights switch on automatically as they pass, lighting a meandering path between the trees. They reach an extensive wooden outbuilding: compost toilets, showers, laundry. Somebody has left their sheets out on the washing lines overnight. Bea goes in to use the facilities, and Scottie wanders between the pale, damp-smelling shapes on the lines until he encounters a pair of plastic lawn chairs at the bottom of the clearing. He sits. The seat is wet. When dawn comes in an hour or two, these chairs will command a view down the ridge toward the Institute.

Bea rejoins him.

"You all right?" she asks. "Ready to go?"

Scottie shakes his head.

"What is it?"

"I've been thinking about what Louis wrote about me in his diary. I didn't recognize myself. I didn't recognize anything he said about when we were young. You see, Louis and me, we basically took a lot of drugs back then. We all did. But we weren't total addicts, we weren't criminals. We weren't out to hurt anyone. We were just taking our time growing up. Making the same mistakes lots of people make.

"It hurt, reading what Louis wrote. Not just because he lied about me. The thing is, despite everything, I still remember that time fondly. And even if I regretted it . . . it would be for *me* to regret, you understand? It's not just his past, it's mine, too." Scottie sighs. Bea squeezes his hand. Her skin is dry from the hand sanitizer in the compost toilet. "I thought we were friends, but he makes like we were just strangers passing time together. He describes meeting me recently in the Berryman, and I don't recognize the person he's writing about. The words he has me say. Did I really say them? Possibly. Did I mean what he thinks I meant? No."

"He's sick, Scottie," Bea says. She's struggling to roll a joint in the darkness. "He must be sick to do what he did . . ."

"I feel like he's wiped me out. Replaced me in his head." Bea nods. She knows what that feels like. She doesn't want to talk about it. "It's so hard to face, Judy, when there's nothing in the future but this . . . monster . . . this monster that's coming . . . I can't afford to lose my past as well." Bea passes him the lit joint. "I mean, fuck." He inhales. "You know?"

Bea holds Scottie's hand in her own. She holds on for a long moment. Flaming specks of hashish tumble out of the joint and fizzle on the damp leaves. He listens to her breathing.

She inhales. She feels the responsibility of the moment. She has an urge to tell Scottie that she loves him, if only because he clearly needs to hear it. Not so long ago she'd have done so confidently, half as a service, half to find out what it felt like on her lips, whether her impulse was, in fact, true. She'd have dealt with the consequences as they came.

But times have changed. Accuracy feels important.

"I'm sorry," she says truthfully, "about everything."

30

During her extended adolescence, Judith Bea never thought of herself as a thorough and careful person, nor did she aspire to be one. She was a dreamer and a doer who came up with grand schemes. This was the most desirable type of person to be, the most desirable way to be described.

Uni was consequently full of adventures. Much dreaming, much doing, and even more weed. She planned on traveling the world after she graduated: Peru, Vietnam, Zanzibar. But things didn't work out. In the months preceding the planned trip, her boyfriend Jesse fell into a strange psychological spiral. He started smoking more weed than he sold, spending more and more phone time absorbing the opinions of fringe individuals. After flirting with a few conspiracies—chem trails, embryo injections—he settled on the complaint that feminism was a conspiracy to destroy men. The edges of his personality started to sharpen: He presented new, overbearing behaviors. He wanted more from her: more latitude, more comfort, more compliance. He claimed to be becoming a new, stronger man, but Bea didn't understand why a strong man would need her to behave like his mother. He seemed, in fact, to be regressing, stage by stage: He covered his walls in soft porn, took up playing soldiers with other man-boys, stopped eating his vegetables, started throwing tantrums.

In retrospect, she should obviously have ended it then; hearing similar stories, she'd felt little sympathy for the women involved; but somehow, in her case, she felt compelled to stay and try to heal the wound that must have given rise to this new Jesse. Because this wasn't him. This guy in a tie who threw his plate of tofu on the floor wasn't the same guy she'd fallen for in first year.

Embarrassingly, it was actually Jesse who ended it. He met someone else, indulged in a few weeks of drama, and finally packed it all in, leaving for the long-planned world trip with an attitude of martyrdom. For Bea, left behind, taking a job at the ALI wasn't the most immediately attractive choice. But sometimes promises got broken, and she needed a job, and even in her disappointment she'd admit she was lucky to get this one.

The Archive for Literary Investment was a dry prospect, though. It didn't scream *dreaming and doing*. She didn't namecheck it when she met people at parties.

In the first weeks she used to get baked on cheap hashish every day. Usually at lunchtime, but sometimes in the morning, too. Trying to push everything back to a bearable distance. Telling herself: *This isn't your life, it's a game you play. Your life is an adventure you'll be having next year, in Peru*. She didn't allow herself to make friends with her colleagues. Not that there was anything wrong with these people, whose only real flaw was that Bea couldn't bear the thought of becoming like them.

This went on for months. Waking and baking, and not making friends. Dreaming of adventures. Outside of work, she started a very casual thing with a guy called Scottie. He lived in some kind of hand-built commune outside of the city and only came into town occasionally. He asked little of her, although there was a vagueness in him that provoked her to offer whatever he wanted. Aside from his strange hostility toward vaccinations, he had nothing in common with Jesse. It was a nice break, her thing with Scottie. But she saw no future in it.

Then Cléophe came to the ALI. Bea didn't get what the big deal was at first. On the day of her elevation at the ALI, when Mr. Holmes gave her an NDA to sign and Jan showed her the cold room and breathlessly explained she'd be working *directly under Monsieur Carrette*, Bea thought he was being pretentious. Only once they were working together did she start to get it, to understand the value of being thorough and careful.

In everything he said and wrote, Carrette had this method of organizing things so that their . . . *thingness* shone through. That was how Bea would describe it, and she knew it sounded silly, but she didn't know a better way. He could take a letter Archimboldi wrote, or just a *word* in that letter, and make Bea feel as though she could define it. Not that she expected to perfectly understand whatever it was—no, but as much as possible she had its parameters mapped out: its qualities, what it meant, how it fit in the world. And furthermore, he could show her what the rest of the world looked like, illuminated in the light of this one thing, set aflame with perception.

Which definitely did sound silly. But was true. And he'd do this without distortion. His gift was to explain the world as it was, carefully and thoroughly, so that everything seemed to be . . . clear. Crystal clear. Shiny.

And Bea found she wanted to be around him. She wanted to glimpse the world as he saw it, even though she could see what hard work it was to take everything so seriously. Not that he was humorless—quite the opposite, he was *seriously* funny, an idea that made perfect sense in his company, but was hard to communicate at parties, when she felt obliged to explain how she enjoyed her non-dreamy job.

People at parties tended not to ask about Carrette. Indeed, there were two types of people who would latch onto the fact that she worked at the ALI. The first were literary types, who wanted to talk about Archimboldi, aspired to work at the Institute, and were bores. The second were politically conscious people who wanted to educate her about *In Re: Albatross Hung*, and they were earnest and frightened, and left Bea feeling much worse than the first type.

Louis Barrow was the first type. Since they worked at the same place, Louis was inescapable, which obliged her to suppress her instinctive aversion and recognize his good points (he worked hard, for one, and seemed to mean well), concluding that he was *fine, really, and perfectly harmless*. But he tended to fixate on things, and wanted to talk to people (usually Bea) about them, yet the more he talked, the more apparent it became that he was really talking about himself. He would get into Archimboldi, tell Bea all sorts of theories from his dissertation (still in progress?), but every theory seemed to reflect his own triumph or failure, as if he were trapped in a mirror world, laboring without success to touch something real.

Bea felt some sympathy. She thought Archimboldi was a good writer, and enjoyed reading through his correspondence, to the point where she understood what an honor it was to do so. But it was slippery stuff, the Archimboldi material, all nested metaphors and unfinished arguments with absent friends, and she could imagine herself falling into the same traps Louis did if she were ever asked to write something serious about the man. She felt lucky to have Cléophe as a guide. A man who was undazzled by lyrical fugues, who could see through all the magical realist bullshit and match it to an actual life: just the right man to write Archimboldi's biography.

Bea declared her long adolescence over, renounced dreaming and doing, and dedicated herself to being thorough and careful. Her life became undramatic. She barely smoked dope anymore—at least, she didn't embark on the same fantastic journeys as before. Bea didn't want to fantasize. She wasn't interested in telling or hearing *stories*. She wanted the facts.

She started talking in a consciously factual way, as if she were in a contest to see how measured she could be in speech. For example, when Louis said something pretentious and self-serving, Bea would have previously said, "*Oh, he's the most annoying guy in the world*." Now, she'd think instead, *He's a minor annoyance*, and find it satisfying to pin him down in such a *Carrettian* manner.

She wondered whether she was becoming dull, then realized she didn't care. She didn't need to exaggerate and confabulate to find the world satisfying. But she did need Cléophe. It didn't work without him, the whole shining, factual world thing. They never had an affair, but it wasn't as if she didn't try. Lingering looks, brushing of hands, no mention of her own relationship status (Scottie seemed to hint that it was "open"), but just a couple of probing questions as to his . . . Subtle enough that she could take it back if Carrette didn't respond (which he didn't), but obvious enough that she wouldn't look back and regret doing nothing.

This was her situation when Carrette revealed the true direction of his research in the ALI.

Cléophe told her they were going to track down a missing manuscript from the 1980s, and she said *yes, we must*. Because every factual element relevant to the life of this great man (did she mean Archimboldi or Cléophe?) had to be brought to illumination. The book was called *The Truth of Carcosa*. Bea assumed the title was either a joke or a warning, because she'd heard of the Yellow King legend. She expected it to be a satire on Latin American politics.

To find the manuscript, Bea and Carrette went through the correspondence from the period he wrote it: 1984. They read it together. Bea was meant to describe what she saw, creating a detailed catalog that Mr. Carrette could use if he ever forgot anything. There were strict rules about not copying anything directly. And if they needed to say anything to each other they'd include it in the notes, in square brackets, like editors' asides.

It started going wrong quite slowly. So slowly that Bea didn't notice before it was far too late. As for Cléophe—perhaps he never noticed at all.

* * *

There were physical symptoms first. Bea fell into a fever one night after reading in the archive. The air conditioning was relentless in the reading rooms, and the cold room was a *cold* room; with Bea going between these spaces, drinking too much coffee, it made sense that her immune system was low and she picked up a virus.

It made equal sense when Cléophe caught it afterward. They took the weekend to recover, and returned to work feeling better, but as the next week went on, with their working hard and drinking coffee under vents again, it seemed they hadn't recovered properly after all. By Friday they felt like they'd need two weekends to get back to square one.

Bea felt horrible. Achy, hot-cold, with this permanent ashy taste in her mouth. She spent the weekend trying to sleep, but couldn't. She just dreamed. Dream for an hour, a day, a hundred years, unclear whether she was sleeping or waking; come to consciousness ten minutes later, begging for the dawn. She kept waiting for the fever to break, but it never would. Just heat. Discomfort. People standing at the foot of the bed.

The Monday after their second sickly weekend, Cléophe told Bea he was being followed. Given the situation with GMM and the Archimboldi Deposit, they both knew some surveillance was inevitable. But he said the man who followed him was different. He wasn't even a man. Cléophe called him a *Kataluin*.

"What's a *Kataluin*?" Bea asked.

He told her a *Kataluin* was like a spirit: a thing that appeared when changes were about to happen. They forced that change, sped it up, with violence.

Bea replied, "Okay, what do they look like and what shall we do about it?" as if he'd merely added something factual to her world. He described a kind of degraded man, a thin corpse-like man in a black jacket. Bea accepted it. These were the parameters of a *Kataluin*. She was running a fever of 103°F.

"He moves too quickly to see. He moves so slowly it's like waiting for hands."

Waiting for hands? She should have taken his temperature there and then. But she didn't. She wrote it down like important information. Her fingers felt huge, holding that funny sharp little pen, the lines coming out all swirly like clouds.

They set back to work in a daze. Whatever confusion Bea felt about the purpose of their research, she held absolute certainty that it was *correct*. And as she read through Archimboldi's letters, she became increasingly convinced that he, too, understood and shared their vision, that they were circling the same end goal, and at night and during daylight hours she dreamed of this circle, these spirals, where Cléophe and Archimboldi and she orbited this same blank space, like a planet, or a magnetic core.

31

"Joseph, I got your message. We've been playing phone tag a bit. I'm out visiting your area and I've dropped something off for you. I hope you get it." Nadia Eze pauses, grimacing, as her car bucks on a rut in the road. Greenwood Community is behind her, but the main road feels far away. "The people you're with seem pretty tightly wound—do you trust them?" Eze doesn't. The hostile woman at Greenwood Community was the first person she's spoken to in four days. She's been staying in her car, observing from a distance, confirming signs of mass movement from rest stops and bridges. It's been a tense, instructive trip and she can't wait to get away. Still, she doesn't feel right leaving Sol alone. "Not sure how much longer I want to stay in this part of the world, but . . . meet me at the quarry at midnight tomorrow if you want a lift to London. Either way, good luck."

Rounding the final bend before the path leaves the woods, some instinct prompts her to switch off her car lights. The instinct is right: She quickly sees that the gateway to the quarry is blocked. A police car sits, silently illuminating the undergrowth with blue pulses.

Eze puts the car in reverse. She tries to recall the angle of the turn, tries to navigate the ruts by touch—but the rear left wheel pops over a ridge at the edge of the road and sinks into a gap on the other side. She tries to pull the car forward again, but the axle is canted now: One wheel spins in the air, the other slips without purchase.

She's stuck, half on the road.

She thinks for a while, weighing her options. Finally she puts the car back into reverse, and the wheel—which was slipping uselessly in the opposite direction—finds purchase and jolts the chassis into the undergrowth behind. Stems and branches scrape the bodywork.

She grabs her bag and climbs out, clambers over the ridge and back onto the path. Her trainers brush through humus and squelch in clay. When she looks back, she can see the pale outline of the car from the road, so she gathers armfuls of leaf mold and throws them against the hood and roof.

She hears voices down the hill. Combustion engines. More vehicles are entering the quarry. She considers running back to warn Greenwood Community that a raid is imminent. At that moment, she hears wheels crunch and burble nearby, and realizes the police car is coming up the road.

She dives off the road and throws herself down an overgrown ridge. She scrapes her shin and bruises her knee, rolls helplessly for a frightening few seconds, then hooks her arm around a root and stops her descent. She listens to the sounds above. The car moves slowly; then she hears a radio bark; the car stops, idles, and finally reverses to its original position.

Eze considers and abandons the idea of climbing back up to the path. She laboriously twists herself round onto her back, arm still hooked tightly around the root. Looking down she sees, through high fencing, the floor of the quarry below the hill.

Vehicles have parked there: two vans with blacked-out windows, and a truck hauling a trailer.

The truck is strange. It resembles one of the low, squat vehicles used for towing jets around airports, and it has a bulbous, boxy load on its back. The trailer looks like a gas canister—or something similar, something Eze remembers from black-and-white images in textbooks: a relic of backward times; an iron lung.

32

One document in the 1984 Deposit was different from all the others. It seemed like the least promising one, to Bea: an academic paper, summarizing proceedings at a conference on semiotics held in the 1970s in a place called Restevo.

Carrette didn't flag the document as valuable, and Bea didn't fully understand it. So when she first read it, she created a very broad description. A single paragraph. Semiotics wasn't her field.

A few months later Cléophe was out chasing down rare book dealers by himself, and Bea could stagger into the ALI two or three days a week; Carrette instructed her to look again at the Restevo Conference.

She looked again.

Everything had changed.

It was amazing, Bea thought, the way the mind worked. She understood the paper perfectly, with a newfound clarity that didn't feel earned. As if it had come on like an atmosphere. Risen from the wetlands or descended from the deep black sky. The Restevo Conference was supposed to be about the connection between language and the world. There was an underlying understanding that language was a closed loop, and could only refer to itself (like Louis, Bea supposed). This idea didn't mean people couldn't communicate. If Person A and Person B both had closed loops in their head, those loops could run parallel for a stretch and imitate each other and ideas would get shared that way and they could call it a relationship, if they wanted.

But if we accepted that language was separate from the world of things, it meant accepting that *saying* something didn't make that thing real. Because there were no magic words. And most people who thought they understood the connection between language and the world (nature, God) were romantics or religious maniacs, and they sought to create sublime and transcendent moments with their words; but they were fooling themselves if they thought they could write it down and make it real, all that beauty or whatever.

So ran the first part of the conference proceedings, laying into all the monks and hippies who wrote freeform poetry and thought they were magicians, when really they were charlatans and their power was all momentarily enticed from the imaginations of the people who read them. This much Bea understood, despite the technical language and diagrams.

But then, it seemed, something in the conference changed. Because abruptly ideas were being discussed that completely contradicted what had come before. A new theory appeared about the connection between language and the world. Certain words, it turned out, *did* have power in and of themselves. Certain words *were* magic. And these scientists thought they worked in a systematic way.

What exactly these magic words did, Bea couldn't figure out. But certain terms kept popping up. The first was passenger. Then Cipher. Node. Seeding. Reaping. Accession crisis. Deferral.

A *passenger* was somebody, or something, trying to travel from one place to another.

A *Cipher* was somebody who helped the passenger. It was unclear whether or why they *wanted* to do so.

A *node* was a word or set of words that act as a target for the passenger. They were also like translators, encryptors or decryptors, or fuel, or buffers. They had to be written down, according to the scientists. It didn't work if they were spoken.

Seeding was the first stage in creating nodes. It was described in a few different ways. Sometimes it was compared to viruses, sometimes to quantum physics. In theory, apparently, the passenger could disseminate information of a near-infinitesimal size a near-infinite distance, but it required near-infinite longevity and patience to reach the point where reaping became possible. Seeds were like information, but also like intelligence itself. As if they were a virus: alive and dead, parasitic, contingent.

Reaping was the second stage in creating nodes. When seeds reached ideal conditions they would coalesce and reconstitute into nodes. This happened with the help of Ciphers.

Then finally there would be an *Accession crisis*, when the nodes became active (whatever that meant) and the passenger transited to the target location.

But if something went wrong, if the transit failed, it was called a *Deferral*. There was a lot of energy spent in a Deferral, apparently.

This much Bea understood, the second time she read the Restevo Conference proceedings. This whole new vocabulary became alive in her, and she sat back in her chair in the reading room, thought about dangerous words, and shivered.

33

Eze is down by the quarry bed, watching through the fence. She sees figures in black clothes file out of the first van. They move without discipline, milling around as if unsure what comes next. A woman wearing an anorak and headset gets out of the second van. She walks past the militia toward the back of the truck, where she opens a panel door and operates some kind of interface. Lights start to glow on the side. She pulls some heavy switches and a set of floodlights comes to life. The light wavers; she makes some adjustments and the light comes back stronger. A vivid yellow glow. The payload on the back of the truck is evidently some kind of generator.

It's at this point that Eze notices the quiet.

No engines are running. The generator—or whatever it is—isn't chugging or spouting smoke. The quarry bed is eerily quiet, in fact: The militia stand silently watching Anorak Woman work the controls. Eze can hear a muffled thudding, simultaneous with the jiggling of the trailer's umbilical wires.

A man in a zip-up sweater and headset gets out of the second van. He looks like a motivational speaker. He starts talking quietly to the militia members, shaking hands and touching their elbows and shoulders. Anorak Woman stands by the truck, watching some counter or meter. Occasionally a jolt from the cylindrical trailer is strong enough to make it rock on its suspension. When the militia members notice this, they fall back into silence.

Pep Man fetches a plastic crate of whisky and disposable cups. He pours measures of the spirit, which the militia members drink gratefully, but quietly, still eyeing the trailer. Now Anorak Woman unlocks another panel, containing a rack of tools mounted on charging points. She whistles, and the militia members hurry over, and one by one receive a blocky, black thing shaped more like a rechargeable drill than a gun, which these objects undoubtedly are, based on the excitement and reverence they provoke. The militia line things up in their gunsights. They murmur enthusiastically, investigating the weapons' triggers and buttons. A couple pose for photos, which Pep Man quickly prevents.

The canister thuds and rocks. The connecting tubes waver. The floodlights remain strong.

Pep Man calls the militia into a huddle. He says things Eze can't hear, and the militia members grunt in collective agreement. Then they all put their arms in the center, and the circle breaks up, and they pull masks up over their faces. The masks feature animal faces: wolves, tigers, bears. Over by the gate, the police car starts its engine and the group follows it slowly up the path between the trees.

They don't all move at once. Two, in particular, are slower than the others. One wears a monkey mask, while the other wears a shark mask. Shark and Monkey pour the last of the whisky into their plastic cups. They drink, and speak quietly. Anorak Woman returns to her van, leaving them alone.

Ignoring Shark's warnings, Monkey walks right up to the canister-shaped trailer. He stands at the end furthest from the umbilical wires, and stares down. There's a shadow there—a shape that Eze had assumed was a rivet. But she sees now that it's actually a small, circular window. Monkey stares down at the window. The cylinder vibrates. Monkey jumps back.

Then somebody in the main group calls out, and Shark and Monkey run to rejoin them.

34

Bea woke up one day in her miserable little pauper's cottage sicker than ever before. Nauseated, the walls billowing in. She started looking for pain meds and when she couldn't find any in the bathroom she thought to try the kitchen, where she discovered she had a package.

It was about the size and shape of a book. Although addressed to Bea's house, the name at the top said Cléophe Carrette. There was no chance in the world Bea would open it. Not because it wasn't addressed to her, but because if she did, she suspected, her skin would bubble and blister and peel off her fingers and the muscles and tendons would writhe and shrink and the bones would snap and crumble, and she'd be conscious of every moment of molecular tearing like a billion miniature chemical wounds as her body popped and spattered into flame.

So she called Louis Barrow. She decided to make him take it away and burn it. Not because he was particularly brave. She just thought if anybody would do her a favor like that, it was him.

But as she waited for Louis, her fear subsided and she started to feel silly about asking him to destroy something like this, and then she felt very unprofessional indeed, since this was obviously a document that Cléophe had entrusted to her. But it couldn't stay in the house. It would have to go to Cléophe. Direct. Louis could take it.

Louis came to her door, all eager to please, and she forced herself to carry the package outside, half expecting it to explode in her hands, but it didn't—in fact, everything felt very normal and the parcel didn't burn his hands or anything. After he left the nausea subsided and the walls edged back into their normal places, and Bea felt so relieved that she threw up and then slept for a day.

Louis delivered the package.

Then it happened. An event she was unable to describe to others because she still hadn't properly described it to herself. Bea's first bereavement.

After she saw the photos of Cléophe's body, Bea knew that everything she'd imagined happening to her—the flames, the tearing—had happened to him. It didn't take her long to realize what a Deferral really meant. The package may have contained a book, but most importantly it contained a *node*. She thought to consult the Restevo conference paper again but the ALI administrators caught her photocopying the wrong files. She should have known she'd be terminated immediately. Perhaps she invited it. Still, job or no job she needed to find out more. She tried to explain things to Louis Barrow, but he was no use. She tried to visit her local library, but it had burned down. She found another library on the other side of town and persuaded the librarian to let her in, and eventually she found an old encyclopedia full of entries that had since gone behind the National Firewall. She looked up Restevo, linguistics, conferences. There was no Restevo linguistics conference. The only mention of Restevo she found was a public health disaster, some kind of terrible calamity in the 1970s where hundreds of people died. She found newspaper articles on microfiche. *We must work hard to make sure no Restevo ever occurs again*, officials said. On the way home her bus was pulled over and the driver was bundled into a van. The world was falling down around her. It was time to drop out of it.

She thought to get to London. Things were different there, apparently. At least she was less likely to stand out in the street. Since Carrette's death she'd started to notice looks that previously she'd missed. The people around her seemed less friendly, more homogenously white. She found herself tying her hair back, wearing a face mask. She asked herself, *where were the other people like her?* And the moment she asked the question, its ramifications echoed coldly through her. Because despite myriad tiny incidents, she'd always thought she was like everybody else. The people who looked at her coldly were exceptions, not the norm; the creeping feeling she got when strangers examined her hair . . . that was just *some* strangers, *sometimes*. But now . . . had she been a stranger in this city all along, and failed to see it? She felt embarrassed. Humiliated by the image of herself bumbling ignorantly about, her difference on display to all these unsympathetic eyes.

No, her memories weren't false, the people had changed. They'd liked her once; now they'd turned against her. But how could the change be so extreme if it hadn't been coming all along? Then a certain *Carrettian* clarity arose within her, and she understood that yes, both everything and nothing had changed. The strand of racism had always been there, hidden within the crowd, hidden even from some who expressed it now. And just as it was coming to her attention, so too was it coming to theirs, like a suppressed memory, like a forgotten dream. And she felt grateful to Carrette, her teacher, to have enabled her to pin down the problem, determine the *thingness* of the thing. *So, then*, she asked herself, giddy, nauseated, floating in a treacherous stratum of false calm, *where were the other people like her?* They'd gone to London, perhaps.

Then her mother called. She was a little confused, a little upset. She'd just been removed from the neighborhood committee. She didn't understand: She got along with everyone so well. She was so put out about it, she thought she'd take her Provence holiday a bit earlier than planned. In fact, she was wondering, would Judy want to come with her this time? The vacation house was big enough. They might stay a few weeks together. A month, even.

No, thank you, Bea said, falling easily into her mother's bright, disingenuous mode. She was fine and quite busy, but her mother should go. Go now. Just jump on a plane, why not? The airports were open, right?

Her own decision to flee was so precipitous she didn't even take the time to buy proper luggage. Just grabbed a rucksack and a garbage bag of clothes and boarded a bus. Waiting for too long for the vehicle to get moving. Wondering whether the tattooed driver was a real driver or one of *them*—who were they exactly, the "Hasturian Guard" she'd only just learned about and yet were everywhere, directing everything?

Then as Calendral Road slipped away beneath them, a sense of mounting excitement and dread; the sudden realization that her life depended on getting to London.

Then the roadblock. A wave of nausea, like a punch in the gut.

Looking around for an exit. Windows that open. Those little hammers for smashing a way out.

And the man sitting across the aisle leaned over, his face swam into her vision, his eyes fixing on hers.

"My name is Joseph Sol," he said. "I know who you are, and I'm on your side. I need you to do something brave. I need you to trust me."

35

Behind the diner where the bus pulled up was a wooded bank descending to a stream. After hurrying from the bus, Sol and Bea hid there, out of sight from the road. Sol's memories of that time were fractured. They might have stayed there for hours. It was a clear day, and sunlight passed between the boughs and bright buds, and at one point a dozen helicopters passed overhead, churning toward the coast. Sol and Bea talked, quietly and urgently. Sol told her what he'd been through—excluding the itch on his arm—and Bea responded with the story of her own time with Cléophe Carrette, their parallel search for *The Truth of Carcosa*. It wasn't an easy conversation. It was, frankly, too much. Sometimes they'd stop, abruptly, overwhelmed, and stand and listen to the birds in the trees. Look at the incongruous beauty of England in spring. In more lucid pauses they took stock of their situation. They couldn't stay here. Sol wondered how extensive these woods were; could they walk away from the city?

And what, Bea countered, walk to London? It would take a week. And the countryside wasn't safe.

Yes, Sol agreed, the countryside wasn't safe. Things were happening there. He remembered Eze's fragmentary warnings: trucks in the rest stops; troop mobilization. He wished he'd paid attention to the news. Even a week ago there were still regular updates from the Emergency Cabinet; not so much recently. He excused himself and walked down to the stream and called Eze, but she didn't answer. When he returned, Bea was hugging her knees, staring at nothing.

"I need to show you something," Sol said. "One last thing."

It was the document on Donaghy's phone. He pointed out the diagram of power lines radiating from a Xanthic Spectrum power plant. He described its similarities with the machine he'd seen in Higgins's office, the grotesque demonstration he'd witnessed, of Higgins drawing energy from Donaghy's body and the fragments of manuscript inside the "humidor."

The final piece of the puzzle.

"So it's about power," Bea said, flatly.

Sol nodded.

"It's not about books, or magic, or alien planets. It's about charging people's fucking phones."

The strange new vocabulary became clear to them then: The Xanthic Spectrum plan for perpetual energy required a state of perpetual "Deferral," and Deferral needed "nodes" and "Ciphers"—and nodes were pages and scraps of *The Truth of Carcosa* and Ciphers were the people who read them. Smoke was rising from the city. Ciphers were people. Somewhere in the woods, trucks were moving.

People.

At that moment, Bea's phone rang. It was her boyfriend, a guy called Scottie, finally returning her call. Half an hour later, a young, bearded man had pulled up in a mud-spattered van. Sol waited while Bea spoke to him. He listened, and looked Sol over, and eventually nodded, waving him onboard. That was how Sol and Bea were granted admission to Greenwood Community.

* * *

They arrived in a clearing with a large hand-painted sign that read GREENWOOD COMMUNITY: GENUINE TRAVELERS WELCOME. Here

Scottie, who turned out to be an open and sincere young man, formally welcomed Bea and "Mr. Sol," then gave them a tour of the site.

In truth, Sol found Greenwood Community ramshackle. Bea, too, seemed unenthusiastic about the longhouse, shed-like dwellings, and narrow fields of spindly legumes. A few people showed an interest: A young woman wanted to pray with them; an older man called John explained the democratic processes on which the entire community apparently depended, as if it were a microcosm of a mythical England, then sang them a song.

Sol had encountered this before. His mother turned to a number of institutions after his father's death, including a weekend in a self-sustaining women's shelter. Sol's main memory was the tension his own male, near-pubescent presence caused. Ultimately his mother removed the family before the notion that Sol carried his father's seed of evil within him could be cemented; nonetheless he recognized the forms and modes of communal living, and his polite responses to the residents' quirks became automatic. Bea, however, was visibly discomfited by the instantly personal questions and comments about auras.

One person, a woman named Fran, provoked a swift negative reaction from Bea. Some kind of authority in the community, Fran seemed very familiar with Scottie; Sol had assumed Scottie was Bea's established boyfriend, but Fran somehow cast the solidity of their relationship into doubt. Perhaps Bea's sudden intrusion into Scottie's home life wasn't something they'd planned for.

Scottie showed them to their sleeping quarters. Bea would share Scottie's subterranean dwelling ("actually very comfortable"), while Sol had a traditional laborer's cabin. Then, after they'd bathed and eaten lunch (taken communally in the longhouse and punctuated by ritual song and impromptu pipes from a guy who apparently *always* wanted to play the pipes), Sol lay on his bunk and took stock of his body. He felt exhausted and unreal. Sol recognized the aftereffects of trauma: He was processing the toxic physiological load of adrenaline and cortisol. Back when he was the footage man, half of Sol's clients were PTSD sufferers. Sol knew the symptoms: hyperarousal, dissociation, blunted affect. Was this unreality merely a symptom of trauma?

Was the itching in his arm psychosomatic?

(Had he seen, undressing just now before the polished steel mirror, the tracery of a sign on his abraded skin?)

He leapt up and hurried out to find Bea, who assumed his fear was the same as her own and was relieved to see him, and it was so comforting to be afraid together, to agree together that something must be done, that it was possible to ignore, in the ever-extending short term, the mark on his arm. So it remained hidden.

36

The quarry bed is quiet. Eze squeezes between two bars of a damaged fence panel and moves as quickly as she dares toward the parked truck. She believes Anorak Woman is still in her van, so keeps the truck between the van and herself, but is nonetheless vulnerable, under the fierce umbra of the floodlight. Although Eze tries not to disturb the scree, her footsteps sound crisp and clear to her. The only other sound is the soft thudding from the trailer, and the rubbery scrape of its umbilical connector.

She reaches the far end of the canister, passing a broad, embossed logo, painted over with white gloss: "Xanthic Spectrum." She reaches the window: a circular porthole the diameter of a coffee mug. The interior is dark. Eze's own reflection bounces as the cylinder shifts.

She pulls her flashlight out of her pocket. She holds it close against the thick glass.

Initially the beam only illuminates the glass itself, and she must carefully adjust the angle until the light is cast on the contents beneath. It's a fiddly, frustrating task, requiring patience and intense focus, and by the time she catches a glimpse inside, her face is directly over the glass, free hand shading her view.

Then she sees it.

And she falls back, onto her haunches.

She hears someone cry out. She realizes it was her.

Behind the truck, the van door opens.

Eze scrambles to her feet. She's perhaps a couple hundred feet from the main exit gate. The van is less than thirty feet away.

But she doesn't run.

With trembling hands she pulls her phone from her bag, fiddles with the screen until she finds the video app, and presses it against the porthole window.

Anorak Woman's head appears around the side of the truck. Her eyes widen and she talks into a radio handset.

Eze holds the camera to the porthole for as long as she dares—not enough, she feels certain—then dashes for the gate. Behind her, Anorak Woman hurries to the weapon rack, unlocks the panel, and retrieves a blocky gun.

Eze pumps her legs and for the first few moments of running she feels like she's flying. Then she loses her wind (far too quickly!) and starts to struggle.

Anorak Woman unfolds a black steel stock out of the back of the gun and rests it against her shoulder. She drops into an easy, practiced firing pose and centers the running woman with the needle on the end of the muzzle.

She whispers to herself as her finger squeezes on the trigger: "Eeny, meeny, miny . . . moe."

Eze perceives a flash behind her, before light shoots past her left flank in a curving beam, and a high-pitched, broken shriek blares like a staccato steam whistle. Phosphorescent sparks appear from the ground nearby.

Adrenaline fills her body and she swerves into an arc that wends toward the gate. Behind her, Anorak Woman eyes the blackened, glassy scorch mark and makes some adjustments to the device.

Eze has gone beyond fear. She moves with the cold certainty that every step she takes should be her last, receiving instructions from a calm-voiced inner pilot that tells her to zig, to zag, to duck at random moments. Anorak Woman fires again: three, four bursts of light and whistling screams.

But no heat lands on Eze. She feels no pain. Some miracle lifts her, some powerful and sympathetic wind pulls her forward, and as she rounds the post of the open gate, her nervous system rewards her with a memory, long forgotten, of running with her rucksack on her shoulders, from the school door all the way down the muddy path to the playing field, where her friends are waiting for her beneath the conker trees, ready to play in the endless after-school hours of a city to which she can never return.

Anorak Woman takes out her tablet and checks the data from her weapon. Overall, she's unimpressed with the result. It's unclear whether the range of the beam is shorter than expected, or some other distortion affected the trajectory. She thinks, maybe that last shot got her. Her data readout indicates feedback, so some kind of contact was made—perhaps, she conjectures, the back of the head, just as she rounded the corner. So maybe not such a bad result after all.

37

"Ciphers are *people*?" Scottie asked, incredulous.

They were in a clearing the community treated as a reflective spot, with camp chairs and a fire. Sol and Bea had been walking him through the whole conspiracy. He'd seemed impressed by Sol's video but doubt continued to flicker over his face.

"People," Sol repeated. "Carrette was a Cipher. My partner Donaghy was a Cipher. Think about it: To generate energy on an industrial scale, you'd need an industrial supply of nodes and Ciphers. An industrial supply of people."

Scottie burst out laughing.

"This is ridiculous. Nobody would agree to such a plan. Imagine it!"

"Scottie, how many people died in the Iraq War?"

"I don't know. Thousands?"

"Hundreds of thousands."

"So?"

"War for oil," Bea said. "Joe's saying people die for resources all the time."

"Yeah, but they're, like, overseas."

"You mean they're not real people?"

"I meant, it's not direct. We don't round up a hundred people and stick them in a battery and plug them into the power grid."

"But would we if we could?"

Scottie shook his head. "No," he said.

"What if it was a hundred people, and you could power the city for a week?"

"It would never happen."

"What if it was five people, and you could power the city for a year?"

"Well . . ."

"Bad people. Pedos. Cannibal Nazi lizard men. People who *aren't real people*."

A thoughtful pause, as Scottie lit a joint.

"I mean, okay. I see the logic." Scottie inhaled. He held the smoke in for a long time. "Fuck, man," he squeaked, eventually. "The Hasturian Guard already talking about raiding the prisons, you know. To protect us from, um, grooming gangs? That's what they claim."

"They're drawing a line between people who matter and people who don't."

"There's another consequence, Scottie, that could be even worse. If Xanthic Spectrum gets it wrong just once, then there's an Accession. That means an entity that exists in a different part of space-time will come to occupy *this* space-time."

"Like an alien invasion?"

"Maybe. Or maybe not. Maybe something simpler and messier. Like what happens when something appears very quickly where it wasn't meant to be. Like a bullet in your brain, maybe."

"What is this *entity*?"

"Cléophe called it the Yellow King."

"That's weird," Scottie said. His voice was thoughtful, without a trace of shock or scorn. He pulled out his phone. "The Yellow King is a broadcaster. He makes these videos about how immigrant smuggling gangs are stealing children's blood . . ."

He showed them a clip of a man in a kimono surrounded by graphics of ancient aliens and swastikas. Sol recognized him. The man had a high, reedy voice and spoke in a drawling American accent about *exterminating the infected.*

"Are you telling me Mr. Carrette was into this guy?" Scottie asked.

"Never!" said Bea. "This man's just a phony."

"Wait—"

Sol snatched the phone and paused the image. He examined the background and the little "Credits" section under the video, which was full of links to further propaganda. He saw something he recognized.

"New Ministries Holdings," he read out. "Do you know who they are? Nadia Eze showed me their name in a big list of companies that work with GMM. They fund fringe groups like the Hasturian Guard. Nationalist groups, extremists."

"Weird coincidence," said Scottie. He relit his joint.

"I don't understand," Sol said.

But he did. He understood, perfectly illogically, that the conspiracy theorist in the kimono and the tall bony man he'd glimpsed in Higgins's office and the unknown entity in the void of space were one and the same thing. His universe was infected, seeds of annihilation replicating and reiterating into foul extrusions. Part of him cherished this irrational knowledge and yearned for the entity that was its progenitor. That part of him extended from the mark on his arm and connected to the network of his nervous system. It pulsed. It whispered. It itched.

"So how do we stop them? GMM, Xanthic Spectrum, New Ministries Holdings—all these bad guys."

Scottie asked this question with a storybook simplicity that made Bea smile. Sol, his focus elsewhere, managed a pained grimace.

"These are big companies," he heard himself say. "They're operating at dozens of different levels at once. You don't just stop that."

"Actually, I think it would be simple enough," Bea said. "The whole process depends on nodes and Ciphers, and it seems they don't actually have a ready supply of nodes."

"So the whole thing stops if you destroy . . ."

". . . the remaining copies of *The Truth of Carcosa*."

Bea and Scottie smiled at one another. Sol wanted to find it sweet. He wanted to get caught up in the romance, the adventure of it all.

"So where are they?" he managed to ask. "What clues did you find in the archive?"

The smile died on Bea's face as she searched for the answer. It was as if she felt she ought to know, the answer was on the tip of her tongue, but . . . nothing.

"It was Carrette who found that last copy. I didn't even know he had it. I think I could probably retrace his steps, if I was back in the archive. But I can't go back."

"What about Louis?" Scottie asked, triumphantly. "He still works in the archive. He could help us out."

"Louis Barrow?" Bea asked. "Can you trust him?"

"Of course! He's a mate. Bit odd, mind. But a friend's a friend."

* * *

In the moments when Sol's itch intensified it took great self-control for him to conceal it. But in the days that followed everybody around him was distracted, trying to understand what news there was, reaching out to families, debating what, if anything, could be done. And while the itch was constant, its power waxed and waned; he could appear healthy. At night he dreamed of

Jennifer Donaghy, crawling on the floor; and felt Dulcie's hand pressing his own.

The three met frequently in the clearing. They discussed ideas for contacting Barrow, either by phone or in person. But until they could think of a safe way of approaching him, no plan was confirmed: It was too risky for Bea or Sol to head back to town; in fact, Sol didn't feel comfortable using his phone in the Community. He'd walk out into the woods and connect to a VPN and glean what information he could about the outside world (garbled, unreliable), then call Nadia Eze.

Eze never answered the phone, but she'd reply if he left messages. Her understanding of the situation seemed reliable. She informed him about the general strike, the blockade of Scotland, the Emergency Cabinet's increasingly ineffectual decrees. She told him about a covert diplomatic mission distributing EU passports for those who needed to get out. Eventually, a week before the mobile network went down and the Hasturian Guard started their shortwave radio broadcasts, she gave him a lead on Louis Barrow.

"He spends time on the *Aldebaran Gazette*. He's been publishing his essays on the Yellow King there. If you want to catch his attention, you can do it there. But Joe, it's not a savory website. I don't know how well you know this guy, but the other people posting are HG for sure. I don't know. Be careful."

38

Back in the clearing where they first formed their plans weeks before, Bea picks up the folder marked "Item Descriptions, JB & CC" and feels unexpected tenderness. Even now, it smells the way the cold room smelled, of acid and fust. The scent recalls others: coffee at break time, biscuits, woolens hanging beside the office door.

Scottie sits in the radius of the hurricane lamp. He takes the document and hands her a far fatter wad of papers.

"Louis's report," he says.

She flicks through the papers and realizes that half is in printed text and half is Louis's own handwriting. She recognizes the handwriting; and that recognition, she realizes, is tainted with sadness. She actually misses him. The old version of him, at least. She misses everybody from that simpler time.

But that world has ended. As will this one.

She sits and pulls a heavy quilt over her knees. She reads. Her hand seeks out Scottie's. She squeezes. He squeezes back.

* * *

An hour later Scottie has piled the *Correspondence 1984* description at his feet. He stretches.

"We saw Prism Consultancy advertised in the GMM video, right?"

"Yeah."

"And Prism Consultancy was Dr. Adriana Bredsky's company. And she was—what, experimenting on Archimboldi? Using some kind of mind-fuck technique to turn his memories into a kind of map, or instruction manual?"

"Based on what she learned from the Restevo Conference, yes."

Scottie reaches over and pulls the Special Report out of Bea's hands. He flicks through until he finds the page he wants, then shows her.

"Look," he says. "Louis was treated by Bredsky, too."

"No . . ." She scans the pages as quickly as she can, her lips moving.

"And look," Scottie points out another paragraph, "look at what he found while he was poking around in her office."

She reads the words *Node/Cipher Cultivation Project: 1984*.

"You know what that is, right?" she says. "That was the 'treatment' she was giving Archimboldi. She was helping him tap his creativity, but not in the way he thought. It was planned from the start . . ." She reads on for a short while, then gasps. "Holy crap."

"What?"

"Look at the stuff about the Live Information Node, the LIN. I remember Bredsky said the LIN was a part of Archimboldi's 'treatment.' It was apparently some kind of machine . . . a computer that . . . *connected up* to Archimboldi? And look at what Louis says: It was still there when he visited Pentorgan House, but it was a surveillance system."

"How does that work?"

Bea shrugs. She reads more of the report and her eyes go wide.

"The LIN is a PanOp Insights product. More proof about the consortium: PanOp Insights, Xanthic Spectrum, GMM, Prism Consultancy . . . You see it, right, Scottie?"

Scottie nods.

"Everything in here points to Pentorgan House," he says. "And so does everything in Louis's report. Pentorgan House is where Dr. Bredsky took Archimboldi, and then, later, Louis. Like she was grooming him for another 'project' of hers."

"But, for whatever reason," Bea says, "it didn't happen."

"Yeah, but it didn't mean the damage wasn't done," says Scottie. "Pentorgan House. That's where Louis's going, Judy, to find whatever copies of *The Truth of Carcosa* Dr. Bredsky left stashed there. If we're going to stop him, that's where we need to go, too."

39

Sol's been telling Fran about his time at GMM for a while now. It's a heavily censored account. He's admitted that he was suffering a mid-life crisis of sorts. He's sketched his first day in the office, painting himself as a quixotic fool, set adrift from the reasonable ambitions of his previous relationship, impelled to prove himself against the worst thing he knows.

He's told her what he learned about *In re: Albatross Hung*, and of the dossier he put together with the names and addresses of GMM's victims. He's described O'Dowd, a tall man with a serious mustache. He's described himself simply slipping away one day, as if early one morning from the castle grounds, a loyal retainer waiting below with a horse and a bundle of provisions.

He's carried Fran with him as far as the bus to London, where he encountered Bea. He reaches to the point where Scottie pulled up beside the diner and beeped the horn. He tells how Bea petitioned Scottie for aid; how Scottie listened and looked him over and eventually nodded. That, he concludes, is how he gained admittance to Greenwood Community: a reward for an act of kindness in the dangerous outside world.

"Yes," Fran says. "But knowing how bad it is out there, why did you go back to the city today?"

This catches Sol off guard. He doesn't have a ready lie. And Fran catches the flicker of his eyes as he hesitates, and he knows he's busted.

"Supplies," he says weakly.

Fran doesn't answer. She looks tired and disappointed. For a long time she just stares at Sol. After she finally breaks contact, she doesn't look Sol in the eye again.

"So you're all lying. You and Scottie and Judith Bea—you've been lying to us all along. Hiding something."

"We don't mean to—"

"But you're worse, because you've been hiding something from them, too. And you've put us all in danger, just by coming here."

Sol's stumped. All he can do is appeal to her hospitality. "Scottie told me this is a place for healing and sanctuary. I thought . . . Fran, I don't know where else to go."

"Scottie's a good person but he's credulous. I'm not. And I could let it go if these were ordinary times, but things have changed. Everything's fucked, out there. You understand that? We're lucky here, because we don't depend on the system, we've got our own supplies. But being prepared doesn't mean being a soft touch. Because where does it end?"

"What do you mean, where does it end?" Sol asks.

"I mean who's in, and who's out? Mr. Sol, there are people I love, and there are people I don't. And you're on the far side of that line."

"Why?"

"I don't trust you."

"I didn't realize you were the only authority here."

"Of course I'm not."

"Just because *you* don't like me doesn't mean I have to leave."

"No. But I'm calling a meeting."

Fran makes her way to the front entrance to the longhouse, where a gong is hanging. She starts banging the gong with a little rubber drumstick on a rope.

“I think I need to find my friends,” Sol says.

“Stay, go, whatever. If you hide in the community we’ll find you. If you leave, then good riddance.”

* * *

The pealing of the gong rings out steadily as Sol takes the back door out of the longhouse and the short mulch road toward Scottie’s dwelling. Around him, doors open and people move in the dim light. He hears low voices. He steps down the little trench stairway and slaps the hanging carpet that substitutes for a door.

“Judy?” he calls. “Judy, we’ve got a problem.”

No response. He pushes the carpet aside and peers into the darkness, hoping his eyes can adjust. Nothing. The smell of clay, weed, and stale human habitation.

He hears more voices outside. The crackle of a radio.

He exits and follows a path that links the settlement to the bathroom block. Low electric lights switch on as he passes. He feels suddenly cold. The hairs are standing up on his arms and the back of his neck.

The toilet block is a squat square shadow before a pool of white. The white planes flicker, deform, and reform, and Sol recognizes sheets hanging to dry.

Over in the main settlement somebody raises their voice.

Perhaps they’re laughing.

The doors to the toilet block hang open: four black holes in the facade. He approaches the first, knowing that it will lead only to a stall smelling of cedar mulch and feces.

Still, his body is on high alert. An alarm in him is ringing, although he’s not sure why.

The first stall is empty. So is the second. As he steps out, he finds himself unwilling to look too closely at the row of white sheets billowing before him. He's fighting an apprehension—something out of a film he saw, perhaps—that he'll see a shadow.

Why is he suddenly so tense?

Of course you have reason to be tense, he tells himself, *they're threatening to throw you out of here*.

No. The danger's here. Now. Something's wrong.

He edges into the darkness of the third stall. He doesn't mind the funk. It reminds him of stables. Safe places.

The radio crackle.

The sound he heard outside Scottie's shelter—it was a walkie-talkie.

But nobody in Greenwood Community uses a walkie-talkie.

He backs out, slowly, quietly. He turns around. The jellyfish pallor of the hanging sheets drifts before him. Shards of darkness intrude as a faint breeze lifts and dies. As Sol stands, watching, stock still, the darkness takes form.

A clothesline.

(Footsteps)

A garden chair.

(A suppressed breath)

A man. A man in black, standing still. Trying to stay hidden.

Sol wants to run but he resists the impulse. Instead he steps *oh-so-lightly* off the duck-walk and onto the grass, putting more laundry between himself and the intruder, and he moves—skips, tries to hover—down a row of pillowcases and behind a looming white nightdress and into a chair—it tumbles, he gives up sneaking, he snags a clothesline and flips onto his back, scouring the grass, a gasp escaping his throat. He sees light: a flashlight switched on amid the fabric. He finds his feet and runs as the intruder hauls down sheets and cuts through clotheslines until the flashlight beam runs freely across the tree line—

But catches only a pair of swaying boughs where Sol has pushed into the woods.

He's halfway between the settlement and the bonfire clearing when he first hears screams.

40

Fran bangs the gong for thirty seconds, then leaves the drumstick hanging on its string. The first citizens of Greenwood Community start to appear before the longhouse: an old couple in woolly hats and a young man in a wheelchair.

"What's happened?" asks the older man. "Has the bomb gone off?"

"John, we'd have seen it if it was the bomb," the older woman mutters. "We'd have heard it."

"Maybe they just did London. Did they do London?"

"It's okay," Fran says, "we're holding a meeting."

"It's the middle of the night, Fran," the young man complains.

"It's an *emergency meeting*," Fran states, loudly and clearly.

"Oh, God, this is it. The four-minute warning . . ."

More people emerge into the light, looking sleepy, cold, and bad-tempered. Fran starts to regret her decision.

"It's an EMERGENCY VOTE," she keeps declaring nonetheless, "an EMERGENCY VOTE to keep us safe."

Some people complain. Fran bangs the gong until they can't be heard anymore. Some bearded individual steals the gong. It turns, for a wonderful moment, into a farce. Fran is chasing the gong-wielding beardy. The old man sits with his head in his hands. Somebody in a burlap sack is laughing. Black-uniformed figures move through the trees. Fran gets into an argument with a pair of sisters. Somebody is playing a pipe. A childish voice asks, "Who are they?"

Police lights freeze the tableau.

Everybody turns toward the source of the blue pulses, as a single figure in a police uniform walks down the path between the bean stalks. The officer takes off her hat. Beneath it, she has a blonde ponytail.

"Evening, ladies and gentlemen," she pronounces, staring at the ground. "I need to know who's in charge here."

Fran looks around, finds a sufficient number of expectant stares, and steps forward.

"I am," she says.

"Uh, excuse me," says the older man, John, sitting on the floor. "I thought this was a democracy."

"Stand over there, please," the officer tells Fran, pointing to a clear spot in front of the longhouse.

"I'd be happy to talk to you, officer, when you show me a warrant for entering private property."

"Do you think I'm joking?" John continues. "This is a serious question. Who died and made you queen?"

"Stand over there, please."

"Where's your warrant?"

"Well, Fran?" John asks.

"John, we can discuss this all day but I'm the one who's actually trying to solve the problem, aren't I?"

"That doesn't make you the leader."

"Are *you* the leader?" the officer asks John.

"We don't have a leader, but I am quite influential."

"Will you stand over there, please?"

John moves to the spot indicated by the officer.

"Now you, too, madam, if you're a leader, too."

"Well, okay," Fran says, anxious not to be displaced, "but I'm going to need to see a warrant."

She joins John in the empty space by the wall and turns back with an expectant look on her face, but the officer has already put her hat on and walked away. From their positions in the woods, the Hasturian Guard open fire.

41

The Crown Leviathan rep observes that the beams deviate from true in line with the Ent-Grav Hypothesis at a factor of two, unexpectedly suggesting the presence of a Primed Cipher in the vicinity. At this range, the effect appears to have a weak impact on accuracy. The right-hand beam connects with the chin of Target One—an older male, slightly stooped, once strong—with immediate and visible catastrophic effect on the integrity of the dermis, maxillofacial and phalangeal muscles, maxilla, mandible, and larynx. The bottom half of his face disintegrates in a shower of sparks.

As for Target Two—a younger female wearing a red kerchief—it's a miss. What should have been a perfect shot is spoiled at the last moment when she turns unexpectedly. Regrettable.

Each gun is fitted with sensors and cameras and relays. Their data appears on his tablet moments after each shot. A quick glance satisfies him. He signals for those around him to proceed in doing whatever else they mean to do. Despite the failure of the second shot, he has what he needs. Everything else is a bonus.

The police officer walks past him, back to her waiting vehicle. Despite the screams, the flashes, and the high-pitched whistling of the weapons, he notices the look of contempt she gives him. He makes a note—a memo to headquarters *re:* police cooperation and morale.

* * *

Back in the bonfire clearing, Scottie and Bea hear fireworks. The whistle of rockets and the cheers of a crowd. For a nonsensical moment, Bea imagines the population of the city below has united in celebration.

Then she sees Sol running down the road toward them, and the fear in his expression changes everything; she realizes that the crowd isn't cheering, they're screaming, and the sound is coming from Greenwood Community.

"What's happening?" Scottie demands.

"I don't know! There are men in the woods! I'm so sorry!" He collapses to his knees in the ashes. "They must have followed me. I must have led them here. I'm sorry!"

"What are they doing?"

"I don't know. It sounds like they're breaking up the community. I'm sorry—you're going to have to find a new home."

Bea shakes her head. "No," she says. "It sounds worse than that. It sounds like they're hurting people."

"This is all my fault," Sol moans.

"Shut up!" Scottie snaps. "Let me think. Okay. Stay here. I'll be back in just a minute. Just a minute."

"Why don't we just run?" Bea asks. "Through the woods, right now."

"And go where? Town? It's fucked, there's no food. I'm going to get the van. There are supplies in the van."

Neither Sol nor Bea protest further. Scottie slips up the narrow footpath through the woods toward the chaos of sound.

* * *

Fran is in a bait ball. The bait ball is a mass of human bodies circling counterclockwise. The people on the edge are exposed to the fire. Each one of them must reach the center, where they might be sheltered by their companions. The center keeps drifting over the trampled bean field, and the bait ball shrinks as those on the outside are struck down in blinding white explosions. The smell of fear, sweat, and burnt hair. Fran has seen nature documentaries. She knows what happens to bait balls. But instinct keeps her pressing into the scrimmage, toward the warmth of the bodies around her, bodies that were once people she knew and loved, and might become so again, if they can only regain their wits, if only they can stop.

But we can't stop. We don't want to die. I don't want to die.

An explosion closer than ever before. A human shield crumples beside her. In a moment of inspired madness, she dashes out of the crowd into the blackness where the predators hide. For a few precious seconds nobody fires. Then the nearest Hasturian Guards—one wearing a monkey mask, the other a dog mask—fire simultaneously.

Something unexpected happens.

Instead of forming a right angle, from Monkey to target to Dog, the beams converge just before the point of impact to form a Monkey-Dog boomerang. Energy blows back up the muzzles of both weapons. Dog's gun explodes, disintegrating his hands. A discharge arc interfaces with Monkey's midriff, and a bright white shape grows from a smile to a yawning grin, and once the sparks have died, Monkey's intestines slop out onto the ground before him, sizzling gently.

Monkey falls to his knees. Dog, screaming, runs into the bushes. The Hasturian Guard, who've witnessed the event, stop firing their weapons.

"Huh," says the Crown Leviathan rep. He checks the data on his tablet before blowing a small whistle hung around his neck.

"Cease using the Beta models, please," he orders. "Revert to the clubs."

Meanwhile, Fran has passed into the welcoming darkness between the trees.

* * *

The police officer walks back to her patrol car, parked beside a hand-painted sign. The blue lights illuminate childish drawings of smiling faces and animals.

She climbs into the front seat. Her jaws won't stop tensing. She double-dosed her pep pills in anticipation of the assignment, and now the pills are punishing her. She pulls a little prescription bottle out of the glove compartment and shakes a couple of downers into her palm. Dry swallows them. Gags.

From her seat, she can see the Crown Leviathan rep in his half-zip jumper and headset flicking through tabs on his tablet. She allows her disgust and loathing to take over. The muscles in her neck spasm as if she is sobbing, her face forms a rictus of sadness, but no tears come to her eyes. Instead, a low animalistic growl escapes from her throat.

She holds her face in her hands for some time, listening to screaming and orders.

When she looks up again, she sees a bearded man in a dirty jacket climbing into the cab of the van parked nearby. He sees her too, and freezes, for too long. Blue light catches the fear in his eyes. Then he gets moving again, fiddling with the cabin light, the ignition. The screams drown out the sound of the engine firing.

She watches, motionless, as he pulls the van out across the parking lot and drives away.

This isn't her first raid. GMM agents became constant features in immigration raids years ago. They started out doing ride-alongs. Then at a certain point, the power of their writs shifted, and the police were the ones riding along with them. Protecting them as they did . . . whatever it was they did. In people's houses, in the estates, out in the marshes.

Then the vigilantes joined, and the raids became rougher. She remembers the first time she saw someone die. They were caught up in a scrum outside some pub. Stamped in the throat. She watched them asphyxiate.

An English person, this was. Not even an immigrant.

Then GMM introduced the other reps, from Xanthic Spectrum and PanOp Insights. Testing new products—cameras, mobile generators—that they promised the police would be using one day—although there's no sign of that yet. And now Crown Leviathan, who makes guns.

And now this.

Apparently some "Trusted Citizen" of the Hasturian Guard handed in a screed against this hippie shantytown. It ticked every box in the Hasturian conspiracy playbook: people smuggling, blood sacrifice, liberal plots against England. The Guard jumped on it, and her captain insisted on her going as a liaison, just to keep up the pretense of partnership, hold the Guard off from trashing the police station for another week, maybe. Once they'd rendezvoused with the creeps from Crown Leviathan, with their sarcophagus "generator," she'd realized what the mission really entailed.

She doesn't understand why they are killing English people. She got it, what they were doing before, because the immigrants were taking the piss. She understands the concept of a hostile environment. But this, she doesn't understand. She takes the downers back out of the glove compartment, and almost swallows a handful, but at the last moment—as if on a whim—retrieves instead her little packet of pep pills, crushes one against the dashboard, and snorts the bitter, chunky powder.

A few seconds later a new sense of purpose lifts her out of the car and to the trunk, where a locked box is kept, and as sparks of energy run through her spine she loads two handguns with old-fashioned bullets, and walks back to where the Crown Leviathan rep is crouched over his tablet. She holds the muzzle over the nape of his neck, perceiving every individual hair with razor-sharp clarity, and pulls the trigger.

42

Scottie drives as quickly as he dares. Lights off, he can see almost nothing in front, but feels the road's familiar ruts beneath the wheels, and rolls with them to where he knows the clearing will be. He feels the vibrations of stones and sticks grumbling beneath the tires. He hopes that's all he's rolling over.

In the pale clearing he can see the embers of the fire and the silhouettes of Sol and Bea waving at him. He turns a wide loop and they jump in the van, and without a word he accelerates back up the path.

"No lights?" Mr. Sol says. Scottie shakes his head.

"What's going on up there?" Bea asks. Scottie shakes his head.

The van lurches in a way he didn't predict, and he spins the wheel and wallows in potholes for a stretch, then settles onto a smooth road, and then thuds hard into something that grunts and falls over. He stalls.

He turns the engine over until it starts again. They sit for a while in neutral.

"Turn the lights on," Sol says. "Just for a second."

Scottie flicks the lights on. The path ahead is clear, except for a single, empty, leather sandal. Emerging from behind a bush just off the path is a bare foot.

"That's Fran's sandal," Sol says.

"Just fucking move," Bea barks, and they roar forward, lights on full beam, tearing up the road to the fork, and as they pass it Bea and Sol try to peer past Scottie to where lights and noises—gunfire now, and flames—blaze and blare from between the trees like a distant funfair.

They leave the lightshow and follow the path off the hill—too fast, now, skidding at the corners—down the steep road to the quarry gate.

⁂ ⁂ ⁂

Anorak Woman's gun is partially deconstructed, its parts laid out on a tarpaulin, a sensor attached to the internal instrument that may be misaligned. She's trying to interpret the sensor's readings when Scottie's van rolls into the quarry.

She isn't obliged to act, but has time to push the components of her weapon into their brackets and fix the barrel back onto the stock, adopt a disciplined firing stance, and train the bead onto the side of the vehicle as it passes.

No obligation, but it's fun to learn how things work.

But when she pulls the trigger, the gun doesn't fire. Instead, a single spark emanates from a ventilation grille in the side of the stock. The spark, as it flutters to the ground, seems to resemble a leaf, or a fragment of parchment, seesawing on the breeze.

From the back of Anorak Woman's mind comes the faintest warning signal, and her eye drifts down to the tarpaulin at her feet, on which lies the last component she failed to reinstall into her weapon. A nondescript polygon designed to absorb energy. In recognition of its vital importance, it's been injection moulded in red plastic, but the yellow light of the generator has diminished the contrast against the tarpaulin.

Sol senses the change. He feels it like a shock wave, as if invisible plates have strained and slipped, a crack opened up in the container of their world. Turning in his seat, he perceives the shape racing from the tree line. He gauges the *Kataluin*'s trajectory across the invisible fracture line.

It gains definition as it draws near Anorak Woman: from a shadow to a silhouette to a puppet of vibrating planes, an already disintegrating caricature of a human cadaver. Heedless, she examines the barrel of the gun.

The *Kataluin* drapes fat white fingers over the nape of her neck.

Deferral. Violent and instant. A flash precedes the shock wave that rocks the vehicle. Scottie grips the steering wheel and accelerates toward the gate, Bea shuts her eyes, but Sol doesn't look away. He gazes directly at the explosion.

Is it a face he sees in the expanding orb of flame? Are those dark hollows eyes? Do those tongues of flame form a crown?

Can he see the Yellow King, snarling behind the thinning barrier between worlds?

Heat pulses through his body out of the mark on his arm. That *itch*.

Scottie hurtles toward the open gates, where a familiar tarmac road is waiting under ordinary electric lamps. Half a mile down the road Sol spots someone limping along the rest stop. She ducks away at the sound of the vehicle, but as he catches sight of her face, disbelief and joy wash over him.

"Pull over," he says, "that's Nadia."

"Who?" asks Bea.

"Pull over, she helped us."

They pass the woman, whose hooded sweater has a hole scorched through the back, exposing a burned patch of scalp. Scottie seems hesitant to stop.

"She can help! She can get us where we need to be!"

Some way up the road, Scottie finally brings the van to a halt.

He clears his throat. Tries to swallow. He has trouble. It's like there's something there, something sticking. He makes a long, chugging, gargling noise that finally resolves into a burp, and then he throws up out the window.

He bursts out laughing.

"I just killed Fran," he says. He giggles. Vomit comes out of his nose. "I just saw Pete, you know, the guy who's always playing his pennywhistle? Kind of annoying? I just saw Pete get cut in half with a fucking laser gun. I saw . . . I saw people running, my alive friends running over my dead friends. And I killed Fran. I hit Fran with a van. Her blood is on the front of this van." More laughter. Bea waits, but he doesn't stop laughing. She starts to fear he won't stop laughing.

Sol climbs out of the van. He walks back along the slightly curving road until he can see Eze, and Eze can see him. He waves. Eze freezes, raises a cautious hand, and waves back.

* * *

An hour later, in a wreckage-clogged rest stop, Eze shows them the footage on her phone.

Through the narrow judas hole, through thick layers of plexiglass, the camera light illuminates the contents of the cylinder.

A human face, female, eyes wide, mouth open. Shadows flicker around the edges of the form. Sinuous shapes attend to the edges of the lips, the nostrils, the eyelids, like hagfish on a deepwater carcass. It is only after repeated viewing and concentration that the shapes reveal themselves to be flames. Dark flames, moving slowly, lifting the corners of singed flesh.

The woman in the cylinder is burning in slow motion. Her eyes are open. Her skin is twitching. Sol recognizes her. Her name, he remembers, is Mona Trent-Mach. He remembers handing her a Silver Bullet on the street outside her workplace. He remembers the satisfaction he felt, knowing that he'd both proved himself and bested her. He can't remember what she did to annoy him, but he remembers thinking, as he handed the subpoena over, *there, that's what you get*.

Evidence

Collected and transcribed by
the Truth and Justice Commission.

Legal Declaration

Distributed by airdrop

UK Ministry of Defence

Attention: Proscription and Dispersal Order

By order of General Witherspoon, Commander of the Armed Forces and Lord Protector of the United Kingdom, membership of the following groups, and all associated subdivisions and affiliates, is hereby **PROSCRIBED:**

- The Hasturian Guard
- English Patriotic Defence League
- The Proud Carcosans
- England Expects!

Members of the above groups are hereby ordered to **SURRENDER** at the nearest convenient location. Persons who turn themselves in peacefully within the next week will be afforded the privilege of a civilian trial.

Following this grace period, association between current and former members of proscribed groups will be **PUNISHABLE BY DEATH**, along with the following activities:

- Recruiting
- Pamphleteering
- Unauthorized broadcasting
- Unauthorized dispersal of goods
- Gathering together

The conditions of the National Curfew remain unchanged. **LOOTERS WILL BE SHOT ON SIGHT.**

Note Verbale

A semiformal, unsigned diplomatic communication between embassies

FROM: The Embassy of Bolivia
TO: The UK Ministry of Foreign Affairs OR the equivalent military bureau

The Bolivian Embassy presents its compliments to the Ministry of Foreign Affairs and has the honor to invite their attention to the following matter.

The Bolivian party protests the mistreatment of its peacekeeping forces and the attempted prevention of their fact-finding mission in England. It draws the attention of the Ministry of Foreign Affairs to the internationally agreed treaties permitting access and protection for a UN-mandated peacekeeping force on UK soil, following recent events. The Bolivian party remains committed to its mandate to investigate allegations of the most serious kind, up to and including ethnic genocide. It reserves the right to exercise measures in accordance with international law to protect its citizens.

The Bolivian party requests an urgent official response to the footage recently circulated that purportedly evidences the torture and/or death of a human scientific test subject, and repeats its previous request for access to the MoD-Xanthic Spectrum Campus.

The Embassy avails itself of this opportunity of assuring the Ministry of its highest consideration.

From Yellow King and Friends [transcript]

Broadcast out of Harrisburg, PA

YELLOW KING [YK]: Welcome, brothers. Welcome, my international brethren. Welcome to the last untainted beacon of truth. We've got a hell of a show in store for you today. We've been working hard, I'll tell you. Been doing a lot of digging, a lot of research, and we've uncovered some scary facts that you aren't going to believe. If yesterday you thought the international globalist cannibal conspiracy was serious, by the end of today's show you'll be crapping your pants. Or at least, you would be if you didn't already have a plan. You got a plan, right? Well, if you need help deciding which and how much guns and gold to buy, stay tuned for Preppers' Paradise, coming up. But first, something from across the Pond. You've all seen the footage. The "footage" of a woman, a person, allegedly enclosed in a . . . would you call it a box? A microwave oven? Toaster? Basically, there's this . . . bitch, in a kind of space-age toaster, getting toasted. Would you agree that is what it looks like? And what we're being told, this footage comes out of England. And it's come out—surprise surprise—just when English folks are finally solving their illegal immigration problem. How's that for timing? Some liberal snake has leaked this footage of some bitch in a toaster, expecting their American fellow travellers to go all bleeding heart and go, we've got to get over there to little old England and intervene. And we're supposed to believe this? Well, now, listen up. I've got a real-live Brit on the line here.

His patriot name is King Louis and he has got a take on this. Are you there, Louis?

KING LOUIS [KL]: Good morning. Delighted to finally talk to you. Long-time streamer, first-time caller.

YK: Glad you called, pal. What's your take on this footage? Do you think it's real?

KL: I think it's very interesting. I think with psy-ops, the most important effect you can generate is something called the "reality effect." Now, that comes when you make a blend of both real and fictional events, artifacts, and statements.

YK: Yeah, but is it real?

KL: Well, I know for a fact that technology exists that will do what you see in that video. When the woman's skin is . . . peeling off . . .

YK: You've seen that before?

KL: Oh, yes. It's Carcosan technology. What you're witnessing there is a Carcosan energy transfer.

YK: Okay. What?

KL: Carcosan energy. I'd be surprised if you didn't know what I'm talking about, given that you've invested so much into your Yellow King persona.

YK: Okay, hold up. I didn't realize I was talking to a True Believer. Maximum respect to you. Are you in the Hasturian Brotherhood?

KL: The Hasturian Guard. Yes.

YK: A rebel with a cause! Maximum respect! God bless you, and God bless what you're doing. I hope you're keeping safe. Especially now your people are being persecuted. I take it you're on the run?

KL: I'm—

YK: Don't tell me. Let's focus on the footage. So who's the bitch? Who's the lady getting transferred?

KL: How should I know? Some immigrant, I expect.

YK: She looks an awful lot like a crisis actor to me.

KL: Maybe, I don't care.

YK: You don't care? That's a surprise.

KL: It doesn't matter to me whether she's real or fake, alive or dead.

YK: You don't care if she's fake?

KL: We live in a marketplace of realities, as well you know, and I adhere to the truth that affords me the most leverage.

YK: King Louis, can I ask, have you been posting on the *Aldebaran Gazette*? What you're saying sounds familiar.

KL: I have been uploading my manifesto in recent weeks, yes.

YK: Oh, wow. I've been reading that. I saw all that stuff about, what do you call it, Cipher Theory? I tell you, you have some mind. Folks are pulling their hair out about you. I've wanted you on the show since I saw your post about the Lethal Chamber. What a neat idea. Hard to persuade people to use it, though!

KL: I was never advocating that the Lethal Chamber should be built.

YK: Oh, sure.

KL: I was just letting people know about our foundational texts.

YK: You've made a real impression. You know, I kind of just want to shoot the shit with you.

KL: Well, Mr. Yellow King, I have a bone to pick with you, too, from a theological perspective. It is strange to me that, if you've been paying attention to my writings, you sell guns and gold on your program. It implies to people that they have a chance of surviving the coming Accession. But, Mr. Yellow King, there can only be two survivors: the Yellow King of Carcosa himself, and the Cipher whose genius permits his entry into this world, and of course, ultimately those two become one . . .

YK: And who's this genius Cipher?

KL: It's me, of course.

YK: And when are you going to be achieving this Accession? Just so I know.

KL: You've got maybe a week.

YK: You heard it here first, folks! Time to build your bunker!

KL: It won't help. None of these baubles will help you. You can't fight it and you can't wish it away. This marvelous syncretism of costumes, code words, reality signifiers—enjoy it as I do, all will fall in the face of true Carcosan power.

YK: [Laughs] King Louis, I know a week is a short time, but can you answer a few questions from our viewers? Our switchboard is lighting up. Folks are real riled up.

KL: Why not? It's not like I'm going anywhere today.

YK: My man! Our first question is from WhitePower_69, who wants to know about the crisis actor in this video . . .

From Lawyers and Liars and Thieves and Murderers

by Nadia Eze

Distributed by dead-drop across the UK

. . . The attached interview recording took place last week. The interviewee is a former clerk to the Emergency Cabinet, part of the "soft moderate" faction purged in the last month of the regime's existence. He recounts the negotiations, threats, and ultimatums that ultimately led to hard-line Hasturian Guard representatives taking seats on the cabinet, even when their stated aim was to dissolve the UK government entirely. While I acknowledge that no "soft moderates" have existed in the UK government since the Immigration Emergency Referendum, and the clerk's work for the non-democratic, corrupt, and deplorable cabinet must be condemned, I consider this interview to be invaluable for the oral history I'm collecting. Please spread.

I need more accounts, primarily from victims and witnesses of the violence that has swept our country, but also from those who saw firsthand how the decisions of the responsible parties were made. This second category of witness statements I am prepared to accept anonymously. Please leave files in the drop-site listed below.

As usual, here's a list of crypto accounts accepting mutual aid donations and the locations of food and aid drops in the coming month . . .

From *The Patriot*

Published in London by New Ministries Holdings

Turning a Corner

Witherspoon: Nothing Is Off the Table

By *Patriot* Correspondents

General Witherspoon is on a roll. Three challenges faced our new Lord Protector of the UK in his mission to restore stability, prosperity, and sovereignty to our nation: reestablishing order, securing much-needed economic stimulus, and striking a treaty for the eventual withdrawal of international peacekeepers. For Witherspoon, these were three challenges set, met, and bested.

You might forgive him for taking a well-earned rest following his latest flurry of diplomatic and trade talks, but the general—who famously sleeps only three hours a night—insisted on addressing our reporters directly.

His latest message is for the people of England. For those who've stayed true in the face of adversity, it's a message of hope.

For past and present members of proscribed groups such as the Hasturian Guard, Witherspoon offers an olive branch:

"Come in from the cold. We're offering second chances. Considerate sentencing. Amnesties, for some. We want, more than anything, to move past this period of disturbance. Nonetheless, we must demonstrate to our allies that we're serious about some of the excesses that took place in the most heated moments of recent history. Justice must be done, and seen to be done. But we aren't unfeeling. Really, nothing is off the table."

Witherspoon's generosity is not, of course, unlimited.

"There are those among us who never loved England, who don't love it now, and who perhaps never will. To them I can say nothing. My actions will communicate."

There's been much discussion regarding the cause of the past year's disturbances, with many pointing the finger squarely at foreign agitators. Witherspoon sees restoring confidence in the news media as an essential first step toward normalization. Many commentators have called for strengthening the National Firewall, but Witherspoon takes a more nuanced approach: Here, he has reform in his sights.

"Of course, I've seen the footage [purporting to show the death of a scientific test subject] circulating. It is very upsetting. My first instinct is, of course, that it must be a deepfake. But my approach is that we must investigate all allegations, in order to determine that they are illegitimate. I should rather have a situation where members of a regulated press can be held accountable for their actions, than the kind of wild west of rumor and speculation that occurs when the scope of permissible discussion is too narrowly drawn. So yes, I am in favor of reform."

Witherspoon's recent deal with New Ministries Holdings burnishes his reform-minded credentials. Six new channels will feature content reflecting the needs and interests of today's English citizens, and counteract the stifling effect of decades of top-down liberal broadcasting.

As Witherspoon attests, it's time to let England roar: "A healthy forum for debate is essential; in fact, it's an English tradition. I've made it clear from the beginning that this is a caretaker administration. Once the conditions are right, and our international obligations are met, I'd welcome reopening the legislative chambers. One day, we can even start talking about elections."

Perhaps then our hard-working general can finally take a little time for himself!

43

One Monday morning, Nat Collins, manager of Excis Property Maintenance, becomes aware that a water safety inspection is due at Pentorgan House. Since Pentorgan isn't part of her portfolio, but that of an absent colleague, she's not surprised by the reminder letter, although she finds the tone slightly affronting. The author might have taken recent disturbances into account before stamping "FINAL NOTICE" over the letterhead in red ink.

Still, she reasons, legionella is no joke. And now that the army has taken charge, perhaps the country can finally get back to business as usual. Perhaps she should welcome the "FINAL NOTICE" tone as a marker of normality.

She calls the number in the letter and sets up an appointment with the inspector. They'll meet at the gates to the property and Collins will facilitate access.

The next day, three hours before the scheduled appointment time, the inspector arrives at the Excis offices and asks for the keys to Pentorgan House. He's a sullen middle-aged man with a complexion Collins regards as Mediterranean, wearing an outfit like the ones American mailmen wear. Collins explains that his request doesn't fit the original arrangement, and besides would be impossible. The inspector asks whether he can take the key anyway, since he's now in the area, but is due back at central in just a few hours. Collins declines.

The inspector agrees to wait. He isn't very nice about it. This, Collins finds difficult. She likes to cultivate pleasant relationships with honest tradesmen of all creeds and colors, and has no ready defense when her politeness isn't returned. She takes her lunch, eyeing the inspector's van out the office window, and scanning the news. She reads another interview with General Witherspoon. She feels unsure about the general's assurances. It's very well suppressing certain vigilante groups, since they clearly went too far, but how will the general address the immigration problems that gave rise to them? Collins remembers her interactions with the local Hasturian Guard. They seemed well intentioned, and were certainly polite, which means something; although, since the tide has turned, she's prepared to accept the new consensus that they were a bit misguided.

Finally she puts down her fork, retrieves her maintenance pack for Pentorgan House, and leads the inspector toward the property.

After an hour they reach Pentorgan village: small houses clustered around a crossroads, and a cattle shed in an excavated gully. The corrugated steel walls are covered in spray-painted signage in a sloppy, childlike hand: WATER, MEDICAL, NATIONAL INNOCULATION CENTER, DON'T WORRY IT MIGHT NEVER HAPPEN ;-).

The sight of this Hasturian Guard handiwork embarrasses Collins. What will happen to the members now? They must be at home, hiding. Collins supports a general amnesty. Let the Guard rejoin society, and scrub off all that paint, so this troubled period can be forgotten. A couple more miles of country lane, rising into bald, worked hills, ducking through unkempt strips of woodland. Let bygones be bygones.

They pass a row of depots and quarries, then finally meet a gate in a tall chain fence with an array of weatherproof signs, among which Collins identifies Prism Consultancy LLC, the owners of Pentorgan House. The surly inspector waits while Collins fishes out a heavy key and unlocks the padlock. He sits in his van on the other side of the gate while she locks up again. Of course, she'd refuse to allow him to close the gate. But a decent person might offer.

Never mind; they drive through an estate of warehouses, steel barns, and yards. No lights on anywhere. The concrete is pitted with potholes, stale rainwater rippling in the breeze. Hard to imagine an English castle here, such as Pentorgan House is supposed to be.

Then they round a windbreak strip of pines, climb another rise, and meet a wall. Sixteen feet of mossy ancient stone. Above it, glimpses of gables promise real English heritage property as they roll around the perimeter to the inner gate.

It turns out to be two gates: a chain-link construction on the industrial side, and a wooden gate on the castle side, with wilderness between.

The wooden gate is heavy, and again the inspector makes no effort to help. It's as if, Collins thinks pettishly, he's resisting every urge to be sociable or decent. She walks the gate closed and looks out for the first time properly on the grounds of Pentorgan House. It couldn't be more different from the industrial Mordor outside: green and fresh with lawns of moss and chamomile. Healthy box hedges, borders flashing with color. Such flowers! The rain up here is mist, and Collins leads the way round landscaped corners, and every vantage affords a gorgeous view. Just sometimes—between boughs—a gantry or strip light from the estate below intrudes on the view, and Collins regrets the modern world.

The house itself is an ugly thing, squat and muscular, brick and stone. There's evidence of age and refurbishment, and a moat of sorts—really a pair of ponds, with tiled edges, flanking the wings. The road swings past the ornamental front drive—gravel, urns, chains on stanchions—and into the trade parking lot in back. The rear of the house has a single-story courtyard of functional buildings, covered with CCTV cameras. Collins parks, gets out, and stretches as if she hasn't already jumped in and out of the car a dozen times.

"This way, please, sir," she trills. She sets off, and the inspector pulls a nasty-looking duffel bag out of the cab and follows. Collins is a little surprised at how slow the inspector is in approaching the house, as if put off by its brutal architecture. But the swarthy inspector, Collins decides, is unlikely to be sensitive to such things; his is more likely a work-shy reluctance, anticipating a considerable job of work.

She chuckles at this wicked thought, then feels guilty, and ushers the man onward with a warm smile, saying, "Isn't it lovely? What a treat, to be able to sneak into places like these. It's really one of the perks of jobs like ours."

They locate the boilers and AC access hatches in the various wings and annexes. The inspector is, after all Collins's cruel thoughts, very thorough, inquiring after the nature of various overhead tubes—most of which transpire to be connected to the electric or telecoms system. He stops frequently, as if in profound, even pained thought, and Collins wonders whether he isn't a deep and serious man after all, keenly aware of his responsibilities. She leaves him to his work.

Collins wanders from the shadow of the house to find the garden outlaid before her, and feels such *relief*, like a previously unnoticed sickness lifted, that she decides that, while she loves these gardens, she doesn't care for Pentorgan House at all.

Her revulsion is such that when she climbs into her car to await the inspector, she actually moves it to the back of the parking lot, where a low parapet looks out over trees and industry. She positions herself to face the house—it feels safer, somehow—and rests her eyes for just a moment.

* * *

Collins awakens to the inspector tapping on her window. She rolls it down, blinking and swallowing phlegm. It's going to be a bigger job than expected, he states, adding reproachfully that he prefers not to be misled. It's absolutely infested. He'll have to run a half-dozen cycles before anybody can go anywhere near that water.

Collins assures the man there was no intent to deceive on her part. She rubs her eyes, wonders how long she was asleep. Is the sun really about to set?

The inspector, not comforted, complains that he'll be spending another evening away from his family. In fact, since he lives in Birmingham, it may be morning by the time he gets home.

Collins can only apologize, yawning and checking her phone. It's dinnertime. Properly, she should supervise this job. Properly, therefore, she has two options: Send the tradesman home (to Birmingham!) and ask him to come back tomorrow; or stay up all night onsite herself.

Yet there's something in the light up here she finds desperately sad. The sense of a day wasted, and creeping cold, and miles to travel before she can rest. She starts to feel an unreasonable fear of driving back over those strange roads after dark, without the reassurance of the Hasturian Guard.

She hands over the keys, asking the inspector to drop them at the office on the way home. Despite the night of hard work that awaits him, he seems satisfied with her decision. He escorts her out, unlocking each gate and beckoning her through, like, she thinks yawningly, very much a gentleman.

* * *

Collins is gratified to discover next morning that the keys have been returned. Wednesday and Thursday pass without notable incident, except for the strange news that the Army's investigating what they're terming "crimes against humanity." Collins hopes they'll be fair, and look into the behavior of *both* sides, although General Witherspoon's press conference demonstrates an alarming bias against the Hasturian Guard.

On Friday there's another problem at Pentorgan House. A tree comes down on the property and the security system alerts her that the house has lost power. The backup generator requires manual ignition, and it has to get fired up today. So Collins cancels her afternoon viewings and once again navigates the unlikely route between the hills, and up the concrete causeways, and onto the graveled drives of Pentorgan House.

The sun starts to set just after she arrives and the house is a crouching mass of blue beneath a green-streaked, fleecy sky. She again feels the dread of driving home in the dark. It upsets her to admit this fear. It makes her feel lost, childlike.

Happily, the backup generator is in the annex, not the main building. Collins locates it in a bay that smells of diesel and cut grass. She starts it, checks the fuel gauge, locks up, and trots faster than she should to her car. As she drives off, she notes the emergency lights, pale green, in the visible rooms.

By Saturday morning the tree's been removed and power restored. Collins makes a final, somewhat unenthusiastic trip out to throw the breakers and turn off the generator. She makes sure to do it early, before lunch, to avoid the creepies. However, the journey strikes her as being utterly unremarkable, and Pentorgan Estate, too, holds no magic today. It's a piece of material investment whose infrastructure needs maintaining, and she carries out her routine tasks methodically. It's a burden, she thinks, to leave all this property in a perpetual state of readiness. As if the owners are going to fly over from the U.S. at any moment, rush in, turn on all the lights; and demand cooked food and ice in their drinks.

Throwing breakers in the utility shed, she toys with the idea that she's bringing the whole house TO LIFE. A kitsch and harmless fantasy passes before her eyes of her own self in nineteenth-century costume, throwing the mad scientist switches—clunk, clunk, clunk—crying "IT'S ALIVE! IT'S ALIVE!"

44

Rewind.

The footage jumps and flickers as Nat Collins of Excis Property Management reverses her sedan back and forth between Pentorgan House and her office. Hedges and gates and scarred earth rush past. The cattle shed with its slogans and labels. Finally we return to the moment where Nat is standing on the threshold of Pentorgan House, breathing in fresh garden air. Pause.

Play.

Joseph Sol retrieves a large binder from his duffel bag and starts to draw a diagram of the interior of the building. He sketches quickly, his ballpoint pen scoring the paper, and sweat rolls down his forehead. He adds red lines representing the thick white cables of the security system, the Live Information Node, and its blocky cameras. He works feverishly, and sometimes his eyes close while his pen still sketches, and sometimes he rests his head against the wall while a spasm—nausea, heat—runs out from the itchy spot on his arm.

Fast forward.

In the cool evening air he steps across the parking lot, exhaling with relief. He raps on Collins's car window and stutters through his story: It's a big job, he's stuck here all night, does she really want to stay all night with him? She falls for it. Blinking, barely conscious, she lets him keep the keys and heads out. He follows an hour later. He meets Scottie and Bea in a rest stop and hands over the keys. Divested of his burdens, he's overtaken by exhaustion and crawls onto a mattress in the back of the van and closes his eyes.

Fast forward.

Scottie has felled plenty of trees, and he identifies the candidate for knocking out Pentorgan's power supply. Disguising the sabotage is unnecessary; while the army maintains order in the cities, the countryside is rife with rustling and theft. The hours between the blackout and resumption of auxiliary power are crucial. Bea and Sol wait in the van for Scottie's signal, which turns out to be redundant, since the floodlights over the concrete yard go out. They sit for a second, taking in the melancholic evening darkness. Then they move. Sol drives and Bea does the gates. He drops her out back of the house and returns to retrieve Scottie.

Bea crosses the verge to the spot where her hand-drawn map indicates a door should be. She moves under the canopy shadow. At the door she sees the first CCTV camera: huge, blocky, and white, its form plain against the brickwork. It's older than any piece of kit she's seen. Sol described the cameras as being like prototypes; to Bea, it looks like a cheesy movie prop. She recognizes the logo, however: PanOp Insights.

She counts keys on the ring until she finds the one that should unlock the deadbolt. It does so. A night bird is calling. She taps a code copied from the maintenance pack into the keypad. The mechanism is battery operated and still functioning. The unit chimes and unlocks.

The hallway inside is pitch black. She shines a flashlight on institutional green walls, a scuffed white skirting board, a slick floor. It smells of old mops. The corridor stretches forward, then divides at a "T." There are doors on either side with reinforced glass portholes. The number of doors doesn't match the map Sol prepared. A minor error, but not promising. On a whim, Bea pulls out the maintenance pack and checks the map printed inside. The doors don't seem to correspond with that map, either.

She moves up the corridor, no longer confident. But when she takes the right-hand turn as prescribed, the corridor does indeed meet a door at an odd angle, as per both maps, indicating the point where the new annex meets the old house. There's the step up, shown on both maps. The door requires another key, third on the ring, which also works. No errors there.

The air inside is cooler, with the taint of damp and mold. Sol's map predicts another T-junction, but instead there's a cramped half-turn stairwell. Climbing, Bea finds the T-junction above. Strange. Is there a mezzanine below, unmapped?

The central part of the "T," Bea understands, should lead to the front, with the left and right forks leading to the east and west wings. Whether this is accurate remains to be seen. She goes right, and passes deep, narrow windows with a view of hedgerows that catch her flashlight. The doors have big steel handles and steel slots that once held labels. Consultation rooms, dorms, or group session rooms.

With Adriana Bredsky in prison, Prism Consultancy LLC is in stasis, awaiting legal clarity. Its real estate has been mothballed. Nadia Eze couldn't say exactly how long ago the last clients made use of Pentorgan House's facilities. She discovered an ancient, archived website advertising corporate teambuilding and high-end retreats, and hinting at large, institutional customers. Eze also dug up details of the LIN, the Live Information Node that Dr. Bredsky apparently used as both therapeutic device and security system. Miraculously, Eze managed to find a manual. Bea has it in her rucksack. It's printed on paper with perforated edges reminiscent of some bulky pre-laser printer. The title page reads:

XXXXX PRISM CONSULTANCY XXXXX

XXX LIVE INFORMATION NODE XXX

XXXXXXXX VERSION 1.2 XXXXXXXX

Bea's first task is to locate the hardware at the center of the LIN. She takes the second left turn, up a narrow staircase—and again finds she's been misled by Sol's map. This staircase ends abruptly in a flat ceiling. Bea doubles back, tries the third left, climbs similar stairs, and reaches a dark little landing.

The flashlight illuminates four doors. Bea counts five keys and unlocks the rightmost one. It opens with a breath of fusty air. Pitch black. Bea locates the light switch by instinct: a hanging cord, like a bathroom fixture. The mechanism is stiff, and the click resonates; and nothing happens, of course. She shines her light further into the room. It turns out to be a windowless closet containing the LIN core, an installation of chunky white moulding and fat white wires resembling plumbing. Facing the boxy little monitor is a heavy wooden chair with armrests, leather upholstery, and a rotating seat.

Bea creeps in and deposits her kit bag on the floor. She sinks into the captain's chair. She must now wait until the power comes back on. Then she'll put her study of the LIN manual to use.

45

Sol parks the van in a little shaded spot just inside an open gate with a view of the road and, in the distance, the graffitied cattle shed. All is quiet.

"Do you think things are going to get better?" Scottie asks.

Sol doesn't answer.

"You know," Scottie prods, "because of the news and stuff."

"You're not supposed to be using your phone, Scottie."

"You don't think GMM is still after you, do you? I mean, they must be done by now. Somebody will have put it together, what they did. Them and Xanthic Spectrum and everyone. Someone will have sussed them out. You can't just fuck up a whole country and get away with it."

"I don't know, Scottie. The Hasturian Guard are finished. But we don't know what those companies are capable of doing. Remember, Eze said Prism Consultancy used to work with the MoD. And the Army is in charge now."

"But things are going to settle down now, aren't they?"

"I don't know."

"At least we have an opportunity now to nip it in the bud, right?"

"Nip what in the bud?"

"Accession."

Sol twitches.

"Sure."

"We're doing well, Mr. Sol. We can get in there before Louis. We can destroy those books, wherever they're hidden. We're in a good spot, right now, aren't we?"

"I don't know."

"Fuck, Mr. Sol."

"I'm sorry. I hope so, is what I mean. I hope we can do this."

"Yeah, I think we're in a good spot. I think our odds are good."

They sit in silence for a while. Sol's fingers play over his shirt-sleeves until he notices them and slips them firmly into his pockets.

"How long have you been seeing Judith?" he asks.

"Nearly a year."

"Good for you."

"We're not going to get married or anything."

"No?"

"No, man."

"Don't you want to?"

"Judith doesn't. She says every time she thinks about our future she remembers that the world is ending and it makes her cry."

Sol recalls the graffiti on the side of the cattle shed.

DON'T WORRY it might never happen ;-)

According to Eze's latest dispatch, distributed via SIM cards and USB fobs in a word-of-mouth network of dead drops, a lot of agricultural infrastructure was used for the "processing" of the Hasturian Guard's prisoners and other people picked up by different groups, exchanged like currency, drawn into a "new, chaotic archipelago of control" that formed after all the old institutions failed.

NATIONAL INnoCULAtion Center

Eze has been a real friend. Her footage of the woman in the cylinder—of Mona Trent-Mach, Sol reminds himself—has had impact.

Her network distributed it widely, until finally it apparently reached the UN, and "medical torture" got added to the litany of crimes being discussed diplomatically.

Perhaps they made a difference.

Perhaps that makes up for it.

The moment of delivery. Waxy paper rolled into a tight tube. Her name in copperplate font. The smug look in her eye.

Sol digs his fingernails into his arm. Pain overrides tingling heat.

"Well," he says, wincing. "One year is quite early to start thinking about the future."

Sol and Scottie sit in quiet and darkness for a few minutes more. Then, up the road a ways, Sol spies light: the rhythmic flashes of a car's headlights navigating a narrow lane.

46

Bea hears a single squelch on her walkie-talkie. The squelch means the maintenance woman, Collins, has passed Scottie and Sol on her way to the house. Bea must wait another twenty minutes. Against all reason, she's afraid to make a sound, and has to remind herself to breathe. Then, without warning, there's a series of little clicks and pops, and a gentle whirring sound starts up.

Little red and yellow LEDs start flashing in arrays on the floor. Then something within the LIN starts chuntering away. Bea doesn't dare move yet. Collins must leave, and lock up, and pass Scottie's van, so that Scottie can send two squelches on the walkie-talkie.

After another interminable wait, this too happens.

She gets herself set up, equipment laid out, instructions in hand. Time to work.

The LIN operating system is text-based, just words on a screen. The screen is tiny, with a thick layer of glass whose curvature magnifies the center: green text bulging on the black background.

Bea works. She finds the LIN strange. The directories have weird names. The actions she can perform are phrased in an alien manner. It's as if the individual who coded this machine had no understanding of human intuition. The keys are sticky. Clicky. Time passes with keystrokes and motes in the stale cupboard air. Then the camera feeds get activated.

There are nine of them. They map to Sol's floor plan—approximately. Front entrance and driveway. Annex entrance exterior. Some lawn and parking lot—nothing Bea recognizes, unless the image has been flipped. A cafeteria, probably in the annex. A corridor that must be in the west wing, although Bea saw no camera there. A view of the old wine cellar, with its trapdoor entrance. An office, probably the main one, probably in the main house. An empty room with a closed door.

Bea marks Sol's floor plan with crosses, arcs, and question marks. Even with the uncertain spots, the points of entry are covered by cameras. She presses the squelch button on her walkie-talkie in a simple code that tells Scottie and Sol to wait. She consults the LIN manual again. She suddenly feels tired. Hot.

She wonders, half idly, whether the air supply in this closet might be limited. She cracks the door and sees little green emergency lights in the corridor.

Yet in the screens, she realizes, the grounds appear pale. There must be some form of night vision.

She exits the camera screens (the command is FLUSH) and starts scratching around for the memory files. It's difficult. The word "memory" doesn't appear in the manual. The closest cognates seem to be "absorption" and "sump," among a few unparseable acronyms.

But a computer has to have memory, and there has to be a way of changing it. She looks. She hits a brick wall. She gets lost in nested directions. She checks the manual, and finds a passage underlined by Eze that seems to describe a reset of sorts, which is apparently combined with a kind of accounting of systems ("culture script"), which might perhaps direct her to the files ("deposits") she'll need to overwrite.

The reset is input as a direct command line. Bea copies out the instructions directly from the manual. Types, and stops typing, and hopes.

The machine starts grunting. Heavy, metallic vocalizations.

Black screen.

Then the camera footage blarts up again. The computer says *aeeeeee*.

Views of the front drive, the back door, the cellar fill the screen. The cafeteria. The office. The empty room.

It's no longer empty.

Somebody's in it, standing, facing the doorway, and the doorway is open and they're leaving.

The lawn and the parking lot. The central corridor.

Another corridor. Empty.

Which is the empty room? Where does it connect to? Which camera will catch its inhabitant next?

How close are they to the LIN room?

The screen goes black.

The computer says *uh nuh nuh nuh*. The cafeteria comes up again and it's full of men in robes. Priests, in fact. Eating out of pale little bowls.

Then the front drive. Covered in snow.

The central corridor busy with people wearing lanyards and others in jogging outfits. Doctors and patients. The haircuts look funny—mullets and big bouffant dos.

This is old footage.

Then the images cycle again. Empty rooms and full rooms. Faster and faster. The LIN is throwing up old data as part of the reset. Bea sees soldiers. Cars pulling up and leaving. Someone running between the lines of box hedge. Someone cleaning the cellar. Faster. A dancing circle on the lawn. A beating in the cellar. Figures struggling in the room that was once empty. Furniture rearranging. Framed pictures appearing and disappearing from the walls. A man pulled from the moat. A man—she recognizes Salvatore Archimboldi, gaunt, unshaven, drenched to the skin—carried along the central corridor by short-haired youths in military sweaters. Archimboldi placed on a metal chair. Archimboldi attached to wires and probes. Blackness.

The LIN falls silent.

47

Scottie opens up the back of the van and sets up a spirit stove on the edge of the load bed. He hands Sol a couple of camping chairs, which he unfolds and sets up in a semicircle, facing the stove. They have tea, a can of beans, and UN rations of dried tofu.

Sol has a sick feeling. He doesn't want to go into the house tomorrow. He doesn't want Scottie to know this. He asks instead, "Are we all set up? Shall we go over it again?"

Scottie puts down his bowl and picks up his tea.

"We set up the incinerator first. We get it burning nice and hot outside the back door. Then we search. It's pretty simple, really. Whatever copies of *The Truth of Carcosa* we find, we burn straightaway."

"How do we stay safe?"

"We wear gloves. We put the books straight into garbage bags without looking at them. We don't read the books."

"What else do we do?"

"We pull the LIN apart and destroy it."

"And?"

"That's it. It's simple."

"We use our walkie-talkies. We stay in constant communication."

"Well, yeah."

"Yeah, Scottie, it's simple, but that doesn't mean it's easy."

"Okay, Mr. Sol."

Sol doesn't want to go inside the house. He can't deny what he felt when Collins showed him around earlier in the week. The pull he felt in certain parts of the house. The books, Sol knows, are definitely there.

And he wants to read them.

Read is perhaps not the word. Absorb. Be absorbed. Satisfy the crawling on his skin, quiet the whispers in the white noise. Manifest the crawling visions that linger in his mind every morning, before dissolving into waking sunlight.

He shifts his weight, tries to change his train of thought. He reminds himself of first principles. "Listen," he says to Scottie. "Remember what Judy told us about Accession?"

"Yeah."

"Go on."

"A broken box, and a puddle."

"Tell me the whole thing."

"Are you okay?"

"Just tell me again. I need to hear it."

"She said, imagine you're sitting inside a box. A little steel cube, so small that you basically occupy all the space inside it. You have nowhere to go, nothing to look at but six walls, but you're safe. That's planet Earth. And somebody comes along and decides to *get inside your box*. And because they're very strong, they can push through the steel walls of your box, they can force themselves in, *even though you are still inside it*. That space you used to occupy is just a mess of chum and slurry. That is what an Accession would look like. A broken box and a puddle. That's what Judy said."

Sol bites down on his lip until he tastes blood.

"And we don't want that, do we?" he says.

* * *

Bea eats her rations in the cafeteria. The main lights remain off, but the emergency lights create a greenish ambience. She must rest in the LIN closet for at least a night—perhaps all weekend—before somebody restores main power, and they can search the property freely.

Her eye keeps moving to the CCTV camera above the benches. It is—should be—inert. The age of the system makes her doubt that there's any kind of live outbound feed sending footage to Prism's caretakers. But there are no guarantees, and even without a live feed she doesn't want to leave any trace, since the three of them may need to do something like this again. At GMM properties, for instance. Or the ALI.

Thinking in terms of positive action helps. It keeps the creepies away. It makes Bea feel less inclined to focus on her solitude in this gigantic, ticking house. Or the things that used to happen here. Magical rites and psychotherapy. Soldiers and priests.

Getting away, she reminds herself, will be tricky. The puzzle—a nicely concrete puzzle—is how to shut down the LIN with enough time to disassemble it before setting off any alarms. Impossible? Maybe they could leave parts running, take it apart in bits like surgeons, altering its perception while it's still conscious . . .

No light flashes on the CCTV camera. It doesn't change at all. Its shape—which resembles only superficially a light-starved tuber root or tentacle—doesn't shift or waver. Or creep.

Bea opens the LIN manual again. Immersing herself in work should take her mind off the fact that she's alone in the dark. But the longer she spends with the LIN code, the more unnerving she finds it. Trying to understand its perverse syntax and oddly fleshy, digestion-fixated vocabulary, she finds herself visualizing the operators of remote drones in cold, dark places: the bottom of the ocean, the vacuum of space. She finds herself imagining lonely people like herself, transmitting signals—weak, buffeted by hostile atmospherics—trying to get some dumb robot to return.

“Fuck it,” Bea whispers to herself. She proceeds calmly enough to the nearest exit, props the door open behind her, and breathes in the damp courtyard air. From her handbag she produces a long-stashed joint, crumbly and dry.

She lights up—the tinder-dry paper burning too fast, too-hot flames making her choke—and reminds herself, as her dilating pupils cause the sky to flash blue: This will make you sleep.

48

The morning starts with protein bars and energy drinks. Then, just before the blue dawn resolves into true daylight, Sol and Scottie tour the neighborhood to establish that the lights have come back on. They signal Bea, and hunker back down to await the maintenance woman.

She passes, looking fresh and breezy in sunglasses, driving with a smoothie in her hand.

Signal.

Twenty minutes later she passes the other way, a merry pair of brake lights and a whisper of exhaust. The house is theirs. They signal Bea, roll back up to the gates, and unlock and relock every barrier until the house looms before them. Bea rushes up, with hollows under her eyes and an anxious smile on her face, and Scottie climbs out of the cab to embrace her. Sol feels sick.

* * *

Sol and Scottie will search. Bea will observe from the LIN closet. But first, as planned, Scottie must fire up the incinerator. They've purchased a garden waste incinerator that promises a reliable flame but requires construction. Scottie is methodical to the point of being slow, taking pains to lay out pieces on the gravel surface for inspection before screwing them together with a little Allen key. Sol, watching him, starts to feel antsy.

"I'm ready to start looking," he says.

"Great," Scottie says distractedly. "I'll have this set up in twenty minutes. I'd say it'll take half an hour to get a good burn going. Then we can put the lid on and let it sit."

"I'm thinking it might be worth having a quick scout around outside."

"Yeah. This will be ready in 50 minutes."

"I can go by myself."

Scottie puts his tools down.

"That's not the plan, though, Mr. Sol."

"Yeah."

There's a moment of silence, and Scottie starts working again.

* * *

In the LIN closet, Bea slumps into the captain's chair and scans the images on the monitor. She can see Scottie and Mr. Sol in the top corner of one of the views. But something's interfering with the feed. It keeps freezing, Sol lurching from one spot to another, like a fly circling Scottie's inert form.

At the same time, perhaps to compensate for whatever is slowing the processing speed, a new component starts up in the machine. It chugs and slurps in an oddly liquid way. She can't trace the origin of the sound, as if the component is working on a different plane, perceptible but untouchable. It revolts her.

* * *

Sol feels a powerful urge to get moving. He paces around the van. He even jumps up and down, swinging his arms and rolling his shoulders, trying to work some of the energy out of his body. Frustratingly, however, he soon discovers that Scottie has actually started disassembling the incinerator again.

"Do you want a hand?" Sol asks, and he picks up a section, which swings apart and showers the ground with loose nuts and bolts.

"No, man," Scottie says quietly. He shakes his head, pulling the Allen key out of his front shirt pocket. He looks at Sol, doubt growing in his eyes.

"Look," Sol says, cracking his knuckles, "I'm going to look around the grounds. I'm not going in the house. Just the grounds."

"Um," Scottie says.

"Don't worry. I'll be back to start the search properly."

"Okay . . ."

Sol walks away, brushing absently at his arm. Scottie realizes Sol doesn't have his gloves on, or his garbage bag, or his walkie-talkie. He shouts, but Sol chooses not to hear him.

⁂

Nat Collins has only to drop her keys through the letterbox at Excis Property Maintenance, then the whole weekend is hers. She's returning to the car, having completed this errand, with thoughts of the Ration Salad recipe she's been meaning to try, when somebody catches her arm.

"Miss Collins," a familiar voice says.

She looks up into familiar eyes, and understands immediately what's happening, and—after making a split-second, instinctive decision—what her duty is.

She nods, beckoning the man into her office.

Collins locks the door and closes the blinds. She leads the man back to the administration room, offers him water and a seat.

He drinks, thirstily. He has bushy eyebrows and thick, strawberry blond hair. His skin is greasy, his eyes are sunken, and he's leaner than he used to be. Collins knows the man as Mr. Bull. He operates a transport company in the commercial estate. He led the local chapter of the Hasturian Guard.

"Thank you," he says, after draining the bottle.

"Are you hungry? I think we have some biscuits." Mr. Bull nods. She heads to the kitchenette. "I hope you like chocolate digestives," she witters, pouring biscuits over a plate. She brings it back into the office and places it before him, and watches him eat, two at a time. He swallows and chokes, and she hands him another bottle of water.

"Thank you," he repeats.

She puts her hand over his. This is the first time they've spoken in any real way, but Collins has seen Mr. Bull at rallies, marches, and charity events; the intimacy doesn't feel strange. It feels right.

"Whatever you need," she says. He nods. When Collins speaks next, she barely knows what she's going to say until she's said it; barely knows the depth of her feeling until the words are spoken. "I think it's a *disgrace*, what they've done to you. You were only ever doing what you knew was right, and most working people agreed with you from start to finish." He nods. "Are you alone?" He shakes his head.

"I have some visitors from across the country," he says. "Things are worse, out East. They're looking for somewhere safe. I don't want to put you at risk, Nat, but I know you've got access to a few places. And we need somewhere to go." Collins nods, absorbing the importance of the request. The fact that Mr. Bull called her by her first name. "I don't just mean a bolt-hole. We need somewhere to regroup. Somewhere big, and out of town, and unlikely to be bothered by the owners. It's not like we'll do any damage. And of course, when things swing around, we'll be able to cover it anyway."

"Things are going to swing around," Collins affirms, nodding vigorously.

"So can you help us?"

"Well . . . how many are you?"

"It's best I don't tell you too much. Not that I don't trust you, Nat."

Collins feels herself blushing. She studies her hands. "I can think of one place . . ." she says. "I was just out there this morning, so I know it's in good order. For what you want—what *we* want—I think it'll be perfect."

* * *

Bull climbs back into the backseat of the car, keys in hand. The Zealot fixes him with one of his stares from the passenger seat.

"Well?" he asks.

Not for the first time, the Zealot's insolence rankles. Bull directs his response to the tall, bony Hasturian Guard in the driver's seat. "I got the keys. I hope this is worth it. I hope I'm not breaking cover for a couple of malfunctioning ray guns."

The Zealot absorbs the news with a discomforting grunt of pleasure. "Believe me, Bull, it's worth it," he murmurs.

The driver, Spider, nods. His face is gaunt to the point of being skeletal, and he gratefully receives the chocolate digestives and water Bull hands forward. Since they met a few days ago, Spider has acted as the Zealot's translator, mediator, and sometimes—after his weird arguments about the divine rights of kings got out of hand—bodyguard. Bull doesn't quite understand the hold Louis Barrow—the Zealot—holds over other Guards. He's read some of his apparently amazing philosophy posts on the *Aldebaran Gazette*, has overheard him holding forth in propaganda livestreams; he sees him as a kooky fellow traveler from the early days of the Movement, not the kind of serious soldier he needs on-side now. Still, the promise of advanced Crown Leviathan weaponry has Bull playing along for now. The kind of guns the Zealot promises could help his chapter hold off the anticipated purge. And whatever credence he gives this promise is all thanks to Spider.

"*Well?*" the Zealot demands. Spider, his mouth full of crumbs, starts the engine. They're in a family car requisitioned in the days of plunder and feasting. Bull hands a little printed map to Pentorgan House to the Zealot, who glances at it as if merely to confirm something he already knows.

"Won't need this," he says. "I've been there before. Oh, I know the place. Oh, yes." He slams his palm against the dashboard and laughs, leering at Spider. "I'm going home, mate! Going home!"

* * *

Sol starts with a circuit of the exterior wall. Why not? It's a nice enough day for a walk. Bracing. Spits of rain on the breeze. A gravel path accompanies the wall for half of its circumference, then swings inward. Sol walks onto the verge, then behind an overgrown rhododendron plantation, then between damp rushes, then between plants that have died back to a knot of grey limbs.

He pays attention to his arm. The skin on it. The hairs on the skin. The air between the hairs. He senses nothing strange. Just fluid motion: wind blowing outside; blood pulsing inside. He sees the van in the distance. He sees Scottie, working away. Waves. He hits the gravel path again.

He's going to be okay. He's going to do right by his friends. He can handle whatever comes: dreams, whispers, sickness. He knows right from wrong.

* * *

"Judy? The fire's ready." Bea pauses by the squawking radio, unsure how to respond. The squelching of the LIN processor distracts her. "The fire's ready, over."

"Are you going to start searching?" she responds.

"Yes, but . . . is Mr. Sol with you?"

"No. Isn't he with you?" Bea scans the screens again. She finds Scottie, standing in the top corner of one screen beside the smoking incinerator. She sees no sign of Sol in the other feeds.

"He wandered off."

"Why?" Bea asks.

The screens flicker. The processor grunts. Bea feels the lurch in her stomach of a plan gone awry.

* * *

The whole ride up, Louis feels it. The fusion of his own anticipation with the vibrations of the cosmos, a million billion excited molecules swirling in the fluid motion of the spheres, he watches from his car window, murmurations gathering in the afternoon light, and he knows it's coming, the hills and rills want it, the trees, the animals, the insects gummed to their grille want it, they want to be witness, they love him from afar, they wish they could know him, they never will, there is only the one who will, the King will know him, he is rushing, the King will know him, he won't be lonely anymore, this is his bridge, his route to Accession, nobody can know his bridge but him . . .

He tries to keep the rocking to a minimum, tries to chant only under his breath. He can't wait to unmask, to leave these subpar minds behind, these terrestrial thinkers with their antiquated notions of nation and personality. He passes landmarks from his journeys to and from residential treatment—the cattle shed, now daubed with messages of hope—and his heart leaps, but it's a melancholy leap, for even as he greets them he is bidding farewell, as he must all ordinary things, the sweet among the sour, for a Cipher is smooth and neutral, a Cipher is a zero through which all filth and beauty passes alike, a cosmic cloaca, a sphincter of the stars, ha ha!

The man behind him clears his throat. Spider gives Louis a warning look, and he suppresses the laughter that's leaking from him. Spider is very stupid, but useful on this planet. Louis wants to be rid of this other man, John Bull or whatever, as soon as he can. Perhaps he'll throttle him. The sky is so beautiful: a fabric rent by the motion of giants, grey upon blue upon gold.

And then they're outside a tall fence with a tall gate, and John Bull is bitching about having to get out and unlock everything, but Louis does something *quite persuasive* he can't quite recall afterward, and off John Bull scurries to do King Louis's bidding, walking the gates and beckoning the car through into a rain-slick industrial zone that Louis barely recognizes, or cares about, since a rising tension resolves into nausea the moment they roll through the gates and he knows, he KNOWS the book is near, he can practically see the lines on the ground and sky through which the *Kataluin* trace their paths.

The engine thrums beneath him and they roll onward over mirror-wet paths. And what will it be like, the moment of Accession? Long has he considered it, the first contact, the tilt-turn-drop, out of this world and into the next. Impossible to witness, of course, and speculation is fruitless, but nonetheless he sees himself walking down a line of saluting dignitaries to board a futuristic spacecraft—stupid, *stupid*, he knows—nausea grips him and his head sinks between his knees and the car stops and Spider is talking and some . . . some eddy in the current of energies redirects the sickness from Louis so he can lift his head and see that they've parked in the most beautiful garden, just as he remembers it, the lawns glowing from within and the borders bleeding into fractal tendrils—he blinks—the tendrils draw back and the house, blooming like a blot—here comes the sickness again—welcomes him.

Breathe.

When lucidity returns, he's leaning against a slate-topped wall beside the car, and John Bull is counting keys on an oversized ring, like the keys to a giant's castle, saying to Spider "You need to get the boy right." Spider hands Louis a near-empty plastic water bottle and tells him to drink. The water is bitter and Louis recognizes the taste of the pep pills raided from the police supply.

A short while later he can stand, and walk, and talk—and he *does* talk, explaining to his oafish companions elementary semiotics and *fin-de-siècle* French poetry and the state of play of Archimboldi Studies and the fascinating, FASCINATING, textual play in *The King in Yellow* and the Necronomicon and Cipher Theory. That is, he repeats in a dry-mouthed shorthand the salient elements of his Special Report and its countless offshoots that he published in the *Aldebaran Gazette* as they navigate a surreptitious route through the grounds and the garden—*oh it is BEAUTY, ultimately BEAUTY ALONE that facilitates intergalactic space travel AKA LOVE*—avoiding the bulbous white LIN probes that Louis understands to be the King's own nerves, monstrously sprouted on this planet like a teratoma—a *terra*-toma, *ha ha!—shut up, Louis*—and his dick starts swelling in his pants as he remembers Dr. Bredsky, her attention on him, moving the LIN probe across his skin, cultivating the certainty that HE IS THE ONE and THIS IS HIS TIME.

⁎ ⁎ ⁎

Bea moves through the bare little office, running her hands over the shelves to confirm they're empty. At the back of the office is a little concealed corridor. It too contains only shelves and the marks of heavier items, long gone. She stops over by the window and scans, quickly, in case Sol is out there. Nothing but lush green lawns and shrubs.

"Judy?" She jumps. No, the office is still empty. The voice is from the walkie-talkie on her hip. "Judy? Come in." Something in his voice warns Bea to take note.

"What is it, Scottie?"

"I'm by the van." His voice is wavering. He sounds like a little boy.

"Yes?" she says.

"There are people on the lawn." She says nothing. She's frozen. "Three people. They're dressed in black."

"Hasturian Guards?"

"They're here, Judy. They're here."

* * *

Sol's arm itches. He pulls up his sleeve and looks for the mark. He can't find it. He sees nothing but red scratches from his nails, a detail he understands to be quite strange. Thinks about itching and scratching. The moment the ghost sensation is relieved by true contact. Abrasion. Pain?

The house is near now, and Sol is walking another loop with the moat on his right. Wondering what he is doing here.

A stroll in the garden.

There is a voice, an over-the-shoulder voice, narrating his walk through the gravel paths and box junctions and beds, but when he looks back there is no one there.

"Dulcie?" he asks.

Silence. He laughs.

People get caught up, he thinks, in the space between the itch and the scratch.

Then: *What are you talking about?* Something is wrong.

He shakes his head to clear it, but it moves so slow, and he feels his hair waving, suspended, in the fluid, and he's forgotten, by the time the action is complete, what it was for, what it was. A quiet over-the-shoulder voice, Dulcie's voice, tells him, *You're in trouble*.

49

They surprise Sol on the slippery walkway beside the pond. John Bull is quick in producing his sawed-off shotgun, but its appearance doesn't have the expected effect. Sol registers the gun, complying with Bull's demands to kneel, put his hands behind his head; but he doesn't give his full attention. He keeps looking out, at the tree line, the borders, the koi pond, the eaves.

Louis understands. He hears the flurry of birds in flight. A convergence. The energies are drawing in. The shadows are ripe with skittering.

Bull squats in front of the kneeling man. He's done this before, with the same shotgun, in a dozen yards, outhouses, and back rooms in the last two months. When he speaks, his trigger finger flexes.

"I'm only going to ask you once, mate. How many are you, and where are the others?"

Sol looks past the man.

⁎ ⁎ ⁎

Bea sees in her screen the steeply angled view of the pond: Three strangers have Sol trapped. The four men are arranged in the foreground, dark water and a gravel path upstage, a rhododendron plantation like a black border at the top of the composition.

From this border, a black spike starts to descend, cleaving the screen in two. It accelerates like dripping molasses.

⁎ ⁎ ⁎

"Look at me," Bull orders. He stands and taps Sol with the muzzle of the shotgun, hard enough to chip a tooth. As blood drips unnoticed from his lips, Sol tries to look at the man before him. But his eyes keep returning to the wall of rhododendrons across the pond, where a shape is coalescing.

The Corpse Man. The *Kataluin*.

Bull, frustrated, swings the butt of the gun at Sol's nose. Cartilage crunches. Blood spills out. Still Sol won't break his gaze. Finally Bull ignores his good sense and looks at the spot that has transfixed the prisoner. He sees nothing: just leaves, bobbing in the breeze.

Sol looks up at his captors. He sees no recognition in the face of the burly, red-faced man with the shotgun, nor the skeletal thug in a bomber jacket behind him.

But the pale, doughy, rabid-looking individual—*Louis Barrow*, the over-the-shoulder voice asserts—catches his gaze. He knows. He sees it, too. A triumphant grin is spreading across his face.

The ghostly figure in the rhododendron launches across the gravel, resolving into the shape Sol knows, the fusty black and soapy white form and half-walking, half-dancing gait, and this parody of locomotion carries it over the lip of the pond and across its black surface, a V-shaped ripple following and growing and falling out of focus, lily pads bobbing, and Louis dashes forward, arms wide, welcoming.

Louis plunges into the pond, up to his midriff. He struggles gamely against the mud and water. His face still beams with expectation and triumph as the *Kataluin* passes him by, extends a billowing finger to a spot on Sol's arm, and disappears.

* * *

In Bea's video feed, the black spike drips downward until it reaches Sol, then spreads out around him until all other detail is lost. There is only Sol, kneeling in darkness. The LIN starts jabbering like a broken robot.

Bea checks the other feeds. Nothing has changed. There's been no eclipse, no flood: The garden and the empty rooms remain in the other streams of footage.

She returns to the black feed. Sol hasn't moved.

Gradually, highlights start to emerge in the blackness.

* * *

It takes a moment for the extent of the catastrophe to become clear to Louis. The light dims, the wind drops, the static energy—the glorious, stomach-knotting power that had held the garden suspended like an underwater tableau—dissipates. Louis, disenchanted, is left standing waist-deep in cold water on a cloudy day. The faintest whiff of smoke hangs in the air.

He wades to the edge of the pond and grabs Sol by the chin. Sol doesn't resist. His eyes are dull. Louis wants to weep.

"What did I do wrong?" he asks. Sol shows no sign of understanding. Louis releases him, and asks the air, instead: "Where did you go?" No answer. Then he starts thrashing about, beating the surface of the water with his fists, bothering the water boatmen and gnats, yelling: "It was just getting started! Why can't I help? Why *him*? Who is he? Who the fuck even is he?"

He slaps the surface hard enough to send a crest of water over Sol's head and chest. Sol remains impassive, dripping, unblinking as a statue.

"Watch it, psycho," Bull says, wiping pond slime from his chin.

"It was meant to be *me*, you cretin!" Louis screams, slapping another spray of water Bull's way. Then another, and another: *splash splash splash*. "It was meant to be *me!*" he whines, "*I'm* the one who understands, *I'm* the—"

Bull's shotgun blast cuts Louis off. A fountain of white and red foam rises from the water around him as his belly is opened up, and warm innards slide out and cold pond water slides in as his legs buckle and he crumples into the indifferent embrace of the silt.

For a period he is aware, behind the adrenal numbness, that nothing more will replace this envelope of cold.

"Um," Spider says, and Bull turns and empties the second chamber into his neck, detaching the head except for a flap of skin and a few knots of muscle—spine waggling, here—so the head rolls back and hangs—pendulous, blinking, upside-down—off his shoulder blades for a short while until the rest of his body relaxes its tense posture and folds to the slate paving.

Bull turns back to Sol.

"Understand I'm not here to play games, yet? How many are you, and where are the others?"

Sol, unflinching, slowly turns his head. Blood pours from his nose, diffusing into the pond water still dripping off his face. His eyes don't focus on Bull. Two slim tendrils of vapor—smoke?—appear to discharge from his tear ducts.

"Fuck this," Bull says, and breaks the barrel of the shotgun to reload. He burns his fingers pulling the first shell out, and spits on them before dealing with the second, but the saliva makes the cartridge slippery, and everything gets fiddly, so he fails to track Sol's movements as he spins and grabs both ends of the weapon; fails to respond properly by pulling his hand out of the hinged joint, so that when Sol pushes the gun's components back in place with sudden force, two knuckles remain in the gap between stock and barrel.

From now on it's pure panic and pain for Bull. He yanks one of the knuckles free, but the breach joint comes down more snugly on the remainder, his middle finger, and the crushing pressure grows, and no matter how he scrabbles with his free hand against Sol's arm, face—gouging his thumb in the eye, watching the blood from that torn orifice evaporate into an impossible trail of ruddy-black smoke—Sol never relents, barely grunts. It's like fighting a burning doll. Bull dodges left and right, but moving sends fresh waves of pain through his caught hand. There is no sense to the assault, no tactics: He is merely being driven backward—and when he can move backward no more (his ankle buckles and he falls to his haunches), the man-thing with the burning eyes simply keeps pushing the two ends of the gun inward, until amid the sensation of throbbing pressure, Bull perceives a gristly pop and hears a click and looks down to see that the impossible has happened: Where once there were two halves of a gun, there is now a whole gun. Where once there was a whole hand, there is now . . . less.

Somebody is screaming.

Sol doesn't stop. The gun, now complete, thumps against Bull's chest. Bull has two limbs to use now, and he scrabbles to push the weight away, but now the Sol-thing is straddling him, exerting an unrelenting downward force, and the stock rolls slowly upward over Bull's ribs, hesitating briefly on the clavicle, then plunging down onto his throat.

"Judy. Judy. Judy."

"What is it, Scottie?"

Bea can barely hear the radio over the screaming of the LIN.

"They're all dead."

"What?"

"A man with a shotgun killed two of them."

Bea tries to remember if she heard any shots. Maybe. The machine is loud now.

"Then Mr. Sol killed the man with the shotgun. Judy, I think he's lost it. There's something wrong with him. He's not acting right. It looks like he's . . . on fire."

"This doesn't make any sense."

"Judy, what are we going to do?"

"He killed someone? He's walking around? He's *on fire?*"

"Yes, Judy!"

"But he's not moving in the camera feed, Scottie. He's . . . he's somewhere else."

Bea looks again at the feed. The image is of Sol, standing stock still, in the middle of a crowded pavement, while people mill around him.

⁎ ⁎ ⁎

Sol, who feels like he's just awoken from a nameless stretch in limbo, stands on the corner of Avenida Antioquia in El Cabracion's central district. The sun's glow illuminates the windows of hulking, Germanic piles. The foot traffic is a mass of shadows, swaying limbs, flashes of hands hauling suitcases. Fat, round-muzzled vehicles flow steadily down the road. Across the road Sol sees the old man, Salvatore Archimboldi, his hair wild, his eyes red, standing before the curb as if paralyzed. He wants to cross. He dares not.

A tram bell rings, and as the ponderous, snub-nosed vehicle swings into view, Sol understands the problem. The plane on which the traffic is moving is not properly aligned with the road. At the east end of the road, car wheels barely touch the concrete; by the time they reach the spot where Archimboldi stands, their wheels are half submerged in the road surface; while at the west end only their humped roofs are visible above the tarmac, slowly descending into the grey as if into a river of ashes.

"Can you help me?" Archimboldi asks. Sol hears him clearly over the traffic. Archimboldi is carrying a small suitcase. He keeps lifting the suitcase, then dropping it again onto the pavement.

"Can you help me?" Archimboldi asks, again, and Sol is now beside him—in fact, they are sitting together on a wooden bench with flaky blue gloss paint. They are watching these great old cars, like yachts, like whales, diving through the road surface. They are watching the sky fade from orange into fantastic purple. They are watching the grim Germanic buildings turn black.

"What do you need?" Sol asks.

"I need to get out of here."

* * *

Scottie observes Sol's body wander away from the pond, back along the side of the house. It's merely Sol's body, Scottie feels certain—not Sol's entire self. The body moves like a puppet, without grace, as if unfamiliar with the capabilities of its own limbs. It trails a cloud of smoke.

After Sol has rounded the corner, Scottie counts to three (then five, then ten, wavering in his determination), then finally forces himself forward to investigate.

He gets as far as the edge of the pond. Here he can pick out the details of the cadavers. They look like broken toys. The man with the crushed chest and bloody hand is a stranger. The crumpled thing on the pond's edge, who looks as though he collapsed in the crab position, is hard to identify without getting closer than Scottie is willing to do. But the pale man floating in the pond's peaty water, attended to already by the ghost koi, is his old friend, the traitor and collaborator Louis Barrow.

An unpalatable blend of emotions rises in Scottie and he turns back.

"Scottie!" his radio bleats.

"Hey."

"I can see you. What happened down there? Do you know who those people were?"

He looks up at the chubby white CCTV camera affixed on the wall above.

"It's Louis. Louis's dead, Judy. We're safe."

"Um, I don't know if we're safe . . . I think there might be something wrong with the machine here. Did you see where Mr. Sol went?"

He points toward the corner.

"Maybe the front door?"

There's a long period during which the only sounds Scottie hears are the fish moving around Barrow's body. Then the radio crackles again.

"Um," says Bea's voice. "Um, I think we have a serious problem."

A golden VW Beetle with an illuminated TAXI sign pulls up at the rank beside Sol and Archimboldi. The driver has bloodless white skin and wet hair. He leers at Sol while Archimboldi transfers suitcases into the hood from a gigantic pile in the middle of the square. The suitcases are old and dusty, some perished leather, some cardboard. Archimboldi carries them in armfuls, like empty props.

“I feel sure these aren’t all mine,” Archimboldi says, as he drops another load into the car’s gaping hood. “Well, are you going to help?”

Sol picks up a suitcase—it’s unwieldy, as if loaded with mercury—and hauls it to the Beetle. He notices a label in what looks like Italian, and an address, which includes the word “Restevo.” He drops it in the hood, where there’s still space for plenty more.

“I know this word, *Restevo*,” he says.

“There are many things here one will recognize,” Archimboldi tells him. “I believe recognition is, in fact, fundamental to the success of the project.”

“What project?” Sol asks.

“Why, this is my bridge. My route to Accession.”

The luggage heap has gone and Archimboldi slams the hood shut, then gets into the back seat. He looks surprised when Sol slides in alongside him. Nonetheless he signals the driver and they sit in the cool space with its scent of leather and stale tobacco. The suspension creaks as they roll forward between the Centro’s hotels and municipal buildings and into the embassy district. The streets are thick with armed guards wearing black tactical clothing and animal-themed face masks.

The car picks up speed.

Archimboldi peers hopefully out of his window, which is far smaller than it ought to be, more like a porthole or a judas hole, so that he has to angle one eye then the other at the glass, which he does in quick succession, bobbing like a bird, grunting like an old man.

“What can you see?” Sol asks. Archimboldi doesn’t reply. Sol tries to look past him but there’s no view, no other way to see out of this cabin, which is sealed up like a pressure chamber, padded with stained white leather, so he tries to shoulder Archimboldi aside, and they struggle until the older man relents, and gives him the view through the peephole.

Sol sees blackness. The deep, vast blackness of space. What stars are visible cannot be named. Hanging like a jewel in this embrace of darkness, rapidly growing, is their destination.

* * *

Bea sees it in the feed, pixilated and rippling with cathode radiation: Joseph Sol sitting in the cabin of some vehicle beside Salvatore Archimboldi. The two of them peering through a porthole that grows to encompass the screen, and within it, rotating before the inky curtain of infinite void, a shard-shaped entity, a corrupted jewel overlaid with a net of lights—pulsing, circulatory—with marbled, slowly shifting fluid beneath.

She knows, without further instruction, that what she sees is Carcosa. She understands instinctively that they've lost Sol. She cycles through the different feeds again: the annex entrance, the wine cellar, the office. All these spaces remain unchanged. It's only where the LIN's cameras are trained on Sol—the physical location of Sol's body—that the vision reappears. Sol's vision.

She switches back to the front entrance. The feed still shows the view from the vehicle's porthole, only the shard has grown: Bea sees infrastructure: endless spaghetti helices of rails and roads with ceaseless ant-like movement visible. Sol and Archimboldi are descending toward a new planet.

* * *

Deceleration pushes Sol and Archimboldi into their seats, hydraulics whine and sputter, the walls thrum with mechanical pops and the grinding of machinery, thrusters barf, sparks creep across the porthole, the cabin fills momentarily with white vapor, which is sucked out again with an ear-cracking pop, and the VW Beetle pulls up outside a broad open gateway. The driver jumps out and opens the door and Archimboldi spills out.

This isn't the embassy district. They are somewhere unlovely and suburban. The sign above the gate reads VILLA MONACO. The skies around are filled with soot and smoke. An unfamiliar, greenish sun rends the clouds in fleeting moments.

The moment Archimboldi steps out, guards appear and start hauling suitcases out of the hood. They ignore his confused protests and pass the cases along a human chain that stretches up the driveway of Villa Monaco toward a distant building. No guard will engage with his remonstrances, and they barely resist when he seizes his luggage back, but he cannot overcome their ant-like will: When he puts a suitcase down, another guard simply picks it up again; if he knocks a guard to the floor, another takes his place. Archimboldi follows the progress of the suitcases up the long gravel drive.

Sol follows Archimboldi.

* * *

"Scottie, what's he doing?"

"He went around the corner."

"Yes, I know. But I need to know what he's doing."

"Can't you see him on your camera?"

"I . . . it's complicated. I don't think these are ordinary cameras. What they're showing me is more like . . . what he's *dreaming*."

"You think he's sleepwalking? With his head on fire?"

"Like that, maybe. The LIN shows me what he's dreaming, but I can't see what his body is doing. Do you understand? I need you to follow him, tell me where he's going, what he's doing."

Scottie jogs to the outer edge of the lawn, then tracks around the house by the tree line. He sees Sol standing at the grand front doors. At this distance he looks bewildered and alone, like a supplicant before the gates of a grand castle. The smoke exuding from his head billows like incense around a censer.

Scottie watches Sol shamble forward—yes, he does seem like a sleepwalker—and raise his fist, and knock.

And knock, and knock, and knock.

Bea hears the beating on the door as though it were resonating through the house. She quickly realizes this can't be the case. She breaks down the sounds: It's not the distant knocking that she hears primarily, but something far closer—the LIN's own echo, sympathetic clicks and snorts following each knock.

And the LIN is responding to Sol in other ways. With each blow, staticky flares of light appear in the video feeds. She cycles the feeds: annex entrance; cafeteria; Sol following Archimboldi up a long cinder path; office. The sympathetic flares occur in all real-world feeds, but in her adrenalized state Bea's brain is working overtime, and she becomes alert to certain differences. Some areas flare more than others. She watches the cycle through again: annex entrance; cafeteria; Sol presenting a gigantic passport to a guard and being led into a narrow room; office.

The differences in the flares are consistent.

This is information. She can read this. She can map this.

She pulls out her floor plan and lays it on a side desk. She's already labeled the areas covered by the LIN feeds; she now marks where the flares are most pronounced.

They're in a cluster. Something in this cluster is resonating louder than anywhere else. It can only be one thing.

"Scottie," she says into the radio, "you need to go to the stairwell between the annex and the main building. The books are there. They're there and they're waiting for him. You need to get there first."

50

The waiting room is clammy and hot. Condensation covers the windowpanes while the walls are tacky with some other substance. Archimboldi occupies a child-size wooden bench, his knees up at his shoulders, his arms hugging his chest. "I'm in trouble," he says.

"Tell me where it hurts," the doctor says.

She's wearing a stained lab coat and oversized leather boots. Her eyes aren't kindly. Sol, seated on a bench by the wall, watches her pull down a harness from an alcove in the ceiling. It clicks and screeches as she manipulates its rusty joints. It's hung with pieces of equipment: white tubes, probes, pumps. She applies probes to Archimboldi, slinging wires across his body as if dressing a Christmas tree. The equipment activates and the air hums and the smell of burnt hair permeates.

"I'm in trouble," Archimboldi says again.

Her fingers depress illuminated translucent buttons. Audible vibrations alter wavelength. She snaps fleshy latex gloves onto her hands. The machine gurgles.

"Tell me where it hurts."

* * *

"Unseemly, isn't it?"

Sol immediately recognizes the person speaking as Cléophe Carrette. Carrette is dressed, like the doctor, in a dirty white lab coat, although he appears to be naked underneath. He, too, is seated on a child-size wooden bench, holding a numbered ticket.

"No doubt Dr. Bredsky didn't intend to embed herself and her machine, the Live Information Node, into the structure, but it was perhaps an *inévitabilité*. The whole bridge is built of trauma—I mean this in the strictest, technical sense, *bien sûr*—and this contraption of hers cannot have been easy for our architect to . . . experience. So it has become a part of the structure."

The doctor draws a semiopaque, waterproof curtain across her half of the room, obscuring the machinery and patient.

"This structure—you mean this house?" Sol asks.

"No. I am referring to a broader and more encompassing structure. The Accession bridge *entier*. My Accession bridge. I'm sorry, I must apologize. Introductions: My name is Cléophe Carrette."

"Joseph Sol."

"Nice to meet you. You are probably a ghost, but it's worth having conversation when you can, isn't it?"

Behind the curtain, a drilling sound starts up, then snarls, and a spatter of liquid hits the plastic. Carrette's leg is jiggling. He grips the ticket anxiously.

"The Accession is happening now?" Sol asks.

"I hope so."

"It's not what I expected."

"*Non*. Nor I. Theoretically, we mustn't be surprised. What the Cipher experiences and what the rest of the world sees are two different things. Even in a Deferral, we can assume the Cipher's consciousness engages to some degree with the Accession bridge even as their body is consumed with fire."

"I am a Cipher? Is my body . . . ?"

Carrette looks sharply at Sol, as if discomfited, even offended, by the suggestion.

"This I cannot tell you. I know only my experience, which tells me that in fact *I* am a Cipher. I hadn't intended to become one, but arguably I left myself open to *persuasion* with my undisciplined handling of materials. And now it has happened, I see no sense in indulging in regret. I mean to walk the path before me, follow the markers laid by our architect here toward union with the King. I'm lucky, because I happen to have carried out a lot of research into Archimboldi. I believe I can navigate his design. Up to a certain point, I have been correct in my predictions. The foundations, the overall schema of what he built—with the help of this *machine*—remain. We sit, *par example*, in a reasonably faithful replication of the morning room of Villa Monaco, converted by the CIA into a triage area of sorts. It is as he remembers, with just a couple of adjustments in the style of Pentorgan House, the site of his therapies."

Carrette indicates the waiting room with its steamy windows and sticky walls.

"Nonetheless, you catch me in a moment of doubt—doubt that your appearance has not ameliorated. What surprises me, although perhaps I should have expected them, are the *additions*. For example, when I was first *called into the bridge*, I was wearing a sweater, and some *slacks*. Now, as you will see, I am wearing the same type of gown as our good Dr. Bredsky. I'm prepared to accept that somewhere on my journey I perhaps changed clothes and forgot. But I also have this strange feeling—this *seen-again* feeling—that I've been here, in this room, in my other clothes, feeling uncomfortably hot."

Fizzing and moans from behind the translucent curtains.

"Then there is yourself, for instance. You, my friend, are an addition. You have about you a sense of something *primaire*, fresh, while this room, these . . ." he holds up his hands, his nails unkempt and grimy, ". . . these other elements are stale. Secondhand."

An inner door opens and Carrette springs up, ticket outheld. But instead of the ticket inspector he seems to expect, a small girl in leggings and a My Little Pony jumper stands just inside the doorway.

"*Alors*, another addition," Carrette says, lowering himself to the bench. Sol looks again at the child. His eyes open wide and a sound catches in his throat.

"What is your name, sweetheart?" Carrette asks.

The girl says nothing. Her eyes are huge. Slowly the door closes between them.

"Her name is Sara," Sol says. "She's my sister."

"Ah, I see," says Cléophe. "So you understand me—you see how you have brought your own addition to the bridge."

"I don't understand at all," Sol says. "What are they doing with my sister?"

"Don't worry. That is not your sister. I can only assume, based on your age, that your sister is an adult woman, no? That girl is a fragment. A memory, perhaps. Just like you."

Sol finds it hard to accept this reasoning.

"So my sister is safe?"

"None of us are safe. The world is tumbling into cataclysm, my friend. But she is not *here*. Nonetheless, I do find it troubling, understanding that this is *my* bridge to Accession—and following the credo that *no one can walk my bridge but me*—when I encounter these additions, with their texture of *primaire* experience. If I assume *you* are a Cipher who passed before me, and failed to complete your journey to the King, and were *immolated* like the other victims of Deferrals, then it would stand to reason that *your* clothes should be dusty, *your* details should be changing. And yet it is I who suffers these declensions. These *unheimlich* adjustments."

Carrette looks closely at his dirty fingernails. He sighs.

"So, okay: I must incorporate these painful realities into my comprehension. I can do so. I'm no coward. Since I know I am not a ghost, then it must stand to reason that this structure operates in a manner independent of linear time. That we might do better to regard it, against all instinct, as merely one instantiation among many. And having made this adjustment, I am prepared to accept the possibility that, although I haven't failed in my Accession effort *yet*—since I am still here, engaged in that effort—there may have been a version of myself who did, in fact, fail."

From behind the curtain, a low buzz like a tattoo gun, and soft whimpers.

"And now we reach the rather exciting conclusion that my own effort—or efforts, why not—toward Accession have been incorporated into the bridge structure itself, such that any new instantiation—each fresh *tilt*, as it were, at the prize—will reactivate my own effort, alongside the scattered additions, these scraps of memory, your lovely sister, the dubious priests in the east wing, my rock collection, the unhappy masses below the orchard, et cetera.

"Every time a person attempts Accession, these elements will be recreated, with still greater complexity, until it succeeds.

"Just imagine how those foolish critics would feel—all those pretenders to the Archimboldi Chalice—if they got a mere inkling of what *The Truth of Carcosa* encompasses? They'd be falling over themselves to define it in long-winded terms: a *collaborative, iterative, repeating instantiation of total sensory experience*—they might write a few papers about that, no? And they thought *Mulberry Sands* was good! This—this is a perpendicular infinity." Carrette laughs, long and low. He itches some uncomfortable patch beneath his lab coat. Slurping and squelching from the other half of the room. "Yes," he says finally, "I will make my way to the King. I will make a success of this."

The inner door opens again. This time a uniformed functionary walks out and surveys Sol and Carrette, who once again stands and displays his ticket.

The clerk, however, dismisses Carrette with a wave of her hand and nods at Sol, who recognizes her beneath her peaked cap and shiny black visor.

"Follow me, please sir," says Jennifer Donaghy, smirking.

As Sol leaves, Carrette calls out:

"A warning, Mr. Sol. If my theory of the Accession bridge is correct, and it is an instantiation that has occurred many times before, then you must understand that repeated iterations of even the simplest patterns ultimately tend toward chaos. Whatever Archimboldi's bridge looked like in the beginning, we can expect it to have grown into something quite different by now, and with added complexity grows the tendency to internal friction. Civil war, *mon ami*. Be careful."

* * *

Scottie navigates the corridors through the annex to where he knows the entrance to the main house should be. And is. Which is a relief.

He cannot hear banging on the front door, which might mean the banging has stopped. Perhaps Sol is already in the house. This possibility doesn't upset him as much as the entirely unreasonable fear he developed as he passed the corpses by the pond and realized that one of them—the lanky carcass whose head seemed to be folded under its back—was still twitching.

Fingers clenching and unclenching.

He reaches the door and counts keys on the ring. There's nobody behind him. None of the corpses have risen. Louis hasn't waded out of the water, trailing murky droplets, and followed him to the annex door. Scottie counts the keys on the ring. He can't remember the number to count to. If Louis comes up behind him now, he'll be trapped. But there's nobody behind him. Louis is dead. He'll be trapped if he can't count to the right key. But he can't remember the number.

Somebody behind him? No.

Try them all?

Count keys. It's the fourth key. If Louis traps him he will put his clammy fingers on him. The third key. His cold wet mouth. Count.

* * *

On the LIN monitor, the feed for the front entrance returns. One of the double doors is hanging off its hinges: splinters on the lobby floor, bloody marks on the walls. It appears Sol simply beat his way through the door.

This fact terrifies Bea. It is so utterly unreasonable. The door, Bea knows, was unlocked. It opened *outward*.

Still worse, the bloody marks appear to be steaming.

She moves through the feeds again. She sees Scottie unlocking the door to the main house. Scottie looks frightened. She cares for Scottie, in this moment, when he looks frightened. She *cares* for him a lot. That would be the factual way to pin it down. The *Carrettian* definition, careful and thorough.

She advances the feed. She reaches the feed that should show the central corridor, and sees instead Sol following a uniformed guard through narrowing spaces, dimly lit passageways with sharp corners, steep spiral stairways, ladders, and vents. They move perhaps twice as fast as they should. The fast-forward progression is fascinating. For a while she watches, fixated, until the original feed blinks back: an empty corridor in weak sunlight, a set of bloody footprints—reeking with some dark vapor—marking progress.

* * *

Scottie enters a space that smells of mold and echoes with the tiny sounds of vermin. A spiral stairwell leads, he remembers, up to the ground floor of the main house. But Bea said to check the stairs themselves. Scottie's momentarily baffled, until he notices a painted metal door like a fuse closet, pulls it open, and finds a cavity behind.

A narrow passage the height of a child. Its walls are unpainted, the mortar between the bricks dissolving to paste, the floor pungent with rat piss.

This must be the place.

Scottie closes the door carefully behind himself and follows his flashlight beam forward. He hears his own breath and footsteps. A beating heart. The air here is full of spores, and somewhere above, he believes he can hear something thudding.

The flashlight beam meets the corner of a cardboard box.

Two boxes. Both sealed. Both printed with the logo *Albatross Hung*.

The proofs. Found them.

Footsteps above. Bassy through the fundament of the house.

Then hammering on the metal door behind.

51

The halls are thick with human bodies both moving and still. The workers fill their trolleys with corpses until the load beds are piled high with limbs and flesh. The trolley wheels squeak and wobble as they roll over the tiles. Where the bodies block the route, four or five workers together will lift the trolley, careful not to unbalance its cargo, its hanging hands and lolling heads on floppy necks. Where soldiers block the way, the workers must submit to checks and searches and beatings and burnings and sexual assaults and summary executions. And once the soldiers have had their fun, the surviving workers pick up the remains of their colleagues and load them onto their trolleys, piling them higher and rolling them further. The trolleys get jammed in impossible lines. Doctors in white coats climb over the rills and drifts of moving and unmoving human meat. They have no treatments to provide. There are no windows, only doors to closets and cupboards and further corridors. There are notice boards. A rota. Announcements every minute or so. The supply of human flesh is inexhaustible. Everybody wears a uniform until they're dead.

"How are we going to get through?" Sol asks Donaghy.

Donaghy flexes her fingers in her leather gloves.

"We're going to have to cut our way through," she says, with relish. "It's terrible, but it's the way of the world: The King's chamber is past this clotted area, and we aren't going to make our way there unless we exercise, despite the best of intentions, the violence we so deplore."

She fits her peaked cap securely over her head. The visor comes down to cover her eyes and reveal her mouth, with its teeth and its cartoon tongue, licking lips, cartoon hungry.

* * *

Bea runs out of the LIN closet and down the staircase toward the sound of the hammering. She trips on the last few steps and twists her ankle; the pain comes slowly but intensely, and she's briefly halted until her adrenaline overrides the sudden sick weakness in her leg. She moves, wobbly, toward the hammering of fists on steel.

Rounding the corner she gets a view of the back stairwell. Sol must be there. She can't see him, but she can hear the sound of the blows, unrelenting, almost elemental, like hurricane winds slamming a loose window. Surely Sol has wrecked his hands. Bea can't help but imagine them after each impact: bloody stubs, splintered bones. When she reaches him she will find a wild-eyed ghoul with flaps of skin trailing off his broken limbs.

When she reaches him, what will she do?

She has a box cutter. Bea always thought box cutters were nasty weapons, used in nasty crimes. The slicing action of their curt little blades made her feel squirmy. Now, wielding it on her way to confront a full-sized adult going apeshit in the stairwell, she wishes she had something bigger. Something that might keep those battering bloody hands away from her body.

As she approaches the stairwell, the shadows within it resolve into form. Perhaps she sees Sol's head—or maybe two heads. A plume of smoke. At a certain distance the atmosphere starts to feel charged. It makes the hairs on her arms tingle, brings a near-sneeze sensation to the root of her nose. She walks slower, as if she were wading through some fluid thicker than air. Her leg no longer hurts but it wobbles like jelly as she reaches the shadow, the squirming thing in the stairwell, the Sol-thing.

The Sol-thing has a broken wrist. His hand flaps uselessly, but his arms don't stop swinging at their target, a steel door below the stairwell, and the percussions resonate through the swampy air. His eye sockets billow smoke. His cheeks are a bloody swollen mass. His nose has been knocked in. She feels a wave of pity for this meat sack, this person under remote control. She imagines the possibility that he might return to himself, wake up and discover the damage wrought against his body.

Maybe there's some way of reaching him? Maybe some spark of consciousness would recognize her voice?

"Mr. Sol," she says quietly.

No reaction. Perhaps he can't even hear her.

Bang, bang, bang, his limbs slam against the door.

"Mr. Sol!"

She's close now. She could reach out and touch him. He might understand her touch.

It happens quickly. She doesn't realize just how close she is until Sol's raised fist comes bearing down huge in her vision, and instinctively she raises the box cutter and although the fist makes contact—she falls against the stairs and the back of her head bounces, CRACK, *oh fuck, that's real*—the mean little blade makes contact, too, and gouges Sol's arm from elbow to wrist and the wound wells with blood. While the world comes over white for Bea, it doesn't recede completely and she stays conscious to see the little battered hatch fly open, knocking Sol aside, and Scottie in the doorway beckons her inside, and she totters to him and they close the door and she isn't dead.

52

Sol hauls himself over the concrete lip of the shaft and lands on grass. He lies, exhausted, beside the well-head. He's climbed a long way to escape the violent corridors through which Donaghy led him. He's aware of their presence below, as if a cutaway diagram could reveal their busy detail at any moment. This place is an orchard, he believes. It's dark. He sees silhouettes of savagely coppiced fruit trees and a scree of wreckage, as if from an aviation disaster. From beyond tall walls he hears engines roaring and gunshots. There's a pale path between trees. He follows it.

In a clearing stands a windowless concrete tower. From a hundred feet away, it appears to be perhaps four stories tall. But when Sol gets closer, he sees that it's in fact ten stories tall. He walks another few steps and understands that the tower splits at its peak, like a serpentine tongue, into a gigantic "Y." He takes another step, and realizes that the two peaks themselves are forked, as if the tower were a tree. As he progresses, the structure of the "tower" reveals itself as an iteratively diverging matrix, like a lung, stretching into the blackness above the orchard in a fractal progression that might resemble the unwinding of a fern or a tentacle. Carrette's admonition returns to him: A simple pattern repeated enough times tends toward chaos.

How many iterations have come before him? How many would-be Ciphers have added their own tower to this structure?

A sign above the door at the foot of the tower reads LA PROFUNIDAD. A steady ant-stream of guards and prisoners emerge from the orchard, and the door opens periodically to allow guards to rush prisoners inside. Violence is in the air: panicked shouts and beatings and gunshots. But nobody touches Sol. He walks unmolested through the doorway—the metal door clanging behind him—and ascends the narrow concrete stairwell within, with its reek of blood and feces, stale urine and fear sweat, and he passes tiny doorways leading, he knows, to tiny, tiny cells, with the interned and their fears and memories and mean hopes within, looping like a generator; he doesn't look through the peep-holes; he fears to see a face he recognizes, a face who might recognize him and say, "I met you once, you called my name and handed me a piece of paper." He walks endless diverging stair-wells, moving always upward, his stomach lurching on occasion as if the floor is swaying, tilting, wavering above great depths, and sometimes he hears a rumble below or above like something falling apart.

* * *

The explosion is closer this time. Sol sees a flash up ahead and feels first the percussive pressure wave, then the blowback rush of wind. At the site he finds a cavity ripped in the wall, the edge of the stairwell projecting over sheer blackness, air streaming into the void. He stands in the gap, gripping the edges, and sees soldiers crawling over La Profunidad's coral-like network. They wear breathing equipment and carry guns. They fire at one another from between parallel and diverging branches, suspended in nothingness. He witnesses an explosion breach another hole in a nearby wall, sees debris and bodies hurtle into the blackness.

A flurry of white papers flies past him on the wind. A page catches on his shoulder and he retrieves it. It reads:

RESIST CORPORATE OLIGARCHY!

~~XANTHIC SPECTRUM—PANOP INSIGHTS~~

~~CROWN LEVIATHAN—PRISM CONSULTANCY~~

CARCOSAN ENERGY FOR TRUE CARCOSANS!

In a fork between two stairwells, Sol sees the first piece of graffiti. Written in white chalk or paint, it reads: ONLY THE KING WILL SAVE YOU. At the next junction, dozens of bills have been pasted onto the wall beside an empty, doorless cell. Printed and written in various hands, the bills represent competing factions; many have been defaced or torn down, and there is a pool of black, dried blood on the floor beneath.

HASTURIAN GUARD OR
TERRAN TURNCOATS?

DO THEY STILL STAND
FOR THE KING?

And:

ALDEBARAN HERESY: BURN ON SIGHT

And:

GIOVANNI, METTI & METTI:
YOUR DEPENDABLE ALLY IN THE FIGHT
FOR CARCOSAN VALUES

And:

What Would the KING Say?

Sol hears footsteps in one of the stairwells and ducks into a doorway as a pair of soldiers scramble down the stairs. They have humanoid bodies and wear black uniforms, but their heads are those of beasts: a wolf and a boar. Wolf is unarmed and injured; Boar carries a small, futuristic-looking sidearm. They run as if routed, never looking back, and seconds later a band of helmeted humanoids follows in pursuit. At their head, wearing a mechanized combat suit and carrying what looks like a flamethrower, Sol recognizes Higgins.

The old GMM grandee looks younger, in an artificial way. His hair is no longer grey but shocking white, his skin pink and slick with sweat. He pauses at the junction and sniffs the air, the sensors assembled around his headset trembling. He turns toward Sol.

“State your allegiance,” he snaps. Sol shrugs. “What is your attitude to Accession? Are you of the Aldebaran Heresy? The Hasturian Guard? Are you a Terran Agent or a Carcosan Trueblood?”

Sol can find no words. He wouldn’t know where to start placing himself in this conflict. He knows only what Carrette told him: Iterations tend toward chaos. Higgins stares at him coldly, no trace of recognition in his eyes. After a couple of seconds he shrugs, and raises the muzzle of the flamethrower.

At that moment, the wall explodes.

* * *

"What the fuck what the fuck," Bea keeps panting, clutching the back of her head as she shuffles to the back of the tunnel. Scottie stays at the door, at first, bracing against it until he can persuade himself that the steel will hold firm against the battering. Then he joins her.

"Was that Mr. Sol?" he hisses.

"Yes, fuck, yes, it's him."

"I found the books."

"Fuckedy fuck my head . . ."

"I found the books and we have to get them out of here."

"Yes, let's go!"

"But this tunnel doesn't lead anywhere, Judith."

BANG BANG BANG goes Sol's fist on the door. The sound resonates through the brick walls, bringing down showers of mold and bug shit.

Bea takes out her phone and struggles to activate the flashlight. When it finally comes on it's so bright her head spins and she has to sit down.

"I don't have time for you to pass out, Judith!"

"Wait up. Wait. Fuck . . ."

She drops the phone and holds her head. The door doesn't stop going BANG BANG BANG. Scottie starts to cry.

"Tell me what to do, Judith. Tell me what to do!"

She breathes heavily. She rests her head between her knees.

"Find a way out," she hisses.

"There's no way out! There's only one door!"

"Then why . . ." she slurs, between weird, jerky breaths, "why . . . did they build it?"

Then her eyes roll up to the back of her head.

* * *

The initial breaching charge is followed by a series of sharp, stunning explosions, before the raiding party swings through the opening on rappel lines. They are beast-faced humanoids wearing rebreathers and carrying light arms, and Sol just has time to see Higgins immolate the first wave of attackers before the venting atmosphere sweeps him out into the void.

His body spins slowly as he clears the nearest concrete spurs and drifts down a channel between rotating boughs; sporadic explosions light up junctions like firing synapses; and the colossal scale and complexity of La Profunidad's structure becomes apparent to Sol over the course of several hours. La Profunidad is an artifact of chaos—a concrete tumor at war with itself—and yet Sol has the leisure to recall Carrette's analysis of the Accession bridge—collaborative, iterative—and recognize the repetition of certain building blocks, architectural gestures, or synaptic chains, and conclude that, yes, this impossible construct might be Iteration 1,000 or 10,000 of something that, at Iteration 1, wasn't impossible to understand.

He has leisure, over the course of the next few days, weeks, months, to consider the validity of more of Carrette's pronouncements. His existence is, of course, impossible: He ceases to breathe; yet he doesn't die. His body freezes into crystal; he doesn't die. He leaves La Profunidad far behind; and eventually—over the course of years—his memories of it themselves ossify, become objects in the void, along with all other memories, impulses, and concerns: pain and frustration, attachment and desire, the neurotic garbage of personality, vented and frozen and moving on unhurried trajectories in and out of perception. Years cease to have meaning. Celestial motion progresses. The reality of the concept of "perpendicular infinity" becomes apparent.

* * *

Scottie shines his flashlight over the brickwork from the steel door to the end of the corridor, a rounded little alcove covered in rat shit. He sees no secret doors. No holes. They're trapped.

He returns to Judith, who's started shaking, with foamy spit spilling from her lips and her eyes rolled back. He tries to move her into the recovery position. Her neck is all floppy and her limbs get caught up against the walls. He cannot stretch her out without help, or if he tries to do it alone he could hurt her more. He has to keep her airwaves open.

BANG BANG BANG BANG

He gets up again. He tries investigating the wall again. There must be something he missed, something he didn't understand.

But it's just bricks. Bricks in a brickwork pattern with musty old cement in-between. Bricks, and more bricks, and—

An archway. It is bricked up, certainly, but there's a different pattern between the brickwork around the archway and the filler. The filler bricks haven't been laid with a running bond; they've just been piled up, one on top of the other, by some incompetent bricklayer.

It could be possible, if he's strong, to knock through the filler bricks. And if he's lucky, the archway could lead somewhere with an exit. He just needs to be lucky, and strong. And he needs Judith to wake up.

The BANG BANG BANG at the door panel hasn't let up. In fact, the door is buckling: Scottie can see a chink of light shining beneath the top of the frame. An angular plane of light, growing between each blow, busy shadows behind.

53

On Day Four-Gamma-Twelve of the tri-lunar calendar, Asteroid Year Thirty, a comet lands in the Hali Basin Demilitarized Zone. It makes ground into deep drifts of soft red dust, leaving a squid-shaped indentation, elaborated by the rapid melting and evaporation of ice. It thaws. It opens its eyes.

Sol stretches his limbs. He hasn't moved for a timeless eternity. His muscles are stiff.

It's dark, but there are stars. The stars are strange. Once he can stand, he tries walking. Once he can walk, he moves immediately toward a glow visible above distant dunes.

* * *

They feed and water Sol in the Oasis Church of the Yellow King. He eats reconstituted rations beneath murals depicting the journeys of the prophets. A wild-eyed preacher instructs the lame and sickly faithful to lay their hands upon him. They clothe him in charitable donations: unseasonable jeans and a faded Banana Republic shirt. They supply him with a rucksack filled with tradeable items. The preacher pulls off his own Kevlar vest and places it over Sol's shoulders, mumbling a final benediction. They stuff his pockets with forged papers and point him in the direction of the Peace Wire and—weeping, praying—wave him goodbye, good luck, King's grace be with you, boss; please bring this nightmare to an end.

* * *

With Scottie's first effort to kick a hole through the brick wall, he aims toe-first and sprains his toe, and is crippled by pain for a while. Then he stands again and swings the foot—pulsing, already swelling into his shoe—heel first at the bricks. No impact. The bricks stay solid. They are bricks in cement. He is never going to make a hole in the wall by kicking it.

He thinks about methods. Tactics. He thinks about all the tools he wishes he had. A crowbar. A screwdriver. A pen.

He decides to pull Judith closer to the archway. This will make it easier, once the hole is made, to move her through it. But she's heavy, and he fears hurting her, so he lets her down again after a few seconds' effort. She can wait until the hole is made.

(A chisel. A fork. Dynamite.)

He decides to move the crates of books closer to the archway. This, too, will save time in the long run. He slips the crates over the damp soil floor. But they, too, are heavy. After shifting one, he leaves the second for when the hole is made.

However that is going to happen.

(A garden hoe. A sledgehammer.)

The Sol-thing is still banging on the door. The gap between the door and the frame has grown. Alongside the slamming sound, Scottie can hear a wet slap. Blood. Flecks and spatters of blood are flying through the gap. A fingertip. Sol is sacrificing his extremities to get through the door.

(A plastering trowel. The front end of a large car.)

Sol hasn't stopped once. He won't stop. He won't waste time shifting things around or worrying about tactics or methods. That's why Sol will break through his door, while Scottie will stay trapped in the tunnel, will have to face him and whatever comes with him when he does smash his way in.

(A spanner. A wrecking ball. An Allen key.)

Will the monster pull him apart? Will he beat him to pulp with his wrecked arms? No, it's the Deferral that'll kill Scottie, the energy will burn him alive (an Allen key) or worse, there will be a full Accession and whatever is waiting to come through will come through and leave him as a broken box and a puddle (THERE'S AN ALLEN KEY IN YOUR FRONT SHIRT POCKET).

Scottie feels his shirt pocket. His fingers trace a hard little L-shape: the Allen key he used to put the incinerator together. Sleek and strong, an almost perfect shape. A miracle of design!

He kneels before the archway, selects a brick close to the floor, and starts scraping at the cement beneath it.

* * *

Before they hand him back his papers, the peacekeepers warn Sol that they have no jurisdiction inside the Court of the King, that any trouble encounters would be his responsibility, and that while it's undoubtedly a dangerous, chaotic place, he shouldn't rely on the false security provided by a big team of guards, since a show of power that threatens any of the factions inside is likely to provoke a response. Don't drink the water, they tell him, and don't engage the services of the sex workers.

Mindful of this, Sol rearranges his clothes so that his Kevlar vest is hidden beneath his Banana Republic shirt. He wears his rucksack, full of candy bars and cigarette packets, backward, covering his chest.

It's long past dawn and the heat is fierce. Aldebaran's red glow illuminates the sand, and the parched silt, and the trash dunes that border the Court's peripheries. Before crossing the barbed-wire barrier of the Peace Wire, he hands the peacekeepers cigarettes.

“King’s grace be with you, boss,” they say.

Sol walks in.

The initial scrum of beggars and peddlers is thick but disorganized, and Sol shoves his way into the settlement. The Court of the King is a tent city, with chain-link divisions and watchtowers of scaffolding. The streets are of packed sand, with open sewers running down either side, and at every crossroads barrels of trash swelter and hum in the heat. A representative of the Royal Guard in ragged shorts and bare feet presents himself to Sol, offering to accompany him through the district in exchange for the first of many packs of cigarettes.

Progress is slow and sometimes violent. They must navigate disturbances—a fight, a distribution of grain, a funeral procession—and pay their way through impromptu turnpikes. But in this district, at least, people pay less attention to Sol than might be expected. Most are too busy lining up—for water, fuel, food, medical help—to pay more than fleeting attention, throw more than occasional insults or greetings. An hour’s walk within the tent city, an ancient wall rears up. The wall is perforated with passes. A faction called the Guards of Court holds these passages, and Sol is obliged to hire a new minder, a heavily armed ten-year-old child, to guide his way.

“Where do you come from, big nose?” the child Guard of Court asks as they descend the stone steps into the ruins of the old city.

“From outside the wire,” Sol says.

“Did you see my papa there?”

“Who is your papa?”

“My papa is a peacekeeper.”

“What does he look like?”

The Guard of Court thinks about this. Between flapping tarpaulins and skeletal tower blocks, Sol sees glints of something—perhaps the palace, perhaps satellite dishes—in the ruddy distance.

"My papa is very big," the Guard of Court says eventually. "He wears a shirt like this." She points to her own football shirt.

"No," Sol says, "I'm afraid not."

"Huh."

"Is there anything you'd like me to tell him, if I ever do see him?"

The Guard of Court thinks about this for a while.

"Tell him I'm ready for the King. And I hope he is, too. And if Mama won't forgive him, that's too bad. But there's only one opinion that really matters, and that's the King's, so I hope he's ready."

* * *

Bea swims to consciousness to the sound of hammering and scraping and tumbling blocks, and in the early moments she faintly suspects she's working in an underground construction site and her expertise is required to deal with *some new stupid thing*.

Then she remembers.

She sits up—her head throbs—and sidles crabwise to where Scottie is pulling bricks out of the wall. The gap behind the archway Scottie is excavating isn't entirely dark; in fact, from the glints of light visible, she surmises that the space beyond could be the wine cellar, which—she remembers excitedly—has a trapdoor exit of its own that leads to the moat and the parking lot where the van is. Where the incinerator is.

Scottie looks at her. There are tears of relief in his eyes. She runs her hand down his dirty cheek and starts helping clear the bricks.

When the gap is large enough to push an arm through into cool open darkness, she moves to try and grab the second crate of books.

It turns out her ankle hurts—how did that happen?—and this slows her down (how are they going to carry these things through the cellar?) but she does push the crate to join the other beside the growing cavity. Scottie starts squeezing himself through the hole just as Sol finally stops battering the door and clambers over the dented panel.

⁎ ⁎ ⁎

In this district a street battle is occurring between the King's Guards and the Revolutionary Yellow Guard. Sol's guide, persona non grata to both factions, leads him down covered walkways and the passages between pavilions, crisscrossed with guide ropes. Shots resound in meaningful tattoos.

Eventually the walkways become unnavigable and they start to move through the living spaces, entering the flaps of tents or climbing over the sills of ruinous windows, distributing candy bars and threats to the residents huddled behind barricades or prostrate on the earth, holding hands or praying.

Finally they reach a plaza of sorts, a wide-open space flanked by mud buildings, with scaffolding and canvas and sandbags and militia and people, cowering and running and rallying to flags and loudspeakers. The chaos of the entire Court is concentrated here, and gunfire is unceasing. They move between stampeding crowds and projectiles, throwing up puffs of dust and sand. The guide puts her small rough hand in Sol's and pulls him through deadly open spaces toward a raised lip in the dust, which resolves into something like a bunker, with long, low windows.

"Down there, boss," the child says.

Sol peers into the slit. The shadows are impenetrable. He unhitches his rucksack, and lowers himself down onto his belly.

"Wait," the child says. "Are you really going to see the King, boss?"

"That's what I came here for."

"Are you ready?" Bullets throw up dust clouds nearby.

"I've been getting ready for a long time."

"How long?"

"Long."

"You know He can end all this, right?"

Sol nods. "Do you want it to end?" he asks.

She nods vigorously, her eyes locked with his own. "Please," she says. "Please."

He squeezes in, hitches his rucksack back on, and moves into the shadow.

* * *

Scottie stands in the cellar and readies his arms for the first crate of books. As Bea pushes, the box slowly extrudes from the aperture, until it tips off the edge and Scottie feels its full weight in his arms. He staggers a little. His toe hurts. His legs are weak.

Nonetheless, he manages to get the box to the trapdoor without complication. Then he returns to where the second crate is already hanging halfway out of the aperture, when from beyond the tunnel wall he hears a thud, and a scream, and suddenly white light illuminates the edges of the box, and with a heavy plosive *crump* it blasts out and slams Scottie squarely in the chest, driving him against a rack of wine bottles, and he hears the crack and tinkle of breaking glass, and feels pressure on his back, and as he slides to the ground, he smells burning sausages.

* * *

The King's Chamber is an expensively decorated drawing room, filled with artworks—paintings, ceramics, fetishes. There is an armchair and sofa, wrapped in a clear plastic film. Leaning against the back wall, beside a closed door, is a pair of shoulder-height gas canisters. Oxygen. Framing the door like a kind of portico is a structure of inflated clear plastic. An airlock. Sol can hear the hiss of the gas canisters and the whirr of a pump.

On the coffee table sits a shoebox-sized container, primitively constructed out of metal. The container is designed to open outward like a briefcase, and has been opened, and inside is a dull aluminium panel with a switch in the center. It's a big switch with a fat handle, like a circuit breaker. The near side of the switch, where the handle rests, is unmarked. The far side, where the handle *wants* to be, is labeled GO.

Dulcie is sitting on the sofa, her mass causing the plastic to stretch and crease. She looks younger than when she and Sol parted. Her clothes seem more confidently chosen, as if she's visualized the vigorous new person she wants to be, and has carefully chosen an outfit to represent that. Her hair is new, too. She may have had Botox.

Sol feels obliged to look down at his own outfit, which has changed once again. He's wearing slightly grubby jeans, a T-shirt that seems to have become too tight for his belly, and a dark jacket resembling a courier's uniform.

"Sit down, sweetheart. You must be tired." He does sit. It's almost automatic, as if he's had a difficult day at work. "How do you feel?"

Sol wants to say something pithy. He understands in the abstract that this isn't Dulcie, but some cynical replica, intended to produce in him a certain emotional response; nonetheless, he wants to collapse into her bosom and weep. She may be a ghost, but it's good to speak to somebody sometimes.

"I'm tired," he says, with wavering voice.

"I need to talk to you about something, sweetheart. It's about *time*." He nods miserably. He wants to put a brave face on it, but he can't. He's dreading what he knows she'll say. "There's a man you've already spoken to, a friend of ours called Cléophe Carrette. I'm tempted to call him our resident philosopher. He has an understanding of the way time works here, that I believe he explained to you. Do you remember?"

"He called it a 'perpendicular infinity.'"

"That's right. I need you to understand what that means." Dulcie speaks the same way she announced their divorce proceedings; Sol feels the same dread wash over him. "It means this isn't going to end, Joe. You're going to exist in this envelope of experience forever. Not only you, but everybody you've encountered, every spark of consciousness that contributed to the Accession bridge. You're never going to wake up. Unless . . ." Here she indicates the button exposed in the briefcase. GO. "You can complete the Accession process."

He shakes his head.

"No, Dulcie . . ."

"Hear me out, Joe." Sol wants to interrupt but he can't. He's paralyzed by a sudden and desperate need to believe Dulcie—and believe *in* Dulcie, believe he's not alone. "You've seen the slogans written on the walls. The people want this, Joe. They're suffering and they want it to end. And you, as the only person who has the power to end it—for you to sit with this privilege and do nothing—isn't that cruel?"

Sol nods. As he speaks next, it's like he's giving something up. It's a sweet feeling.

"I am aware of their suffering," he says. "And even though I know this is a strange place, I'm not so arrogant as to assume that nothing I see is real, nobody I hear is real."

Dulcie smiles. "You're a good man, Joe," she says. She puts her hand out over his. The warmth of her touch fills him. "Joe, what was it like, being alone all those years?"

Sol is surprised to hear himself sobbing. It's as though something that barely started to thaw is now melting wholesale, glaciers crashing into the waves.

"It was horrible. Horrible. I found ways of coping. You always find a way to cope. But I was *trapped*, Dulcie, in my own mind. I watched the stars moving. One star, passing through my vision for a hundred years. I thought about my life. I thought about you and me. Replaying conversations we had, when it was all falling apart. And I felt guilty. But then I reasoned it through, and felt other things: angry at you, then grateful that we'd known each other, or sad or relieved that we wouldn't meet again. And after I'd thought about that one moment, ten times, a hundred times, it started to *calcify* in my mind. It would seem harmless, inert. Like a pet rock, which I could pick up or put down if I chose. But if I snapped it open, broke through the surface, all those feelings would bleed out again, you see? Just as strong as before. As if nothing had really changed. And all my memories were like this. I was like someone in a sculpture park, with this collection of ancient fossils, and I'd go between them, touching them, comparing them, teasing away at them, and occasionally breaking through to see if the inside was still fresh, see whether I could still hurt. And I always could. I never lost that.

"I had ten million conversations. I'd get lost in them. That was scary. Not to be lost, but to realize that you'd *been* lost—you understand the difference? Waking up is always worse. You know, one moment you're a rock gardener showing special guests your collection of . . . *memory rocks*; and the next moment you realize the truth again. You're alone in the darkness and you can't move and there's no end."

Dulcie sits beside him now, she has embraced him, pulled his head onto her breast, and with every movement they make, the plastic sofa covering crackles and *plarts* beneath them. Finally Sol pulls away. His fingers are at the sides of Dulcie's head, in the soft hair behind her ears. She's so realistic.

"I wanted to say something pithy to you, Dulcie. Something to put you in your place, like I'm immune to your torture. Because I *know* you're not real. And I know what's happening to me. I'm being placed under what some might call *intense psychological pressure*. I'm not weak. I'm still here. I've been trying so hard. And no, I'm not going to pull this lever, sweetheart, I'm just not. Not today. Not for as long as I can. But *infinity*, Dulcie? Forever and ever? Infinity frightens me. It scares me like nothing else. I can't pretend it doesn't."

She moves in toward him. Her lips pass his cheek and reach his ear. He can feel her warm breath, the electrostatic field of her living presence.

"Why don't you just get it over with?" she murmurs. "You've already proven your point. You're so strong. You don't need to show me. I know."

One hand is on his thigh. The other hand gropes for his, and entwines with his fingers, and draws it downward—oh, she will guide him between her thighs—but, he realizes, she has placed his groping hand onto the device on the coffee table, the lever labeled GO.

He caresses the lever and she catches her breath. He rolls his palm over its handle and she shivers deliciously. She straddles him. The plastic beneath them pops and crunches like calving glaciers. He seizes the lever end in the palm of his hand, feels its heft, its roundness. She freezes above him. Waiting. An ecstasy of anticipation.

Waiting.

For a long time.

"Well, go on," she urges.

Sol does nothing.

"Ram it home, baby. Come on, let's go."

She bounces a little, and the plastic sheeting farts.

"Maybe later, eh," Sol says.

"What's wrong with you?"

"I guess I'm tired."

"Pathetic."

"Can you get off me, please?"

"No."

"Dulcie."

She growls like an overworked hard drive and draws her painted nails across his face. She scrapes raw tracks down his cheek and pulls away four pennants of papery skin gummed to her ragged fingernails. He feels hot dampness on his cheek, and as the pain wells up, so too does a wave of nausea—but Sol's right hand, which is free, goes instinctively to his jacket pocket and comes out brandishing the object whose presence he's never entirely forgotten, over all these years, but whose importance is only now becoming real: Fran's gift to him, his toothbrush.

He jams the toothbrush into Dulcie's midriff and a pulse of force flings her over the coffee table and onto the sofa opposite.

Plastic quacks. He waves the brush head over the wound on his cheek and the pain lifts and fingernail shards drop from the healing skin into his collar.

"No pain, Dulcie," Sol says. "Not if I don't want it."

Dulcie glowers at him.

"Where did you get that?" she asks, pointing a ruined fingernail at the toothbrush.

"This? This is called a focus. Lucid dreamers use them to gain control in situations where they would otherwise be powerless. Somebody taught me how to use one."

He can't stop looking at Dulcie's nails, bent backward and dripping with plasma. He points the toothbrush and fixes them up.

"Impressive," Dulcie says. "You know this changes nothing, right? Remember eternity? Remember infinity? Remember being alone in the dark?"

Behind Sol comes the sound of mail through the letterbox. Dulcie stands, adjusts her clothes, retrieves a pamphlet from the floor and tosses it onto the coffee table. Crudely printed on yellow paper, it reads:

PERMIT ENTRY OF THE KING
THE POPULATION OF CARCOSA CALLS TO HIM
TO END OUR SUFFERING
THE TORTURED THE STARVING THE FURIOUS THE TRAPPED
OPPRESSED AND OPPRESSORS ALIKE
WE BEG FOR THE MOMENT WHEN
YOU SHALL RELEASE US

"You'd be a hero to these people if you gave them what they wanted. Only you can do it. You want to be a hero, don't you? You used to want that."

Dulcie delivers her lines slightly less convincingly now. Her whole appearance seems more doll-like, backsliding into the uncanny valley.

"Dulcie, I never wanted to be a hero."

"Oh, come on, Joe. I get it now. I've had a bit of time to work on myself, and I've realized I was holding you back from what you really needed to become."

She nods for slightly too long, relaxing back into her chair.

"I used to shout at you," Sol says. "I used to rant and rave."

"Yes, you were very frustrated. My attitude toward the work you did was unacceptable."

"Remember when you said I was tilting at windmills, like a little boy?"

Dulcie covers her mouth with her hand.

"What a horrid thing to say," she says.

"I called you a bad feminist, and you said I was mansplaining feminism to you, and we didn't speak to each other for two days."

Dulcie nods, wide-eyed, a smile plastered to her face.

"I was *definitely* in the wrong."

"Not really. Not at the bottom of things. You just wanted me to deal with what happened, with my dad . . . you wanted me to process my trauma without placing myself at the center of it."

She twitches.

"An unreasonable thing to demand of you."

"I knew you were right. While I was working at GMM, I knew it was a kind of game, in a way."

"You did *heroic* work at GMM."

"I'm not going to do it."

The pump mechanism supplying the airlock suddenly makes a guttering sound, like the snore of a restless sleeper. Blockage in the pipes, perhaps. Then it sighs and returns to normal. But once he's identified it, Sol cannot unhear the sound of breathing.

"Yet. You're not going to do it *yet*. But I'll show you something, Joe. I'm going to change your mind."

She stands up. The plastic-wrapped cushion whistles back into shape. She pads over to a tall, narrow closet—her bare feet are filthy—and steps entirely inside it. She closes the door behind her.

The gas pump sighs. The letterbox craps religious pamphlets onto the welcome mat.

Dulcie backs out of the closet, towing a trolley of AV equipment. On the top shelf is a television monitor—white, clunky, old—and beneath it a stack of redundant tech: video recorders and mixers and unidentifiable gewgaws with wires poking out the front and back.

"I'm going to show you where you are, Joe, and what you're doing."

She presses the remote control's single button, and footage starts to play.

The TV screen has a low-res, pulsing quality. Bea is on the screen. She's all pale and uplit by the on-camera light, but doesn't seem to be aware of the camera or its light. She's in a dark space, a tunnel, trying to push a heavy box through a hole in the wall. She keeps looking back, to a shape up the tunnel that isn't immediately obvious but slowly comes into focus: a man wearing jeans and a T-shirt and the ragged remains of a jacket. All of the clothes are black with blood. The man's arms, which he holds out before him, terminate in flaps of skin and flesh and dirty extrusions of bone, all of it smoking. The man's face is lost in a billow of smoke but Sol knows who it is. It's him. Joe Sol. The version of himself that remains on Earth.

The monster staggers toward Bea, stumps outstretched, but before he reaches her, a jagged channel of light explodes from the side of the box, zigzags up the tunnel, and meets his chest. Sparks cascade from his back, and his form is backlit as his feet leave the ground. The box is forced out of the aperture and Bea, who has been caught in the aura, falls to the ground.

There are screams. The camera moves close into Bea's face, illuminating the scrapes and smudges of ash and emerging red burns. Her eyes are wide. The camera tracks over the earthen floor of the tunnel, through a brickwork threshold and into a stone-tiled room beyond. The tiles are wet with some dark liquid and littered with shards of green glass. There's a boot. A trouser leg. Scottie, lying against a smashed wine rack, confusion and pain on his face.

* * *

Scottie knows he's hurt, possibly seriously. There's a slow-growing ache in his lower back, and a wetness running down his flanks and buttocks that's too warm to be spilled wine. And there's glass everywhere.

But his body can still move, and while it can he'll help Judy, who's still in the tunnel, screaming. He gets up, pushes his head into the tunnel, and reaches Judy, who tells him "Don't worry about me, grab a box and run."

So he hops—his sprained toe complaining now—back to the fallen crate, seizes it, and lifts—oh, his back shrieks with pain—and takes a step or two, and his knees start to fold, but he tells himself *you have to do this, you have no choice*, and when that doesn't work, he switches to *call it done*, *pretend you're remembering*, *remember how you carried the box to the incinerator*. This seems to work, and he remembers himself all the way out of the cellar and through the cool air to where he remembers the van and the garden burner, and he remembers hot coals and licks of flame.

He tears a nail opening the crate. The contents are hardback books in waxy dust jackets. He sees the title, *The Truth of Carcosa*. He registers elements of the cover illustrations, but understands nothing, sees only something appalling that his eyes don't want to rest on. He pulls a single copy out of the container—realizing that he isn't wearing gloves, remembering nostalgically the precautions he discussed with Sol—and hurls it onto the coals.

The terror of having touched this toxic substance washes over him, yet his fingertips aren't stinging or steaming; none of the influence has affected him.

Emboldened, he seizes two books at once, understanding as he does so that the cover in fact features the facade of Villa Monaco, a location for which he feels an instant and powerful familiarity; and as he hurls the books into the incinerator, one flaps open and the knowledge of the page that is exposed—a sequence of physical torture committed by a CIA operative—wriggles through Scottie's consciousness like a slippery parasite.

He heeds the warning.

There are no gloves nearby but there is a thick plastic sack, and Scottie shields his hands with this as he feeds more books into the incinerator.

He thinks it works. No more insights intrude on his work. He stirs the burning books with a poker to make room for more. It's a job of work and it takes far too long. He listens for Bea's footsteps (shouldn't she be just behind him?) but hears none. He listens for screaming or thuds from inside the house. But all he hears is the wind, and oblivious birdcall, and the crackle of flames.

A less-panicked part of Scottie wonders whether he can sense the books' power diminishing. Whether there really is a lessening of heaviness and nausea as they burn. But he's in no state to identify it, with the pain and weakness of his body, the sudden clenches originating in his lower back, the shards of tooth enamel he keeps spitting in bloody gobs from his mouth.

Finally the last of the books are heaped up over the fire, and Scottie gives the pile one last squirt of lighter fluid before limping back toward the house.

The leaves keep rustling. The birds keep singing. The house looms large and the cellar door yawns open at the bottom of its slippery slate stairwell and Scottie slides and stumbles but—*does—not—fall*—then picks up the pace again because he can hear things clattering around inside. It must be Judy, but *what is she still doing in there*? She should have brought her own box out long ago.

"Judy?" he hisses.

Something tumbles. Something cracks, rolls, smashes.

"Judy?"

"I need help," comes a whispered reply.

Scottie walks into the shadow and finds the cellar devastated. Several rows of wine racks have been overturned, reinforcing a makeshift barricade built against the hole in the wall. Bea sits at the base of this obstruction. The book crate is lying at her feet, while with her upper body she braces against a wooden panel—some section of a closet or desk—which is knocking and pulsing, as the Sol-thing tries once again to break through.

Scottie grabs a long plank and tries to slam it like a pike against the panel. At the last moment he falters, unwilling to risk hurting

Bea, but the weight of the object pulls it toward his target, and then the nose of the plank pierces the panel and seems to bounce on something soft, and they hear a muffled snap.

Everything goes still.

Bea looks back at Scottie with something like hope in her eyes.

"Did you get the fire going?" she asks.

"Yes."

"And they're burning?"

"Yes." Bea smiles. Scottie loves her. "Let me help you up," he starts to say.

Then the plank starts to jiggle. It bounces up and down in the crack, producing a maritime creak. It jumps back out an inch or two, and blood oozes from the aperture.

"Take the box and run," Bea hisses at Scottie.

"No, not this time. You take it. I'll keep him here."

"You've already done it once, you know what you're doing."

"I can't leave you here, I couldn't live with myself if—"

"Oh, for fuck's sake, Scottie . . ."

She pulls herself up from the collapsed barricade and the extent of her injuries becomes clear. She's been burned across her left arm and flank, up to her ear. Her clothes are scorched, and the skeletal wiring of her bra is digging into the raw skin beneath. Most of the burned flesh is a boiled plum color, but there are parts where yellow blisters are already rising.

She sees Scottie flinch.

"*What?*" she snaps. "Don't worry about it, it doesn't hurt."

But she herself refuses to look at it. She holds her hand behind her back as she limps to where the box is lying.

The plank keeps shifting. A few elements of the barricade start to slide away.

"Hold it down, then!" Bea says.

Scottie gets to the base of the pile before his strength suddenly gives out and he falls to his knees.

Bea gasps. The backs of Scottie's shirt and trousers are drenched in blood.

"Fuck, Scottie, you're hurt!"

He crawls up the barricade and applies his weight to a point he judges will give good leverage.

"Scottie . . ." Bea says. She sounds on the verge of perfect panic. The thought of hearing her lose control frightens Scottie. But the thought of hearing what she might say about his injuries terrifies him more.

"Just *go*!" he screams.

She goes. Sobbing, stumbling, the fatty goo that was the skin on her left hand sticking to the cardboard and peeling off in scraps, she hauls the crate of books out of the cellar and up the stairs to the green expanse beyond—such a gorgeous lawn—and she sees, like a distant gleaming beacon, the van and the squat little incinerator, with its plume of smoke.

She makes it halfway across the lawn before she hears crashing behind her. Soon she hears the scuff of footsteps on grass. She's not alone. She doesn't want to turn and see it. Perhaps if she keeps moving she won't have to.

But her strength is failing. And her left hand is in agony. And when she tries to adjust her grip the smacking wrench of burned flesh being pulled away fills her with nausea, and she drops the box.

And then she has to look.

The Sol-thing no longer has clothes. Its skin is red and striated with blisters like raspberry ripple ice cream. Its shredded arm stumps have been sealed with flame. The dangling remains of its genitals are oozing gore. Its head is an angry cloud. It has a pair of broken legs—the left dragging a kinked ankle, the right sporting an exposed fibula—and every motion should provoke a twinge of agony; yet it runs toward her.

Scottie's pale, frightened face emerges behind, hobbling to catch up, mouthing something, perhaps screaming. He loves her. He doesn't want her to die.

But he has no chance. The Sol-thing is upon her, and when it reaches a few feet away, the lid of the box pops open and another arc of lightning flares out to meet it, and as the flash envelops her, Bea hears her own voice saying coldly, *that was the lightning*.

The moment collapses inwards toward memory.

She is a child and the sky above Provence is storming. She sees the lightning flash against the wall of the vacation house. Window shapes, with patterns of running water. After each flash, she counts, as she has been taught to do—*one ten thousand, two ten thousand*—to determine whether the lightning is moving away or coming closer. And while her mouth is talking, in the back of her mind she tells herself: *that was the lightning* (three ten thousand). *Here comes the thunder.*

Here comes the thunder.

"YOU CAN STOP THIS," a voice tells Sol. The voice is sourceless, but nonetheless he turns to see that the door behind the airlock has opened.

Behind the door are flames.

No, not flames. Sol approaches to get a better view. What he first thought were flames are something else: flares of color ranging from ruddy umber to gold to citrine yellow. They move with fluid grace around a central spot of blackness. He's looking at the iris of a colossal eye.

It blinks.

"THEY ARE EXPERIENCING GREAT PAIN," the voice says. It speaks slowly, with the gravitas of a slamming mausoleum door. "BECAUSE THE ACCESSION IS FAILING. YOU ARE LETTING YOUR FRIENDS DOWN. YOU ARE LETTING ME DOWN."

The eye disappears from the doorway. Moments later a gigantic set of lips, with gleaming yellow teeth, replaces them. The lips move when the voice speaks, although the sound and motion don't align.

"TRUE ACCESSION CAUSES NO SUFFERING. THERE IS NO FIRE OR EXPLOSION. IT IS A SIMPLE, PAINLESS PROCEDURE FOR MY MAJESTY TO STEP INTO YOUR WORLD. THE REWARDS FOR YOU ARE BEYOND MEASURE. YOU NEED NOT BE LONELY, MR. SOL. CONSIDER TRUE COMMUNICATION. THE UNION OF YOUR WORLD, YOUR MIND, YOUR LANGUAGE, WITH MINE."

Sol flicks his toothbrush at the TV trolley and it slides around until the screen faces the door. He points at the monster in the center: handless, naked, with strips of barbecued skin flaying off his body.

"Look at this," he says.

The mouth disappears into blackness, and the blazing eye returns. The pupil fixes on the television screen.

"I'm dead," Sol says flatly. "If not now, then in minutes, maybe seconds."

The eye blinks.

"YOUR FRIENDS MIGHT LIVE. THROW THE SWITCH. LET THEM GO."

"They might get away anyway. The explosion might throw them clear. There's always a chance."

"ARE YOU WILLING TO WATCH THEM DIE?"

Sol feels a flash of anger. But it passes through him quickly, leaving something like peace in its wake.

"If I have to."

He realizes that the footage on the screen is running slower than it was at the start. Now his horrible body moves as if wading in deep water, the flames dancing like ink trails in a pond.

"You're slowing it down, aren't you?" he says.

The eye blinks.

"YOU NEED TIME TO CONSIDER YOUR DECISION. I CAN MAKE THIS MOMENT LAST A VERY LONG TIME."

"Can you make the footage stop?"

"YES."

"Prove it."

The footage comes to a halt.

Sol walks up to the monitor and stands in front of it. He stares intently at the pixels on the screen. Everything is wavering.

"THIS TORTURE CAN BE INFINITE—"

Sol fires the toothbrush and the door slams shut on the eye.

He returns his attention to the screen.

He scans the pixels, left to right, right to left. Everything wobbles in his vision. The electrostatic force of the old machine causes his hair to stand on end.

Everything is wavering, but is anything changing?

He watches. He waits. He can wait. He's proven that he can wait for a long, long time.

If anything changes—anything at all—then all is not lost.

All hope hinges on this.

* * *

And then it happens. A single pixel, switching from white to grey in the corner of his vision.

Sol exhales a breath he didn't realize he'd been holding for hours, months, years. He laughs with delight. Tears of victory roll down his cheeks.

"You can't do it, you old fuck! You can't stop time! I'm not here forever! I'm not here forever! I'm going to die, and it's going to end, and you're going to fail, again!" He dances around the room. "I'm going to *die*! *Die, die, die*!"

He stops dancing.

The plastic-covered couch suddenly disgusts and infuriates him, so he flicks his toothbrush and replaces it with something nicer: an upholstered easy chair in mustard yellow, familiar from his past. He sits on it. He gets up again and stares at the endlessly exploding monster on the television screen again until he's confirmed more signs of movement.

Then his attention falls on the equipment below the monitor.

He points the toothbrush at the video machine and flicks it, turns it like a key, and the front panel falls open. He executes a similar gesture toward the other gear. More panels open, wires and gubbins spill out. Some resemble the equipment Sol saw on the walls of Pentorgan House.

"I wonder how this works," he says out loud.

There's a rope of wires running out of the back of the unit to the closet door. Sol lifts a length off the floor, and hauls the skein out of the closet, drawing it in arm over arm. It pulls sockets and pieces of hardware with it: chipboards, keyboards, unidentifiable interfaces, rubbery connectors oozing coolant. He stands over the coiled mass of equipment. It's as if he's pulled a nerve from its fleshy envelope and drawn all the sensory organs out with it.

He hauls the mass closer to the coffee table and places a keyboard and a tiny LCD monitor upon it. They sit there—inert, slightly greasy—until Sol waves his magic toothbrush over them, and the wires throb, and a light green cursor appears on the screen.

Experimentally, Sol presses what appears to be the "return" button on the keyboard.

The wires twitch, and the following text appears on the monitor:

XXXXX PRISM CONSULTANCY XXXXX

XXX LIVE INFORMATION NODE XXX

XXXXXXXX VERSION 1.2 XXXXXXXX

"Huh," says Sol. He glances back up at the TV screen, which has barely changed. He looks back at the monitor. He doesn't know exactly what he's looking at. The backward text, however, feeds a slightly crackpot notion in his head: By using this equipment, he is operating somehow from *within* the Live Information Node.

A crazy idea, of course. Probably disprovable. And even if he found out it was true, what would it mean?

He doesn't know.

But he has a very long time to find out.

Epilogue

The GMM lawyers want to run the investigation from the outset. They act as if their *Albatross Hung* writs are still the silver bullets they used to be, addressing the officers without respect to rank, demanding access to the scene and witnesses. Inspector Lee is polite but firm, showing the GMM agents his MoD letter of warrant and explaining that it supersedes any previously recognized authority. The constables who escort the agents from the grounds of Pentorgan House are less diplomatic.

It's time, they tell the suits, *for police to be police again*.

They really want it to be true. They want to do real work again. The last few months are a locked box that they never want to open again.

There are two main sites of interest. The first is the pond, with its three male bodies, most likely Hasturian Guard fugitives. Victims of a violent death, Lee notes with some satisfaction. The second site is the lawn where the explosion took place. Here the first responders discovered the charred remains of one corpse and scooped up two potential witnesses, one male, one female. Both have suffered what the medics identify as "life-changing" injuries, with odds of survival placed at 30 percent (male) and 65 percent (female).

There's a good officer up from CID, and she gets started quickly on connections between the two sites of violence. Bagging and tagging and marking maps, she demonstrates a commendable work ethic, although Lee suspects it is driven by guilt. Holding up her map after an hour of work, she reports on the trail of damage across the property.

"We can assume the three pond deaths occurred first, with the perpetrator then moving through the house, with some struggle, some pyrotechnics here, here, here, finishing up back outside again, beside the garden incinerator."

"One perpetrator?"

She shrugs. She looks as though she hasn't slept in weeks.

At that moment, a techie calls Lee upstairs to the third site of interest. It's a computer suite with an old-fashioned system hooked up to the grounds' security cameras.

The techie, Schwab, explains that she found a way of running the security tape (despite the computer's "prehistoric, creepy" operating system), and discovered anomalies in the footage.

"Anomalies?"

"Images that couldn't possibly have come from these security cameras. The anomalies show up on different video feeds, but they all connect to each other. They make a sequence."

"Like a message?"

"Like a movie. It's not that long—just over ten minutes in total—but it's dense. There are parts of the film that appear to be in fast motion. If you slow them down, so that the action moves at normal speed, this movie is a lot longer."

"How much longer?"

"Like, a *lot*."

"How does that work?"

Schwab shrugs.

"I've collected the footage into one file. It runs seamlessly."

"Show me."

Schwab loads the film on her device, instructs him on manipulating the speed dial to slow down the key parts, and backs away.

Play.

It's an art film. It follows a middle-aged man attempting to leave a Latin American city. The man is diverted and detained in a luxurious villa that seems to have been taken over by paramilitary forces. He encounters scenes of extreme violence that span the corridors and grounds in and beneath the villa, and ultimately—in a disorienting science-fiction twist—enters a strange concrete structure suspended in the void. He spends a very long time—judging by the motion of the stars in the background—traveling through space without a spacesuit. He lands on a desert planet where the natives treat him with great deference, aiding him on his journey through a fetid refugee camp and finally into a middle-class living room. Here, after a brief tussle with a femme fatale, he stays for another considerable period of time, ceaselessly working on a piece of computer equipment.

Lee notices a flash around the final frames of the footage, so he rewinds and slows right down, revealing, at the very end, a title card of sorts. Words briefly overlay the screen, reading: "IF THIS RECURS, WARN ME. I AM NOT POWERLESS AND NOR ARE YOU."

He pauses the frame. He analyzes the expression of the man on the screen. His mouth is set, eyes triumphant. A man who's solved a problem. Lee sits back. He's been watching footage for half an hour, although he has the unsettling feeling it's been longer.

"What is this?" he asks Schwab, who's been hovering behind his chair the whole time.

"My first guess would be signal intrusion from another source. Given the age of this equipment, I'd say something analogue: an old-fashioned television broadcast. My second guess would be artificial intelligence. The video could have been autogenerated based on the footage fed into the neural network. But that would be assuming that this machine is a lot more powerful and advanced than it appears. And I'm not sure."

"Huh," says Lee. It's a riddle. It has the appeal of a riddle.

"What do you want me to do?"

"Do your job. Make copies. Start your analysis."

"Okay."

Lee is on his way out of the room when Schwab clears her throat.

"Um, Inspector Lee. Have you ever seen anything like this?"

"No."

"Is it going to stay with us? This case?"

Lee shrugs.

"Be nice to work a real case, on our own, wouldn't it?" she says.

Lee smiles.

Be nice not to have led GMM into people's homes.

Not to have handed the holding cell keys to the Hasturian Guard.

Be nice to be able to sleep without drinking.

To stop twitching. Crying out in our sleep.

To have something else to think about.

A real mystery to solve properly.

Something we can do right.

"Tell you what," he says casually, "why don't you make a couple of copies, just in case. Keep one for yourself. Hard copy only."

She nods.

IF THIS RECURS, WARN ME. I AM NOT POWERLESS AND NOR ARE YOU.

On the way downstairs Lee calls the officer who accompanied the survivors to the hospital.

"They still with us?" he asks.

"For now," the officer responds. "I think they're putting the lad in a coma. The young woman was awake for a couple of seconds before they put her down again for surgery. Anything I need to know, sir?"

"Not yet. We're still putting it together."

"Good luck, sir. It's a nasty one, this."

"Have they been checked in properly?"

"Their IDs haven't been processed yet, if that's what you mean. They're John and Jane Doe."

"Good. There's a problem with those IDs. Don't hand them over. Keep them with you."

"But nobody here knows who they are . . ."

"I'll worry about that. I want you to stand down now. You've done your job. Return to patrol. I'll speak to you back at the station."

The moment he hangs up, his phone rings.

It's the call he's been half-expecting all day: headquarters telling him to let the GMM agents back in. Their own, freshly minted MoD letter of warrant has just circulated. Lee will afford the GMM suits all the help they need, including access to the witnesses and sole possession of the electronic evidence.

He huddles the constables and breaks the news as softly as he can. Nonetheless, it has a visible impact. The morale leeks out of them like a vital gas, leaving them deflated, foul-tempered.

They will drink tonight. And fight. They want so badly to be the good guys, bloodshed is inevitable.

Pushing the wooden gates aside to let the GMM agents in, he keeps his eyes to the ground. Most of the suits ignore him. The last one, a younger individual, lingers a while.

"I'm sorry," she tells him. "For what it's worth."

He gives her a wry smile.

"I wasn't all that surprised. Only a matter of time before you were back on top again."

She shrugs, pulls the case notes out of his hands, and walks past.

Lee watches the GMM suits fan out across the lawn with mobile devices and sensors, taking possession of the evidence and standing the police down. He sees Schwab's face in one of the windows of Pentorgan House, and surreptitiously signals for her to leave by the back door. The GMM suits gather around a garden incinerator and start sifting through its contents.

IF THIS RECURS, WARN ME. I AM NOT POWERLESS AND NOR ARE YOU.

Lee's first step will be to remove the witnesses from the hospital before GMM can track them down.

His second, to deliver the footage to somebody who can read it.

And then he will recruit whoever in the station still dares use the word "justice." Together, perhaps, they can solve this one case, if nothing else.

Acknowledgments

Special thanks to Natalie Butlin, who championed my work before I had an agent, and without whom this may not have happened. Thanks to Justine Mann and the staff of the British Archive for Contemporary Writing, where the seed of this novel was sown in 2019. That archival placement was funded by the UK Arts and Humanities Research Council. Thanks to them.

Thanks to my agents Harry Illingworth and Helen Edwards. Thanks to my editor Mika Kasuga for believing in this book (and supervising the necessary cuts), as well as Ardyce Alspach, Mahalaleel M. Clinton, Alison Skrabek, and the rest of the team at Union Square. Thanks to Lynn Northrup for the copyediting. Thanks to Nick Bradley for moral support, Jimmy Kelly for good advice at the right moment, and Chris Richford for the etheric visual resonance. Thanks to the various employers whose tacit patronage made this novel possible. All due acknowledgment to the novel coronavirus SARS-CoV-2.

The name “Salvatore Archimboldi” is an allusion to Benno von Archimboldi, from Roberto Bolaño’s *2666*. I use it in recognition of my debt to that author, whose work was influential on a deep level.

Thanks to my family and friends for being consistently supportive. Deep thanks to my wife, Meghan, for being an early reader, constructive critic, and cheerleader throughout the years.

About the Author

Jacob Rollinson was born in England in 1984 and has lived and worked in China and the UK. He completed a creative and critical writing PhD at the University of East Anglia, and his fiction and creative nonfiction have been published in NewWriting.net, *Moxy*, *Spoonfeed*, *Critical Quarterly*, and the *Brixton Review of Books*. His novella *Late King in Yellow Woods* was published in 2021. He works as a librarian.

Thank you for reading this book and for being a reader of books in general. We are so grateful to share being part of a community of readers with you, and we hope you will join us in passing our love of books on to the next generation of readers.

Did you know that reading for enjoyment is the single biggest predictor of a child's future happiness and success?

More than family circumstances, parents' educational background, or income, reading impacts a child's future academic performance, emotional well-being, communication skills, economic security, ambition, and happiness.

Studies show that kids reading for enjoyment in the US is in rapid decline:

- In 2012, 53% of 9-year-olds read almost every day. Just 10 years later, in 2022, the number had fallen to 39%.
- In 2012, 27% of 13-year-olds read for fun daily. By 2023, that number was just 14%.

Together, we can commit to **Raising Readers** and change this trend. How?

- Read to children in your life daily.
- Model reading as a fun activity.
- Reduce screen time.
- Start a family, school, or community book club.
- Visit bookstores and libraries regularly.
- Listen to audiobooks.
- Read the book before you see the movie.
- Encourage your child to read aloud to a pet or stuffed animal.
- Give books as gifts.
- Donate books to families and communities in need.

BOB1217

Books build bright futures, and **Raising Readers** is our shared responsibility.

For more information, visit **JoinRaisingReaders.com**

Sources: National Endowment for the Arts, National Assessment of Educational Progress, WorldBookDay.com, Nielsen BookData's 2023 "Understanding the Children's Book Consumer"